CHAIN OF DESTINY

James ran a slightly trembling hand over her smooth and shapely breast. 'Margaret – you are beauty incarnate! And I treated you like . . .'

'Like a master, James,' she murmured. 'So that now I am your mistress indeed. Am I not?'

He frowned down at her. 'Mistress . . . ? Why do you say that? Mistress – that you never wished to be. Nor should. Wife, not mistress . . .'

'I say it because it had to be. But now there is no denying it. This is my place . . .'

'No!' Vehemently he said it. 'Wife I said I would make you – and I shall. Mistress, no! Not you.'

'Not wife, James – that cannot be.' Earnestly she besought him now. 'Your wife must be . . . other. The Princess of England, perhaps. The Margaret you must marry is Margaret Tudor, James – not Margaret Drummond. For the realm's sake. For both realms' sake. That there may be peace, not war . . .'

Chain of Destiny

Nigel Tranter

CORONET BOOKS
Hodder and Stoughton

Copyright © 1964 by Nigel Tranter

First published in Great Britain 1964 by
Hodder and Stoughton Limited

Coronet Edition 1977

Printed in Great Britain for
Hodder & Stoughton Paperbacks, a
division of Hodder & Stoughton Ltd.,
Mill Road, Dunton Green, Sevenoaks, Kent
by Richard Clay (The Chaucer Press) Ltd., Bungay, Suffolk

ISBN 0 340 21238 1

PRINCIPAL CHARACTERS

In order of appearance

KING JAMES, THE FOURTH OF SCOTS: eldest son of James Third; aged fifteen.

SHAW OF SAUCHIE: Tutor and former governor of the young King.

ROB BRUCE: younger son of Bruce of Airth, a property near Stirling.

PATRICK HEPBURN, 2ND LORD HAILES: later Earl of Bothwell. One of the
leaders of the revolt against the late King. Head of the Lothian family
of Hepburn. Lord High Admiral of Scotland.

ALEXANDER, MASTER OF HOME: later 2nd Lord Home. Grandson and heir of
the first Lord. Another leader of the revolt. Chamberlain of Scotland.

ARCHIBALD DOUGLAS, 5TH EARL OF ANGUS: the famous Bell-the-Cat, head
of the powerful house of Douglas, who looked upon himself almost as
an independent prince. Self-appointed Guardian of the young King
and his brothers.

WILLIAM SHIVAS: Archbishop of St. Andrews, Primate of Scotland, a former
astrologer, favourite of James Third promoted to this high position.

ANDREW, 2ND LORD GRAY: High Sheriff of Angus. A sinister figure, friend
of the Earl of Angus, and suspected by some of the murder of James
Third. Another of the leaders of revolt.

WILLIAM ELPHINSTONE: Bishop of Aberdeen, a former Chancellor of
Scotland and the wisest statesman of the realm at this period. Founder
of Aberdeen University.

ROBERT, 2ND LORD LYLE: A leader of revolt, nephew to Lord Gray. A former
ambassador to England.

MASTER GEORGE HEPBURN: Vicar of Linlithgow. Master of the Rolls. Later
Bishop.

JOHN, 1ST STEWART EARL OF LENNOX: Keeper of Dumbarton Castle. Distant
cousin of the King.

THE LADY MARGARET DRUMMOND: daughter of 1st Lord Drummond.

MARIOT BOYD: daughter of the Laird of Bonshaw.

MAGGREGOR OF GLENARKLET: a Highland chieftain, friend of the King.

COLIN, 1ST EARL OF ARGYLL: chief of Clan Campbell. Chancellor of Scotland.

JOHN, 1ST LORD DRUMMOND: a friend of the former King. Steward of the
royal earldom of Strathearn. Father of the Lady Margaret.

SIR ANDREW WOOD OF LARGO: Scotland's most famous sailor and ship-
builder.

JOHN MACIAN OF ARDNAMURCHAN: Chieftain of a branch of the great Clan Donald.

JOHN CATHANACH MACDONALD OF ISLAY: Chief of Clan Ian Vor, a claimant to the vacant Lordship of the Isles. In revolt.

MARSALA MACIAN: daughter of MacIan of Ardnamurchan.

ALEXANDER MACDONALD OF LOCHALSH: nephew of John, last Lord of the Isles, and leader of the Clan Donald federation. In revolt.

ALEXANDER: illegitimate son of King James by Mariot Boyd. Later Archbishop of St. Andrews.

PERKIN WARBECK: Pretender to the English throne, claiming to be Richard, Duke of York, one of the Princes said to have been murdered in the Tower of London. Later confessed to being imposter.

O'DONNELL, PRINCE OF IRELAND: Earl of Tyrconnel.

DON PEDRO DE AYALA: Spanish Ambassador.

THE LADY ELIZABETH HERON: wife of Sir William Heron of Ford Castle Northumberland.

JOHN, 2ND LORD KENNEDY: later 1st Earl of Cassillis, known as the King of Carrick.

THE LADY JANET KENNEDY: daughter of above, known as Flaming Janet, mistress of Angus.

ROBERT BLACKADDER: Archbishop of Glasgow, churchman and diplomatist.

MARGARET: infant daughter of King James and the Lady Margaret Drummond.

THOMAS SAVAGE: Archbishop of York. English emissary.

THOMAS HOWARD, EARL OF SURREY: Earl Marshal and Lord Treasurer of England, later 2nd Duke of Norfolk.

THE COUNTESS OF SURREY: wife of above. Chief Lady-in-Waiting to Princess Margaret.

PRINCESS MARGARET TUDOR: Daughter of Henry Seventh of England, sister of Henry Eighth, wife of King James.

PRINCE JAMES STEWART: Duke of Ross and Archbishop of St. Andrews, younger brother of King James.

ALEXANDER, 3RD LORD HOME: son of the 2nd Lord. Cupbearer to the King and Warden of the Marches. Succeeded father 1506.

ARCHIBALD, 2ND EARL OF ARGYLL: Chancellor of Scotland. Succeeded Colin, 1st Earl, 1493.

ADAM, 2ND EARL OF BOTHWELL: succeeded Patrick, 1st Earl, 1508.

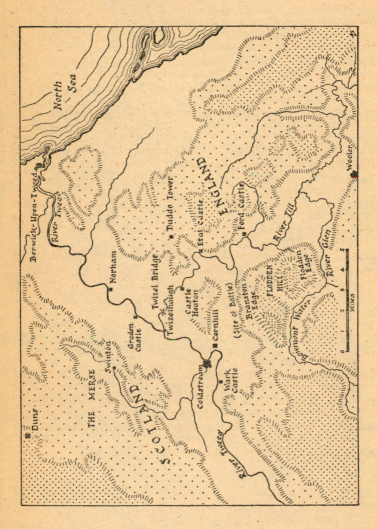

PART ONE
Chain of Destiny

1

THE young man cut short the woman's gabbled incoherences with a strangely authoritative gesture. Unspeaking, he pointed to the rough plank door, but there was almost as much pleading as command in his glance.

The miller's wife, still spilling a disconnected flood of words, backed away from the youngster, reaching a hand to draw her silent and apprehensive husband with her. The two men at the door opened it wider, to let her out, and the jostling crowd outside, mill-hands, men-at-arms and passers-by, pressed closer to peer in. Angrily the richly dressed gentleman in half-armour waved them back.

". . . he said that he was a priest, lord," the woman insisted. "By the Rude, I swear it! A dark man, wi' piercing eyes. In black mail. A lion on his briest. A red lion . . ." She turned on her husband. "A red lion, was it no', Beaton? Speak up, man — speak up. You saw him . . ."

The miller of Bannockburn at the same time both nodded and shook his head, mumbling. His watery eyes were drawn and held by something that lay on the floor at the other side of the small, dusty, cobweb-hung room. He found no words.

"A bishop, it might ha' been. An abbot, lord. A great one, to be sure. Och, I was crying for a priest, like he said. *Him.*" She faltered a little, and her glance slid across the room. "He said to fetch a priest. And this one told me he was a priest. The dark one. Wi' the lion on him. Wi' yon on him, belike he was of the King's company. Save us, I didna ken, lord. Hoo could I ken? He went and kneeled there. On his knees, just. He bent close. Then — ah, God in Heaven — out with his whinger, a great black dagger! '*I'll* shrive you!' he says . . ." The shrill gasping voice rose higher, and broke.

Tensely controlled, but vibrant with emotion, the youth spoke. "Sir," he said to the gentleman at the door, "have her out, in God's name!"

Nodding, the older man gripped the woman's elbow and

roughly propelled her through the doorway, the miller stumbling after. He made to close the door in all the staring faces.

"You also, sir," the young man jerked. To add, low-toned, "I pray you."

The other, a man of middle years, the sternness of his features in the scholarly mould rather than the military, despite his half-armour, raised heavy eyebrows. But something in the other's beseeching expression, at odds with those tight lips, moved him. He inclined his bared head briefly, signed to the armed servant who stood expressionless at the other side of the door, to accompany him, and strode out.

The rickety plank door closed behind them. The young man was alone at last.

With the need to keep up appearances for the moment removed, he was of a sudden no longer a young man. Shoulders drooping a little, tight lips slackening, he was abruptly the merest youth, little more than a boy. He was, in fact, only fifteen years old – although young folk admittedly matured fast in the forcing days at the close of the fifteenth century.

The youth moved across the uneven stone floor, caked with old flour dust, oats crunching beneath his tall spurred riding-boots. Of medium height, slenderly but well built, he had a pleasant open face distinguished by large eloquent eyes under a wide brow, a long, straight, strong nose, and a firm, even obstinate chin, countered by a wide and generous mouth which had been only transiently tightened. Under auburn hair which fell to his shoulders, it was a countenance that held the promise of very masculine good looks to come, of strength and weakness both, of a strong will yet a questioning doubting mind, an impatient impetuous spirit and a warm and compassionate heart.

At the far side of the little room, he knelt on the hard dusty floor, to stare down blindly, lips working. It was only after a while that he got it out.

"Mary, Mother of God – speak for me. Sweet Jesu, Kind Jesu – have mercy on my soul!" he whispered.

He reached out a hesitant hand to draw back fully the rough woollen cloak which part-covered the features and upper half of the body that lay outstretched there. The face he revealed was both notably like his own, and notably different. The wide brow was there, the great dark eyes – glassy now – the straight nose and long upper lip. All the same. But the chin was different, even rigid as it now was, more rigid than it was in life, pointed instead of squared. And the mouth was small, not wide, and the lips though blue now were almost womanly in their shapeliness. It looked a strangely young face, almost immature, in its set alabaster whiteness — the boy had never seen it look so young as this, so that the man who lay there did not display his thirty-seven years.

Long the youth stared, from swimming eyes, biting his lip. He sought to close those great glazed eyes, but could not, and blamed his fumbling reluctant fingers.

"Sire," he whispered. "Father." How seldom had he used that second word, in life. "Father, I willed you no hurt. No harm. I swear it, by Saint Ninian. I but rode with them. They said that I must. For the weal of the realm. They said that no hurt would touch you . . ."

The graven lifeless face, the pinched nostrils, the empty eyes, seemed to cast his whispers back at him with even worse than disbelief — with utter indifference.

"It is the truth," he insisted thickly. "I thought you safe. Fled from the field. Gone to the port of Airth, where the *Yellow Carvel* lies. I did not know . . ."

A mouse scuttled from a hole and peered at him from a corner, and even those little black beady eyes were a relief to meet, after the glassy stare of the others. Sighing, the boy rose to his feet, auburn head sunk, and crossed himself. The gesture reminded him. Stooping again, he picked up the golden cross of Saint Andrew which lay on the dead man's chest, a handsome trinket of saltire backed by the saint's figure, the only item of richness and distinction about the body — for the youth himself was more notably dressed than he who lay on the floor. Gently, diffidently, he sought to detach the ornament, having difficulty in getting the gold chain over the stiff neck and head. He was about to place it about his own neck when of a sudden he choked, as his glance fell on the back of his hand. It was smeared with dark and sticky blood.

Horrified, urgently he wiped and rubbed it on the crimson velvet of the short cloak which hung from one shoulder, over his belted doublet. A stain remained on his skin, and he eyed it askance. Then he examined the body, lower down than heretofore, and moved aside gingerly the woollen cloak still part-covering the trunk and legs.

The darkly sober stuff of the doublet was horribly soaked and

13

clotted with blood, now almost black; but this could not wholly cover and hide the gaping holes and rents in the clothing – many of them, slashed all about the lower chest and abdomen, through which the blood had oozed and congealed, witness to the savage and prolonged fury of the close-range attack.

At the sight, the youth all but spewed. Swaying a little, momentarily dizzy, he lurched the pace or two over to the bare stone wall, there to lean head on arm, eyes closed, breathing deeply.

For a while he stood thus, until the nausea ebbed. His eyes open again, stare at the rough masonry as he would, he still saw only the ghastly pattern of those stab-wounds, and groaned.

"Shame! Shame!" he cried. "I did not know! I did not know! To do this . . .! God's everlasting curse on he who did it! Aye, and God's curse on me, also – for I . . . for I . . ." He banged his fist on the harsh stone. "I raised this hand against you – Mary-Mother plead for me! But . . . not this! Not this!"

As the paroxysm faded, the speaker, staring upwards, saw now other redder blood through the evil haze, the grazed knuckles of his own right hand. Only semi-aware, he perceived that he was clutching a chain that hung there, a rusty length of chain hanging from a great nail on the wall. This room had evidently been the harness-room of the mill, and pieces of old and broken saddlery and leather strapping hung from hooks. Releasing his grip on the chain, with a strange satisfaction the youth saw the round marks of its links imprinted on his skin, red and sore where he had clenched it against the masonry. Rubbing those marks almost abstractedly, he stooped once more and drew up the miller's tattered and now blood-stained cloak over the body, over the face with those indifferent staring eyes.

"God rest you," he muttered. Then, raising his head, "God save . . . the King!" And as he said it, the face wore no child's expression, no boy's, but a man's, grim, determined, but with a quality almost of bitter irony. He reached up, and took down that rusty length of chain, and deliberately tied it like a girdle around his waist, one short trailing end hanging down over trunks and hose, the other and longer end he wound round and round his hand and bare wrist. He moved to the door.

Free hand on the latch he paused, glancing back, to take his last look at the father whom he had little known, had been taught not to respect, and had never understood. He raised the hand to his brow, in some involuntary form of salutation – for, after all,

14

the corpse was James Stewart, third of his name to be King of Scots. And by the same token, he himself, James Stewart likewise, was now James the Fourth. God save the King, indeed.

Squaring those shoulders again, and lifting his chin deliberately, markedly, he turned, opened the door, and strode out.

The little crowd was still there, clustered in the cobbled yard of the mill beside the brawling Burn of Bannock, though standing back a respectful distance from the pacing dignified figure of the gentleman in half-armour and good broadcloth. The armed attendant stood nearby, watchful, hand on sword-hilt, and by the water side, where they might drink, the groom held the four horses which still steamed with hard riding, that warm June day of 1488 — and he was watchful, tense, also. For this Scotland was a land where life itself might hang on a man's keen eye, ready sword-hand and swift heels, any day of the week, especially in this company, and nowhere more notably than here within a couple of miles of the King's town of Stirling.

Seeing the youth emerge, very much the young man again, his Tutor, James Shaw of Sauchie, halted his impatient pacing. "Let us be off, James," he jerked. "This is folly. There is nothing that we may do here. It is dangerous. If my Lord Lyle discovers that you are missing . . ."

"Reward the man who brought us the word, sir," the other interrupted. "Reward him well, for he has earned it. Give him a silver merk."

"A merk! Nonsense, James! It is too much. A shilling will serve — not fourteen . . ."

"Is fourteen shillings too much for risking a life? Give it, sir. And, if you please . . . not James."

"Eh?" The man frowned, tutting. "My lord Duke of Rothesay, if it please you . . .!" he began.

"Nor my lord Duke, sir. I am King, now — and I must remember it. As must you, and all men." That was said simply, soberly, without vaunting or any sort of boyish triumph, a quiet statement of fact.

Sauchie blinked a little, coughed, shuffled his feet, and then bowed jerkily. Recollecting, he took off his bonnet. "Your Grace," he got out, thickly.

James took a few quick paces forward, to lay an impulsive hand on his Tutor's arm. "Your pardon, sir," he said. "Do not take me

15

amiss. Here is no cause for pride, God knows! But . . . my state is changed. Of a sudden. You must see it. The man who . . . who struck those, those . . ." He swallowed, but with a visible effort recovered himself, tensely gripping the chain and raising his head. "The dastard who struck those craven blows, who slew his liege lord helpless, has changed all. All. Changed more, I swear, than he knows! I shall find him, I vow, and all the saints of Heaven are my witness! And he shall pay the price."

"Aye. No doubt. To be sure." Sauchie was staring at that chain, round the young man's waist and wrist. "What a God's name is this? This . . . this ironware? Fetters." He actually pointed. "What means this?"

"A memento. A prompter," his former charge answered briefly. "You have taught me to use prompters, sir, for many a lesson. This will serve to remind me of . . ." He jerked his auburn head towards the harness-room that he had left. ". . . of yonder. Of this day. Of my duty. I found it hanging there. Above him. To my hand. A memento, lest I forget." James twitched the chain with a jolt that must have hurt his bare wrist. "Aye, lest I ever forget." He turned away, to scan the crowd. "The woman — where is she? I must question her."

"James . . .! Your Grace! There is no time. Not now. There is danger here. We must back to Stirling. At once. Before you are missed . . ."

His urgings were ignored. "Reward the man, as I said, sir. Yonder he is, by the tree. Have his name. He has served me well, and may serve again." James had picked out the miller's wife in the throng, and beckoned her. "Mistress — here. To me."

She came doubtfully, still dragging her shambling husband with her. The crowd pressed closer.

Before she reached him, James was speaking, eager, impatient. "This man?" he demanded. "This assassin? You said he was a priest? A bishop or abbot, maybe? Bearing the King's device — a lion rampant . . .?"

"I do not know, lord. He *said* he was a priest. But, to do such evil . . . to slay the King . . .! Och, it could not be. No true priest of God . . ."

"Priests have done evil before this!" he interrupted. "There were priests on the field, on both sides. But none, I think, would wear the Lion of Scotland. You are sure of the lion, Mistress?"

16

"Aye, sir—aye. A red lion, as I mind it. You saw it, Beaton man. Tell the lord. Guidsakes—can you no' speak?"

Moistening slack lips, the miller found words. "Aye. A lion. But no' red. White. White on red, it was. An ill, black-a-vised man. A devil, sir—nae priest! A black beard to him . . ."

"*White*, you said? A white lion. On red, not gold? You are sure, man? White on red? Not red on gold?"

"Aye, lord. White it was. On red. On his briest, just . . ."

"Woman—was it red or white, the lion? Which?"

"I . . . I canna mind, sir." She shook her unkempt head. "I wasna heeding to the likes o' yon. But . . . but white, belike. Aye, now I think o' it—a red coat over his black mail. Wi' the lion front and back. White . . ."

The young King's eyes narrowed as he gazed over her head, out across the green slanting braes that rolled down to the level floodlands of the Carse of Stirling, to the blue narrowing Firth of Forth sparkling in the June sunlight, and beyond to the steep shadow-slashed ramparts of the Ochils. "My Lord of Gray bears gules, a lion rampant argent!" he said slowly. "White on red. And his beard is black as sin itself! My noble Lord of Gray, who ate at my table last night!"

Shaw of Sauchie frowned. "Unwise talk," he urged warningly. "Have a care, a mercy's sake, how you speak!" His glance slid round the listening gaping crowd. "Gray is a great and powerful lord. He would never stoop to . . . this. You cannot heed the babble of these numskulls on such great matter as this. Moreover, there are others who bear lions on their arms—Angus himself. March. Glamis. Home. Bickerton, I think. Aye, and Mowbray. You cannot take the word of a chattering hen-wife. And she knows not her own mind . . ."

"See you to yonder man and his reward, sir—and leave the woman to me," the young man directed. Never before had James Stewart spoken to his Tutor thus. "Mistress—tell me the way of it. From the beginning. Think back. How went it with my father, two days ago? Tell me all, and fear nothing."

The miller's wife rubbed her mouth with the back of her hand, as though to school her lips to eloquence. "I tell't you, lord. It was just past noon. Two days back. The day o' the battle. I was at the dam. To draw water, wi' my pitcher. I heard the horse coming hard down the hill yonder. Frae the moor. A great grey beast it was. Hard-ridden, or bolting—I ken not which."

17

"Just the one? He was alone?"

"Aye, sir — alone. This one man only. I think he couldna hold the beast in. Down he came. Och, I was fear't he was coming right at me. I dropped my pitcher, and broke it. The brute was near on to me . . ."

"Yes, yes. But the King?"

"Och, it was the dam, lord — the water. The beast wouldna jump the dam. It shied and reared, nigh atop o' me. It threw him. The rider. He fell. Near into the water, he fell. We carried him in yonder, Beaton and me. He was sair hurt. When his wits came back to him, he called for a priest. For to confess, he said. I askit him who he might be, and he said 'I was your King this day, at morn.' Aye, is that no' what he said, Beaton? Och, I ran out then, sir, fair vexed. I cried for a priest for the King. This one was there, with others. He said he was priest enough for the King, and where was he . . .?"

"He had followed him, then — this man? From the battle?"

"I'd no' ken that. I think no'. It was a whilie after. This black-avised man wi' the lion — he was looking at the King's great grey horse. At the waterside. Others wi' him, but he was chiefest. I didna see where they came frae. When he said he was priest, I brought him to the King. Alone, he came. Wi' just Beaton and me . . ."

"Aye. And then?"

"He hunkered down beside the King. Close. He askit him if he was like to recover o' his hurt. The King said he didna ken, but belike he would. But if he was priest would he shrive him? 'Aye, that shall I do right heartily!' the black man cries. And, sweet Jesu — out wi' his whinger . . .! Ah, Guidsakes! Guidsakes . . .!"

James moistened his lips, but said nothing.

"What could we do, lord? What could we do? We are but puir folk . . ."

"Aye. And after? What of this devil? This dastard slayer of his helpless prince?"

"He laughed, sir. Aye, he laughed. Near knockit us ower, he did, as he went, laughing. He took horse wi' the others, and rode off. Yonder. The Stirling road."

The youth looked, without seeing, where she pointed, northwards. There, against the towering blue background of the Highland hills, the rock of Stirling, flanked by its climbing grey streets and crowned by its proud royal castle, soared abruptly above the green plain two miles away. But after only a moment or two his eyes focussed keenly enough on a rolling cloud of dust rising from the same road, from the dull pall of which occasional gleams shone metallically in the June sun. He frowned, but did not speak.

His Tutor was as sharp-eyed and more eloquent. Hurrying back from giving reluctant largesse to the young man who had sought them out whilst hawking amongst the Torbrex knowes, and brought them here, he pointed also, and shouted.

"Look there! They come! A plague on it—they come. We are too late. Did I not tell you! We should never have come here. It was folly. I said so. You would not heed me . . ." Shaw of Sauchie had changed his direction, and was hastening to the waiting horses. "Come, you. Perhaps there is yet time. Down the burn-side, to the low ground. Under the hill there, in the marshlands, we could be hidden. Win back to Stirling unseen . . ."

"No," James declared, with quiet decision. "That we shall not. I am the King now, and shall run from no subject of mine."

"But . . . keep your wits, in God's name, James! King you may be, now—but in name only. These lords are great and powerful men. And fierce. Well you know it. They ordered that you were not to ride out of the Stirling demesne. Lyle, Home, Hepburn— they are hard and wrathful men . . ."

"They are my subjects," the youth said, setting his jaw stubbornly—and looking the younger for it.

"You say that! When *he* lies in there? They were *his* subjects also, I'd mind you!"

James flinched a little. He looked down at the hand gripping his chain, and then up again. His eyes met those of the young man who had brought them here, only two or three years older than himself, and who had now moved across to his own horse which still stood steaming beside the four beasts from the royal stables. He saw, or sensed, encouragement, sympathy, loyalty, in those friendly grey eyes set in the long hatchet-like countenance, and nodded his head.

"We wait, sir, for whosoever these may be," he said flatly.

The older man tugged at his small pointed beard. "My head may pay for this . . ." he muttered.

"Not while mine remains on my shoulders. Never fear." To halt further efforts at persuasion, James looked across at the young man again, who stood beside his sorrel mare but evidenced no intention of mounting and riding off. It was a good horse, and though the rider's clothes were plain and well worn, they had been of fair quality. "Your name, sir?" he asked.

"Bruce, Sire. Rob, they call me. Youngest son to Robert Bruce of Airth, yonder. And . . . your leal servant. Your Grace's true man."

James flushed slightly at the obvious warmth of sincerity in the other's voice, at the infectious enthusiasm—and at this, the first bestowal of his monarch's style of Sire. "I thank you," he said thickly. "My first. Aye, my first. You have served me truly already. I think that I shall require more service yet, Rob Bruce! By Saint Ninian, I do!"

"Always, Sire. It is yours to command. As am I. For aye."

Head lifting, brow clearing, with the sudden impulsive decision that was so typical of him, James actually smiled. He swung on the armed servant in the royal livery who stood watching. "Your sword, man." And, as his glance rose beyond the man, towards what was now clearly a large and hard-riding cavalcade approaching fast along the dusty highway, he added impatiently, "Quickly."

"Eh . . .?" The other stared at him, doubtfully, and then looked at Sauchie. "My sword?"

"Aye. And quickly, I said." James took a pace or two forward, free hand outstretched. "Hurry, man."

Drawing the heavy weapon, the man-at-arms seemed unsure what to do with it. James took it from him eagerly, turning back to Bruce.

"Come," he ordered. "Here. To me. You bear a proud name, Rob Bruce. Here on this ground—Bannockburn. I shall make it prouder!" And as the other came up, "Kneel, Rob man."

Bruce looked wonderingly from the young King to those around him, and over towards the advancing horsemen. But he knelt as he was commanded.

"What folly is this, James?" Sauchie exclaimed. "Here is no time for mummery. For play-acting. I' faith, 'tis we who will be kneeling ere long . . .!"

"My first act as King, it is," James asserted, his voice breaking a little with excitement. "As well that these should see it," and he gestured to the oncoming company. The sword was too heavy for easy gestures, however, and he had to release his other wrist from the coils of chain, to use both hands on the long hilt. "An augury, is it not? This name, to pledge me his leal service and life, in this place? Bannockburn. At this moment." James raised the sword, to bring the flat of it down a little harder than intended perhaps on the young man's broad shoulder. He raised his voice likewise. "Arise, Sir Robert!" he cried.

Colouring in turn, confused, stammering, Bruce got to his feet, as James held out his left hand to him, still marked with the rust and impressions of the chain. He reached to return that boyish grip, recollected, and stooping jerkily, awkwardly, kissed the far from clean fingers instead. He mumbled incoherent words.

What he said was lost, as were Shaw of Sauchie's further strictures, in the thunder of hooves and the clank of steel, as the newcomers pounded up. There were at least fifty heavily armed men in the party, mainly savage-looking and unkempt Border moss-troopers on shaggy mounts, led by two richly dressed men in chased and engraved breastplates, but wearing velvet caps instead of morions or helmets. Two Standard-Bearers rode directly behind them, before the soldiery, carrying fluttering banners showing colourful devices. Scotland was a notable place for streaming banners.

The country-folk and bystanders scattered like chaff and ran incontinent before the onslaught of rearing, pawing, violently drawn-up horseflesh and shouting men. No consideration was shown for man, woman or child. Even James and those close to him had to draw back hastily to avoid being ridden down. No respects, no greetings, were offered to any. The two leaders reined their caracoling steeds almost on top of the shrinking Laird of Sauchie, with scarcely a glance for his young charge.

"Fiend take you—what means this, Sauchie?" the elder bellowed. He was a big, florid, dark-haired, handsome man, not yet middle-aged but seeming to be overfull of blood; Patrick, second Lord Hailes, he was head of the powerful Lothian house of Hepburn, and one of the principal rebels against the late King. "You had your orders. The boy was not to leave Stirling bounds. God's death, man—how dare you bring him here!"

"It was not my wish, my lord—I swear it. I advised turning back. From Torbrex. To the castle. We were hawking. But the tidings were . . . were . . ."

"You advised! *Advised*, fool? Since when were you told to advise? You were to govern. Control. If you cannot do that . . ."

"He did not bring me here. I came of my own will, despite him." That was James Stewart.

"Quiet!" Hailes did not so much as look at the speaker. "Why came you here, Sauchie? Out with it. What a pox is your game?"

"No game, my lord. In truth. This man brought us tidings. This Bruce, here . . ."

"My Lord of Hailes." High and clear the King's young voice rose, even though there was a tremor in it. "Hear me, I . . . I command you! I came here because I must. Because I could do no other . . ."

"My Lord Duke commands us, hark you!" That was the other nobleman, a younger man in his late twenties, lean, angular, sandy-haired, with a hawklike face and keen darting eyes, on whom the rich clothing sat but awkwardly. He grinned, and still in the saddle, swept off his jewelled velvet cap mockingly. "Your Highness finds us all ears, I swear!"

The boy bit his lip, but maintained his head high. "I hope so, Master of Home," he said. "For there is a deal to hear. Much demands attention here. Yours, and mine."

The grandson and heir of old Lord Home grimaced, clapped on his bonnet again, and turned away. Hailes it was who answered.

"Quiet, boy," he ordered. "Your time will come, no doubt. But not yet. Sauchie — I have little love for men who fail me . . ."

"My lord!" The knuckles of the hand which still held the drawn sword gleamed white, as James called still further upon his store of courage and hardihood. "The Master of Home had the civility to uncover to me. I'll thank you to do the same!" That came out with a rush.

The Hepburn turned to stare from the youth to Home and back again, clearly astonished. "Uncover, did you say?"

"Aye. Is not the custom? To uncover before your King?"

"King, hey!" Hailes hooted rudely. "God's Body — you go too fast, cockerel! Because we set you up under the banner of Scotland on yonder field two days ago, it doesna make a king of you. When our hands place the crown on that head o' yours, it will be time enough to uncover, boy. Mind you that."

"Another hand has done that for you, my lord."

"Eh . . .?"

"My father . . . the King . . . lies yonder." James gestured to the harness-room behind him. "Cruelly slain." His lips trembled, and no more words came.

The noblemen stared from the boy to each other, and then to Sauchie. At that man's agitated nod, they flung themselves down from their horses, and went stamping to the building, armour clanking. Home, in the lead, flung open the door.

James stood where he was, set-faced, eyes fixed on the distant line of the hills beyond the Firth. Sauchie fidgeted and shuffled, tugging at his wispy beard. Young Bruce moved closer, to stand directly behind the King, but said nothing. The company of moss-troopers talked, laughed and jeered, caring for none.

Presently Hailes and Home emerged from the hovel, their expressions markedly changed. Not that there was shock or sorrow or awe reflected therein, for they had hated and despised the man who lay there, and death however violent was commonplace indeed; but preoccupation and calculation showed on their frowning features. The Master of Home now carried in both hands a huge and long-handled sword of antique design.

"Here's a pickle!" Hailes jerked, to no one in particular. "God's Body—this changes all!"

"He is stiff. Cold. He has been dead for long," the other said. "Who did it, think you?"

"That remains to be seen. Whoever it was has kept it quiet. Why?" Lord Hailes tapped at his prominent teeth thoughtfully. "Who would gain? That we should not yet know that the King is dead?"

"All thought him escaped with Wood in the ship—the *Yellow Carvel*. To Fife. Or to the North. That he was now with Huntly or Forbes . . ."

Hailes looked across at the Tutor, ignoring James. "How heard you of this, Sauchie? What brought you here?"

"This lad, my lord. This Bruce. He sought us out—whilst hawking at the Torbrex. He swore that it was the King . . ."

"How did you know this, fellow?" Hailes demanded of the young man. "What a pox was your part in this . . .?"

"My lord." It was James who spoke, and strongly however jerkily. "I ask you to address Sir Robert Bruce more fittingly . . . since his prince has but new honoured him with knighthood." He swallowed. "And, speaking of courtesies, do you owe none to your new King? If not to the person of he that *was* your King!"

The big man all but choked, his red face purpling. But, by the time that he had found his tongue, choler was giving place in his

23

glance to speculation, appraisal, even a glint of wry humour. He rubbed his chin. "So ho!" he said. "Thus it goes, does it?" And with a grin that was only half-mockery, he took off his velvet bonnet, held it to his steel-clad chest, and inclined his head. "Your Grace's most humble servant!" he declared.

The boy's eyes, large, urgent, anxious, but with their own shrewdness, met those of the Hepburn, and held them for significant moments. "I rejoice to hear it, my lord," he cried. "You have a strong shoulder . . . and I am yet young. May I lean on it, my Lord of Hailes? For my comfort and the weal of my realm?"

If the other's lips were laggard, clearly his mind was not. Searching the youth's face, with its strange mixture of uncertainty, sensitivity and determination, he calculated swiftly, visibly. "M'mmm," he said.

"You are the first of my lords to pledge your fealty, The *first!*" James repeated, with notable emphasis. "I am . . . well pleased that it should be so."

Hailes drew a deep breath. "Aye," he said. "Sire — my shoulder is as yours, henceforth." He strode forward, took James's hand, and raised it to twisted cynical lips.

"Good!" the boy exclaimed, too eagerly. "Good. All true men will have cause to rejoice in this, my lord, I swear."

Immediate rejoicings were not evident there and then, however. The Master of Home looked, narrow-eyed, from Hailes to the King, still clutching the great sword. He did not speak, but suspicion and reserve were in every line of him. None could fail to sense it.

James did not. "Master of Home," he said. "Your own noble house, I am assured, has ever been a prop of the Crown." If the boy flushed a little at this barefaced lie, he nevertheless still held his head high. "You, sir, I trust, will likewise be my true support. My . . . my left hand. You and your most ancient house."

It was Hailes' turn to look frosty. The Hepburn rise to power was of only comparatively recent origin, from a mere Lothian lairdship — whereas the Homes were descended from the princely Cospatrick Earls of Dunbar and March, descended from King Duncan's son, of a line that had been great before the Normans crossed the English Channel. The Master cleared his throat, and bowed stiffly.

"I am yours to command, Highness," he said.

Hailes snorted a coarse laugh, but before he might make other comment, James went on quickly.

"I rejoice at that, sir. In that you both will uphold me. Be sure that the Council, *my* new Council, will say the same. Will . . . will perceive the realm's good fortune. And take due action." Leaving that hint of high office to sink in, he changed the subject. Pointing to the sword which Home still held, he said, "I think I know that great brand, sir. How did you come by it?"

"It was yonder, Sire. In there." The Master gestured towards the harness-room. "Under him. Under the King. He lay on it. The Bruce's sword it is, I think. King Robert's. Which he bore once on this same field, near two hundred years ago. He — your father — bore it less worthily, it seems, three days back."

James bit his lip. "He was not a man of war," he said. "The sword was never his friend, his choice. Whether it shall be mine, whether it *must* be mine, God knows. I do not." He held out his hands. "*This* sword, at least, must be mine. Heaven helping me, I will use it justly."

Hailes grinned. "It is a mite large as yet, Sire! You must needs grow a little before you are man enough for this one! Meantime, perhaps I may wield it for you, to good effect, however. Give it here . . ."

"My thanks, my lord — but no! That is the King's sword. None may wield it save the King." Hoarsely the youth asserted it. "Master of Home — give it to me." Taking the great heavy weapon, five feet in length, the two-handed hilt of it alone more than a foot, he stared down at it a little askance. There was blood on it, clotted and dried and black — but only a smear, and half-way up the broad of the blade. It was royal blood therefore; no foeman's blood stained its point or sharp edges. Shaking his head, the boy turned right round abruptly, and thrust out the weapon to young Bruce behind him. "Take it," he said. "*You* take it. Your ancestor's, it was, as well as mine. Your namesake's. None could carry it for me more worthily, I vow. From now on you are my Sword-Bearer, Sir Robert Bruce."

That young man, taking the weapon, said something falteringly. James was not looking at him however, but at Hailes and Home.

Neither nobleman actually protested. Hailes barked a laugh, and shrugged, whilst the other pursed his thin lips tightly and stared straight ahead of him. The young monarch let go his breath in a long quivering sigh. It was the first test, and he had won.

"I have a — a duty for you, Sir Robert," he said, turning back to Bruce. "A notable duty. Your first. We ride to Stirling. But . . . my father. The King. His body . . ." James cleared a thick throat. "It . . . he must be looked to. As is seemly. Proper. See you to it. Bring him to Stirling. To the Castle. Decently and in order. On a litter. You understand?"

"Yes, Sire. To the Castle . . .?"

"No, by the Mass!" Lord Hailes put in. "Do you want a riot? All the town in a stramash? Do not bring him to Stirling."

"But secretly? Covered. None will know . . ."

"All Stirling will know within the hour. Think you these gentle marchmen of ours will hold their tongues?" He gestured towards the waiting moss-troopers. "We should have the town in an uproar. Men at each others' throats. *His* faction against ours. I care not for a little blood-letting. But for a better cause than over yonder . . . corpse!"

The boy blinked, clenching his fists. Home intervened.

"A church," he suggested. "Our late liege lord would lie safest in a church. Saint Ninians is but a mile off. Put him there, under guard . . ."

"No!" James cried. "Not that. He shall not be hidden away like some felon! He was King of Scots. He must lie in honour now, at least. He loved Cambuskenneth. The Abbey. He shall lie there. Where my mother lies. Take him to Cambuskenneth Abbey, Sir Rob. Tell the Lord Abbot to guard him well. In the King's name. Then come to me, at Stirling Castle." He turned to Sauchie. "Sir — reward the miller here. And his wife. For their trouble. A silver merk, likewise . . ."

"Faugh!" Hailes broke in. "Waste no time with such cattle! Come, Sire — we have spent overlong in talk, as it is. Mount, and let us back to Stirling, in God's name! We have much to do."

"Do as I say, Sauchie. These are my subjects as much as are you, are they not, my lord? They sought to aid a man in his dire need. They merit their King's regard, I think — even if their reward be less than yours!"

Hailes gobbled like a turkey-cock.

"Shall we ride, then, my lord?" James suggested.

Home spoke. "See you — none must know of this. Yet. That we have the King. That His Grace has now the crown. Not until

26

we are prepared. Until we have time to take steps. Necessary steps . . ."

"Aye, we must work fast," Hailes agreed.

James looked from one to the other, but said nothing. He moved over to his horse.

As he mounted, Hailes called out. "That chain you have round your middle? What tomfoolery is this?"

"No foolery, my lord. That is my memory. It goes with me henceforth. Lest I forget Bannockburn Mill. And what brought him to this. And us — God forgive us!"

2

Surely never had there been experienced in all Scotland's vivid and colourful past a scene at once so gay and splendid, yet so hag-ridden with guilt; so brilliant on the surface yet so sombre beneath; so full of praise to God and fear of men, joy and hope walking hand-in-hand with suspicion and dread. The proud and ancient Abbey of Scone, heart and palladium of Scotland, had witnessed nothing like this in its chequered history.

The spreading parklands by the silver Tay were a kaleidoscope of colour and movement, strangely mottled and splashed with heavy black. Tents and pavilions and booths had been set up by the score, the hundred, below the Abbey buildings, and above them banners and ensigns innumerable fluttered in the breeze. Shrines, temporary fanes and calvaries had been erected to the Virgin, to Saints Andrew, Ninian, Duthac and others, on every eminence of the park, under every group of trees, where teams of monks and singing boys chanted or made soft music. Minstrels, fools, tumblers and acrobats were there to rival them – although it would not be until later, after the ceremony, that these would truly come into their own. Assuming that such stage was ever reached. A tilting-yard had been formed on the level haughland, with lists and a decorated stand for the ladies and principal spectators; and at the far side of the park, a racecourse for those with different tastes. There were pits for cock-fighting, even a bear-garden, and a ring, well barricaded, for bull-baiting. Nothing had been stinted, nothing overlooked, however short the time for preparation.

Yet amongst and besides all this gaiety a very different note sounded constantly, incessantly, ominously. For one thing, the Abbey bells rang out in slow booming monotony, not in joyous pealing but in knell for the dead. The black and purple hangings of mourning were draped everywhere on shrines and pavilions even, incongruously, on bull-ring and sports arena. Each group of monks interspersed their music with repeated masses for the soul of their late liege lord James and prayers for God's mercy on his successor and unworthy servant, also James. By order of the King. Men walked warily therefore, however their women might laugh and skirl, and none were far parted from their weapons however splendidly they might be dressed. Uncertainty, suspicion, fear, stalked abroad against the lovely background of the Highland hills. Groups of men-at-arms, brilliant in their lords' heraldic liveries, stood waiting, watchful, ready. Each new arrival, noble or laird, bishop or abbot or burghal representative, was noted, his allegiance and power assessed. Scone, that sunny breezy Coronation day of 26th June 1488 had as much of calm and assurance as a powder-barrel with a lighted fire near by.

As strange as the scene itself perhaps was the fact that all its dichotomy, its essential dissonance, was so largely the responsibility of one individual, and that a youth, a mere boy. For King James had inevitably, if not deliberately, set the tone of this great gathering by insisting first that his Coronation should be held thus early, only a bare two weeks after his father's death; also that, although all was to be carried out in the finest style and regardless of expense, nevertheless every great lord and all those connected with the Court were to be dressed in black—as he was himself—in mourning for him who, he declared, so many of them had helped to slay, himself again included; that all of his nobility, great churchmen and representatives of the burghers, should be commanded to attend—including those who had been the late King's men until a fortnight ago, and therefore sworn enemies of the rebel lords who had won the field of Sauchieburn and who now held sway around him.

So everywhere about the precincts of the great Abbey colour clashed with sombre black; men eyed each other askance; choirs sang of adoration and glory and forgiveness, while guests calculated, whispered and weighed chances; and the youthful central figure of the King himself, though he sought to greet and smile at all, was little better than a prisoner, ever hemmed in and guarded by a set of grim and jealous nobles fearful even now that he might be snatched from their care by others and so lose them power and privilege and preferment.

Nevertheless, uneasy and false as was the day's rejoicing, it represented a major triumph for young James Stewart. For it was all his own doing. None of those who sought to govern and use him had been in any hurry for this Coronation; none had sought the presence there of enemies and rivals; certainly none of them mourned the late King, or shared the boy's sense of guilt and remorse over his death. Most of them, in fact, had urged vastly different courses on the young monarch—and would have enforced those courses upon him had they been able. That they had not was a tribute to the youth's wits and determination. Deliberately, skilfully, he had played off one against another, using their own deep jealousies, ambitions, greeds and vanities, to prevent them uniting to impose their wills upon him. Although he was the King, his position was desperately weak. He was a minor, many years from the age when he might insist on personal rule; his country was hopelessly divided, many hating his very name, and although he had been used as figurehead by the rebel lords against his father's misrule, he personally meant nothing to most of them; and in an age when might was unquestionably right, the Kings of Scots had no standing army, no personal forces of their own, with which to carry out their policies, but were dependent on the unruly levies of their nobles and the musters of the townsfolk.

Yet certain advantages James had, in the situation into which he had been thrust, and he made shrewd enough use of them all. He was the fountain of honour and source of power, however little of it he himself might be permitted to wield. Since all must be done ostensibly in his name, so long as he withheld his name little that was legal and lasting could in fact be done. The Privy Council, the ruling body of the kingdom, automatically dissolved itself at the death of a monarch, and only the new monarch could appoint successors, even though the Estates of Parliament must eventually approve them. The great offices of state, the plums of power and patronage, were in the grant of the King, and since there was no Council available to insist on certain nominees, James's own signature was the only essential authority. And from that first day at Stirling, he had shown that however youthful and inexperienced, he was not to be bullied or cajoled into signing against his judgement. That his judgement was not infrequently at fault was beside the point. He was making many mistakes, taking foolish and headstrong decisions, undoubtedly. But by using the opportunities to his hand, by playing on both the strengths and weaknesses of those who had him in their physical power, he was steering a course, his own course, however erratic and sometimes short-sighted, not others' courses for him.

As he had perceived that grim day at Beaton's Mill, he might build up his shaky throne on the two arrogant nobles who had come there to constrain him — and on their mutual envies and suspicions. Patrick Hepburn, Lord Hailes, coarse, impetuous, ruthless, but an able soldier and a strong man, he had appointed Master of the Royal Household, Keeper of Edinburgh Castle, Warden of the Mid and West Marches, Great Admiral of Scotland and governor of his young brother the Duke of Ross, next heir to the throne. To counter all this, the Master of Home was now Lord Great Chamberlain, Keeper of Stirling Castle, Warden of the East March and governor of the still younger prince, the Earl of Mar. It made a nice balance. Both coveted the Chancellorship, the role of chief minister, but James had held back and put off. In consequence these two former comrades-in-arms now eyed each other like dogs seeking the same bone, whilst between them the boy picked his careful way. Lesser appointments he had filled on the same principle, so that what had been a strong faction, more or less united and bound at least by mutual interest sufficiently to lead a successful army, had become a pack of rivals resentful of each other's winnings, call themselves a Court as they might.

James's very arrival on this strange if spectacular scene precipitated a clash in itself. The magnificently robed Abbot of Scone, with a gorgeous company of prelates, priests, acolytes and choristers, was waiting to receive the sombrely clad Court party at the Abbey gatehouse and to escort the King to the great church itself. But the youthful monarch had other ideas. When he could make himself heard above the fanfares of massed trumpets that saluted his presence, he so informed the churchmen.

"My Lord Abbot," he said. "I thank you for your welcome. But I am not yet ready to enter God's house. Worthy I fear I shall never be — but *ready* I must be." Dressed in black velvet, he dismounted from his splendidly caparisoned horse, and so all the throng of lords and knights behind must needs do likewise. "There are shrines here set up, that will prepare me. Or so I hope. Will you attend me?" He gestured towards the seething parkland.

"But, Sire," the Abbot protested, astonished. "What need have you of such? Such trumperies? My Lord Archbishop awaits you yonder, at the High Altar. With all the bishops and fathers of Holy Church. If further preparation of Your Grace is necessary, surely it is for them to give. Not . . . not these monkish pedlars of indulgences? These are for the commonality, for the poor . . ."

"As am I, sir! And I have my own poverty." Eagerly the boy sought to explain to the prelate. "Do you not see — before I can stand at the same High Altar where once my father stood, I must do penance? I have done it already, God knows — but not enough. Not enough. And I must be seen to do it, of all. By my people, and his. The blood-guiltiness must be washed away. Surely you understand . . .?"

"Holy Church does not require such, such extremities of Your Grace. Not here. Not this day . . ."

Sighing, James shrugged. "Come!" he said, and turned to walk towards the nearest group of trees, under which a shrine had been erected.

Grinning at the churchmen's discomfiture, the dark-clad courtiers followed after, laughing and chattering. Hailes and Home kept close at either side of the King, but only a pace or two behind strode the other youthful figure of Rob Bruce, in black likewise, and bearing over his shoulder the great sword of his ancestor.

After those first malicious grins, any smiling that was done on that progress through the crowded haughland was done by the King himself, occasional quick and nervous smiles and nods to groups and individuals whom he passed, gentry, friars, merchants, townsfolk, even packmen and Highlanders. All these stared, some few hastily remembered to uncover, but none returned his anxious smiles save only a cluster or two of giggling girls. Perhaps therefore James was hardly to be blamed if thereafter he seemed especially to select young women to smile at. The folk of Scotland were not used to kings smiling on them, moving amongst them, or indeed seeming to notice their existence.

At the first shrine the royal party came to, a mere ramshackle booth with makeshift altar erected to Saint Mungo, and a seedy friar in stained and patched habit displaying a relic of bone in a box, James surprised all by actually kneeling down before this scarecrow — to the latter's extreme alarm and embarrassment undoubtedly. None other save only Rob Bruce at his back followed suit. Into the shocked silence, the King in a clear determined voice sought the friar's intercession with the saint upon a sinner who had helped to encompass his father's downfall; and if possible his benediction thereafter. The monk's gabbled assurances, genuflexions and lavish blessings were all but lost in the mutterings and exclamations of amazement and little-disguised disapproval from all around. The Abbot of Scone's lip-curling distate almost reached the stage of disgust. James rose, to take from young Bruce a little bag of coin, which he handed over to the astounded friar, with the request that he should of his goodness say masses for the soul of the late King, cruelly slain, and the salvation of his own, in peril.

He moved on, flushed and pink, with perspiration beading his lip but his chin jutting strongly, while the ranks of censure and scandal fell in behind.

Hailes did not trouble to lower his voice to proffer his advice. "Sire — enough of this play-acting, in Christ's name! Let us on with the business that brought us. There are too many in this park whose looks I like but little!"

"I came here to take certain vows before God, my lord. Before I take them honestly, I must do what I deem right. Fitting."

"Fitting! Then keep your kneelings for the church, I say . . ."

"This talk of your father, of the late King, is foolish — danger-ous," the Master of Home put in. "His death lies not at your door. Or ours. It was unfortunate — but a consequence of his own misrule. To make this much of it smacks of implication, of blame. Nothing could be more harmful for Your Grace's cause."

"It is my soul that I must think of, on this my Coronation day, sir — is it not? Rather than my cause?"

"Soul!" Hailes cried. "A pest — leave you old men and clerks to worry about souls, my Lord James! You have a realm to rule. At your age you should have more solid meat to bite on than souls!" He turned a fleering eye on the cleric. "Eh, my Lord Abbot?"

The prelate, in a difficult position, pursed his lips and said nothing.

James nevertheless stopped at the next shrine, a more ambitious canopied baldachin to Saint Michael, with chaplains and choristers from the late King's own Chapel Royal at Stirling. Again he knelt, muttered a prayer and sought benediction, before handing over another purseful of silver.

If the Abbot had been disparaging before, now he was so offended as to be driven to protest — for the Chapel Royal was a parvenu and rival establishment of James Third's that had drained off much good revenue and custom which might well have come to Scone. "Sire!" he exclaimed. "Your royal liberality and bounty should not be squandered and mis-spent on such as these — upstarts, pretenders, parasites! This ancient foundation, key to your kingdom, is pinched and straitened, impoverished of its due sustenance . . ."

"God in Heaven!" Hailes burst out, gazing about him at the rich cattle-dotted parklands and trim gardens, the noble church and spreading monastic buildings, all in excellent order and maintenance. "Do you name this impoverishment, man? The kingdom cannot show finer . . ."

"We do what we can on scant means," the other said primly. "God's service suffers. Would you deny Almighty God . . .?"

James moved on, leaving the argument fierce behind him. He made his way, past the entrance to the jousting-ground, towards a third shrine, set beside a fountain that played amongst statuary of eye-catching indeceny — a permanent feature of the park this, it seemed. The young King's eyes did not fail to be caught. Pausing involuntarily, his glance slid from women's breasts that streamed water sideways, to male organs spouting it upwards. Moistening his lips, he considered and admired. He looked round, to catch Rob Bruce's eye. On its return his regard caught that of another pair of eyes, dark, gleaming and bold, belonging to a handsome gipsy-like girl who stood near by watching, a dirty child clutching at her skirts. A none-too-clean tartan plaid part enfolded her shapely person, covering one shoulder and leaving the other bare save for the thin stuff of a bursting bodice which sagged low. Frankly the Highland girl smiled at him. She tossed a glance over at the statuary, and then came back to him. One eyebrow rose, and her lips pouted into a red circle, as she studied him from under lowered lids. James grinned.

The party behind was now almost upon them, a little held up by the hot debate of Hailes and the Abbot. Close at the King's back Rob Bruce coughed, and when that had no effect, actually tapped the royal doublet lightly between the shoulder-blades with the long sword-hilt, James took a lingering farewell of those dark challenging eyes, raised a finger an inch or two, almost imperceptibly and passed on. He looked back after only a few paces, and found the young woman's glowing gaze still upon him.

Plumping down precipitately on his knees before the shrine a little way beyond, it is to be feared that the monarch's devotions were less intense than heretofore, despite the fact that this fane was dedicated to the blessed Saint Ninian whose guardianship had ever been especially acknowledged by the royal house. They were briefer too—and Saint Ninians' earthly nominees on this occasion might well have found cause for offence, for on taking the usual purse from Bruce, James hesitated, opened it, and extracted one of the silver merks therefrom, to hand this to Rob and jerk his head backwards towards the young woman's position, whilst he presented the ravished remainder to the bowing priest."

Home glanced sharply at Hailes, but the latter was too busy congratulating the Abbot of Scone on his handsome sculptural decorations to notice the incident.

There was a diversion. Down from the direction of the Abbey buildings a great figure came striding, scattering people before him like chaff, a train of lesser characters hurrying in his wake. This man, huge, hulking, greying, with craggy harried features and a nose like the beak of an eagle, was by no means dressed in the prescribed mourning. He wore the richest of clothing, indeed, but with a sort of slovenly flair. At sight of him, all around the King fell silent, even Hailes ceasing his baiting of the Abbot.

James perceived the newcomer's approach as soon as any, but he did not pause to wait for him as did others, moving on deliberately towards a Calvary set on the first rise of the Mote Hill. Only Rob Bruce kept place close behind.

"James!" a deep and rasping voice bellowed. "Y'Grace—what is the meaning of this? Fiend seize me—what do you here?"

The youth squared his shoulders. "Greetings, Uncle," he said, his voice as calm as he could make it. "I see you well, I hope?"

"A plague! You see me hot, boy! I am not used to kicking my heels waiting on bairns! If the pack in yonder church are prepared to wait your pleasure there, under that damnable clanging bell, I am not!"

"So you come to bell the King, Uncle? You who once so notably belled the cat?" James smiled in what he hoped was friendly fashion, to counteract the half-scared titter of amusement from the listening, watching throng. "I shall not keep you long, my lord of Angus. I have a vow to discharge. A vow of my own. Before I make those others at my crowning. I cannot make the pilgrimage that I would have wished, to Saint Ninian's fane at Candida Casa. But at least I can do this. I can confess my fault before these shrines. These lesser shrines. In the sight of all men. It is a vow, you see, Uncle . . ."

Perhaps Archibald Bell-the-Cat, fifth Earl of Angus, was not the most hopeful individual from whom to seek sympathy for the keeping of vows and undertakings generally. Nor was he truly the King's uncle—though as a great-grandson of the Princess Mary, daughter of King Robert the Third, he might claim some sort of cousinship. He was chief of the great House of Douglas, and the most powerful man in the kingdom. A thorn in the flesh of James's father, he was not so much one of the company of rebel lords as in permanent and independent competition with the Crown. On the late King's death he had, without waiting for anyone to appoint him, announced himself as guardian of the King—and no one had dared, at least publicly, to say that he was not. Had James been younger still, undoubtedly the Earl would have declared himself to be Regent, and taken over the government. Only a year at most had saved Scotland from that fate.

"Vows!" Angus barked. "Belly wind! While you make vows and confess your piddling sins, boy, must Douglas wait? 'Fore God, he will not! Enough of this child's-play . . ."

"'Fore God he will, my lord! Since he is but Douglas and not the King of Scots, wait he will!" Blazing-eyed, fists clenched, the boy faced the huge man, white-faced, but unflinching, resolute, even though he trembled.

For moments they stared at each other, whilst around them scarcely a breath was drawn.

Perhaps it was inevitable that it was the youth's glance which wavered and fell eventually before the man's hard glare. James cleared his throat. "I . . . I have but one more orison to make, my lord," he said. "At yonder golgotha. If you will accompany me? It will take but a moment . . ."

"No! I have waited over long already," the Earl grated. "Come with me, now. To the church."

The boy looked down at his gleaming knuckles. "After," he said thickly. "After I have done what I said I would do."

"Christ God! Then do it without Douglas! Do all without Douglas!" Angus cried, and swinging on his heel he stamped off. Hastily men fell back before him, to give him and his following ample passage, as furiously he roared for his horses, his men, to be away from this accursed place.

James looked after him for a few seconds, biting his lip. Then he turned to stride on firmly towards the canopied crucifix on the Mote Hill.

"So we now have Angus to reckon with!" the Master of Home

exclaimed. "I' faith — here's a costly tantrum! We shall all pay for this folly."

Hailes rubbed his chin. "I wonder . . .?" he said. "We had Angus to reckon with, anyway. And I'd sooner have yonder old bear across the ring from me than sitting at my side!" He laughed shortly. "Our young liege lord may lack much, but it seems that he does not lack spirit! We will be wise to reckon with that also. His father, I vow, would never have spoken Angus so! Aye, by the Rude — I doubt if even Patrick Hepburn of Hailes would so starkly have belled Archibald Bell-the-Cat! For so warm a kneeler and prayer, young James has a firm jaw to him."

"Aye — and a warm eye for a wench, likewise," Home added, glancing back towards the Highland girl. "Here's a steed in need of careful handling, it seems."

The trumpet fanfares within the great church were deafening enough not only to make James's head throb but to bring down dust and dried bat-droppings showering upon the illustrious throng from the high roof-timbers, speckling the King's black velvet. Sitting alone, up near the High Altar, surrounded by the gorgeously robed prelates, the youth felt isolated, uncomfortable, distracted, his mind filled with none of the elation, the holy fervour, or even with the urgent desire for such, that the occasion warranted. Would Angus cause trouble, he wondered, rather? Had he been a fool to so antagonise the most powerful man in his realm? But he had to do it, to make a stand — or allow Bell-the-Cat to dominate him always. To have obeyed, to have gone meekly with the Earl, in front of all . . .! In front of Hailes and Home. He could not have kept those two at arm's length, after that. They would have thought to do what Angus had done. In front of Rob Bruce, whose simple homage he needed, relied upon. Aye, even in front of that girl. She had looked at him as a man. Not a king or a lord — only a man, splendidly a man? He could not have knuckled and submitted to Angus, after that. She had looked straight at his manhood . . . and that manhood had risen to her challenge. She had smiled towards those statues. Her eyes had spoken him plain. Deliciously plain. They were warm, kind, eager, those eyes. She had lifted a shoulder towards him. Her breast with it. She had actually pointed it at him. The shape of it, full, round, proud, the nipple prominent through the thin straining linen stuff . . .

37

James moistened his lips, and shook his head sharply. These were no thoughts for this place and this moment — God forgive him. He ought to be praying, confessing, seeking strength. At least listening to the Archbishop's intonings. He had a foxy face, had Archbishop Shivas — foxy, and hungry too. Hungry for what? What else could he want that he had not already got? Could it be that he hungered after righteousness? Not that. Righteousness was not what those quick darting eyes sought. They said that he was in league with the powers of darkness. Certainly he was a notable astrologer. Knew much of matters occult. He had had great power over the King, his father. As a child James had never liked him, recoiled from him. Assuredly his father should never have appointed him Archbishop of St. Andrews — one of so many ill-judged appointments. They said that he could bring up the spirits of the dead. Could he? Was it possible? If so, might he not bring up his murdered father, then? Now, perhaps? Here, before all? Here, where once he had sat likewise, waiting, the heavy crown on his head, in this same chair . . .

James rested his elbows on the arms of his throne. Not that — God, never that! Saint Ninian — save him from that! Saint Fergus, patron of this Scone — save him! Saint Andrew of Scotland . . .!

The Archbishop was advancing to the altar, hands high, not even glancing at James. The jewels that encrusted his mitre and cope sparkled and glittered in the dusty sunlight. No black robes for William Shivas. The rings on his thin fingers blazed. Shivas was watching, admiring the dazzle and play of light on those rubies and diamonds and emeralds — that's what he was doing. Praise God, he was not raising spirits! He was moving his fingers to make those jewels flash — James could see it plainly. Thanks be to Ninian! And Andrew! Aye, and Fergus. Fergus must not be forgotten. Perhaps it was part of his own doing? Perhaps his orisons and confessions and masses had been sufficient? To permit his father's unquiet soul to lie in peace?

Straightening up, for the weight of the crown tended to force his head and neck forward, the youth stirred uncomfortably in his seat, the same elaborate square chest-like chair of carved and gilded wood that once had contained the Stone of Destiny. Fairly long in the leg as he was, his feet would not have touched the floor had it not been for the footstool in the image of a recumbent lion — for this was a high chair, built to enclose the tall stone that itself had been seat-high. Not like the ridiculous squat box on legs that the arrogant Edward of England had had constructed to house the lump of Scone sandstone, the sham Stone of Destiny which he had so proudly carried off to London two hundred years before, and which successive English monarchs had sat on so hopefully since. James would dearly have liked to have had the true Stone of Scone, Scotland's ancient talisman, beneath him this day. But there had been no time to search it out, to send search-parties seeking for it. That is a thing that he would like to do, himself. To find the Stone. In its cave. There were various beliefs as to where it lay hidden. At Moncrieff Hill, not far away. At Dunsinnane. He himself believed that it was much farther off—in distant Skye, of the Hebrides. Where King Robert Bruce's friend, the Lord of the Isles, had taken it for safe keeping when the English ravaged the land. That is a thing that he would do. He would go himself to the Isles, to see that great chief, and find the Stone. Bring it back to Scone, where it belonged . . .

James hitched himself round on the wide seat, twisting his body, trying to ease the position of the iron chain at his loins. He had been prevailed upon to hide the chain now, and wore it next to his skin. Hailes said that men, not knowing its true significance, would esteem it a sign of servitude, would be offended at it. Home said that a chain was not a suitable symbol for the king of a free people like the Scots to wear. So now he hid it, but wore it still—for he would always keep his vows, God willing. It hurt against his skin—but that, to be sure, was as it ought to be. Better thus. Yet it was a plaguey awkward position, down there—the trailing end of it got between his legs. Holding this heavy sceptre in one hand, and the orb in the other, he could not adjust it. Only try to twist himself . . .

They were chanting, now—all the bishops and priests and monks. Should he be chanting also? No one had told him just what to do. Just to sit there, after he had repeated the answers, the vows, and been anointed, with the crown on his head, holding the orb and sceptre. He should feel other than this, he knew. The Lord's Anointed! He should feel differently, filled with strength for his great task, his mind uplifted. Yet he could only think of trivial things. He could not even pray . . .

The Earl of Erroll, the Lord High Constable, had not come. So Hailes was bearing the Sword of State, in his place. Erroll had been loyal to his father. But he should have been here today,

39

Constable of Scotland. James would have wished Rob Bruce to be well forward somewhere, with that other sword – but they had squeezed him out. He could not see him in the great throng. Buchan, too was missing – Hearty James whom he loathed, his true great-uncle. The other brother, John Stewart, Earl of Atholl, was there in front, a stern and silent man, ageing now. But there were many notable absentees . . .

The service over at last, James found himself counting and naming those significant absentees, as the long procession of his nobility came up, one by one, to kneel and do homage to him, their liege lord duly crowned. All had been invited, commanded, to attend, on his own personal assurance of goodwill and safe-conduct, whatever the past. But how many had kept away. The Earl of Huntly, the Gordon chief, the King's Lieutenant of the North. The Earl Marischal. Crawford, who had been Chamberlain, and whom his father had but recently made Duke of Montrose. The Lord Glamis. And Forbes. And Lindsay of the Byres. The Earl of Glencairn had died at Sauchieburn, of course – as had the Lords Erskine and Sempill and Ruthven. But the tally of absentees was grievous. Especially from the north, the "loyal north" . . .

James was abruptly jolted out of his reverie. A hot flush mounted to his brow as he stared down at the man now kneeling before him. Almost he jerked his two hands away from between the palms of this splendidly-dressed nobleman as he stooped to murmur his homage in the prescribed formula. He was dark, this man, dark of complexion, dark of eye, black of beard, of middle height and middle years, a hard, muscular, thin-lipped man with a long chin made longer by the black spade-beard – Andrew, second Lord Gray, High Sheriff of Angus. Gray! Gray, who bore a white lion rampant on a red field. A black-a-vised man with a black beard, the miller's wife had said, with a red coat over his mail!

The kneeling lord looked up, to meet the intensity of the young monarch's gaze. Coolly he stared back, unwinking. Then raising a curving eyebrow towards first the prelate who now held the sceptre on one side of the King, and then to the other who held the orb, he inclined his head with a slight sardonic smile to James, and moved away unhurriedly, to make room for the man behind.

The boy followed him with his urgent glance, even as the pair of palms of the next lord took his hands between them, hands which he strove hard to keep from trembling. Could it be he? Gray was a close crony of Bell-the-Cat, partner in that last traitorous plot with England. But he had led the second line of battle in the rebel army at Sauchieburn. Could it be he?

It is to be feared that the King paid but scant attention to the remainder of the flower of Scotland, queueing to bend and declare their allegiance and fealty. Over and over in his mind he sought to recollect all who might bear a rampant lion on their arms, who were dark and black-bearded, and who were likely to have been in the vicinity of Bannockburn that fatal day. Always he came back to Andrew Gray.

At length the proceedings were over, and pushing aside the clerics who would have prolonged them with additional solemnities, James, divesting himself somewhat unceremoniously of the crown and trappings of royalty, hurried out into the June sunshine, eager for movement and activity, eager for food. But still he had to hold himself in, to school himself to patience and gracious comportment. For now he had to be presented to the folk outside, the less privileged, the late-comers and the commonality, who had been unable to gain admittance to the church. This was mercifully brief, however. His young brothers, the Duke of Ross and Earl of Mar, were brought to stand on either side of him, the crown, sceptre, sword and orb were held aloft behind him, while the Lion banner of Scotland was unfurled to flap above. More fanfares were trumpeted. James bowed and smiled, the Archbishop sketched a perfunctory benediction, and everyone perceived duty to have been more or less accomplished. Truth to tell, anyway, the less privileged did not seem to be greatly interested, no vast crowd having assembled. On the other hand, the Abbey parkland was now seething with life and animation, brisk as any Saint Johnston's Fair, the noise therefrom quite drowning anything but the efforts of the trumpeters.

By unspoken mutual consent the realities of the situation were accepted, and a move made down to the lower ground by all save the most pompous and stuffy.

James led the way to the jousting yard. This had been set up on his own orders, for of all activities he loved the somewhat outdated tournament, the romantic knightly sport of personal combat, of tilting in the lists, of skilful horsemanship and swording. At these, he had trained himself to excel, young as he was —

and with no approval on his father's part, who had judged such a relic of barbarism. Today unfortunately it was not considered fitting that the newly-crowned monarch should take personal part; but at least he could watch and judge and applaud. And eat whilst so doing. The Abbey kitchens had been given explicit instructions on this score.

So whilst a succession of knights, lordlings and champions did clangorous battle for the edification of such as were prepared to watch, either out of interest or because clearly it was the King's wish, an *al fresco* meal was served on groaning trestles there in the open at the side of the lists, which did Holy Church considerable credit despite the Abbot of Scone's declared penury. In view of the short notice given, it was a notable feast, and went on for three hours. In appreciation, the now comfortably replete sovereign ordered the Abbey's hitherto somewhat neglected relic of the head of Saint Fergus to be encased in silver, at the Crown's expense, and other suitable recompense made to the establishment's coffers — at which the Abbot smirked and purred like a satisfied cat, and the Lord St. John of Jerusalem, newly appointed Lord High Treasurer, muttered darkly.

James was less impressed by the standard of jousting and chivalry, and swore to young Sir Rob Bruce that this was something which he would set himself to improve. Poor handling of horses and weapons, doubtful sportsmanship, and lack of dash and vehemence, seemed painfully obvious, at least to the youthful enthusiast. He itched to be down in the lists himself, to demonstrate how it should be done, and even held a whispered debate with Bruce as to the possibilities of slipping away unobserved, borrowing some unidentifiable armour, and taking part himself in the tourney, unannounced and incognito. But Hailes and Home and the rest were never far from his side, and they would strenuously disapprove, he knew. Moreover, as Rob pointed out, there were no champions taking part today of a calibre suitable for the King of Scots to ride against. Another day, let it be.

In a different matter, however, James did assert himself. Toying with the leg of a roasted goose, and scanning the throng below him during one of the waits between jousts, his keen eye spotted a tall thin and stooping cleric, noticeably drably clad amongst the colourful crowd. He had been, as all that afternoon, more or less involuntarily looking for the Lord Gray. Now his eye lightened, and glancing at his lordly watch-dogs to see if they noticed, below his breath he instructed Rob Bruce to go to summon the cleric to his side.

As he approached, with the young man, the inevitable opposition developed.

"Sire," Home said loudly. "See who comes! The Bishop of Aberdeen has the temerity to approach Your Grace. This is an outrage . . .!"

"I have requested the Lord Bishop's presence, sir."

"Do not receive him, my Lord James," Hailes urged. "He is a dangerous man. If he were not protected by his cloth and mitre, I'd have him in closest ward!"

"But *I* would not, my lord. If it is dangerous to be honest, then this realm is in parlous state indeed!" James rose, and stepped forward to greet the newcomer, actually stooping over his hand to kiss the episcopal ring. "I rejoice to see you, my Lord Bishop," he said. "I am glad that you came to my crowning . . . for I feared that you would not. Welcome to my table."

"Your Grace is kind. Generous," the other acknowledged, with a faint smile. "I thank you."

He had a soft and gentle voice. A gentle manner, too. Despite these, however, there was little that was soft about William Elphinstone, and his gentleness in no way invalidated a calmly shrewd mind and an innate strength of purpose and character. Tall and thin-faced and stooping, he was a man in his late fifties, with grey, thinning hair, lined, almost haggard, features, but eyes notably blue and lively. Until a few days before, he had held the highest office in the land, under the Crown — that of Lord High Chancellor of Scotland, chief minister of the realm. It had been one of the few wise appointments of the late King; had he made it earlier, instead of only in the February of that same year, much of history might have been otherwise.

Taking Elphinstone's arm impulsively, James led him to sit at the table beside him. Looking around at the frowning men who thronged him, the King frowned also, raising his chin.

"I would speak privily with my Lord Bishop," he said. "On . . . on matters spiritual. I will be obliged, my lords, if you will ensure that all others keep their distance."

Elphinstone shook his grey head as the others fell back, with black looks and angry muttering. "I fear that was hardly wise, Sire," he said, sighing. "You must not offend your friends, for the sake of an old done man."

"Are you not my friend?" James demanded. "And how friendly are these hungry lords, think you?"

"Hush, lad! If I am your friend, I must needs counsel you to watch your words. You are King now, Sire — and have a somewhat carrying voice! The King, you must remember, must control himself before he can control his kingdom. And of all his subjects, his own tongue can well be the most unruly and treacherous!"

James bit back the words which sprang to his lips, and stared ahead of him.

The other touched his arm. "I am sorry, lad. Forgive a prating priest who cannot forget his preaching. I would be having you a very Solomon for wisdom, before you have scarce warmed the seat of your throne . . .!"

"I'd rather be a David, sir!"

"Aye. No doubt. That I can well credit. I hear that Your Grace has begun by slinging a stone at the Douglas Goliath!"

"I had to. He came commanding me, shouting his bidding. At the King. You would not have me truckle to him?"

Elphinstone sighed. "No. Surely not. But until you are secure on your throne, lad, you must be careful whom you offend. God forgive me if I seem to advise you to dissemble, to be less than honest. But a monarch must rule through those who wield power around him. Particularly the monarch of this Scotland, who depends on the levies of his lords for his strength, and has no great forces of his own. If you offend my lord of Angus, it is all the more necessary that you do not offend these others here."

"They will not be so greatly offended so long as I have offices of state and profit to give out," the youth declared. "So I play one against another. Hailes I have made Master of my Household, Great Admiral, Warden of the Marches, and Keeper of Edinburgh. The Master of Home I have appointed Chamberlain, with other offices, with Stirling Castle to keep. Lyle is Justiciar. Lord St. John is the Treasurer. But they all look for one office above all. Others too. The office *you* held. The chiefest. That of Chancellor," James leaned close, eagerly, "I have said nothing. I have controlled my tongue in this, at least, my Lord Bishop. I do not intend that any of them shall have it. I have kept it, you see, for you!"

The other turned to consider him, wonderingly. "My Lord James!" he said. He shook his head, at a loss. "This is . . . extraordinary. You are good, kind. But it is impossible."

"It is not. It is in my gift. Until there is a Parliament. To ratify it. By then, you could be secure . . ."

"No. No, lad. It will not do, generous as it is. My thanks — but no. It is not to be considered."

James stared down at his own tight-gripped fingers. "You will not serve me? Me, and my realm? As you served . . . him! Is it . . . is it because of what I have done? Because of him, my father? You hold me guilty? Of my father's fall? You think me a . . . a . . . what is the word? A patricide! Damned . . .?"

His wrist was gripped in a surprisingly strong grasp. "James! Sire! Never say it! The King's death lies not at your door."

"I rode in the field against him. When these rebel lords rose, and took me from Stirling Castle, I did not refuse. I signed their proclamation. They told me that I must . . . but I could have refused. I did not. I believed my father to be wrong, to be wasting his realm, to be selling Scotland to the English king. He was naming my brother Ross as heir, above me, the elder . . ."

"Yes, yes. He was headstrong. Mistaken in many things. Though not in all . . ."

"I did not wish him harm, sir. I swear it! By Saint Ninian's self. Only that he should change his course. Never that he should lose his crown. And, God's mercy — not his life . . .!"

"I know it, lad. None with any understanding would believe otherwise. Do not fret yourself, Sire." The Bishop shook his head. "Many are to blame, before you, for the King's death. Even I myself, I think, have more responsibility than have you. For I was his Chancellor. I carried out his policies — policies that perhaps spelled his end. I sought to better them, yes — to lead him out of what I considered error. But still I must bear responsibility for much that was ill done. My conscience will not let me forget it. So . . . it is not possible that I serve as Chancellor again, Your Grace. Your lords would never have it — and rightly. Nor would my own poor honour."

"You do not think me greatly guilty, then?"

"Would that I thought myself as little so."

"Thank you, thank you!" the boy said, warmly. Then he sighed. "But I am sorry that you will not be Chancellor. Of all men, you I would most trust. Your advice I would most gladly take. Who, then? Who, of all these that want it, is to have the office? Who will not misuse it for his own gain?"

45

"Since you esteem my advice, Sire – I would say, give it to Argyll."

"Argyll? The Campbell! Who is now in London, envoy to King Henry? That sour old man! What has he done, to be Chancellor again?"

"It is not so much what he has done, as what he has *not* done! He is sour, yes, but with his own astuteness. And if he is old, he is no longer ambitious. He was your father's Chancellor, before me, for five years. He has learned much, of a difficult task, by hard experience. He was not in rebellion against the late King – so that many on your father's side would accept him, who would not accept Hailes or Lyle or Gray." The Bishop glanced round at the watching lords, none the less suspicious for being just out of earshot, "If Argyll is Chancellor, none of these can be Chancellor! None therefore can become too powerful, too strong for you. They will not love him . . . but he is old and sour enough not to care for that. He will do your work for you. Give you time, lad, to find your feet . . ."

"Aye, I see it. You are right, my Lord Bishop. As always. Argyll it shall be. It is a shrewd move. But you? You will still advise me? As thus? You will not deny me your guidance, sir? For I need it."

"Always it is yours for the asking, Sire. Never fear. So long as God gives me breath. And wits . . ."

"Good! Good! A place must be found for you in the Privy Council." James paused, his eyes busy searching the company below. "You mentioned Gray, just now. Andrew, my Lord Gray of Foulis. He of the black beard and the white lion! I believe him to have a black heart also. I think . . . I think that he killed my father!"

The older man stroked his shaven chin. "That could be a dangerous thought, my Lord James," he said, after a little.

"Dangerous for Gray!" the youth answered hotly. "If I can prove it."

"Dangerous for you. Dangerous for all the realm, I think. Must you prove it, Sire?"

"Why? 'Fore God – would you have me do otherwise? Let my father's death go unavenged?"

"Yes," the other said simply.

"But . . . but that would be the part of a craven, a weakling! If Gray basely drew steel on his liege lord when helpless, when he was seeking the consolation of a priest . . ."

"Say rather the part of a wise monarch, with a cool head as well as a stout heart. See you — nothing that you can do will bring back your father, lad. May he rest in God's peace. Now you have your father's shaken realm to rule, to guide, to unite — and it is sore rent and riven. Do not rend it more. As you will do, if at this stage you pursue the Lord Gray. For he is powerful, and allied to others equally powerful. He is uncle to the Lord Lyle. Good-son to your own uncle, the Earl of Atholl. Related to Keith, the Earl Marischal. His daughter is married to my Lord Glamis. Attack him, and you attack all these. You cannot afford that — your realm cannot, today. Most serious of all, Sire — he is close to Angus. They work together, Bell-the-Cat and Gray. Already, I hear, you have publicly outfaced Angus — perhaps rightly. But do not further enrage him. Do not drive him to show his strength against you — for his is the greater, I fear. Douglas can put five thousand men in the field within a week. Ten thousand in a month. With Gray and Glamis and the others, that could be doubled. Your throne cannot risk such challenge, lad. Not yet."

"But . . . even if this is so, must I forget it? Forget what Gray has done? To my own father?"

"Forget? I cannot think that you will forget. Even forgive? But if Gray did this vile deed, Sire, leave him to his own conscience. To God's repayment. Today you have taken solemn vows to cherish and preserve this realm of yours. You will not do it by forcing Gray to defend himself against you, however just the cause. By him raising half the land in arms." Elphinstone laid his hand on the boy's hunched shoulder. "That might be the act of a bold man . . . but never of a wise king, a true monarch to his people."

"Lord!" James almost groaned. "Must being a king make of me a poltroon and a dissembler, then?"

"It must make of you a father, rather. A father to your people of Scotland. Who can take the long view. The view of the greater good for all. Who can overlook the lesser evil to himself, for the greater good for them. Can you rise to that grace, Your Grace?"

"God knows — I do not!" The King grimaced, and then shrugged, and grinned wryly. "I am something young for that sort of fatherhood, I fear . . .!"

CHAPTER

3

"Tush, man!" Lord Hailes hooted. "Where's your judgement, you that's High Justiciar? Kate Carmichael may be all very well for you and me to throw a leg over when we feel like it, but she's double the boy's age! Old enough to be his mother."

"What harm in that? She is experienced in the business, which counts for a deal." The Lord Lyle, handsome, elegant and supercilious, distastefully edged a little further away from the drunken snoring Lord Kennedy, who sprawled in a pool of wine across the long table next to him. "Moreover, she has the advantage that she will keep her head, and do what we tell her. Some younger wenches might not. Might give him their hearts as well as their maidenheads, and be the less use to us."

"You're a cold-blooded fish, Robert, i' faith! Or sound like one." There was little love lost between these two pillars of the throne. "We've got to consider the lad himself. *He*'s not cold-blooded, as we've discovered! He's high-spirited, with a mind of his own. Think you he'll meekly bed down with a woman old enough to have mothered him just because she offers to open her legs for him . . .?"

"So long as she goes about it with some judgement — and her paps are big enough!" the Master of Home put in judicially. "And you'll admit, Patrick, that Kate wears well."

"Aye — she's worn three husbands under the sod!" Hailes agreed. "But will James not see her as an old woman, nevertheless? And choose elsewhere."

"So long as he chooses. We can work on the woman afterwards . . ."

"No!" Lyle declared strongly. "That will not serve. He might well choose some empty-headed young fool with a pretty face. For our purposes the woman must have wits, as well as parts of more immediate interest to a young man. A fool would be useless. As would one too soft-hearted. I still say Kate Carmichael — but if she's over-ripe for our youth, what of the Lady Joanna Maxwell? She's but new married, but she's a hot bitch, and Sir

John's a ninny and scant use to her, I'll swear!" He drew a hand over mouth and chin. "I can vouch for her wits . . . as other parts!"

"As can not a few of us!" Hailes grunted. "But, see you — we can't have the boy contracting a pox! As it strikes me he might, with yon one. Some day, he's got to marry and produce an heir. That is vital for us all. We can afford no half-wits or dizzards . . ."

"Hailes — I do not think that I like your choice of words!" Lord Lyle half-rose. "Do you suggest, by any chance, that I . . . that I . . .?"

"My lords! My lords!" The softly smooth voice of Master George Hepburn, Vicar of Linlithgow and newly-appointed Clerk of the Rolls, intervened soothingly. "Here is no matter for dispute, surely? Let us not quarrel over the ladies, dear creatures, the delight and solace of us all. Since we do not yet know certainly His Grace's tastes in this respect, it behoves us, does it not, to provide a selection? So that he may choose his plaything. We shall, of course, have chosen first, in general — he chooses for himself, thereafter, in particular. Then all are satisfied . . ."

"Ha, Cousin George," a fat voice chuckled from the other side of the table, "there th . . . shpeaks a m . . . modicum of wisdom. But only a m'modicum." The stout man was having a little difficulty with his words, thus late in the evening. "Do not underesh . . . do not underestimate our young Galahad. His prowess. One or two of the darlings may not sh . . . serve to keep him tamed. If he is of so warm an eye as my lords think, then he may need a covey of the plump birdies to hold the bit tw'twixt his teeth!"

"A notable metaphor, Prior John!" the Vicar observed, smiling thinly. The speaker had been John Hepburn, Prior of St. Andrews, now Lord Privy Seal. There were a lot of Hepburns about the Court these days — which was perhaps part of the Lord Lyle's trouble. "If the King's capacity is indeed thus great, then we must seek to satisfy it, for, h'm, the good of the realm! For nothing, I vow, is more trying to a state and its ministers than a superabundance of energy on the part of the Crown! *Amare simul, et sapere ipsi Jovi non datur!*"

"Damned clerk!" the Earl of Lennox burst out loudly from the head of the table, where he lounged as senior noble present and head of the most prominent branch of the House of Stewart next to the royal line. "Speak plain, in God's name! What you mean is that you will so wear out James with women that he leaves such as you free to run his kingdom? Eh?"

"I pray you, hush, my lord!" Anxiously, Vicar Hepburn glanced over his shoulder towards the arras-hung doorway which separated that ante-chamber from the Great Hall of Stirling Castle. He need not have worried about Lennox being overheard from without, save perhaps by Lord Hailes' moss-troopers who stood guard there. The noise from the Hall was sufficient to prevent any lesser sounds from penetrating – music and singing and uninhibited laughter. "Put it rather this way . . ."

Hailes interrupted his kinsman. "Do not fear, my lord of Lennox – the rule will remain in the hands of those born to the task. The Lords of the Council. We have seen enough of rule by upstarts in the reign of the late King. We seek but that a head-strong youth does not set that Council by the ears – that he occupies his mind with other than affairs of state that are too deep for him. On that Council none is more prominent than your lordship's self . . ."

"Faugh! Have you too become a clerk, Hailes? To try to cozen me with words?" The elderly Earl leaned forward, his heavy features purpling. "Think you Lennox is a fool? Witless? Blind? By the Mass, what does he see? Hepburns here, Homes there! Half the offices in the land filled by your Borders brood! And what for Lennox? He may retain his seat on the Council and his sheriffdom of The Lennox – God's death!"

"You keep Dumbarton Castle, my lord – one of the keys of the kingdom. And I mind, you kept to it, close, when Sauchieburn was to be fought!"

"Damn you . . .!"

"My lords – please! I beseech you!" Bishop Blackadder of Glasgow roused himself from a brown study, and starting up from his seat beside Lennox, he accidentally overturned his goblet of wine. The Earl, cursing, had to push himself hastily back from the table to avoid being soaked by the spilling liquor. Into the confusion, the Vicar of Linlithgow's honey-smooth words infiltered and persisted.

". . . and so, may we not reach a decision on this matter in hand? Much may hang on it. Here is what I suggest, my lords. Let us arrange that a selection of ladies offer their favours to our youthful prince. Ladies of differing ages and shapes, and, h'm, experience. By all means let us try him with the Lady Carmichael. Likewise the Lady Joanna Maxwell. It may be that, expert as these are, they will carry him off his feet . . ."

"On his back, you mean?" somebody asked, amidst guffaws.

"That remains to be seen. But I counsel that less ripe fruit also should be presented. I have a wench in mind—the daughter of the Laird of Bonshaw, Boyd by name, here in the train of my Lord of Morton. She is a comely creature with a questing eye. And Bonshaw is indebted to myself in some measure . . ."

"Ha! Holy Church is being generous! Can you spare her?"

"Already trained to bit and bridle by an expert! Here is true loyalty to your liege lord!"

"I concede nothing, good sirs! But Mariot Boyd is nearer His Grace's own age. This will be her seventeenth summer, I believe. Shall I have a word with her?"

"What of the Drummond girl?" Andrew, Lord Gray, stirred himself to ask, out of cynical contemplation of his fellows. "Have I not heard that the boy has been much in the company of one of Drummond's daughters? Which, I know not."

"Sauchie would know. Send for Shaw of Sauchie. Who was Tutor."

"Aye." Gray stroked his black beard. "My new Lord Drummond is notably in need of bettering himself, is he not? He would co-operate, I think."

Sir John, Lord Drummond, was not present at this gathering of those prominent in the new regime. He had been raised to the dignity of a Lord of Parliament only a few years before, by King James Third, with whom he had been friendly enough to have office at Court. He had not actively supported the misguided monarch in his later follies, and so no proceedings had been instituted against him; but undoubtedly his position in the new order would stand much improvement.

The Laird of Sauchie was brought from the Great Hall into the company of the elite, in some apparent trepidation, a man unsure of his present usefulness. "Sauchie," Gray addressed him curtly, not suggesting that he should be seated. "We have heard that His Grace has seen much of one of the Lord Drummond's daughters. If this is so—which?"

Wondering, the former Tutor glanced about him. "Why, my lords—all of them. All five. The Lord Drummond was Master of Horse to the late King, and had lodging here in the Castle. So that his daughters were all but brought up with the Duke — with His Grace. His sons were older . . ."

"Aye, but James was seen more with one than the others, was he not? So I heard."

"With the Lady Margaret, that would be, my lord. She is of his own age — a few months older, only. Three of her sisters are younger."

"You judge him fond of this wench?"

"It is hard to say. They have been friendly, yes. As children are. But I have seen nothing more . . ."

"She has looks?"

"Why, yes. She is growing very fair."

"And wits?"

"She is a young woman who knows her own mind, I think."

"Aye." Gray flicked a hand in brief dismissal, towards Sauchie. "My lords," he said. "I suggest that we send for the Lord Drummond . . ."

As the dance finished, James whirled his buxom partner off her feet, twice round, planted a smacking kiss on her laughing open lips, and letting his fingers trail across her swelling heaving bosom, staggered panting to his seat at the table on the raised dais at the upper end of the Hall. He mopped his brow with the sleeve of his doublet.

"Whe-e-ew! Hot work, Rob! Yon lass I was jigging with was a warm one! Some are warm and some are cool. She seemed to melt under my hands. Like butter." Grinning, he wiped sweating palms on his trunks. "But, Lord — she weighed as much at the end as at the beginning, I vow, for all that!"

"Your Grace should choose lighter pieces."

"Aye. But I like them well-fleshed, man. I like the feel of them, under my hand. The movement of rounded flesh, soft but firm, under the stuff of their gowns. Did you see that one? How she rubbed herself against me? Not only above. As she leaned on me. But lower down also, i' faith!" He stirred, to slightly re-arrange the lie of the chain at waist, under his trunks. "This iron . . . save me, it's like to have bruised her! As well as me! Who is she, do you know? How is she called? I swear I had not the breath to ask her!"

"She is the Lady Joanna, I'm told, Sire. Wife to Sir John Maxwell of Hoddam."

"Wife, heh? Umm." James looked a little doubtful, at that, peering round the crowded Hall, thick with the smoke of scores of blazing torches. "Is . . . is he here? This Maxwell? I did not know . . ."

"They say he is older, Sire—much. And . . . not hearty. He is not here tonight, I think."

"M'mmm. Well . . . but still. Another man's wife. She did not seem . . . such. She was not backward. But I would not wish to, to . . ."

Sir Rob Bruce smiled slightly. "That sort can be hottest. Young, with an old husband who does not satisfy. They have learned the taste for strong meat, and will not be content with capon . . .!"

The King turned to consider him. "You talk as though you knew a deal about it!" he charged. "You—who sit here at this table all night and never so much as touch a woman! How are you so well informed, Rob Bruce? What know you about women?"

It was true that the other had not once danced all evening, and scarcely left the high dais table which he alone permanently shared with James, save to deliver a message or transmit a command. He shrugged now. "I know a little," he said. "There are other women besides Court ladies—and I think them none so different under the fine clothes!"

"Under the fine clothes . . .!" James pursed his lips. "You think not? But you are not putting it to the test, eh? You should be trying out your belief, man! No need to sit at this table all night. You are none so ill-favoured. Plenty of women will look kindly enough on Sir Robert Bruce, the King's Sword-Bearer, I'll swear."

"That may be, Sire. But I do not seek their kindnesses."

"No?" Curiously James eyed this friend whom he had chosen so impulsively. "You do not mislike them, Rob? The women? You are not . . .?"

"I like them very well, Sire. But there is a girl. In my own place. Near Airth. Her favours only I seek."

"Ha! So that's the way of it! But one who holds out, eh? Who keeps you a-begging?"

He nodded. "She likes me well enough, I think. But bids me be patient."

"And none other will serve, meantime?"

"None, Sire."

53

James frowned, and rubbed his chin. "A man should not let himself be too much humbled by any woman, I think," he said. "It is unsuitable."

"You would have me take her, against her will? Like a brute beast?"

"No. Not that, man. Do not be so touchy. But if she plays a man like a fish, holds him off over-long, then let him turn to another until perhaps she comes to her senses." And when the other did not answer. "What is her name?"

Only reluctantly Bruce answered, after a pause, "Mary."

"Mary what, Rob? Come—out with it!"

"Mary Somerville, daughter to the Laird of Plean. I was on my way there when I heard that there was a man slain at Beaton's Mill, by the Bannock Burn . . ."

But James had suddenly lost interest, was not listening. His eyes were following a couple amongst those pacing out the present dance, to a more stately rhythm than the last high-spirited caper. The man was middle-aged but lithely built and splendidly dressed, dark of feature, black of beard—Andrew, Lord Gray. The woman was young, a mere girl, and very lovely.

"Devil seize him—see there!" he whispered, gripping Bruce's arm.

"My Lord of Gray, you mean? I thought that Your Grace was minded, now, to let that pot simmer meantime?"

"But see who he dances with, damn him! Margaret Drummond! Look how he holds her . . .!"

"Less close than you held the Lady Joanna!"

"Tush, man—that's different! When I dance with her, she holds her distance."

"I do not recollect any notable gap . . ."

But the King, leaping down from the dais, was pushing his way through the press of dancers towards the couple that he had singled out. Thrusting himself in front of them, he forced them to a halt. Inevitably others halted likewise, all eyes.

"My lord!" he jerked, tight-lipped.

Surprised, Gray sketched a bow, black brows raised.

"The Lady Margaret. She . . . this measure. She should be treading it with me."

"Indeed? Do you tell me so?" Gray looked from the youth's tense face to that of the girl, still, calm, with only a faint trace of concern on it, like a deep pool with only its surface brushed by a passing breeze. He laughed. "In that case, Highness — the lady is yours, of course. All yours! I yield her up with the best will in the world! Your convenience is most assuredly mine!" He bowed deeply this time, but there was mockery in it. Touching the young woman's arm, he added significantly. "You will add honour to the House of Drummond, my dear, I am sure. Remember it." And turning, he swaggered away through the throng.

"A plague on him!" James said, biting his lip. "That man is . . . evil. What did he mean? By that last? About remembering honour? To the House of Drummond?"

"I fear that I do not know, Sire," the girl said coolly, head held high.

Frowning, and noting the other dancers watching around them, James took her arm and moved somewhat stiffly with her into the measure of the dance.

"That was ill done, I think," she said quietly.

"It was necessary. I could not bear to see you in that man's arms. He is a devil! What was he saying to you? Speaking so close to your ear? I saw him. What was it?"

She did not answer at once. "It was of my father that he spoke," she said at length. "Referring to my father's . . . position."

"Your father! Likely, that! Holding you so! Your father is in Edinburgh, as I know."

"But apparently my Lord of Gray did not. My arm, Your Grace — you hurt it with so fierce a grasp."

"I'm sorry, Margaret. But . . . it was seeing you dancing with that man. When you had refused me."

"I did not refuse you, Sire. None may refuse to dance with the King. I danced twice with you."

"You held me off, Margaret. You know that you did. And when I asked again, you said that you were tired. Asked to be excused . . ."

"I did not relish being held so, in front of all, Sire. By any man. I could not give you what it seemed you wanted. Others, I noted, supplied you afterwards right generously! I am sorry if I disappointed you in this respect, Your Grace."

"'Fore God, Margaret — why do you talk like this? Your Grace! Sire! Your Grace! All the time. Stiff, like any stranger. You used to call me Jamie . . ."

"You were not King then, Highness. You are now. King of Scots. Liege lord of us all. All is changed."

"All is not changed. Not between us, Margaret. *I* have not changed, because I have now a crown to wear."

"By your handling of the Lady Joanna Maxwell, I would say that you have, Sire! And that other—the French envoy's daughter."

Almost he shook her, frowning at her in a mixture of exasperation and perplexity. But he could not maintain that frown, not with the girl so close. For she was very beautiful, with a fair and serene loveliness that melted something within him as a flame melts wax. She was almost as tall as himself, slender, long-limbed, with a figure full of promise yet by no means so spectacular in its contours as those of some others present whom he frankly admired. Her features were as though chiselled by a master-sculptor, although she was only sixteen, her eyes hazel and her hair thick and silver-gilt beneath a gracefully draped black velvet hood. She wore a long tight-bodiced gown of crimson satin, square-necked, the skirt full and elongated to form a train, but raised and divided at the front to reveal a gold embroidered petticoat of white linen.

They danced together in silence for a little. Then, as they worked round near the head of the great room again, James suddenly broke away from the other dancers, drawing the girl after him to the dais.

She resisted, though this was indicated by murmured objection and the backward pressure of her arm rather than any undignified pulling against him. But he was insistent, hurrying her up to the table, where Rob Bruce rose to receive them.

"Sit," the King jerked. "Take wine with me, if you will do no better!"

"This is foolish, Sire," she told him, flushed a little now. "Bringing me up here, for all to stare at." She did not sit down. "This is no place for me. It can only set tongues wagging . . ."

"Let them wag."

"*You* may not care how they wag. But I do. I can less afford their wagging. Let me go . . ."

"No! Sit down. That is my command—my royal command!" James beckoned imperiously to his watching cup-bearer. "Bring wine. A fresh goblet for the Lady Margaret." He glared straight in front of him.

Anxiously Rob looked from the young woman who slowly seated herself, calm-featured yet, with only deep breathing and the flaring of fine nostrils intimating her distress, to his scowling young monarch. James occasionally had these dark moods, when a generous and friendly nature suddenly became clouded over with anger and aggressiveness. In the month of their association he had never yet seen such directed at a woman, however.

"My lady," he said diffidently. "May I offer you a sweetmeat? A fruit . . .?"

"Thank you, no . . ." she began, when James interrupted.

"There speaks Rob Bruce — who allows a woman to mock him, to play him like a fish!" he grated.

The young woman turned a shapely shoulder on the still standing King. "I have heard of Sir Robert. And only good, sir, as yet!" Seriously she considered him. "Your father's castle of Airth was burned, was it not, in the recent troubles? I hope that none suffered . . .?"

James sat down abruptly. "Do not think that you can wheedle and cozen him, Margaret, with your wiles. Wiles which you deny me! He has thought for only one — some Mary Somerville who plays cat and mouse with him. But if he is a fool, I am not! None shall so play James Stewart!"

"I like Sir Robert the better, I think, Sire!" was all that she answered.

The cup-bearer brought wine for the young woman, but she did not touch it.

A guizardry, a sort of charade by wandering players, had succeeded the dance, and was drawing laughs and applause from many. But the trio at the dais table sat unsmiling, stiff, each a little apart from the other. Any of the company who approached that dais were warned off by the King's dark looks — for none might mount it uninvited.

Rob noted that a group of the principal lords, across the Hall, were not watching the players at all, their regard wholly on the King. Heads close, they spoke together frequently. Gray was amongst them, and Hailes.

With the guizardry over, and another and livelier dance, led outrageously by the Court Fool, still not bringing the King from the table, the knot of lords broke up. Presently one who had been with them, the cleric Hepburn, Clerk of the Rolls, came forward, smilingly escorting a young woman. He bowed low, before the dais, and his companion curtsied deeply, remaining so.

"Your Grace, have I permission to present the Mistress Mariot

Boyd, daughter to the Laird of Bonshaw?" Vicar Hepburn asked in his sweet voice. "She is new come to Court. Knows few here. An opening rose from the fair Borderland! A shame, is it not, that such should bloom unheeded . . . save by old men and tonsured clerks?"

James, still glowering, looked down at them irritably. But the cleric was astute. His appeal on behalf of the lonely and neglected was calculated to affect the youth's generosity. Also the hint of young feminine beauty wasted on elderly impotence was shrewd probing. Moreover, the girl in that down-swept prolonged curtsy not only demanded uplifting by the chivalrous, but her forward-leaning posture there below him most notably emphasised the white ovoid prominence and deep cleft of a highly developed bust. He cleared his throat.

"Well . . ." he said.

"Your Highness is ever kind. Mistress Mariot will, I swear, repay your benevolence." Raising her up, the older man assisted the girl to step on to the dais — which she achieved with some heedful lifting of long skirts to reveal a deal of pale-coloured hose — before he backed away.

"Come. Sit here, Mistress Boyd. On my right," James said. His glance flickered along towards Margaret Drummond. "You are welcome. To my Court. And most, h'm, handsome, if I may say so!"

The young woman smiled warmly, gratefully, and fluttered her eyelids, but said nothing.

Mariot Boyd was a considerable contrast to the other girl. A year or so older, she was much more amply built, without being over-weight in any way. She had her own confidence, though of a different order to the other's innate serenity. High-coloured, dark-haired, with gleaming active eyes, she was certainly less beautiful, though with an undoubted attractiveness that had a very positive and challenging quality. Her dress was less rich than that of Lady Margaret, but served to draw attention to its wearer very well, being yellow taffeta slashed in front to show a flowered underskirt, and modestly topped with a shoulder-collar of narrow brown fur above a high belted waist; only, below the collar, the wide scoop-front of the gown was not prudishly filled with any drapery to hide the rounded excellence beneath. Even Rob Bruce's eyes strayed thitherwards.

The Lady Margaret rose. "May I go now, Sire?" she requested quietly.

"No, you may not." James was forceful. "Mistress Mariot —
you will dance with me?"

Jumping down from the dais, the King held out his arms.
Though the drop was but twelve inches or so, his partner made
quite a thing of the descent, and ended by being lifted bodily
down. As they swirled off, laughing, in a skipping, bouncing
gallopade, that invited more support for the female form than
many dressmakers had provided, James was not backward in
furnishing his aid.

Watching, Margaret sighed a little.

"An antic, just," Bruce commented. "More seemly at a fair!
The King is in a strange humour."

"He looks to me for what I cannot give him," she answered,
slowly, sadly. "Not . . . thus. I fear that I gravely disappoint."

"He thinks a deal of you, nevertheless, I believe."

"We have been friends. For long."

"You are still his friend, are you not? He . . . he needs friends,
I think."

"Aye — still. Always." She nodded. "But I will not be his
strumpet!"

"No. That I understand."

She turned to him. "There is something that *I* do not understand, Sir Robert. Why should some of his lords be so concerned
that the King is . . . satisfied? Pleasured in this matter? Provided
with what he seems to seek? Of women?"

"Are they so?"

"Yes. My Lord of Gray made that very plain. And Master
Hepburn — the Vicar of Linlithgow — was of the same party. They
were all together. There is something here that smells strangely."

The other looked down. "Men can be like that, Lady Margaret.
Urging on a younger man. Watching and snickering. Wagering
even, on the results — as at a cock-fight. Unworthy, but common
enough."

"Perhaps. But would such sport pay for lands, office, position?"

"Eh . . .?"

"For such is at stake, it would seem. And my father is deemed
necessitous!"

Bruce shook his head. "This I do not understand."

"Nor I. But there is something behind it. Worth the watching . . ."

The romp over, and James and his partner back, panting, flushed and laughing, minstrels played soft music whilst breath was recovered. Then, after shouted demands by some of the lords, a woman was pushed forward to sing. She made low obeisance to the dais, and then, with an elegant lordling kneeling at her feet and plucking soulfully at a lute, she launched into a plaintive ballad of unrequited love. She sang most sweetly, most tunefully, most hauntingly – but with a subtle lascivious under-tone that grew ever more evident, more notable. As she went on, all over the crowded Hall hearers stirred in a growing and delicious discomfort.

The woman was neither very young nor very beautiful, but she was of an undeniable fascination. Spare, lean, almost hungry-looking, her figure was yet somehow magnetic in its attraction, not so much desirable as so evidently desiring. She used sinuous grace, long eloquent hands, and pointing thrusting breasts, to speak louder than her words, and her great glowing eyes in the thin whitely-drawn face slid from man to man as she sang, and left none unmoved. Her gown of black velvet was almost unrelieved save for an embroidery of sewn pearls, and her jet-black hair, strikingly, she alone in that great chamber wore under the old-fashioned starched lawn wings that seemed to suggest nun-like purity.

Moistening his lips as the singer released his own almost hypnotised regard in one of her circuits, James coughed. "The Lady Kate is . . . remarkable, is she not?" he said.

"Who is she?" Mariot Boyd whispered unevenly.

"The Lady Katherine Carmichael. That was the Lady Crichton. And something other before that. I cannot remember . . . How think you of her?"

"I . . . I do not think that I like her, Sire."

"M'mmm."

"Nor do I, by the Rude!" Rob Bruce added bluntly. "She offers too much."

"But asks more still, I believe!" the Lady Margaret put in quietly.

The King glanced along at her, but said nothing.

When the curious song was finished, amidst uproarious ap-plause – almost wholly masculine – a blind story-teller was brought forward to recount a saga of daring-do against odds, of the time of Robert the Bruce. Normally this would have enthralled James, but tonight he was disturbed and excited, and paid little attention. His regard kept straying to the splendid bosom of the girl who sat so close on one side — although almost as often his glance sought the lovely eyes of her who sat at the other.

It was a lengthy epic, and presently Lord Hailes made his way forward to the dais. On receiving the royal nod to approach, he came and spoke in the King's ear.

"My Lord James — this is plaguey dull, is it not? I suggest a more amusing entertainment. And less crowded. There are too many here." He nodded towards a door at the back of the dais. "In the presence-chamber, perhaps? More . . . intimate. The Lady Kate has a dancer. Some Egyptian. Of notable parts, she says. If *she* says it, I warrant there's something to it!"

James nodded, and rose at once — so that all others must promptly rise also. Perceiving this, and the effect on the blind story-teller, whose voice faltered, he bit his lip, frowned, and sat down again. "Continue, my friend," he called out, and waved the company down. To Hailes he whispered. "See you to it, my lord. I will come when this is done. It would be an ill thing to spoil the old man's story."

Shrugging off his astonishment at such delicacy, Hailes bowed and withdrew. For the first time that evening, Margaret Drummond, however, directed a smile, faint but warm, at the King — though it is to be doubted if he saw it.

At last the chronicle was over, and with some relief the company prepared to dance once more. James directed the three young people beside him to the door, where one of the Hepburn moss-troopers now stood on guard.

"May I go, Your Grace?" Margaret asked. "May I be excused?"

"Why, no. I wish you to be with me," he returned.

"I am weary. Would retire . . ."

"Then perhaps the entertainment will revive you! And wine. If my presence does not! Come." But it was Mariot Boyd's rounded arm that he took.

Already a select group of men and women were assembled in the presence-chamber, a small arras-hung dark room, notably bare of furnishings save for the gilded throne on another double-stepped dais, and a single table, now laden with flagons and goblets. The light was very dim in here, only a few candles being lit. But when James called for torches, Hailes urged otherwise, saying that the Lady Carmichael desired it so for her dancers. Even less might be required.

The problem of seating was solved by bringing in cushions from the domestic quarters. James, from his throne, signed to Mariot Boyd to place hers on the dais beside him at one side, where she could lean back against his chair. After a few moments, as though by an afterthought, he directed Margaret Drummond to do likewise at the other side. When she shook her head, he frowned, and insisted. She obeyed. Rob Bruce took up his stance behind the chair, and the others gathered loosely around. The cup-bearer provided all with wine.

The first dancer whom the Lady Kate brought in was a swarthy young gipsy with a flashing eye and gleaming teeth, dressed in highly colourful rags. He came from Spain, she declared. He danced a wild and stirring morisco to the strange twanging accompaniment of a colleague in the shadows. The second offering was very different, a mime, lively and unrestrained, depicting an eager man most evidently seeking to coax an unseen woman to lie with him — all to a thrumming rousing music in which a drum beat like pulsing blood to a rhythm that mounted and mounted.

In the midst of this, leaning forward absorbing the challenge of it, James became aware of someone slipping in front of him below the dais, to sit at his feet. Occasionally the woman's back touched his knees. It was Kate Carmichael herself. Gradually, as the tension of the dance grew, she leaned more fully against him.

When the gipsy came to his explosive finish, and backed away panting, she rose, without looking or speaking to the King, and went forward again. She extinguished all the candles save two, which she placed on the floor near the tapestry-hung wall opposite the throne. Then out of the darkness at the back, a woman came to join the male dancer, running on bare feet, with long hair loose to her waist. She appeared to be clad in gauze-like clothing, possibly the finest silk, filmy and scanty, through which her figure was clearly silhouetted against the flickering light of the candles, lissome, vital. She commenced to dance to the man.

Kate Carmichael came unobtrusively back to sit at the foot of the throne once more, this time leaning against James's knees quite frankly. As the dance, all languorous grace and suggestiveness, progressed, her hand came up, to rest on his thigh. She rubbed gently, to the rhythm of the music, with the ball of her thumb, on the tight stuff of his long hose. Uncertainly he moved his hand down, and, all the time looking only at the dance, she coiled her long slender fingers in his. She drew his hand down, to her shoulder, to the cool skin at the wide neckline of her gown, and held it there, stroking his finger-nails.

Uneasily the youth stirred, and felt the muscles of her back ripple against his legs. The dancing grew ever more amorous. The cool hand that held his hot and moist one, began to draw it down further, down and down. It reached the swell of a small pointed breast, pear-shaped, firm. She closed his clumsy fingers over the nipple, large, pouting, hard.

James was biting his lip. He could not keep himself from trembling slightly. Urgently he looked about him, in the gloom.

It was at Margaret Drummond that first he glanced. She had risen to her feet, and even as he looked she turned away and slipped past the others into the further darkness. His regard switched to the other side and Mariot Boyd. She was sitting up, wide eyes on him, not on the dance. She looked away when he peered down at her, quickly, but did not move her position.

The Lady Kate's fingers, leaving James's hand cupping her breast, slid up his arm, back to his knee, his thigh, and moved on and upwards. With a choking gasp, the boy jerked back in his seat, pulled his hand abruptly out from her gown, and swung his knees roughly sideways, butting against her leaning back in the process.

Soft and low, but clear enough, a chuckling laugh came from the woman at his feet.

The peculiar dance came to an end with the man and woman sinking to the floor in each other's arms, and there continuing to writhe until somebody used blankets to hold before the candles, thus bringing down a curtain of almost complete darkness on the entire chamber. The music died away in a long shudder.

In the subsequent chatter and exclamation, Kate Carmichael rose and stumbled her way forward in the darkness. There were squeals and giggles and scuffling before the light of the two candles was allowed to shine out again.

James sat stiff and tense on his throne, on edge, a battleground of conflicting emotions, desires and constraints. He was both physically roused and disgusted, excited and yet repelled. He felt unclean – but externally only, not within himself and in his mounting desires; only with an embarrassment for people behaving so for the mere entertainment of others. And because of the Lady Kate. What she had done. Her hard aggressive demanding body — yet older than his own dead Danish mother, for certain. It was horrible, somehow. And yet . . .

People were clamouring for another dance. James, even whilst he felt distaste, yet knew avidity also, to see what they would do next. To know more — more of this strange challenge of the body, between man and woman. He had so much to learn . . .

He stared around him. Margaret Drummond was nowhere to be seen. She had evidently taken the opportunity to slip away, out of the chamber, in the gloom. Mariot Boyd was gazing down, preoccupied apparently with her own soft hands. But when he touched her shoulder, she looked up at him doubtfully, wide-eyed, questioning — but eager too. Uncertainly, she smiled.

Kate Carmichael announced a new dance, by the gipsy woman alone, and amidst laughter extinguished one of the remaining candles. This time, after a prolonged light thrumming, almost sighing, of a drum, the dancer emerged wrapped tightly in what seemed to be a large parti-coloured shawl or small blanket. Presently, as she twisted and shook and swayed to a jerky, oft-repeated melodic theme, swinging one arm wide and then the other, it seemed that she might be naked beneath the blanket — although it was difficult to be sure in the faint light of the single guttering candle. James leaned forward, eyes narrowed, the need to be certain strong, insistent, upon him. He was so peering, practically convinced, after one half-turn towards the light, and willing her to turn again, when he started in his seat as a finger ran lightly down the curve of his chin. The Carmichael woman was back, standing behind his chair this time. She whispered something in his ear.

James was somehow affronted, angry. With a quick gesture of his arm, he pushed her away, vehemently, finally. He heard Lord Hailes cough warningly behind him. The Lady Kate moved silently back into the shadows.

The King crouched, frowning, for a few moments. Then his hand slid down to Mariot's shoulder. He felt her quiver to his touch. Then move very slightly nearer to him. He pressed her closer still. Without hesitation, but not forwardly, she came. He stroked the fur collar at her neck, and after a little felt her soft cheek rubbing lightly on the back of his hand. He waited, his eyes now raised to the dancing woman, now downbent.

When Mariot made no further move, he moistened his lips. Had he expected, hoped for, too much? She was not going to do it? But then . . . did he really want her to? Was that not partly what had been wrong with the Carmichael woman? What had offended him, even as it excited? *She* had taken the lead, unsuitably. He was the man, who should lead. The King, moreover. Should he not play the man's part? Now? Take charge? Was that not better, whatever the result . . .?

Drawing a deep breath, James moved his hand down from the band of fur, down over the smooth skin and into the cleft of that lovely bosom, so round and richly swelling, firm but soft. And warm.

She trembled a little, but did not stir or draw away. His breath came out on a long sigh, tremulous itself. Then, as his hand moved again, searchingly, hers came up—but not to restrain, only to cover and hide his. So they sat, both breathing quickly.

After that, James no longer consciously saw the dance, nor was interested to discover the state of the gipsy or the outcome of her posturings. He sighed, stirred this way and that in his chair, and sighed again.

If he did not really see the dancer in front of him, certainly the youth had no eyes for Hailes behind him, nor perceived that man's urgent gestures, nor noted the gradual and careful movement of the rest of the company, in response, in the three-parts darkness. Heedfully, almost tip-toeing, the women hitching up their trailing skirts, all moved away from behind that dais and throne, into the deeper shadows, towards the door at the far side of the chamber. For a little longer the dancer and musician continued to play their parts, until at a sign from Hailes, now alone at the guarded door, they made an end, bowed low, and picking up their things, hurried away.

It was the girl who first perceived the situation. "They . . . they are gone!" she gasped. "Sire—where are they? All are gone."

"What . . .?"

"We are alone."

Most reluctantly withdrawing his moist hand from its warm nest, James stared. "By the Rude—so we are! Lord—how . . .? When?" He rose, peering around. He strode over, to pick up the single burning candle, and raised it high. "All gone!" He laughed, unevenly, a little too loudly. "I' faith, I do not know the wherefore of this—but it is convenient, is it not?"

Mariot said nothing, but looked up at him, great-eyed, lips parted, receptive. She did not rise from her cushion.

Setting down his candle with something of a jerk, so that it almost tipped over, James went to her. There was no lack of cushions left behind.

"Softly! Softly!" she whispered, when she could free her lips from his burning kisses. "There is no hurry. No hurry, at all. Wheesht now — wheesht!" She was like a mother with too eager a child.

"There is!" he got out thickly. "There is. You are beautiful. Kind. I . . . oh, Mariot!" His hands were on her, fumbling, pulling.

Hushing him, chiding gently, and smiling, she aided him.

There was altogether too much of skirt and petticoat, too much of taffeta and linen, for a man in such haste as was young James Stewart that night. The top came down readily enough, with only a little tearing — but what it revealed made only for greater hurry, urgency.

Now it was his own attire troubling him, the tiny velvet trunks above long tight-fitting hose. It was a race against time and the mounting fever in his blood — desperately he knew it, resented it, but had no means of denying it.

Somehow he won clear of the cloying, clinging, enfuriating material, velvet as well as taffeta and linen — but then, the sight of long white limbs glimmering palely in the candlelight was almost too much for him. Feverishly he cast himself upon the girl. It was all wrong, all wrong . . .!

She cried out, involuntarily, astonishment as well as pain writ large on her features. Not that James saw it. "You hurt! You hurt!" she exclaimed. "What . . . what is it?" She put her hand down, groping. "Iron . . .?" she gasped. "Iron chain!"

The other was in no state for explanations. His fingers, anyway, were gripping into her soft flesh almost as painfully as were the links of chain.

It was the young woman's turn to bite her lips. She sought to move so that the discomfort was less — but not abruptly. Patiently, generously, she schooled herself and helped him.

It was of little avail. Furiously the flood-tide in him rose to burst all bounds. He groaned, as he sank away, foundered, vanquished, lost. "I am sorry . . . sorry . . .!"

"Hush, you—hush!" she whispered in his ear, staring up at the shadowy timbered roof. "Do not fret. There is no harm. No hurry. Wait, you. Sleep, now—sleep. And later . . . later will do . . . very well." She stroked his long auburn hair, damp now with sweat. "There is no hurry. Later . . ."

4

THE King strode back and forwards on the grass before his tent, eager, impatient, armour clanking, spurs jingling. His lords and captains, standing around in the chill thin October sunshine, watched him with varying expressions. The youth was a bundle of energy, vigour, enthusiasm—and the most cheerful man present, despite the news. It was hard to believe that he had ridden eighty hard miles the day before, had feasted and sung and danced half the night away before the camp-fires, and spent its short remainder making love to Mistress Mariot Boyd—only to rise with the dawn, make a circuit of the siege positions around beleaguered Dumbarton town and castle, insisting on the re-siting of some of the artillery, even helping to manhandle the heavy cannon himself, before dashing back to the main camp for breakfast . . . and this news from the north. Patrick Hepburn, who was no longer Lord Hailes but belted Earl of Bothwell by the royal favour, grinned wryly. Their scheme for the wearing down of the kingly energies and for keeping the monarch from interfering too much in affairs of state, by means of a judicious supply of demanding young women, could hardly have been named a success. James had accepted, indeed enthusiastically embraced the women, especially this Mistress Boyd—but diminished nothing of his other activities. On the contrary, each conquest, like each month of his life, seemed only to enhance his vigour and ardour and fervour for living—and ruling.

Words were tumbling from the King's lips. "If we but knew how long we have! Even if we knew their route. And their numbers. Are any of Forbes's and Huntly's people with them? If they are mainly Highlandmen, they will have little of horse and armour? And no cannon. But they will move the faster. A Highland host will travel unheard of distances, even in a day." He halted, to point at the single proud Highlander in his travel-stained tartans. "You, Glenarklet, believe them to be all from the clans? With no cavalry?"

"Such is my information, Sire. Save only for the Earl of

Lennox's own company. But, och, I have not seen them with my own eyes, mind." The soft lilting voice of the MacGregor chieftain was markedly at variance with his fierce and warlike appearance. "I was for wasting no time, when I heard, but rode to warn you. Myself, I have not seen them."

"But you are certain that this report is true? Of Lennox having a Highland army at Balquhidder?"

"Balquhidder is Clan Alpine territory, Sire—and in it what MacGregor is told is sure." That was stiffly formal.

"M'mm. Well . . . no doubt, sir. If they are at Balquhidder, then they will likely come down Strathyre and the Pass of Leny. And so into Monteith, and here. Will they not? How long until they are upon us?"

The other shrugged plaided shoulders. "They could be here this night. But the word is that they are waiting for the Athollmen."

"Atholl!" James jerked, frowning. "A curse on it—my own uncle! But since Buchan, his own brother is in it . . ." He shook his head, and swung on the Earl of Argyll. "My Lord Chancellor —this Highland host must be stopped. We must not be trapped between it and Dumbarton. How many men can you spare me to take north, to halt them?"

The spare, elderly, lugubrious Argyll, chief of Clan Campbell but looking the unlikeliest Highlander, or warrior either, moistened thin lips. "None, Your Grace—not one!" he protested. "We are outnumbered as it is. Lyle and Lennox's son have more men in Dumbarton than we have besieging it! Only your great cannon keep them from breaking out on us. I dread each night, when we cannot see to fire them. Until Home and Maxwell come with their Borderers, we dare not lose a man. Unless, as I have advised before, we raise the siege . . ."

"No! Never that!" James turned to stare at the grey town of Dumbarton, half a mile away, on the edge of the sparkling Firth of Clyde, with its soaring castle-crowned rock rising behind. "These are rebels against their liege lord. They have challenged me, and I have accepted their challenge." He drew a deep breath. "I must go alone, then, my lords. Go north," he decided. "For if Lennox reaches here, to join his son and Lyle, the kingdom is lost."

"What can you do, Sire? In the time . . .?" The cast-eyed Argyll never looked cheerful; this bright chill morning he seemed depression incarnate.

"I must raise men. Somehow. And quickly. My Lord Graham — there are many of your House between here and the Highland Line. You must ride, and raise them. In all haste. All that you can. And bring them after me. Horsed men."

"I have two hundred here, Sire . . ."

"Another two hundred! I need them — must have them. Before nightfall." He turned. "Buchanan — your country is near, also. You can raise more, I swear!"

"Only . . . only a few gillies, Your Grace," Patrick, the Buchanan chief, claimed. "All my fighting strength is already here . . ."

"Tush, man — you could find one hundred more gillies along Lomondside! Mount them on your hill garrons. And send them north. Or, by Saint Ninian, Lennox will have Lomondside and all else!" He swung back on the Chancellor. "Send couriers to hasten on Home and Maxwell, my lord — forthwith. I ride now. Menteith is an old and done man, and craven — moreover I have not time to seek him out on his island. But at Doune I shall find some few of my own men. After that there is my Lord Drummond. How far? Fifty miles? Sixty? And Ruthven . . ."

"I shall ride with Your Grace," the new Lord Bothwell declared.

"No, Patrick. Bide you here. Your moss-troopers are the backbone of the force here — and I'll warrant they'll obey none but you! Besides, I'll ride the faster alone, with but Rob Bruce." That was simple truth. The King's furious horsemanship was already a legend, up and down the land.

Without waiting for protests or good advice, he hurried into his gaily-coloured tent, over which the Lion of Scotland flew proudly. There on a couch of deerskins Mariot Boyd still lay outstretched, flushed with sleep, luxurious and desirable. He strode over to her and caught her up bodily in his arms, against his cold armour, kissing her lips, her eyes, her throat.

"I am off, my dear," he announced, breathlessly, between kisses. "To the north. Trouble with Lennox. The old man. He has raised the clans. Or some of them. Marching south to relieve Dumbarton. He must be stopped. I am for Doune. Then St. Johnstone . . ."

"*Now*, James my lord? At once? Surely not . . .?"

"Yes. At once. Go you back to Stirling, Mariot. You will be safer there. The good Bishop will take you — and will find it no hardship, I swear!" Master George Hepburn, Clerk of the Council, and former Vicar of Linlithgow, was now deservedly Bishop of Brechin. "Await me there."

"But you, Sire? You must be weary . . .?"

"Not I!" He ran his hands over her warm body. "Lord—I could do with you! But . . . there is no time." He raised his voice. "Rob! Rob Bruce! Here! To me!" And to the girl, grinning, and pushing her down to the couch again. "Cover yourself, a God's name! Rob is so almighty proper! Rob, man—where are . . .? Lord! How long have you been standing there? Quick—the horses. And food to carry with us. And my small helm . . ."

James rode, in a lather of sweat, at his usual headlong gallop, and perforce Rob Bruce had to try to keep up with him; a state of affairs to which he now had become accustomed. He had long since given up the thankless task of warning the King of the dangers, not only to himself but to his realm, of such prevailing precipitancy, however expert and dashing. Today was different, of course; every minute might be precious. Moreover, he had to admit that James had an excellent eye for country, for the quickest and surest going, an instinctive sense of location.

They pounded up the fertile valley of the Leven Water, the heart of Lennox, with the Highland mountains towering misty blue before them about Loch Lomond, their jagged summits already streaked with the first of the winter snows. They forded the winding river at the shallows above Murroch, to face the long lift to cross the high rolling moorland north of the Kilpatrick Hills, through Graham country making for Killearn and Balfron. As well the Lord Graham was on the right side in this affair—accounted for no doubt more by his hatred and fear of his powerful neighbour Lennox than by any touching loyalty to his young monarch. James had few illusions on such matters.

This rebellion had not been unexpected—although it had been a shock that the Lord Lyle, one of the victors of Sauchieburn, whom he had made Justiciar-General of the kingdom, should have joined with Lennox in the leading of it. These two had been dissatisfied with their pickings as a result of the change of king and government, jealous of the greater gains of the Hepburns and Homes. Then there had been all those who had supported the late monarch, and who continued to blame his murder on his successor; not all of these had joined the revolt actively, but significantly placed nobles in the north especially had raised the banner, notably the Earls Marischal and Huntly and the Lord Forbes. The latter indeed had ridden through the streets of Aberdeen and adjacent towns with the alleged torn and blood-stained shirt of King James Third fluttering at his lance-head, calling for vengeance. To the standard of revolt had adhered many branches and members of the great House of Stewart itself, unfortunately, following Lennox's lead, disappointed in their royal cousin's inadequate patronage towards themselves. It was probable that most were not so much against the new King as against the faction which had put him in power – but it came to the same thing in the end. Hearty John, however, Earl of Buchan, had gone so far as to approach English King Henry for help against his own nephew – although almost certainly Archibald Bell-the-Cat was the main mover behind this typical piece of treason.

Nevertheless, the real danger was not in the north, or from over the Border, but here in the Clyde valley where Lennox and Lyle hereditorily dominated all. Dumbarton Castle, a royal fortress of which the Earls of Lennox were Keepers, was one of the keys of the kingdom, held now by Lennox's son Lord Matthew Stewart. With another Lennox stronghold, Crookston, further south, and Lyle's Castle of Duchal in Renfrew, these controlled a great and strategic area of the west, linking with the hostile and ever-dangerous Highlands. All could be lost here. James, rising to the challenge, had sent Argyll to take Dumbarton, whilst he himself had gone to invest Crookston and Duchal.

In his own assault he had been successful. The two southern castles had fallen within the week, thanks largely to his skilful use of the new artillery, of which James was an enthusiastic pro-tagonist – the great Mons Meg, his pride and joy, being foremost. But Dumbarton was a tougher nut to crack, for the cannon could not get within range of the castle, without first taking the sur-rounding town – which was garrisoned by as large a force as had the attackers. Moreover James would not permit the bombard-ment of the town itself. The Chancellor had settled down to starve out the rebels, believing time to be on the royal side, with Home's and Maxwell's reinforcements on their way. But now, this. Old Lennox was coming to the aid of his son and Lyle.

Something over an hour's hard riding brought them to the edge of the vast flood-plain of the Forth, the great watery moat that the Lowlands laid down before the towering cohorts of the mountains. Far and wide it stretched in front of them, an empty desolation of marsh and moss and quaking wilderness, fifty square miles of it, stretching all the way from the hills crowding Loch Lomond to Stirling itself, through which meandered and twisted the serpentine coils of Forth. This was why so many battles had taken place in the Stirling vicinity, from Wallace's Stirling Bridge and Bruce's Bannockburn to Sauchieburn itself—for here was the only place where an army might cross from north to south on sure ground, between the waterlogged barrier of the morass to the west and the sea to the east.

Hunting this area out from Stirling, James knew it well, and knew of only the one way across for adventurous travellers—by the causeway through the marsh from near Kippen to the Fords of Frew, and thereafter by causeway again, zig-zagging across the mosses and the tributory Water of Goodie to eventual firm ground at Kincardine. Cursing at having to ride so far eastwards, the King led the way thither.

It was well after noon before the pair of them won out of the green and black treachery of Flanders Moss—for this scrub-grown maze of reedy dykes and ditches and runnels and ponds, where the wildfowl squattered noisily and the roe-deer flitted silently, was no place to hurry through. Horses and persons now mud-coated as well as spume-spattered, they dug in spurs as they reached firm ground, to gallop the two miles to the royal castle of Doune, filched by James's great-grandfather from the Earls of Menteith—one reason why the King did not seek the present Menteith's help in this crisis.

Within the massive walls of Doune, by the rushing Teith, rudely disturbing the mid-day quiet, James commanded the startled Keeper, Edmonstone of Duntreath, to quickly assemble, arm and mount every able-bodied man in the district, and have them ready for him when he returned in a few hours' time. There were to be no excuses, no remissions. He was going on to the Lord Drummond at Stobhall, north of Perth, but he would be back. Yes, it was a long ride, but the kingdom hung on it. No, he would not send a messenger instead—he must see Drummond for himself. But he would be back.

Mounted on fresh horses, the two young men thundered off to Dunblane, where the Bishop thereof was likewise required to have a force of horsed retainers ready for their King's service before nightfall. A hasty prayer and abridged hearing of mass before the altar of the Cathedral, and they were off again.

There was nothing for it now but the long and weary slogging up the high road that went by Allan Water and over the high ground of Tullibardine Moor, to Strathearn and Perth. They called in at Tullibardine Castle, en route, but unfortunately old Sir William Murray was gone on a visit to his son's castle of Balvaird many miles away and had taken most of his men-at-arms with him. However, some good was gained by the call, for it transpired that the Lord Drummond, who was a cousin of Sir William's, was not at Stobhall after all, but much nearer at hand. He had called here at Tullibardine only the day previously on his way to Muthill, a mere five miles away, where he was building a great new castle.

Despite this handsome shortening of their journey, James rode for the next mile or two frowning and with an apparent droop in spirits. Rob Bruce thought that he knew why. Despite the danger to the realm and the urgent need for the help that Drummond could give, more than this had been drawing the King towards Stobhall. Margaret Drummond was there, living at home again, and however much James might enjoy the charms of other women, and especially of Mariot Boyd, he still was in some way in the thrall of this other who would not yield to him. More than one letter Rob had had to find a courier to take to Stobhall, and not to Lord Drummond. Once he had come upon James trying his hand at poetry; he had not got very far with it, apparently, but the title at least was clear and forceful—"To Margaret, Fair but Cruel."

They ran the Lord Drummond to earth amongst a green country of knolls and hillocks and woods about two miles west of Muthill, superintending the masons erecting a tall and handsome tower on the summit of a ridge of rock, with stone being quarried nearby—a scene of much activity. Drummond was a handsome man, of middle years, stockily built, with a leonine head. His surprise at having the King thus erupt upon him with demands for immediate help did not set him by the ears, for he was a vigorous and practical man, better at acting than scheming. Moreover, he still had his way to make in the present royal favour, since his daughter most evidently would by no means make it for him. Almost before James had finished, he was shouting for his minions. He had fifty men-at-arms with him here – the minimum with which any lord might decently ride abroad – mostly put to work meantime to help quarry and transport stone. He sent messengers hot-foot back to Stobhall and Cargill, to raise his main force. Others he despatched all over Strathearn, for he was Steward, Coroner and Forester of that royal earldom. He himself would ride first to Inchaffray Abbey, where the Abbot had a large body of armed retainers always to hand – too large for any churchman, Drummond declared. Thence to the Lord Oliphant at Gask a few miles further, who should be good for seventy, perhaps.

This was the sort of reaction that pleased James. He himself would hurry on to Ruthven, whose young lord, though of doubtful loyalty, should be anxious to please, his father having died on the wrong side at Sauchieburn. They would meet again at the Bishop's palace at Dunblane, as soon after nightfall as might be – for haste was vital. Such forces as could not be raised by then, were to be sent south after them.

Before parting, the King cleared his throat, and considered the mountains beyond Crieff. "Your wife, my lord – the good Lady Drummond? She is well? And your daughters?"

"H'mm. All are in good health, Your Grace." Drummond also stared away at the hills, no more at ease than his sovereign. "Though to be sure I hear but little of Elizabeth's doings, these days." His elder daughter was married, most unfortunately in the circumstances, to George Douglas, Master of Angus, Archibald Bell-the-Cat's son and heir.

"And the Lady Margaret?" That came out with a rush.

Drummond was no more at ease. "A . . . a headstrong girl, Sire. Wilful, I fear. But . . . she is well."

"Good! Good! I . . . ah . . . I will see you at Dunblane, my lord."

Again on fresh horses, the two young men rode on, sixty miles behind them already.

James seemed completely to have forgotten his weariness – although only a few minutes before he had been half asleep over the Bishop's great fire in his palace at Dunblane. Eagerly he leaned forward to question the ragged and not over-clean Highlander who stood at the other side of the table.

"You say that this host is in the midst of the Mosses? Now?" he demanded. "Encamped there, hidden? By some secret way?"

The MacGregor's speech had not been of the plainest. And at the man's nod, "Lennox has come down by the Pass of Aberfoyle — not by Strathyre. He is twenty miles west of us? And less than that from Dumbarton! Hidden in the Mosses of the Forth."

The other nodded. "In Talla Moss, lord."

"How many?"

"Who knows, lord? A great host, just."

"To take a great host through that wilderness! It is scarcely believable. Where even the deer must tread warily! How does Lennox do this?"

"He has guides. Menteith guides. Who know the secret ways. As do I."

"You know . . . ? You can lead us, then? To Lennox and his host?"

"For that Glenarklet was after sending me, lord."

"Sire — I smell a trap here!" The Bishop leaned forward, a plump man, pink and hairless. "I do not trust these Highlanders — not one of them! They are savages. Barbarians. We live too close to them here not to know it. This could be all a trap, to entice Your Grace into these marshes, to your doom."

The MacGregor raised proud and contemptuous eyebrows at the cleric, but said nothing.

"I trust Glenarklet," James asserted. "He it was who warned me of Lennox's coming, in the first place."

"He could be in Lennox's pay, nevertheless, Sire. Other clans are, it seems. Why not these thieving MacGregors?"

"You hear what the Lord Bishop says, my friend," James put to the messenger. "Why should the King trust the MacGregors?"

The other shrugged disdainful plaided shoulders. "Because, lord, our race is royal. More royal than the King's! We are the sons of Kenneth mac Alpine, the first High King of the Scots. Royal we were before the Stewarts had even a name. Clan Alpine will never betray the King."

"M'mmm . . ."

"Insolent ruffian!" the Bishop cried.

"I believe MacGregor, nevertheless," James decided impulsively. "I will go with you, sir."

"Your Highness, I pray you take heed . . ."

"I see a trap in this, Sire — but of another sort." That was the Lord Drummond. "A trap for Lennox. He may be hidden in this Moss — but we might ensure that he never gets out of it."

"My own notion entirely, my lord."

"So said Glenarklet," the MacGregor agreed. "One force to be pressing them against the river. Another at the other side, to be keeping them from crossing. In the darkness . . ."

"You know just where they are camped? You followed them?"

"Not followed, no — we went with them, lord. Himself, Glenarklet, sent us. Nine of us. With the host. He spoke the Lord Lennox fair. We were to be slipping away, after dark. Three of us. My own self to come here, seeking you, the King. One to go to Dumbarton, to warn them there. One to go back to Himself, Glenarklet. Where he waits by the lochside."

James jumped up. "Aye. Good! But . . we are wasting time. Let us be on our way. The night is passing. We can make our plans as we ride, my lords. We have no time to lose, i' faith! To horse, my friends. You, my Lord Bishop — give us your blessing. And your thirty men!"

And so they were off once more, despite more than eighty miles of riding already that day. But this time it was not two young men spurring furiously, alone. Now the Lords Drummond, Ruthven and Oliphant rode behind them, with Sir John Stirling of Keir, Graham of Inchbraikie, the Dean of Dunblane and the Abbot of Inchaffray. Four hundred armed men thundered at their backs. And more would follow.

Back the four miles to Doune they galloped through a night of thin chill rain — there to discover that Edmonstone, the Keeper, misinterpreting the royal commands, had already taken the road, at the head of seventy men. But he was making for the Pass of Leny, below Strathyre. Cursing, James sent Rob Bruce hot-foot after them, along the Callander road, with instructions to bring them to the place where Glenarklet waited at the west end of the Loch of Menteith.

Down to the level plain of the Forth they pounded on, with midnight past. It took almost an hour's hard going to reach the loch, and circle it to the north. Halting the steaming, sweating company in a wood, with the ground already boggy and uncertain beneath them, the MacGregor slipped away into the dark fastnesses ahead, on foot.

"If the fellow is false, we shall soon know now!" the young Lord Ruthven declared, loosening sword in sheath.

"I do not doubt him," James declared, panting. "I think more highly of these Highlandmen than do most of you, it seems!"

"They are as vermin, Sire. Scarce human!"

"They are my subjects, my lord — no less than are you!"

After perhaps ten minutes of impatient waiting, three dark kilted figures loomed out of the shadows. The bonnet of one bore the two eagle's feathers of a lesser chieftain.

"Ha! Is that Glenarklet? Man, I'm glad to see you! We came as fast as we might, when we got your message. Is all . . . as it was?"

"Aye, Sire. The Lord Lennox's army lies yonder, near two miles away, in the Moss."

"How many?"

"I would think near four thousand."

"Lord!" James exclaimed. "So many!" Behind him he heard the alarmed murmuring of his companions. He raised his chin, though none would perceive it. "But what of that? We must make the Moss fight for us!"

"Well said, Sire!" Drummond supported strongly. "And surprise, against a sleeping host, is worth a thousand men."

"Sleeping, my lord?" The young man frowned. "We cannot attack them, sleeping. That would be unworthy, lacking in all chivalry! Let us use the darkness, and all that Glenarklet can tell us, to position ourselves, yes — but it must be fair fight thereafter!"

Drummond stared at him. They all did. "What . . .? Your Grace — what folly is this? Chivalry? This is war, Sire — not a jousting! Lennox is in rebellion against you. These would ravage your realm — rob you of your throne. And you talk of chivalry!"

"These are subjects of mine, nevertheless, my lord — misguided, but still my subjects. Lennox is one of my earls, head of a branch of my own House. They are not rats to be drowned . . .!"

"Four thousand rats!" Oliphant jerked. "And Highland rats at that, with sharp teeth!"

"How many men have you, Sire?" Glenarklet put in, quietly.

"Here, some four hundred. More are to come. Seventy should be here soon. Coming over the mounth from Callandar. The others, I know not when . . ."

"Four hundred only! And Your Grace talks of fair fight! One to ten!"

"I but mean that we cannot attack them sleeping. That I am their King, not leader of some robber band! I must have the respect of my people – their love and respect. Not just their fear . . ."

"What of the four hundred behind you?" Drummond demanded. "Will you have *their* love and respect? Who are to be thrown against ten times their number, to save your throne? When you throw away their lives for, for a childish whim!"

"My lord!"

"I am sorry, Your Grace. I was carried away. But two hundred of these men are my own Drummonds. I did not bring them to see them sacrificed for some notion of chivalry. Would you make widows and orphans of half my people? For that?"

"Holy Church could not countenance the useless death of many of her sons, Highness – for a mere conceit!" the Abbot of Inchaffray announced, heavily.

James bit at his lip.

Again Glenarklet intervened, with his soft lilting voice. "We are wasting time, Sire. Precious time. In this fruitless argument. I think that we but beat the air. This is a Highland host. It will sleep none so sound, I'm thinking. You do not steal upon the clans, so easily! I counsel that you consider rather how you may make your four hundred of some effect against them."

"There speaks good sense!" Drummond grunted, to the agreement of the others.

"Very well. But . . . there must be no unnecessary slaughter," James said, unhappily. "None must die needlessly. You understand, my lords? That is my royal command – no single man must die whose life may be spared. For these are my people, as are you." He spoke through the muttering behind. "Your plans, then, Glenarklet? What do you propose?"

"That you divide your strength, Sire. They are camped on a place of firm ground. Rising like an island, it is, amongst the mosses. Near to the river itself. Ringed it is, with waters – but there is a causeway. Hidden. Under the water. If we can gain that, none may leave the island. Save to the south. Across the river. There are shallows. Possible it is, to cross. A little way to the west. There is where your second force must be waiting. To drive them back into the river. Thus you may have them. For they cannot turn left nor right, for the mires and marshes."

"By the Mass – I like the sound of that!" Drummond cried.

"You think to reach these places undiscovered?"

"Yes. They have guards on both. But on the causeway, only at the island side. The river ford, where they mean to be crossing at daybreak, is guarded at both sides. The company that goes there must wait. Remain hidden and silent. Until they break across. Then attack, when they are scattered and in confusion. Drive them back."

"How can you be sure that they *will* cross, man? They may break backwards. Or sit close."

"They must believe that a great force has come up behind them, Sire. Fires. Many fires, scattered wide. Horns or trumpets blowing. You have trumpeters? Shouting, from far apart . . ."

"Good, I see it all," Drummond broke in. "They will not sit close, I swear. Not with a river behind them. They will cross, to put the river between them and the attack. That is what they will do. So the main fighting will take place beyond the river? To the south. Is there hard land there? For the horses?"

"Yes. The river there winds close to the edge of the moss. A spur of firm ground reaches out. Once there were even houses. A mill. Gartalunane, it is called . . ."

"You shall go there, my lord," James directed. "With our main force. Three hundred of the men. The rest I shall take, to make the gesture of an attack. Any horns, trumpets, to remain with me. Flints and tinder, also. Can they reach this place, Glenarklet? Gartalunane? From here. Speedily?"

"It will take an hour, Sire. To circle the head of this Talla Moss. Seven miles. Eight. But they will be there before *we* reach the causeway, I think. For we must go on foot. Gregor Mor will lead them." He pointed to the MacGregor who had come to Dunblane. "I will take you through the mosses, to the causeway. You can ride some way yet — then you must leave the horses. Ian Glas will wait here, to bring on those who come later . . ."

"Good! We part, then, my lords — and may God and Saint Ninian go with us all. But, remember — the least killing that is possible. Tell your men." James's voice was high, eager, excited. "Lord — I wish that Rob Bruce was here . . .!"

It was an eerie business, making their way through the great benighted moss. They went only in double file, behind Glenarklet and the King, a long, slow-moving coiling column of silent men, with the strictest instructions to tread only and exactly in the footsteps of the pair in front. They had ridden for perhaps half a mile before the going became too bad, and they left their floundering, alarmed and mire-spattered horses at one of the many mounds of drier ground, scrub-covered, that rose out of the marshlands.

Their route would have made astonishing plotting on a map, undoubtedly. Hardly for a dozen yards on end did they ever travel in a straight line, twisting, circling, cork-screwing, doubling back. Sometimes, even in the darkness, the reason for these diversions and detours was apparent, with pools and ponds and morasses to get round, even sizeable lochans, quagmires and reed-grown fens to skirt, runnels, ditches and wide canals to avoid, quaking treacheries of every kind to cross. How Glenarklet picked his intricate and improbable way through it all, and yet preserved a sense of direction, in the darkness, was a mystery – and an even greater mystery to James was how an army of four thousand had ever managed to traverse this watery terrain, in the first place.

The MacGregor explained that this was not exactly the course that Lennox's force had followed. That had been a slightly more direct and drier route a little further to the west. He was avoiding it in case Lennox had, in the end, sent back pickets and scouts to cover his rearward approaches, as a prudent commander might have done. This way, they ought to make their approach unobserved – if they made no noise.

That was not so easy, either. It was not so much the sounds of squelching and splashing, the occasional cracking of dead wood underfoot, or the muttered cursing; these probably would not carry more than a few score yards against the cold, sobbing wind that sighed across the mosses. It was the continual disturbance of the wildfowl that was the trouble; the place was alive with duck in especial, that went quacking off in protest, with a great beating of wings and pattering of webbed feet on the surface of every mere and tarn, as the column advanced. There was nothing that could be done about this, but hope that Lennox's sentries would assume all this movement of waterfowl to be normal at night on the marsh.

The slippery, stumbling, devious progress seemed interminable, and every man was coated in slime and mud, and soaked to the skin. No doubt there was scarcely one who did not heartily wish that his lot had taken him with the main body to Garta-lunane. At length, however, Glenarklet called a halt. They appeared to be on the edge of a wider sheet of water stretching away on either side. In the deep shadows beyond, there was just the suggestion of deeper black looming higher than the normal alder and birch and willow scrub.

"Yonder it is," the Highlander pointed, whispering. "The island. That is where they are."

It seemed scarcely credible that there could be four thousand men over there. So near. No sounds rose above the susurration of the waters and the sough of the wind. No camp-fires glowed. No duck, even, had squattered away for some time – presumably because this vicinity had already been disturbed by the earlier invaders.

"They . . . they have not gone, think you?" James wondered. "Moved on? We are not too late . . .?"

"I think not, Sire. They have marched near thirty miles this day. Weary they will be. They will not stir until dawn."

"The causeway? You say that it is under this water? Deep? Is it here, in front of us?"

"No. It is further to the right. Two hundred yards, maybe. I stopped here, so that we may make our plans. Here is what I propose, Sire . . ."

The project had to be fairly simple, in the circumstances. Perhaps a score of the men were to move away, separately, spreading out, to gather dead wood, dead leaves, dry rushes and the like, to make fires. In the damp and drizzle they would have to seek their fuel under thick bushes, drifts of leaves and so on. And in silence. Many fires were to be made, dotted about wherever they could find dry and solid spots to build them. The trumpeters and men with hunting-horns – there were three of the former, each lord always having a herald-trumpeter to ride with him, suitably to announce his presence – were to be included in this party. Another score were to be merely shouters – the older and less active men, these. To spread themselves along the rim of the mere on either side of the causeway, their task to sound like the commanders of vastly more men than they were. But there was to be no shouting or trumpeting or fire-lighting until the signal was given – a single piercing whistle blown by Glenarklet. Then they were to seem to be an army, and a noisy one. The remaining sixty or so were to be the actual attackers.

The first party was sent off at once. Their task was an uncomfortable one, and would take time. No doubt there would be much falling into pools and holes – but however wet they got, they must keep their tinder dry. Ten minutes of waiting there-after, ears stretched, and Glenarklet led the remainder west-wards towards the head of the unseen causeway, dropping shouters every thirty yards or so.

"Here is the place," he declared, at last — although there was little, in the darkness, to distinguish the spot from any other along that waterside, save for the churned-up mud where many feet had passed, and a single gaunt stump of dead tree. He explained that the causeway, a more or less solid track paved with large stones submerged a couple of feet below the surface, reached out to the island. But it was not straight. It went some sixty yards, then turned in a dog's-leg bend for another twenty, then back again in a curve, finally to reach the opposite shore, nearly two hundred yards from where it started. It was very ancient. Who had built it, brought large and heavy stones all this way, none could say for sure — although some held that it was the Romans, who had looked on these morasses as the ultimate barrier between their settled polity and the unconquerable and impenetrable Highlands. There were some others in the mosses, like this, known to the MacGregors — a secret handed down in the clan from father to son. Glenarklet did not mention that they provided most useful sanctuaries for stolen cattle from the Lowlands, being driven home by raiding Gregorach.

The Highlander whispered his instructions. Every man was to provide himself with a stick, from the thick alder scrub behind. This was for support, for the unseen stones beneath the water would be weed-grown and slippery. There must be no slipping, stumbling or falling here. No single splash or gurgle of water. It might take them half an hour to cross that two-hundred-yard gap — that did not matter. Absolute silence was the vital factor, not time. The causeway was fairly wide, twelve feet perhaps, but its twists were deliberately and cunningly made to confound the ignorant and the unwary. And there were stones missing. One single hasty, unprospected step could ruin all, and by splashing draw attention to their presence, in the darkness. There would be guards at the farther side.

"Would we be better with our boots off?" James asked. "I could grip those stones better so, I think."

"No. For we may not have time to put them on again, at the other side," Glenarklet decided. "And these Lowlanders, fighting in bare feet, would be at a disadvantage. But you, Sire — you are not coming? Joining in this hazardous attack? You, the King?"

"By the Rude, I am! Why not?"

"Because . . . because it is dangerous. Och, if we were caught, half-way, all would be lost. None might get back, at all. One man splashing, and we could be discovered. You must wait here . . ."

"Indeed I shall not! I did not come for that, my friend!"

"This is no work for kings, Sire! The weal of your kingdom demands the King's safety . . ."

"The weal of my soul demands that I do what I ask these my subjects to do, sir! Amongst your clans, do the chiefs hold back when there is man's work to be done? No. Nor do I. Am I not Ard Righ, the High Chief? Enough, sir – lead on."

So that strange procession commenced. The MacGregor went first, moving slowly into the water, feeling his way heedfully, an inch at a time, with the toe of his rawhide brogan, bringing up the second foot to join its neighbour only when he was sure of his stance, balanced with a stick, and so careful as hardly to make a ripple on the black water. He went a couple of yards thus, and then beckoned for James to follow. Behind him came the ranks of men-at-arms, in close order now, each probing with his alder wand and each holding the shoulder of the man in front, five or six abreast, creeping forward so slowly that the dark bulk of them seemed scarcely to move. Deep breathing was the loudest sound men made on that mere. The whistle and beat of duck's pinions overhead was infinitely more evident and pronounced.

The stones were indeed slippery, and rounded. Every step was a hazard. Without the sticks, sliding forward and wedging securely into the crevices between, there must have been stumbles innumerable. Even so, James, probably the most impatient individual present, as he was the youngest, staggered not a few times. Once, having to throw his weight backwards suddenly on the rear foot, it slid, and there was a distinct swash and purl of water. Choking back the curse which rose to his lips, he glanced about him, humiliated. He saw the pale oval of Glenarklet's face turned back to him, but all others were peering downwards into the inky depths, although nothing could possibly be seen therein.

The water was deathly cold on the legs and feet.

So slow was their advance that no one, save the MacGregor, noticed the change in direction at the first bend in the causeway. James had started out intensely aware of the presumed sentries waiting at the other side, sure that they were bound to see their approach eventually, even if they did not hear it. But now, all his concentration was on this grievous business of inching forward on numbed feet over invisible, treacherous stones, rounded and occasionally gapped, without making a sound. He had thought to count every yard; in fact, with inches as the measure of progress, he not only assessed no yardage but did not perceive the turns and bends of their strange roadway.

So that, when some utterly uncalculable time later, Glenarklet's stick came back to tap the King's arm, as a sign to wait, to halt all behind for a space, James had not the least notion how far across they were. The MacGregor moved on alone, and, most encouragingly, swiftly was completely lost to sight in the thick rainy gloom. The assumption was that he had gone ahead to prospect a particularly difficult part of the causeway.

It was a very strange sensation, standing, with the chill water well above the knees, motionless, leaning on sticks, waiting, scarcely daring to breathe, with deep water on either side, all this treacherous stonework behind, and thousands of enemies in front. It was like some cold hell that one of the mad wandering friars might describe — and the hooting of the owls, from far and near, was the mockery of the earlier damned.

Without warning, Glenarklet materialised once more. He came right up to James, close enough to whisper in his ear. "Two men only," he breathed. "Well back from the edge. Sitting. Leaning against trees. Talking."

"Eh . . .? You mean . . .? You have been across? All the way?"

"But thirty yards from the shore, we are. The sentries another twenty. The ground rises. Trees. We must take those sentries. Silently."

"Yes. But . . . must we kill them? Can we not silence them without killing?"

The MacGregor frowned. "This is war. Sire," he protested. "We cannot afford to add to our difficulties . . ."

"If we can get close enough to take them, without sound, without being seen, man — we can do it without killing!"

The other shrugged. "As you will. We all move to the water's edge. Another thirty yards. Then I go forward. Alone. Round to the side, just. To get behind them. If I am approaching them from the direction of the camp, they will not be suspecting anything. They are clansmen, anyway, talking in the Gaelic. I shall

85

speak to them. Take their attention. Give you opportunity to creep up at their backs. But they must not cry out . . ."

"Yes, yes. I understand. Come, then."

Even that last thirty yards seemed to take an eternity to cover. At length, involuntarily crouching now, James stood on firm ground, and soundlessly the men-at-arms crept out behind and around him, dripping water. They laid down their sticks, all peering ahead, uphill, towards the mass of the trees. With infinite care they drew their swords and whingers and daggers, ensuring that no least screak of steel sounded on the night. Glenarklet disappeared again, off to the right.

They waited, still as statues now. They could hear the murmur of quiet conversation ahead.

Quite soon they heard footsteps approaching from the direction of the camp, quite clear, undisguised. Even a cough. Then Glenarklet's voice, not loud but not lowered, giving some salutation in the Gaelic.

James turned to the two men whom he had selected, signing them on to follow him.

They circled to the right, as the MacGregor had done, treading with catlike care lest they snap any fallen twigs. Fortunately, the dead leaves being damp did not rustle. It was a simple matter, after the crossing of that causeway, to work up and round until they were amongst the trees behind the sentries, and then to move in towards them, flitting from trunk to trunk. Their position was made amply plain by the talk, clear and natural if unintelligible, of the three Highlanders.

The last few yards were taken almost as slowly as when feeling their way in the water. James, slightly in the lead, could just see that the senties were standing up now. Glenarklet had coaxed them forward a little way from the tree. The King touched one of his companions, and pointed to the left-hand sentry. He indicated himself and the other. The third man would support them, as would Glenarklet. He clamped his left hand across his mouth, as a sign of what must be done. In his right hand he held a naked poniard.

Drawing a deep breath, he took three final steps, past the tree, aware of his colleague doing the same at the other side. Glenarklet, facing them, suddenly raised his voice, and turned to point eastwards, jerking something in his own tongue.

As the unsuspecting guards leaned forward, peering, James,

86

heart in mouth, jumped. His right arm he threw around his quarry's neck, to jerk tight, his left hand swung to close over the other's mouth. A strangled, choking cry escaped — but only very faintly. Then both man and youth, locked together, overbalanced and fell backwards. Glenarklet leapt like a panther, a hand whipping out his dirk, and almost in the same movement bringing its haft hard down on the falling man's head. With a grunt the guard went limp, sprawling on top of the King on the wet grass.

The other Highlander was similarly, and rather more efficiently, dealt with by the two men-at-arms.

"Good!" the MacGregor commended, aiding James to his feet. "None would be hearing that. Your Grace is not hurt?"

"He . . . he is not dead?" the boy panted, staring down. "You did not kill him?"

"No. Just the handle, I gave him. Tie these two up," Glenarklet directed the others. "Come, Sire."

Although he had been present at the Battle of Sauchieburn, of unhappy memory, this was James Stewart's first blow actually struck in war. He had difficulty in hiding his trembling.

Returned to the waiting company, the MacGregor explained. The woodland ahead was full of sleeping men. There seemed to be no actual camp, no tents pitched. Men lay everywhere beneath the trees, covered with their plaids. Where Lennox and his officers might be he could not say — perhaps well forward, down by the riverside beyond. All they could do was to move up quietly, spread out on a wide front, and then, when he gave the whistle, attack.

James was too excited to protest again about striking at sleeping men.

Forward the sixty advanced, spreading gradually into line abreast, tense, most of them half-crouching, swords gripped fiercely, up the slope and into the trees. Glenarklet, in front of them, halted presently, arm and broadsword upraised. Somewhere in the shadows ahead a voice spoke abruptly, thickly. Nearer at hand a man groaned in his sleep. Thrusting two fingers into his mouth, the MacGregor blew a shrill, high, penetrating whistle, long and shockingly loud and strident after the enduring silence of the night.

Pandemonium broke loose.

In any chaotic situation, a man with purpose and certainty is worth any score without, worth fifty panic-stricken, confused, leaderless. That was the position in the Moss of Talla that night of 11th October 1489. The Highlanders comprising Lennox's force were neither craven nor fools; indeed they may well have been fiercer warriors and braver men than the assortment of bishop's hirelings and lords' minions led by Glenarklet and the King. But they were taken wholly by surprise, scattered through the woodland, bewildered and misled, and left wholly without centralised control and direction. Roused rudely out of sleep, with the impression of a large force attacking them, it was every confused and bemused man for himself.

Not that any notable coherence and organisation prevailed amongst the assailants either — for such was manifestly quite impossible in the darkness of the woodland, surrounded by shouting, fleeing, stumbling enemies, with no systematic commands reaching them. Yet they had purpose and objective, knowledge of the situation, and the sense of each other's support and company. Also the mounting morale of men who have roused panic in others. Moreover, behind them, the high neighing of trumpets and the winding of horns, as well as the shouting and the red blaze of fires, all helped, strangely enough — not only to delude and distress the enemy, but to sustain and encourage themselves, sound and fury though it all was. Even James was heartened somehow by the purely illusory host behind.

Not that he consciously thought about it, consciously thought about anything — chivalrous conduct, the fact that these fleeing men were his subjects whom he was assaulting, or anything else. He was wholly caught up in a great wave of wild excitement, a mounting frenzy of passion, that carried him on almost blindly smiting, thrusting, flailing, scarcely aware of what he did, seeing before him not men with hearts and hopes and affections like himself but scurrying objects, targets for his eager triumphant sword. Reality was whirling, darting, insatiable steel, onward motion, and noise, noise, crazily intoxicating, inflaming, after the enforced silence.

It was a rout, a massacre, and no battle.

Men fought back, of course, even as they fled. Not all were lost in panic. Little groups drew together here and there, and formed islands of resistance, and these were avoided, left behind, so that the momentum of the advance should not be lost. But the main tide surged ahead, southwards, towards the unseen river away from the attack, from the noise, the trumpeting, the blaze of fires, leaving behind plaids, arms, supplies, clothing.

James, stumbling twice as he ran, the second time going down on his knees, realised that he was in fact now running downhill. As he staggered to his feet again he perceived ahead of him, to the right, a tent in an open space amongst the trees that were now thinning, the only one that he had seen. This would be Lennox's pavilion, barred and striped in his colours. Thither the King hurried, tripping over abandoned gear that lay thick here, armour, saddlery, harness, blankets. But the tent was empty. The Earl had gone with the tide, perhaps led it.

Pausing in the flapping entrance, panting for breath, James was about to resume the headlong rush after his companions, when he was aware of a major uproar developing behind them, back whence they had come. This seemed to be much closer than the shoutings and brayings of trumpets from the other side of the causeway. Could it be that some proportion of Lennox's men had rallied, slipped round behind, discovered how painfully thin in fact was the attacking line, and were now about to take them from the rear?

He called urgently, unavailingly, after his own triumphant men, who like sheep-dogs herded their terror-struck flock before them. Their own shoutings would drown all else. Apprehensively he turned back, up that littered slope.

He had not gone far when he paused, appalled. Even in the gloom he could see that a mass of men were coming rushing down, bearing directly upon him, kilted men, yelling. Suddenly the tables were turned. He was alone, helpless in the face of a charging solid body of enemies. It was his turn to know panic. He swung about, to flee before this phalanx that he could never hope to stem, tripped forthwith over a fallen body, and measured his length on the wet ground. Desperately he half-rose, realised that he could never do it in time, and flung himself flat again, dropping sword and clasping hands and arms behind his neck and tucked-in head below hunched shoulders, and so lay.

Pounding men were upon him, kicking, tripping over him, stamping on him. Beneath the feet of his subjects the King of Scots lay, bruised, battered, the wind knocked out of him.

James, in fear and pain and dizziness, was conscious presently that his ordeal was getting worse, not better, but only vaguely aware that this was because it was now feet shod in hard boots that were trampling him, instead of the earlier rawhide Highland brogans. Something in his bemused mind tried to tell him that this was significant, important, but he could not grasp it. Shrinking, sick, buffeted and mauled, he lay, enduring.

At length, blessedly, the pounding eased, died away, Still he lay, fearing more, seeking to make himself as small as possible. Then, as no more feet came at him, he raised his aching, swimming head slowly, cautiously. He appeared to be alone on that tree-clad slope now, save for other dark bodies, flatter than his own. All the noise and fury seemed now to be concentrated down the hill, towards the river.

Painfully he got to his knees. He was sick there, violently, gripingly. At length he rose to unsteady feet, and staggered to lean against a tree-trunk, weak, sore, gasping for air.

For some time he leaned there, loth to move. Then, railing at himself as a weakling, a craven, he forced himself to reluctant action again, and started off on an erratic course downhill, towards the noise and his further duty.

He had gone only a little weaving way when he realised that he went empty-handed. His sword — he had lost his sword. A warrior never lost his sword. That was the final defeat, humiliation. So long as he retained his sword he was not utterly degraded. He must have it. He was the King. He could neither fight nor appear before men lacking his sword. Swaying, he turned back.

The trouble was that he did not know where he had fallen, had lain. Amongst all the bodies and the shadows and the trees and the litter. And bending down to peer and stare and rummage made his head reel. His stomach was an agony, his breast as though constricted within an iron band, the chain about his loins stamped into his flesh. That evil wood swayed and dipped about him. Bodies twitched at him, and sprawled and jerked. They groaned, too — or was it himself who groaned? Time and again the earth rose up to meet him, and dearly would he have loved to accept its embrace, just to lie there and be quiet and still. But he had to find his sword, or be for ever shamed . . .

Swords there were. He found many. But these were all broadswords, heavy Highland brands. They would not serve. None would be deceived. His own, it must be.

Thus it was that Rob Bruce, after that charge and the slaughter at the riverside, coming hurrying up the slope, peering at bodies, running from corpse to corpse, seeking, panting, found James on his knees, dazed, dishevelled, groping, his long red hair matted with blood and mud, still searching, searching, and talking to himself.

"Thank God!" he cried. "The saints be praised! Blessed Mary-Mother, I thank you! James! Sire! You are safe? Christ God, I feared you dead!"

"My sword . . . ?" the King said thickly, "Where is it?"

"What matters it, Sire? So long as you are preserved." Bruce sought to raise him up. "When I could not find you, with the others, I feared . . . I feared . . ."

"My sword! I must have my sword . . ."

"Here, Sire—take mine. What matters it? All is well. It is a victory. And you are safe."

"I . . want . . . my sword . . ." James Stewart sighed, and sank unconscious to the earth.

CHAPTER

5

It was indeed a victory—not great by military standards, but complete on its own scale, and highly significant politically. Indeed few major martial triumphs achieve lasting results such as did the Battle of Gartalunane, as it came to be called. For it had the effect of settling King James the Fourth more firmly and securely on the throne of Scotland than any of his predecessors for many a long day.

That such a relatively minor affair should be responsible for such major results depended on many circumstances quite extraneous to the actual tactical situation. This was a victory of the spirit rather than of mere arms, something that Scotland required and craved for at this moment in her long story. That the very flowering of idealism and quixotry which made it what it was should also hold within it the seeds of inevitable and ultimate disaster, could scarcely be apparent to even the most far-sighted.

Despite his own sense of failure and personal humiliation, James came out of it all a hero, a youthful paladin, a shining knightly figure of gallantry and magnanimity, wounded in person but nobly generous. He, the King, was in fact the only one of the leaders on either side to suffer physical hurt. This, and his reluctance to take advantage of sleeping enemies, with his repeated orders that there was to be no unnecessary bloodshed, a theme unusual enough to be phenomenal, became the talk of the country. The fact that such carnage as did take place, small as it was for a battle of the time, nearly all developed across the river at Gartalunane under Drummond's generalship, after the King's smaller band had put thousands to flight, contributed to the legend which grew to sweep the land. That most of the men with him had been servants of either the Bishop of Dunblane or the Abbot of Inchaffray—since Drummond and the other lords had naturally taken their own men with them to Gartalunane—was seized upon and used to good effect by Holy Church, to the great credit of sundry saints, Ninian in especial, as the almost bloodless victory of true faith. Moreover, the King's final intervention, when he himself had been conveyed across the river, dazed and in pain, to halt all reprisals, all pursuit and hunting down of fugitives, further enhanced the story and set the seal on the young monarch's prestige.

That facts were not entirely in line with the popular version was neither important nor to be wondered at; they seldom are, in major events which move people most and determine the course of history. The lack of slaughter, whatever the royal commands, was undoubtedly mainly attributable to the character of the Highland host itself; a mixed assortment of members of many clans, by no means all mutually friendly, involved in an enterprise of no real interest to themselves and unlikely to be productive of much booty, when utterly surprised and disorganised and left entirely without leadership from the centre, they merely melted away into a landscape infinitely apt for it. On the very edge of their own mountain fastnesses as they were, nothing could be more typical of Highland character, which can be at once so impractically heroic and unashamedly and judiciously retiring. Most of the casualties, indeed, were amongst the Athollmen, only half-Highland levies of James's own uncle, less practised at the hit-and-run tactics of clan warfare.

Lennox and his close associates all made good their escape, with whole skins but sadly diminished fame. Though they made for the Dumbarton area, there was no further attempt to relieve the castle, which in fact capitulated soon afterwards.

The northern lords in arms, soon aware that the tide of national sentiment had so swiftly and unexpectedly set against them, discreetly dispersed. In his sea-girt Lothian castle of Tantallon, so convenient for communication with England, Archibald Bell-the-Cat no doubt cursed mightily, and thereafter carefully cherished the flame of his hatred for some more hopeful occasion. Hearty John of Buchan and his silent brother the Earl of Atholl, sent hasty and vehement messages of loyalty and congratulation to their nephew, and retired modestly to remote places.

James was not seriously injured. A cut on his scalp, a closed-up eye, severe bruising of ribs and loins, and an aching belly, were the worst of it. In a healthy and vigorous youth, such are soon dismissed. After a few hours' sleep in a farmhouse on the edge of the mosses, at Buchlyvie, he made an uncomfortable ride, less headlong than usual, to Dumbarton, there to acquaint Argyll and the others with what had transpired. If his arrival and tidings did not arouse such immediate elation in the royalist camp as the circumstances might have warranted, this could have been due to staleness engendered by the thankless and inactive business of besiegement, so dull and unheroic. Patrick Hepburn, the new Earl of Bothwell, and the Master of Home who had now arrived with his Mersemen reinforcements, were notably cool about the entire affair, and towards the victorious Lord Drummond in particular.

James was in no mood for siege either. After a single night outside Dumbarton, restlessly re-positioning the great guns Mons Meg and Duchal, he was off the next morning the forty miles to Stirling, with only Drummond and Rob Bruce for company. He did not pause at the town itself, but pressed on to the Kirkton of St. Ninians, a mile to the south, where in the old church he gave thanks to his favourite saint, promised a substantial grant of Lennox lands to the astonished priest, heard mass, and prayed for his father's soul and his own forgiveness – watched by his somewhat sceptical companions.

The news of Gartalunane had reached Stirling before him, and the King's ride through the streets thereafter, to the royal castle, a blood-stained bandage still around his bare auburn head, took on something of the nature of a triumphal procession. He sought out Mistress Mariot Boyd forthwith in some satisfaction therefore.

Perhaps he was wearier than he knew, sapped by physical effort and emotional experience. Perhaps the bruising caused by rough, stamping feet was partly responsible – and certainly the chain, trodden into his flesh, was damnably awkward in its siting. At any rate, despite the felicity of the occasion, his bedding with Mariot was less satisfactory than usual, and by the following morning he was on his way north once more, with the Lord Drummond and Rob, making for the former's home at Stobhall.

There he remained for some time, comparatively quiescent for that young man, inactive, with something like the inertia of reaction constraining him. There all who would see the King must seek him – and in the circumstances that was many indeed. Not all relished having to do so in the modest establishment of the but recently discredited Drummond; to say nothing of the inconvenience of the journey north to the silvery Tay. And not all his courtiers and officers of state were so patient and understanding as was, for instance, Bishop William Elphinstone, newly appointed Lord Auditor of Causes and Complaints, when the King was not to be disturbed because he was composing poems of indifferent merit to the Lady Margaret.

The full effect of the curious victory of Gartalunane only became apparent as time went on. For though the public reaction to it was important and advantageous to the King, nevertheless that was more or less immediate and shortlived compared with its effects on James himself. And this was evidenced only slowly.

First and foremost, it helped to lift from James's mind the weight and burden of Sauchieburn. Never would he wholly outlive the sense of guilt, but now the darkest stain of it was largely erased. His people's new and glad acceptance of this legend of personal leadership and young gallantry against odds wiped out their dark apprehension that their monarch had been implicated in the murder of his father. This could not fail to affect James powerfully.

The second long-term effect was that, in raising up a new figure of military esteem in the person of the Lord Drummond, it enabled the King to depend less upon Bothwell and Home. He now had someone with whom to counter their dominance. He did not dare quarrel with them, but he was not now wholly in their power. Hailes, Home, Lyle and Gray—these were the four who had led the revolt which had ended in Sauchieburn and placed him upon the throne. Lyle had put himself outside the pale, by joining with Lennox in this new rebellion. And Gray, that figure of menace, being so closely linked with Bell-the-Cat, and cousin to Lyle, was in a very weak position and forced to lie fairly low meantime, despite the fact that there was no proof that he had had any hand in the recent treasonable uprising. Always, the peculiar weakness of the Kings of Scots was their dependence upon the power of their great nobles; Gartalunane, by a happy concatenation of circumstances, enabled James to balance that power to a substantial degree, to use it instead of being used by it.

Partly to further that state of affairs, partly on the quiet advice of Bishop Elphinstone, but largely because it was his own desire, in accord with his own nature, James followed up his victory with a policy of unprecedented generosity and liberality towards the rebels. Although an immediate sitting of the Privy Council, minus of course a notable group of its members, automatically forfeited all the principles in the revolt, technically dispossessing them of lands and titles and liberty, none of this was actually enforced and no steps taken against even Lyle and Lennox, other than orders to ward themselves in their own houses until the King's pleasure was known. That pleasure, within a few weeks, was revealed as outright pardon to all and sundry. A parliament was held, and guided to decide that all persons and parties whatsoever of the realm should henceforth be at friendship and concord — although sharp justice was promised against any who refused to be in amity and quiet. Lennox and Lyle were even restored to their seats on the Council, as were Atholl, Buchan, Huntly, and the rest. James was taking a major risk, much against the advice of Bothwell and Home. Even of Drummond, in this instance. That he felt strong enough to take it was the measure of this his first triumph. No King of Scots had ever before shown such reckless magnanimity.

If Drummond this time counselled caution, his daughter did not. James was still spending much of his time at Stobhall, a relatively small castle situated impressively on a high tongue of ridge above the winding Tay, nine miles north of Perth. Inevitably he was seeing a lot of Margaret Drummond. Indeed Rob Bruce believed that this was the real reason for his continued presence there, even though the King declared it to be part of the process of weaning himself from the power of Bothwell and Home. The relationship of these two was peculiar. Physically and emotionally, the girl still kept James at arm's length; yet there could be no doubt that she was fond of him. They often walked together in the late-autumn woods surrounding Stobhall, or along the river banks — although these walks not infrequently ended by them coming back to the castle separately, the young woman's lovely head held high, the young man's features either very flushed or black frowning. They bickered and quarrelled inordinately, to the alarm of her father and mother, but there was undoubtedly a basic and mutual attraction and understanding between them which these surface storms did not disturb. Rob noted how, whenever they were in company with other people, their eyes kept seeking and meeting and holding, eyes that were so much more eloquent than their words — though frequently in such exchanges, even throughout an entire long evening in the firelit hall, no single spoken word passed directly between them.

It was on a crisp December day of frost, with snow capping the long line of blue mountains to the north and west, that James and the girl walked along the wooded bank of Tay, making for a flooded haugh some way north of Stobhall, to see whether it was frozen sufficiently for skating. James had a notion that knights jousting for a fair lady's favours, on skates, would be a notable ploy. He had been blithe enough when Margaret had agreed to his plea that she should accompany him — under implicit threat that he would make it a royal command if she did not — but was now less cheerful, for the young woman, on emerging, wrapped in a plaid against the cold, had summoned Sir Rob Bruce to keep them company, with all her own calm authority. That young man much disliked playing gooseberry, but he could think of no good reason for disobeying his host's daughter — and moreover, he was strongly of the opinion that the King ought not to walk abroad in lonely places totally without armed escort, for the kidnapping of monarchs by ambitious nobles was something of a traditional means to power in Scotland. So now Rob sauntered uncomfortably along behind them, at a discreet distance, seeking to concentrate his attention on everything else around and behind him rather than on the pair in front.

Margaret, having ruined James's walk for him, in typically feminine fashion was all graciousness, seeking to smoothe out his frowns by intelligent discussion of his problems — seeking more than that, no doubt, also.

". . . do not heed them, Sire," she was saying. "Even my father. Your generosity is worthy, noble, and will in its turn bring out the nobility in others. It is wise, as well as kind . . ."

"Some call it weakness."

"No — that is wrong. Foolish. Strength, rather. Not weakness after Gartalunane. You have proved yourself in battle, in victory. Before, forgiving your enemies might have spelt weakness, perhaps. Afterwards it is strength, Sire."

"Sire! Sire! Why must you ever call me Sire, Margaret? When we are alone. I have asked you not to. My name is James. Call me so."

"Very well." She paused, and then went on. "Do not heed those who say that in forgiving these others you are forging a sword for your enemies to smite you. I think that you are in more danger from your friends!"

"My friends? You mean . . .?"

"My Lord of Hailes, whom you have made Earl of Bothwell.

And the Master of Home, the Chamberlain. And that proud cleric, the Bishop of Glasgow. It seems that they grow ever more powerful . . ."

James forgot his dudgeon sufficiently to utter a brief laugh. "A king needs more than one sort of friend, Margaret. These are not of my choosing, but Fate's. Still, for my part, I think to play a card or two against Fate! Alexander Home is little danger, I swear, lacking Patrick Hepburn. Moreover, Bishop Blackadder hates them both. So I have prevailed on the Council to send Earl Patrick and the Bishop together on an embassage. To the Courts of Europe. Many Courts. They will be away for long. Not loving each other. Is that not apt?"

Quickly she looked at him. "What embassage is this?"

He cleared his throat. "The Council's embassage it is. Not mine. That they have been at ever since I mounted the throne. To seek a, a princess for me. To wed."

There was a silence. "Ah, yes," she said at length, evenly.

"See," he jerked. "I desire to wed no princess."

"No?"

"No. It is the Council. They keep prating of it. For the weal of the realm. To find Scotland allies, they say. For me, I want none of it. I would not look so far afield!"

"Ah, no. Of course—the Mistress Boyd! Such would bear sorely on her."

He flushed. "Not the Mistress Boyd! She . . . I am not thinking of Mariot."

"Then surely you ought to be, Sire? Your solace and comfort! The companion of your bed!" The girl's head was held distinct degrees higher now, however mildly she spoke.

"No, I tell you!" he cried. "That is altogether . . . otherwise. Mariot Boyd is . . . is . . ."

"Is not to be forgotten, Your Grace. When you seek your princess."

"*I* do not seek any princess. It is the Council's quest. They can send the embassage—I care not. But they cannot make me marry whom I would not. I will not be married off to some wretched foreign woman—or child, more like—whom I have never seen, belike with crossed eyes and buck teeth, who cannot speak our language!"

Even Margaret Drummond had to smile at this depressing portrait of current royal brides. "Some may be less fearsome,"

98

she suggested. "Even though they cannot rival Mistress Boyd's charms. Perhaps, Sire, you will be sufficiently . . . active to have both!"

"A plague on you, Margaret Drummond!" His hot breath rose like a cloud on the cold air between them. "You go too far."

"Yes. That is true. Or, at least, I have gone far enough. On this walk." The girl's lovely serenity of word and poise was as remarkable as it was maddening. "I am weary. I will go no farther. With Your Grace's royal permission." She dipped just the hint of a curtsy, and turning unhurriedly about, swept off whence they had come, looking neither right nor left.

Doubtfully Rob Bruce stood aside to let her pass, staring from her to the King.

James swung about, and kicked furiously at an unoffending tree root. "Ninian aid me!" he cried. "All the saints above have mercy! A curse on all women . . .!"

PART TWO
Chain of Destiny

CHAPTER

6

THE young man, balancing himself expertly against the heave and sway and dip of the ship, sniffed the salt air like a questing hound. His whole attitude, there at the very prow of the tall vessel, leaning forward into the north-west wind, eyes narrowed, typified eagerness, impatience, vigour, determination. The showers of spume, from the short, sharp Hebridean seas slapping against the *Flower*'s port bow, sprayed over him, but far from flinching he seemed almost to revel in its cold lash, shaking his bare head like a dog to rid himself of the salt droplets. The last dying rays of what had been a spectacular sunset stained his comely features to a ruddy hue, but turned his small curling beard darker than its true auburn.

"No war-galleys, Sir Andrew," he declared, not for the first time. "No lights along the shore yonder – no warning beacons. We have done it, I do believe!"

"Do not crow ower soon, Sire," Andrew Wood advised gruffly. "This is no' the Borderland, mind. They'll maybe no' use bale-fires here. And their galleys can maybe see in the dark, better than we can. These are no' decent honest folk we're dealing with, but heathen barbarians. Trust them in nothing, I say." The old sea-dog spat proficiently over the side. "Wait you."

"They are neither heathen nor barbarian, my friend," James said, but patiently, almost wearily, for this was an old, old story, and Sir Andrew Wood, like ninety-nine per cent of Lowlanders, would hear and believe nothing good of the denisons of the Highland half of his liege lord's kingdom. "Misguided they may be – but am I not here to guide them aright? That I shall do, with the help of God and Saint Ninian. But in love, not in spleen and anger."

"Love! Curse me – that's good!" the old man exclaimed, with something between a snort and a guffaw. Europe's most famous sailor held his tongue for no man. He turned, and jerked his grizzled head back towards the shadowy rows of long-nosed cannon ranked along the bulwarks, James's pride and delight. "Strange love-tokens!"

"They are but persuaders," the young man said. "To speak loudly first, so that men may stop to listen to what I have to say afterwards. In love. For these are my people also. And hear me they shall."

James spoke quietly but assuredly, confidently. Five years on the throne had changed him much in certain ways, but in others not at all. At twenty-one he was old for his years in some respects, young in others. But this mantle of evident authority he wore now as of habit and right, however eager and at times boyish he might seem.

Sir Andrew Wood grunted. "So be if Your Grace isna drowned dead first!" He looked in scowling distaste to starboard, where the loom of land towered blackly out of a border of ominous white, near at hand, much too near for any mariner's peace of mind, the savage rock-bound, reef-ribbed, skerry-torn coast of the Isle of Mull, against which the Atlantic rollers surged and shattered themselves in perpetual fury.

The royal fleet had stood well out to sea all day, out of sight of land, and only now was beating in close to the shore, as the sunset's light died over the dark waters, too close to that wicked shore for the shipmasters, on the King's own command, hugging a seaboard that was as menacing as it was beautiful, the most dangerous coast in Europe.

"We could have slipped direct into the mouth o' the Sound o' Mull, from the sea," the Admiral asserted. "This crawling amongst these plaguey skerries and reefs is fool's play . . ."

"And risked running into one of Alexander of Lochalsh's galleys? You know that they are said to patrol the mouth of the Sound day and night, like leashed hound-dogs. I dare not hazard that. One shot fired too soon, and all the Isles will be aflame, the Highlands blazing like tinder. It will be war, carnage, death, then —whoever wins. That must not be, Sir Andrew. So we creep under the shadow of this great island, that we may slip into the Sound unseen, in the darkness . . ."

"To creep and crawl, like cravens —the King's ships! Andra Wood! For a wheen Hieland galleys! Sink me —the first time it is the foe has seen Andra Wood skulking like any cur!"

"But then, these are not the foe, sir! Will you not heed, not learn? These are your fellow-subjects of my realm. They are not even rebels, in truth — not yet. Pray God we do not make them so, before I may speak with them."

Thinly behind them, against the wind, they heard the *Flower*'s shipmaster calling for all hands to be ready for the next tack. Having to beat thus into almost a head-wind was no help to navigation in these perilous waters where barely below the spouting, heaving surface were mountain ranges as jagged and fearsome as those that soared from mainland and isles all around. The look-outs, roped to bowsprit and mastheads, were hoarse with the endless shouting. James peered back.

"I do not even see the *Yellow Carvel*, now. Nor the *Christopher*. Bothwell is lagging shamefully. I told him to follow close. No single ship is in sight. The barges are slow — but there is no excuse for the others . . ."

"I saw a tall ship but a few minutes back, Sire," Rob Bruce told him, from close at the King's back, as ever. "Yonder great cloud darkens all. She was against those islands that we passed — the Treshnish Isles, they called them. The *Yellow Carvel*, I think — the Lord High Admiral's ship."

"*Flower* could aye show her heels to *Carvel*. And *Christopher*, likewise," Wood declared. "Forbye, their masters have belike cut down sail, no' being arrant fools . . .!"

The King ignored him. The new tack set them heading seemingly straight for a great thrusting headland of land that reached out blackly north of them from the main mass of Mull — Cailleach Point. Once round it, asserted their Maclean pilot who was guiding the shipmaster, the worst would be over. They would be able to swing away, east by north, towards the open funnel of the great Sound of Mull, to where it narrowed to a mere two miles across. An hour's sailing, and, if not intercepted, they would be within the jaws of it, with Mingary Castle close by — but hidden by the night's darkness.

The fourth man in that spray-drenched group on the high forrard castle-deck spoke — and in the Gaelic, his soft sibilant voice having to be much raised to be heard above the rush of wind and sea, the groan of timbers and the creak of cordage. "My Lord James," he said, "I would counsel that you turn some way into the Sound, and so approach the castle of Mingary from the east and south. Three miles in, perhaps, it lies from the jaws of the Sound, on the north shore. Some glimmer of light never quite is dying from the north-west sky, here in the Isles at this time of the year. Alexander of Lochalsh's galleys may be sailing the mouth of the Sound and the open sea, but MacIan's own folk on the towers of Mingary will have keen eyes. His own galleys may lie off-shore. Better that we come up from behind them, lest they see our outlines against the north-west, and give the alarm."

"You are right, Glenarklet – that is well thought on." The fact that James answered in the other's own language, and understood what he had said, was a tribute to both of them. After Garta-lunane, MacGregor of Glenarklet had remained close to the King, and proved useful in many ways. James, of all the long line of the Stewarts, was the first to turn his eyes northwards in anything but contempt, fear or wrath. From his earliest days, all but a prisoner on the rock of Stirling, he had gazed out across the level mosses of Forth to that awesome, towering and lovely barrier of blue mountains that represented the frontiers of another land, strange, romantic, exciting, almost forbidden, that other half of Scotland, unknown and challenging, and his eager and adventurous young heart had yearned to know it and its proud and difficult people. Always that challenge had been at the back of his mind, and as soon as he was fairly securely on his throne, he had started to make plans. He would one day be King of all Scots indeed, of the Highlands and Islands as well as the Lowlands. He would unite the warring, mutually scornful halves of his ancient king-dom. One of his first tasks in this self-appointed crusade was to make himself able to speak to the Highlanders, man to man, in their own language – something that even Bishop Elphinstone had thought to be unsuitable, undignified, and taking things too far. MacGregor of Glenarklet had been given this duty, therefore, of teaching James – and incidentally Rob Bruce also – the Gaelic. Ably he had done his work. However the nobles and courtiers might sniff and snort, the King of Scots could now speak with all his people.

Tonight, after years of often impatient preparation, of pre-liminary manoeuvres, laying plans and building ships, the great project was under way.

Hugging the savage coast, the *Flower* crept north as night descended on the Hebrides. Her shipmaster announced that the look-outs reported glimpsing at least four of the royal fleet in approximate line behind, between them and the Treshnish Isles. The host of galiots and barges, of course, being low-set in the

water and making heavy weather of these steep seas in consequence, would be far behind.

Under the lee of Cailleach Point, where they found both shelter
from the north-west seas and wind and cover from possible keen
eyes, the *Flower* hove to, whilst James paced the forrard castle
impatiently. The next stage of the operation would demand the
closest liaison between all craft.

The first ship to join them there was the great *Yellow Carvel*.
She and not the *Flower* was flag-ship of the fleet, flying the banner
of the Lord High Admiral of Scotland, the Earl of Bothwell — for
despite all his unorthodoxy and impetuousness, James was a
stickler for certain forms and dignities, and in fact used these to
bind his nobles closer to himself and for the realm's good. So that
Bothwell was ostensible commander of this expedition and Sir
Andrew Wood Vice-Admiral in charge of fleet movements.

Slowly the other tall ships came in, until there were six of them
lying in the angle formed by the headland, about half a mile
off-shore — a favourite assembly place of the Maclean and MacIan
galleys, according to their local pilot. They dared risk no light
signals, so Wood despatched a rowing-boat to the *Carvel* informing the Admiral of the King's further plans, formally seeking his
approval and requesting him to send boats to inform all other
craft. Patrick Hepburn, who knew nothing about ships and the
sea, but appreciated the Lord High Admiral's handsome revenues
from every trading port in Scotland, would no doubt co-operate.

After a full hour's wait, with only two galiots and one barge
arrived, of the host of troop-carrying smaller craft, James's scant
patience was exhausted. He left *Christopher* to collect and bring
on all the lagging transports, with strict instructions about their
route, whatever navigational hazards, and hoisted sail again with
the four others in close support.

Rounding that long thrusting peninsula was a heart-in-mouth
business, so close to the land, with tide-races and backwash on
an enormous scale to contend with, overfalls a commonplace —
caused by tides building up against sunken ranges — skerries
everywhere and winds unpredictable, rebounding off hillsides
near and far. Andrew Wood swore solidly for half an hour on
end, and even James's heart failed him a little as he realised how
utterly he had placed the fate of Scotland that night in the hands
of a turncoat Maclean pilot.

But at last they were round, unscathed, and running north by

106

east in comparatively uncomplicated seas for Ardmore Point and the mouth of the Sound. The look-outs had glimpsed no watch-dog galleys seawards — indeed a thin rain had started, further darkening the night, and visibility was reduced again. James welcomed the obscurity, whatever the hazards to navigation.

This expeditionary force could be only a limited and partial secret, of course, in the circumstances. The confederation of the sea-based clans of the west, under Alexander of Lochalsh, acting Lord of the Isles, knew well that the royal forces were not far away and planning action. It could not be otherwise. James had siezed the Castle of Tarbert, with its sheltered anchorage, seventy miles to the south, and made it his base, a year before, gradually building up supplies, arms, artillery and provisions. The clans could not fail to be aware of it. Not only so, but he had sent messengers to the great chiefs, Alexander's supporters, summoning them, civilly but firmly, to meet him at MacIan's Castle of Mingary in Ardnamurchan by the end of May, to make their due and loyal submission to their King. It was now the 26th of May. But the fleet had slipped out of Loch Tarbert the night before, under cover of dark, lingered all day on its northerly course well out of sight of land between the Inner and Outer Hebrides, and now was slipping in towards the strategic centre of Mingary, near the tip of the long peninsula of Ardnamurchan, westermost point of the mainland of Scotland — it was to be hoped unobserved. Alexander and his allied chiefs could, it was said, muster over a hundred war galleys and forty thousand broadswords. The King had not one-eighth that number of men embarked, and though his tall ships with their cannon were each probably worth many galleys, his small craft would be like sheep at the mercy of these savage wolves of the island chiefs.

This was all a highly delicate operation, therefore — appreciated the more fully by those who knew the pride and temper of the clans. Moreover, Alexander himself, with his main force, was reported to be at the Isle of Coll, no more than twenty miles off.

In the jaws of the great Sound of Mull, the thirty-mile channel which divided that large island from the mainland, they were into a tide-race again, with the ships being carried eastwards at an alarming pace. The pilot was discernibly anxious about two sets of rocks which they must thread, a bare mile apart, with visibility reduced to less than quarter of that. But after a critical fifteen minutes, he was satisfied that they were past the hazard, and directed the *Flower* to be put about on a northerly course, to start beating into the wind once again. A couple of miles of this, and they could all smell land close ahead of them, wood-smoke and the scent of new heather, on the north-westerly breeze. Presently they could sense rather than see the dark loom of it directly in front. Pinpoints of light, though not many, began to puncture the darkness ahead.

There was no more shouting from the mastheads, bridge or forecastle. The pilot had reduced his own directions to a whisper, and it became infectious. They were only four hundred yards from the Castle of Mingary at the head of its little rocky bay, he claimed – although how he could be so sure was a mystery. Silence was now all important. Fortunately they were to leeward, so that sounds would be apt to carry in the other direction. But the King's orders were explicit and stern. Any man, be he lord or tarry sailor, making unnecessary sound, would suffer the royal wrath. The anchor-chains had been heavily greased in anticipation, and were now let out link by link, painfully slowly. As well that there was little or no current here in the small sheltered bay, or the ships might well have drifted on top of one another before their anchors gripped.

At length, without any sign of alarm from shorewards, the five large ships lay secure and motionless in that benighted bay, in line, each within half a cable's length of the next, after as difficult a piece of seamanship as Wood's skilled captains had ever been called upon to perform. It was over an hour past midnight. They had less than three hours in hand.

Although most men snatched the opportunity for a brief sleep, King James could not. He paced the deck in restless tension, alone. Too much depended on this throw.

At approximately four-fifty next morning James stood, tense still, but no longer alone in this, staring landwards, silent, knuckles gleaming white as he gripped the foremast stay against which he leaned. All around him, on the *Flower* as on the other ships, men stood as still, as tense, waiting. So they had stood for almost forty long minutes, whilst the darkness gradually lessened around them. Dawn had been more than half an hour ago, but on a cloudy overcast morning there had been but little lightening of the gloom as yet. Sunrise would change all – but the effect of sunrise was modified by the ranks of soaring mountains which rose to the east, delaying the birth of the new day over this western seaboard. The clouds in that direction were already tinged with red, but so far spilling only little of reflected radiance down into the great trough of the Sound of Mull, still filled with shadow. When that radiance did surmount the mountain barrier, it would do so swiftly.

The King's glance, like that of most of his commanders, swung watchfully between four main focal points. That distant line of hill-tops to the east; the battlements of Mingary Castle which now loomed out blackly, towering above its own sheer cliff, an eagle's nest of a place, backed by grassy hills; the horseshoe-shaped natural harbour beneath, where at least a dozen long raking galleys could now be distinguished, moored close to-gether; and backwards, southwards, across the mouth of the Sound, where they looked for the remainder of the royal fleet, which had not yet caught up with them. Seawards, visibility was still very poor, and there was no sign of shipping; no life seemed to stir about the galleys; and so far no movement, no hint of alarm, showed from the castle. MacIan's watchmen were either somnolent or less than eagle-eyed.

The slap-slap of wavelets against the hulls, the whistle of wind in the shrouds, and the sad wail of gulls backed by the haunting calling of cuckoos from the Ardnamurchan shore, alone broke the uncanny silence, as hundreds of men stood ready. James nibbled his lip, his comely features barred by a blacker frown than he knew.

At last what they had been waiting for happened. As they watched, the ruddy glow above the long ridge of mountains changed to orange, to yellow. Then, out from a narrow rift in the leaden cloud ceiling a few vivid beams of sunlight shone out, golden, dazzling, fanwise. As though a curtain had been raised, all that world of sea and rock and heather and hillside was illumined by its glow and luminosity. Detail and distance, light and shadow, burst upon every eye.

Blinking, James raised his right hand. In it he held a white kerchief. He gazed fixedly at the castle keep.

For long seconds he stood thus, hand high, as though frozen there. Then the sound of shouting came thinly across the water to them, from the shore, to be followed by the high blaring of a horn from the castle walls. The white cloth in the royal hand swept down.

Pandemonium itself broke loose in the Bay of Mingary. Practically every cannon that James had been able to manufacture, buy, borrow or lay hands upon was in those tall ships of war. And every one of them now crashed out in thundering fury. The *Flower*'s armament blazed first, in an unbroken roar of percussion, spouting flame and smoke, every timber and spar of the vessel trembling to the shock of it. Before the last of her guns fell silent, the *Yellow Carvel* had opened up, belching fire and reek until she was all but lost in the exploding, pulsating clouds of it. Then *Ninian*, as *Flower*'s guns were feverishly reloaded. By the time that the *Cuckoo*, the fifth vessel, had taken up the fusilade, *Flower* was ready for the second round. Again she leapt in the water to the blast of those bellowing iron monsters.

Continuously, sustainedly, the ear-shattering din went on. The air quivered and shook. Strange hot winds buffeted men this way and that, and a hundred hillsides threw back the echoes to join in the hellish clamour. Never in Scotland's story had such a cannonade been seen or heard, such noise and horror let loose. Land and sea seemed to crouch appalled under the deafening scourge of it. Men, on the ships as well as ashore, reeled dizzily, clutching splitting heads. Many fell flat, as indeed well they might. And seawards, the mouth of the bay was wholly cut off by a tall spouting wall of water and spray, as balls crashed into the waves in terrifying succession—for guns were firing from both sides of the ships. Landwards however not a single fall of shot was to be seen.

At last the King, watching from under a hand that held a creased and throbbing brow, as *Cuckoo*'s third salvo crashed out, waved the white kerchief again. The blackened and sweaty gunners on *Flower* straightened up, putting aside their spluttering fuses. The echoes from the enclosing mountains kept up the racket for seconds on end. Then the last rumbling died away, and a quivering, stunned silence succeeded. Almost painful was the quiet now, as the curling smoke clouds lifted and dispersed.

At the King's third signal, a single lone trumpet rang out from the *Flower*'s poop, high, pure, compelling. For moments its immaculate and melodious challenge pierced the battered air. Then it was swallowed up in a tremendous fanfare, as scores of trumpets blared, raggedly at first, coming from all the ships, but settling into a stirring, assured and harmonious flourish of martial music. As this proceeded, up each of the four masts of the great galleons large blue-and-white saltire banners of Scotland were run, with others, and the lesser pennants of individual lords and knights, rising from staffs and shrouds, above forecastles, poops and decks, a most colourful display. Then, up to the topmost tip of *Flower*'s mainmast soared the huge golden tressured Lion Rampant of the King of Scots, to stream proudly in the breeze, while the swelling cheers of all the ships' companies all but drowned the music.

James turned, took from Rob Bruce a simple gold circlet specially brought for the occasion, and placed it over his bare head. He was now richly dressed in crimson and gold velvet, with a short satin-lined cloak handsomely emblazoned with the Lion of Scotland over one shoulder, armour all discarded and neither sword nor dirk at his side. A boat was being lowered, manned only by four sailors, with a golden canopy erected at its stern. Down a ladder to this the King descended, alone, while still the trumpets sounded. James seated himself under the canopy, and the boat cast off and was rowed towards the shore.

How many pairs of eyes watched its progress there was no knowing. Fierce looking men thronged all the sides of those moored galleys now, armed to the teeth. The castle battlements and curtain-walls were black with figures. Tartan-clad gillies seemed to have sprung out of the very earth all around. But all appeared to be motionless, mute, waiting. Even in the royal ships no movement showed. Only the small boat, with the red-haired young man in the stern, provided animation to the scene.

The skiff slipped close past the ranked galleys with their raking prows and gaping banks of oar-ports. James did not so much as glance at them, and no single word was shouted from their crowded bulwarks. The boat grounded gently on a strip of shingle below the castle-cliff, and unhurriedly the King stepped out. Leaving the sailors there, he turned to pace calmly towards the abruptly climbing zig-zag track which led from shore and boat strand to the frowning castle walls.

Only then were other boats lowered from the royal squadron, and filled with resplendent personages, armed and armoured, with flags flying, were headed for the land, led by that bearing the banner of the Lord High Admiral. Still the trumpets filled the young morning with their disciplined clamour.

The slight-seeming lone figure of the auburn-haired young man wearing the gold circlet climbed steadily, stooping forward a little, for the track was steep. More than once he paused, to ease the drag of that unseen iron chain around waist and loins.

At last he was on comparatively level greensward at the top of the cliff. People were congregated thickly here, the ordinary Highland folk of clachan and croft and glen, in stained tartans and ragged saffron, kilts and plaids, silent, all eyes – but they moved back to give the King passage as he turned right-handed to pace on across a hundred yards of grass towards the deep water-filled moat that guarded the castle on its jutting headland from all approach by land.

James saw the blank unwelcoming face of those towering curtain-walls fronting him across the unbridged ditch, aloof, inaccessible, and though he did not hesitate in his steady walking, he moistened dry lips. If the bridge remained up, and he was left there standing waiting, suppliant before all . . .!

But while still fifty yards off, with a creaking of timbers and clanking of chains, the wooden drawbridge was lowered, to cross the gap. Before it was in place and level, a new sound arose to drown the creaking and the distant music from the ships, as a dozen pipers strode out from the yawning gateway on either side of the canted, sinking bridge, blowing lustily. Shrill and high and as challenging as the trumpets, rose their strange insistent strains, as the instrumentalists spaced themselves out along the drawbridge and turned inwards to face each other. King James came to the bridgehead and so stood. A faint smile lightened his features now.

At the other end of the bridge, within the high arch of the gateway, was a group of men, stern-faced, all proud of bearing however various in age, aspect and dress – or undress, for most had the untidy appearance of men but newly roused from their beds. Almost all, however, had bonnets clapped on their un-combed heads, and from none of these less than two eagles' feathers sprouted, while most showed three. Three eagles' feathers marked the bearer as full chief of a clan; two, as chieftain of a sept or branch-clan. MacIan had notable company this morning, it seemed.

For minutes on end all stood waiting. No voice could have prevailed against that strident wailing of the bagpipes. At length the man a pace in front of the other chiefs raised his arm – though this had no apparent effect upon the musicians, who blew as vigorously as ever. This man was tall, elderly, grey-haired, of a grave and noble countenance, with a hawklike commanding eye. He was dressed in a hastily donned tartan philabeg or half-kilt, and plaid thrown slantwise over a saffron tunic, his bony legs bare of hose, with feet thrust into untied rawhide brogans. Yet despite this dishabille, he appeared the very picture of dignity as he leaned upon the basket-hilt of his great broadsword.

The raised hand must have had its effect after all, for the piping died away after a little in bubbling moans. Into the eventual silence, it was the King who spoke, his young voice clear, firm, but pleasantly modulated, almost conversational in tone.

"John mac Alastair vic Ian of Ardnamurchan and Sunart, I greet you warmly," he said. "I am James Stewart, come in peace to seek your hand in friendship and your due leal homage. I pray God to be with us both."

There was a distinct pause, as men stared at each other. The tenor and the tone of that pronouncement, equally with the words themselves, were clearly totally unexpected; even more so, undoubtedly, was the fact that it was spoken in their own language. This was something quite beyond all Highland experience.

MacIan, after a brief backward glance at his colleagues, cleared his throat. "James Stewart," he said, in the Gaelic. "I am honoured. I bid you welcome to my humble house." He stroked his chin. "If Your Highness had warned me of your coming, I should have endeavoured to receive you more . . . fittingly."

James inclined his head. He chose his words as carefully as had the older man. "I understand," he said. "But travel by ship is uncertain. So much in the hands of God! Be praised He brought us here more surely than might have been. And more swiftly." He glanced seawards as he spoke, and his eyes widened a little at what he saw.

Visibility was now excellent in the clear yellow rays of the slanting sunlight. Westwards the Hebridean Sea appeared to be full of vessels. Towards the south the shining waters seemed to be littered with the transports, galliots and barges of the royal fleet, beating into the Sound, inadequately shepherded by the single tall ship *Christopher*. And to the north, scores of long low sinister-looking shapes, rather further distant, seemed to fill all the gap between Ardnamurchan and the isles. It was on these that the King's look lingered. He moistened his lips.

The others did not fail to follow the lines of his gaze, and their murmur rose.

James recovered himself. "I did send you, MacIan, and others, my kingly summons here, for the end of this May month. I rejoice to see you. And still more of my good Highland subjects approaching yonder to claim my friendship and make their faithful duty."

MacIan drew a deep breath, seemed to be about to speak, and then changed his mind, inclining his head instead. A great bull of a man at his back, not much less than seven feet in height and shaggy as one of his own red Highland cattle, uttered something brief and pungent, on a short laugh. None other spoke, or changed expression.

James went on. "No doubt, MacIan, you have a signal? For your friends yonder in the galleys. Some means of intelligence?" He glanced up at the topmost castle tower. "A flag, perhaps? Or a smoke? Some sign. I would esteem it a favour if you would inform them of my presence and kindly welcome. Now. That they be assured of my goodwill and loving affection."

MacIan looked down at the timbers of his drawbridge.

Only a little more loudly, but spacing his words clearly, James added, "You would prefer my own sign and signal? The Master of Ordnance on each of my ships is watching me at this moment. As no doubt they watch your castle from those galleys. Keen-eyed, all. If I raise my two arms, every cannon on my galleons fires. As before. Only, with some small difference as to shot, perhaps! You heard my salute to you, I believe? Perhaps Alexander of Lochalsh heard it also, even on Coll. And so comes. Would you have me repeat it, gentlemen? All the cannon are loaded, and waiting. Shall I raise my arms?"

His hearers did not fail to put their own interpretation on that speech. Hundreds of loaded guns faced Mingary Castle at short range, and there was no reason to believe that they were still primed with blank shot. No single cannon was there to fire back. The King might die amongst the first – but Mingary and all within and around it would not survive him long. A prolonged sigh from a dozen chiefly throats acknowledged their recognition of the situation. MacIan bowed.

"Lord James," he said levelly. "My signal it shall be. Forthwith." He jerked a command at minions standing near, gesturing upwards and seawards. Then he turned back to his visitor. "James, son of James, son of James, son of James, son of Robert, High King of Alba, honour my house. Enter it with my blessing."

Far from being level-spoken, that was almost intoned. "What is MacIan's is the King's."

"As is Donald's, son of Angus, of Keppoch!" a deep voice behind declared.

"And John's, son of Hugh, of Sleat."

"Aye, and Clanranald's!"

With the skreak of steel, the bull-like giant drew his broadsword, gripped it by its tip, and stepping forward, extended its hilt in the direction of the King. "The sword of Ewan, son of Allan, of Locheil, Captain of Clan Cameron!" he growled.

James's own breath came out in a quivering sigh of thankfulness and relief. Emotional always, his voice broke as he spoke. "My friends . . . I thank you! Your bounty I accept. Your hands I grasp. Your words I trust." He strode forward over the bridge.

Without observably being ordered to do so, the pipers fell in behind him as he advanced, extracting new brayings from their instruments. The hand-kissing ceremony within the gateway, in consequence, was performed without words.

The first of the King's party, the Earl of Bothwell, Lord Drummond, Sir Rob Bruce and MacGregor of Glenarklet, appeared at the head of the cliff-path.

The King of Scots sat as MacIan's table in the great hall of Mingary, and sought to keep his attention from wandering. He found it difficult, for a variety of reasons. For one thing, his head was less clear than usual, partly on account of reaction and a sleepless night, but mainly because his host kept re-charging his great goblet with amber liquid refreshment, which was not wine nor ale but the most potent whisky that he had ever tasted, and which these Highland chiefs seemed to quaff like water. Already he noted that Patrick of Bothwell had fallen forward over the table, head on arms, snoring, Drummond was slumped sideways, eyes closed, and others of the royal entourage were no less affected. Secondly, there was a distinct and soothing monotony about the voice of the sennachie who was entertaining them with a lengthy saga in the Gaelic, accompanied by intermittent pluckings at the strings of a clarsach, extolling the epic deeds and high descent, not of the Kings of Scots but of the Lords of the Isles — an account which most of the Highlanders present appeared to know almost word for word judging by the way their lips shaped themselves in anticipation of words to come; yet they remained enthralled, it seemed, however familiar the resounding catalogue — though this may also have owed something to the excellence and strength of the whisky. Then, the window near by was apt to draw James's attention. Out there, the sun shone on as fair a scene as ever eye contemplated, the isle-dotted Sea of the Hebrides, heart-breakingly lovely with colour and light. But not only the scenery drew the young man's gaze; his own fleet of transports, and light craft was now in process of anchoring off-shore, quite overflowing the Bay of Mingary — but a bare mile to seawards the long lines of war-galleys approached still, black, eagle-prowed, raking, menacing, their great banks of oars dipping and sweeping rhythmically and catching the sun with a myriad flashes. They made a sight to distract any eye. And lastly, almost equally compelling to a young man of James's temperament, was a high gallery at the far end of the crowded hall. There, amongst a number of older women, segregated meantime from their men-folk, sat a strikingly beautiful girl, raven-haired, proud-featured, vivid. She had not sat still throughout this strangely timed feast of welcome, like the others, but had moved about, attending to the other women, at intervals leaving the gallery altogether for short periods. When she did, it seemed to James as though the sun had ceased to shine.

Determinedly he strove to concentrate, not so much on the endless panegyric about Clan Donald and the Princes of the Isles as on the tactical situation. It was essential that he did not fall into any day-dream — or worse, asleep like Bothwell and Drummond. The danger represented by those approaching galleys was by no means yet past. He had supped at MacIan's board, and so was safe from ill-usage by all present, by strictest Highland custom; but who knew the temper and spleen of those warriors out there in the long-ships? Alexander of Lochalsh, who now acted Lord of the Isles, was a man whom it would not do to take for granted, or to underestimate. Alexander's approach demanded his every faculty, James knew. And he was more than a little drunk — that he also knew.

It was this last realisation, together with the fear that the condition might conceivably get worse, plus the rather irritating harping on the heroic merits of these wretched Lords of the Isles, that forced the King to eventual action. Perhaps it was contrary to custom for a guest to interrupt the story-teller in full flight — but the fellow had had ample scope, surely. Moreover it might well be time for the King of Scots to assert himself. Waiting therefore until the sennachie paused for breath and a twanging of his strings — having reached only as far as Donald Balloch — James called out a couple of enthusiastic bravos, raised his goblet towards the surprised performer, and sipped in his honour. Then he rose to his feet. All men must therefore likewise rise — but he waved them down.

"MacIan of Ardnamurchan, John of Sleat, Donald of Keppoch, Clanranald, Locheil, MacDougall of Dunollie," he rehearsed slowly, carefully — and prided himself that he had made no mistake nor slurred a single syllable. "Hear me, James of Scotland. Listening to the stirring record and noble chronicle of your high and mighty patriarchs, the illustrious sons of great Somerled, Lord of the Isles, I am minded to adopt unto myself and my own line some of this glory, to our own undying advantage and renown. For the sake of all this realm of Scotland. I have decided how best this may be done."

He paused. He could not have had keener attention from his Highland hosts, however suddenly wary — even though his own people in the main slumbered on, and could not have understood him anyway since he spoke in the Gaelic. James's glance switched towards the high gallery. The dark young woman was leaning forward, watching intently. For a long moment his eyes held hers. Heartened, he went on.

"As is known to you all, the aged and venerable John, Lord of the Isles and former Earl of Ross, penitent for his insurrection against the Crown of Scotland, made voluntary resignation of his titles to my father, the King, near to twenty years ago, and now lives in peace and retirement in my monastery of Paisley, my guest and friend. His sons Angus and John are dead, both. And the natural son of Angus, the child Donald Dubh, is in the keeping of the Earl of Argyll, my Chancellor. Parliament in its wisdom has forfeited the style and title of Lord of the Isles. But Alexander of Lochalsh, nephew of John, assumes it. Claiming it also, they tell me, is John the Warlike, of Islay, his cousin. Here then is an ill tangle, a sad state, as undignified ending to the proud line of the Isles. I do not doubt that you all esteem it so."

He paused again — but not long enough for any present to intervene or seek to amend this distinctly garbled and loaded version of a controversial situation. He raised his voice almost in declamation. "That dignity may be maintained, therefore, and ancient glory be not tarnished, I now declare and pronounce in your noble presence that I, James, son of James, High King of Alba and of all Scots, do hereby take unto myself and my heirs for all time coming the style, rank, dignity and honour of Lord of the Isles, Earl of Ross. I merge and conjoin that lofty designation and distinction in the very Crown of Scotland, my friends. It may rise no higher."

Apart from Bothwell's snoring, there was complete silence in that great stone-walled hall. Men stared from the flushed young speaker to each other, eyes questioning, debating, demanding. Here was an extraordinary development. Were the clans being honoured? Or humiliated? The Confederation of the Isles saluted? Or tricked? What did it mean?

Something at least of what it meant James made clear forthwith — even if this was by no means likely to do away with controversy and heart-searching. "In consequence of which royal edict, my friends," he resumed, "each and all of you who were vassals of that Lordship, holding your lands in fief, now become freeholders, tenants-in-chief, holding direct from the Crown, superiors of your own territories, with all the rights, privileges and revenues thereof. Each becomes a baron of the realm of Scotland. My clerks shall write you all new charters to that effect, in my name."

Now the silence was broken as men whispered, murmured, exclaimed — though none actually protested. It was shrewd persuasion. In one significant sentence, the King had raised the status, powers and wealth of every man present — even if at the same time he had undermined and sapped the life's-blood of the very Lordship, the semi-independent principality of the Isles, which he was on his feet to honour.

James, though still standing, let the chiefs chatter and discuss this bombshell that undoubtedly resounded still more loudly in their ears than had done even the earlier cannonade of artillery. He glanced out of his window again. A small group of the longships were already beached on the shingle of the boat-strand, although the great majority of the galley fleet was now spaced out in a wide semicircle ominously hemming in the royal flotilla in the bay and anchorage of Mingary. It would not be long now until the final test.

He looked up again to the gallery, and had no difficulty in finding and holding those dark eyes once more — indeed they sought and met his with what seemed, even at such long range to be a smouldering intensity. Reaching for his goblet, James raised it to his lips, staring over the silver rim of it towards the young woman. Almost imperceptibly he inclined his auburn head, though never his eyes, and drank. He had quite forgotten the feeling of incipient drunkenness.

Out of the babblement, the heavy growling voice of the giant Locheil prevailed. "Lord James," he called strongly. "Do you say that you will confirm every clan in the possession of the lands it presently holds of John, Lord of the Isles?"

"I do," the King answered. Only for a moment he hesitated. He knew that, for instance, Locheil's Clan Cameron disputed the possession of certain large territories with Alexander MacRanald of Glengarry, not present. Also that his own host, MacIan, held the adjoining lands of Sunart, claimed by Clanranald who sat near by. Here was dangerous ground. "All lands held by charter, I hereby confirm. Lands held otherwise, by intrusion, or loan, or by the sword, will be duly considered by a Council of the Isles that I will call hereafter."

There was some murmuring at this, but more acclaim. A number of chiefs began to speak at once.

They were interrupted effectively—but not by the King. The door to the hall was thrown open, and an old white-haired seneschal appeared. "MacIan!" he cried. "MacIan—here to your hall comes the high and mighty . . ."

He got no further. A steel-meshed arm was thrust in front of him and swept him bodily aside. In his place, framed in the door-way, stood a tall, fierce-looking figure, a frowningly stern man of middle-years, proud-browed, hatchet-faced, archaically clad in a long coat of chain-mail, with over it a loose tunic of piebald calfskin and a tartan plaid. On his head was a helmet of steel, embellished on either side with great backswept feathered wings, in the traditional Viking style. From a silver-studded shoulder-belt hung a long two-handed sword, and he leaned slightly on a mighty battleaxe. Behind him thronged others as proud-seeming and fiercely warlike as himself.

None spoke.

MacIan rose to his feet. "Welcome to my house, John son of John son of Donald," he said.

James blinked. John, not Alexander, he had said? John, son of John son of Donald. This, then, could be only John of Islay,

John Cathanach, the Warlike, Chief of Clan Ian Vor, Alexander's rival for the Lordship of the Isles. He cleared his throat.

"I looked for Alexander of Lochalsh. But . . . do I see before me the hero, John, grandson of the mighty Sir Donald Balloch MacDonald of Islay?" he demanded.

The newcomer raised his eyebrows at this being spoken in the Gaelic. He inclined his stern head a little, but said no word.

"John of Islay, Lord of Dunyveg, Kintyre and the Glens of Antrim!" MacIan implemented carefully – but there was no mistaking the tension in his voice.

Swiftly the King came to a decision. "Here is joy!" he cried. "To meet and greet in person so renowned a warrior!" He thrust back his chair deliberately so that it fell over with a crash, and leaving the table, strode down towards the doorway. Behind him everywhere men started up. MacIan and Rob Bruce hurried after him almost shoulder to shoulder.

"I am James of Scotland," the King declared, as he came on. "Greetings, Cousin!"

All noted that word cousin. It was not wholly rhetorical, for Donald Balloch's father John Mor was a son of the Princess Margaret Stewart, who was daughter of Robert the Second, the first of the Stewart kings. But that the monarch should publicly name any Highlander cousin was something for men to marvel over. John of Islay, ever sparing of words, fingered his beard.

"The isles return your greeting," he said, deep-voiced.

Although that was giving but little away, James was encouraged to continue. This man could field more broadswords than could Bothwell, Home and Angus put together, with much of Ulster his as well as the southern Hebrides. He halted a pace or two from the other.

"Your sword, sir," he demanded.

The older man stared at him, cold eyes narrowed. He made no move.

James smiled. "I had heard that you were ever ready with that sword! But . . . another will serve." Since Rob Bruce and MacIan, like the rest, had laid aside their weapons to sit down together at table, the King leaned forward, past John of Islay, to one of the lesser chiefs who stood at his shoulder, to grasp his sword-hilt. "With your permission, friend?" he said.

This warrior looked doubtful indeed, glancing this way and that for guidance.

"Malcolm MacNeill of Gigha," MacIan murmured, from behind.

"The more honour," James declared strongly, and jerking his wrist, drew the heavy claymore from its sheath with the shrill squeal of steel. "Kneel, John son of John son of Donald," he ordered.

It took moments for the other to consider that, to question, and slowly, warily, to obey. Even so, he only crouched a little, over the battleaxe, tense as a tiger about to spring.

Rather more hastily than was normal on such an occasion, the King brought down the heavy blade on the mail-clad shoulder, having to use both hands to control the weight of it. "I dub you knight," he jerked. "Bear you the accolade worthily. Arise, Sir John de Insulis, MacDonald of Islay!"

Amidst an excited and mounting storm of exclamation, acclaim, wonder and doubt, the proud chief straightened up. Level, unwinking, his eyes met and locked with those of James, and so continued while the noise maintained. Neither sought to speak yet, each weighing the other. James's decision had been taken, but John of Islay had his still to make.

Well might he debate. By this single dramatic gesture the King had brought him to the bar of fateful choice. Accept this knighthood, the only such honour bestowed on any Highlander for generations — possibly since that of his own grandfather Sir Donald Balloch of Islay — and all would inevitably name him the King's man. Accept it, and it would imply that he was a subject of the giver, he who now named himself an independent prince. Moreover, the status of the Lordship of the Isles, which he claimed as great-great-grandson of John the Good, would be affected; none yet had told him of the King's assumption of that ancient title. On the other hand, the honour was a notable one — and, with the acknowledgement of cousinship, could be taken to indicate the royal acceptance of *his* claim to leadership in the north-west as against Alexander's. Alexander of Lochalsh was not knighted. And to reject the accolade thus bestowed could only be seen as outright insult to the King of Scots, nominal treason, war. In this hall of Mingary he could strike swift and sure. The King's life was his; but out there in the Sound, though his galleys ringed the royal fleet, the King's cannon, so eloquently demonstrated, could blow his ships out of the water and batter this stone castle into rubble.

John of Islay stared and weighed and measured. The younger man waited, smiling — but his fingers tap-tapped the hilt of MacNeill's sword.

At last, as the noise waned, the chief handed his battleaxe to one of his supporters, and raising his hands slowly, took off his great winged helmet. "My Lord James," he said, stiffly.

Seeking to keep the quivering relief out of his voice, James flung an arm around the other's rigid shoulders. "Come, Sir John!" he cried. "To the table. MacIan's goodly table. Here is a matter to drink to, if ever there was!"

If drunk he must be this day, James Stewart would have his excuse. He had won a greater victory than at Gartalunane — and no drop of blood shed.

"I WARN you, nevertheless, Lord James," Marsala MacIan said, "it is not wise. It is dangerous. Only sorrow will come of it."

"Wise! Wise! Must always I be wise?" he returned. "I am not King Solomon! I had rather be David, indeed!"

She shook her raven head. She would not play his game of teasing argument.

"A man must play the man, sometimes, whether he be prince or scullion . . . or lover! Or be no man," he went on. "Wisdom is not all." He shrugged, and laughed — although he winced a little as he did so, for his head still ached from the morning's potations. "You are very beautiful, Marsala MacIan. I have no doubt that many men will have told you so."

"Some," she admitted, unsmiling. "When they weary of more important matters."

He searched her features. She was indeed beautiful, with a kind of beauty hitherto unknown to him — dark, slender, finely wrought, still, quiescent, but with somewhere the promise of slow fires damped down, a fatal, smouldering Celtic beauty that challenged a man to blow it to white heat. James was not the man to miss that challenge.

They sat within an open roundel of the topmost battlements of Mingary, watching the sun at its lovely setting amongst the Western Isles, alone — or as nearly alone as was possible in a castle overcrowded as it had never been before. Undoubtedly eyes watched them — it could hardly be otherwise. The faithful Rob Bruce gazed in the other direction from another roundel a score of yards off. But at least none could hear their words.

"Any man worthy of the name would find it hard to think of more important matters when you were near," he said.

"You say so? Would such a speech deceive your Court ladies in the south, I wonder?"

Nonplussed a little, James hesitated, "I do not seek to deceive," he assured.

"Then what do you want of me?" She turned those great glowing eyes full upon him. "Speak plain, my lord."

Unused to such directness, he moistened lips suddenly become ineloquent.

"You did not bring me here, to this place, alone, for no purpose, I think?"

"I . . . I . . . for what purpose did you come with me, then? Unprotesting?" he gave back.

"I came that I might warn you that it was unwise to trust John of Islay," she told him. "Unwise and dangerous."

"M'mmm."

"If it is my bedchamber that you seek, there was no need to bring me here," she added, simply.

James's mouth opened, and shut again. He had experience of plenty of brazen women, thrust before him by their designs and ambitions, or by those of their menfolk; but this Highland girl gave no impression of brazenness — the reverse rather. Reserved, delicate, discriminating, she seemed, a woman who would have to be fought for.

"Would you . . . would you have taken me to your bedchamber?" he blurted out, at length.

"Yes. If you so asked."

He frowned, and looked away. The blaze of scarlet and gold from off the western sea hurt a head that was not yet at its best. "Because I am the King?"

"Because my father has said that all in his house is yours. I am in and of his house."

"You mean that MacIan would give me his own daughter? As he would food, drink, shelter?"

"All his house, did he not say? It is not MacIan's custom to use words lightly." Proudly she raised her head.

" 'Fore God — is it your custom then to bed with your father's guests? You, daughter of a great chief? Like any tavern wench!"

Calmly she met his gaze. "You speak unworthily," she reproved. "MacIan does not offer lightly all that is his. To any man. And I am blood of his blood."

James, looking down, ran a hand over his eyes. "I am sorry," he said. "I ask your pardon." Nevertheless, he was somehow offended. If he could have won to Marsala MacIans' bed that night, he would. He would undoubtedly have used all his wiles to gain it. But this, for some reason, he felt to be unsuitable. It

124

was not conquer and surrender; it was not the irresistible pull of like to like; it was not even desire reciprocated. It was but cold duty and flat acceptance – in a matter that should know naught of such. The man's vigorous masculinity was affronted. He knew an unusual embarrassment.

He changed the subject abruptly. "If I may not trust Sir John of Islay, what of the others?" he asked. "Who may I trust?"

"Trust my father. And Locheil – although he may be ungracious. And Clanranald, I think." The young woman went on with this less personal theme as calmly, as composedly, as though there had been no interlude. "Most of the mainland clans. Some of the Isles. But not John Cathanach. He is a killer."

"A king must make use of more sorts of subject than one," he said. "I shall use his fierceness to bring peace to the Isles."

"All men perceive how you would divide John from Alexander, my lord. To bring down the Lordship. Even as you have used your freeholds and superiorities and charters to wean my father and his friends from Alexander."

James narrowed sore eyes to the colour-stained panorama of the Hebrides. "The Confederation of the Isles must be broken up," he declared. "There is not room in this Scotland for two kingdoms and two kings."

"Perhaps," she admitted. But she sighed as she said it.

"The old Lord leagued with the English against my father," he went on, heavily. "Others before him. That must never be again."

"As did your own uncle of Angus, did he not, my lord? And others."

Surprised he looked at her. "You know of such things? Here. You – but a girl!"

"Is that strange? Do you too esteem us ignorant savages, Lord James?"

"No. Never that. God forbid! But . . ." He shook his head, and left the matter there. "The Lordship's day is over," he asserted. "None must doubt it."

"Alexander of Lochalsh may doubt it. Even though John of Islay plays him false."

"Alexander! Alexander! I think that I hear in your voice some . . . some warmth for Alexander of Lochalsh? Each time you name him."

"Why not? Do I not also descend from Somerled the Great?"

"So does Sir John — whom you name killer and not to be trusted."

"He is unworthy of his line. Alexander is altogether a nobler man. Strong and brave and true."

Closely he eyed her. "And much admired of Marsala MacIan?"

Her alabaster-clear pallor took on just a hint of colour. "He is of age to be my father," she observed.

"Tell me of him, then," James urged. "This paladin. It will be naught to his hurt, I warrant!"

"Have I not told you? He is noble, honourable and strong. But gentle, also. And generous."

"Yet he rose in armed insurrection against me, his prince. As against my father. He devastated Badenoch and Inverness and Ross. He flaunted his galleys almost under my castle of Dumbarton in the Clyde. Gentle, you said?"

"*You* said, did you not, that a man, if he is a man at all, must play the man sometimes — whether it be wise or no? Alexander is all a man. And he is Lord of the Isles."

"*I* am Lord of the Isles," the King corrected her, but mildly.

The young woman looked at him steadily. "In name, Sir. But go amongst the Isles . . . and discover who is Lord! Go to Coll or Tiree or Skye or Barra or The Lews. And ask who is Lord of the Isles!"

He nodded. "That I shall do. And . . . yes, I think that I shall take you with me, Marsala MacIan. That you may learn who rules Scotland! You would enjoy that, would you not? To see your Alexander!"

"I counsel you not to waste your ships' space with women," she returned, with something like a flash deep in those dark eyes. "You will require every man that you may carry, when you visit Alexander!"

"So! I think not." He smiled then. "But I also think that MacIan, your father, was wrong when he promised that all in this house was mine! Here is one, I swear, who is Alexander of Lochalsh's woman . . . old enough to have sired her as he may be!"

She rose up off the sun-warmed stone, head held high. "Shall I take you to my bedchamber now, Lord James? Since you doubt my father's word — and mine? I am ready."

"By Saint Ninian — no!" he cried, starting up in his turn. "A plague on it — I'll have none of it . . . thus! What do you think

126

me? A cold-blooded lecher? Curse you — I . . . I . . ." Restraining his sudden strange fury, James looked away into the now crimson west. "Forgive me. I . . . I am tired. Weary. Last night I did not sleep. I bid you goodnight, Mistress."

She searched his face, picked out ruddy and shadowed by the sunset, and then gravely inclining her head, turned along the parapet-walk and left him there.

Despite that summary rejection and dismissal, James was by no means free of Marsala MacIan's challenge and spell in the days that followed. Always she was at the back of his mind, an enigma, a question-mark, somehow a reproach to his manhood. She did not again suggest intimacy, did not even seek his company — but nor did she avoid it, and in the circumstances inevitably he saw much of her. Indeed, although he did not do so consciously, he came almost to pursue her. He sought opportunity to speak with her, to be in her company, to see her alone. She became intensely desirable to him — but complicatedly so. He went in a sort of fear that she might again offer herself to him, and he be forced once more to reject her; on the other hand, he all but wooed her, manipulated his activities and affairs to make opportunities to do so, and found certain satisfaction in even the least physical touch and contact with her person. He, in fact, set himself to win what he could by no means accept in gift, gratis. He was that sort of man.

Although it was actually a period of deliberate waiting, of strategic inaction, they were full, strenuous and taxing days. Messengers had been sent out from Mingary, not only to Alexander of Lochalsh but to all the clans not already represented there, requesting their chiefs to repair thither forthwith, to enter into bonds of amity and duty and goodwill with their entirely loving liege lord — in the name of James, Lord of the Isles and High King of Alba. Many came in answer to this summons, or on account of more private tidings and warnings received — for news travelled with uncanny speed over those vast and apparently empty distances of mountain, forest and sea; notable characters like Alexander MacDonell of Glengarry, Duncan Macintosh of Clanchattan, Kenneth Mackenzie of Kintail, Colin MacDuffie of Colonsay, and Dunslaff MacQuarrie of Ulva. But it was as noticeable, as the days passed, that not only did no word come from Alexander of Lochalsh, but no representation appeared from the important Isle of Skye, which was almost wholly under his sway, nor from the great and warlike clans of Maclean, of MacNeil of Barra and MacLeod of the Lews and Harris. All these, and many lesser tribes of the Northern and Outer Hebrides, followed Alexander's personal lead, as the southern isles had tended to follow John of Islay. Each day their non-arrival grew the more ominous.

The week of waiting was as hectic a period as any even the energetic and tireless James Stewart had ever known. The Highlanders, however famed for introspection and lack of industry, went in for wholehearted enjoyment of an occasion, and their ideas of entertainment lacked nothing in vigour and enthusiasm. The early June days were not long enough for all the activities and excitements which MacIan organised for his celebrated and numerous guests, and the short night much too brief for all the feasting, drinking, dancing and story-telling that fell to be crammed into them—to say nothing of sleeping. There were tinchels, great organised deer hunts, the quarry not a single stag but huge herds of beasts, as many as two hundred at a time, rounded up by gillies from a vast area, the slaughter being achieved by archery—some experts being proficient enough to have two more arrows in the air before the first struck home, and all finding their marks. There were fishing contests, and hawking; horse-racing and foot-racing—which, when pursued up the steep sides of mountains, was telling work indeed. There were exciting mock-battles between the war-galleys, and races for small boats—at which, it is to be feared, the Lowland seamen put up an indifferent showing. There were trials of strength in the tossing of whole tree-trunks, the heaving of large stones, wrestling, and swimming. There was swordery, with long and short blades, and other weapon-play.

Seeking to maintain some credit for his Lowland dominions, James organised games and contests also—in fist-fighting, in which the Highlanders did not seem to engage; at ball-play and quarterstaff and single-stick and shooting with the arquebus. He sought to teach his hosts jousting, on shaggy Highland garrons, with crude lances of pine-poles—and produced more mirth than chivalry.

In all this, James was apt to have an eye fixed on Marsala MacIan. It was necessary for his own prestige and that of his realm that he should shine before these critical Gaels, admittedly;

but it became still more essential for him to impress MacIan's dark-eyed daughter. No doubt he did both, for all his life he had made it his pleasure and duty to excel in all manly sports, as at the social graces.

· He allowed himself seven hectic, crowded days, therefore — and at the end of them knew only a very limited satisfaction. He had not won the young woman — although one or two others were smiling more than kindly upon him. And there was no word, no sign, from Alexander or any of his close allies. Also, whether significantly or not, quite a number of John of Islay's galleys had slipped away quietly from Mingary Bay, in ones and twos by night. That stern chief made no comment on the fact — but then, he was not the man for making verbal comment on anything; a more unforthcoming warrior and subject it had never been James's fortune to encounter.

At length the King's patience was exhausted. He would wait no longer for any man — or woman. He said so to Marsala MacIan over the supper table that seventh evening.

"Tomorrow," he told her, "I go to seek your Alexander, since he will not come to me. And, since you esteem him so highly, you will come with me, as once I said. You had better, I think, come out with me to my ship, *Flower*. Now. To discover your lodging there."

Closely she considered him. "You go, then? To confront Alexander?" She shook her head, sighing. "Do not do it, lord. Leave him. What hurt does he do you, in his islands?"

"I cannot leave him. He disobeys my summons and flouts my royal authority. If I leave Alexander, I yield the entire north-west. You must know it."

"It will be war."

"No. I shall go in peace. Think you that I would be taking you with me if I intended fighting?"

"Alexander will fight. He can do no other."

"Not if I seek him in peace. It takes two to fight."

"May he spare you time to tell him so!"

"There, you may help me, perhaps. And therefore him also. As envoy. Envoy for peace."

"I will be no envoy for ten-score of cannon!"

"That you shall not be. The cannon I leave behind."

She did not answer that.

"So you will come out to *Flower* with me, Marsala *a ghraidh*?"

"If it is your command, lord," she said.

He frowned. "It is my *wish*."

"Very well."

He signed to Rob Bruce, across the table.

Rob himself rowed them out to the great ship in the gloaming of a grey evening. Gravely he asked, as he assisted the young woman aboard, whether the boat would be required later, or whether His Grace intended to spend the night on the vessel? The gracious reply made up in vehemence what it lacked in clarity.

To the knowing looks of sundry seamen, James conducted his guest to the tall after-castle and poop. The best cabin in *Flower* was not the King's, but was reserved by common consent for Sir Andrew Wood, who had designed the ship. James's was the next best, and though low-ceiled was commodious and well-furnished. His things were scattered untidily about it.

"You will do well enough here, I think," he told the girl.

She looked at the unmistakable signs of his occupancy. "No doubt," she said.

"If there is aught else that you need? Desire? Woman's gear? You will tell me. The ship is yours, to command. As . . . as am I."

She smiled faintly, "Lord James — there is no need to mock me. Or yourself. You command all — including myself. I command nothing."

"Save only, perhaps, my devotion, Marsala. And therefore myself."

She swung on him, dark eyes flashing, with one of her few displays of feeling. "Devotion!" she exclaimed. "Your devotion is a notably shared feast, is it not? How then can it be yourself?"

"I do not understand you," he said, warily now.

"Can a man be devoted to so many women?" she asked. "He can desire many, take many, keep many. But devotion is something other, is it not? Your devotion is not for me."

"Why do you say that? How can *you* tell?"

"Because I am a woman. Pray reserve your devotion for another. The mother of your little son, perhaps. Mistress . . . Mistress . . .? I have forgotten her name. Or if not her, another of the fine ladies who adorn your palaces. Even perhaps the princess that you think to marry!"

"You . . . you mistake. And I think to marry no princess," he said shortly.

"Yet we hear of embassies . . ."

"You hear too much, I vow!" he jerked, grimly. "I had not thought my poor doings would be of such concern here in Ardnamurchan! These embassies for a princess are for my realm's sake, not mine. In the cause of alliances, treaties and the like. Other princes, and their chancellories must be cozened, kept friendly. I . . ." He paused. "But, i' faith—I did not bring you here to discuss statecraft and policies! I did not!"

"Ah, no. How foolish I am! You must forgive me, lord." The young woman looked around the cabin. "There are two beds here, I see. Which do we use, to pleasure you best?"

James all but choked, as she stepped over and felt and prodded one of the bunks.

"It is hard," she commented, calmly. "But no doubt it will serve."

He cleared his throat. "That is not why I brought you," he declared heavily. "I brought you to consider your lodging here. To say what you might wish otherwise. For our journey tomorrow."

"Only that?"

"Only that."

"To be sure. I understand. But your cabin it is, lord. Nothing need be altered because I share it. For a little. As with your devotion!"

"A plague on it! We do not share it. I move otherwhere. In with Rob Bruce." He shook his head in exasperation. "You are hard on a man, Marsala MacIan!"

"Surely not, lord. I deny you nothing . . ."

"And will you cease from naming me lord with every second breath, for sweet Ninian's sake! It is not the Highland custom, God knows!"

She sat down on the edge of the bunk, and eyed him closely, curiously. "You are a strange man," she said at length. "What is it that you want of me? Since, it seems, it is not my body."

He paced the cabin, not looking at her. "I want your esteem. Your kindness. Your love. Is that so strange? You are beautiful, desirable, yes. But . . . I am not a brute-beast, an animal. To . . . to look, to desire, to grapple and straddle, and pass on! Can you not see it . . .?"

"You demand arts and artifices? I am sorry. I should have thought of that. A man so used as you are to nimble, clever women. Sated with the business, no doubt. But, alas, I am not

131

experienced, talented, in such refinements, lord. I am only a simple Highland girl . . ."

"You know that is not my meaning."

"If it is your wish to be tempted and diverted, no doubt of your great experience you will instruct me?"

"No!" he almost shouted. "I tell you, no! Will you nowise understand? You greatly mistake the man I am."

"It would seem so indeed. If I am not to pleasure you, I do not see how I may serve you here, this night. I think that it would be best to take me home to my father's house."

"Yes," he agreed. "That I shall. At once. For there is no profit here. Come!"

"I am sorry . . . for my father's honoured guest," she said.

James himself rowed her back to the shore, curtly rejecting the help of others. No words were exchanged in passage – in part undoubtedly because of the fury which the King put into his oarsmanship, flailing and punishing the unoffending wavelets and hurling the blunt-prowed coble onwards as it seldom can have moved previously. Many grinning men watched, and came to their own conclusions. Sir Rob, perforce, had to find his way back alone.

On the winding turnpike stairway in Mingary Castle, Marsala paused, to turn to her silent escort. "I go to my bedchamber now," she said. "I cannot believe that you wish to accompany me thither? Nor indeed that you any longer desire my company on your journey to Alexander?"

"I sail tomorrow, as I said," he gave back shortly. "You with me. A goodnight to you."

The *Flower* beat away from the jagged, thrusting coast of Ardnamurchan into the prevailing westerly breeze, on a sparkling forenoon of dazzle and high sailing cloud-galleons so much more impressive even than herself. For she was alone, save for two of MacIan's own galleys that escorted her. James indeed had been better than his word; not only the cannon had been left behind, but all the royal fleet – much against the advice of Wood and his captains. The peacefulness of this errand was to be without question.

With the King, now on the poop-deck, were Sir Andrew Wood, Rob Bruce and Glenarklet. These were all that he had brought with him, save for Marsala MacIan – and her foster-mother, whom James had ingenuously included for the sake of the young woman's reputation. Bothwell had been left in command of the main force, and as the King's lieutenant to receive all incoming chiefs.

The island of Coll, where Alexander of Lochalsh was at present said to be established, was a mere fifteen miles or so from Mingary — indeed it could be identified as a dark line on the horizon. It was isolated and not large, and seemed a strange choice as fortress — although it contained the powerful castle of Breachacha, long one of the most important strongholds of the Lords of the Isles. It might of course have other advantages that were not obvious.

With all flags and banners flying, *Flower* tacked to and fro — for Coll lay directly into the wind, and the fifteen miles were bound to be more than doubled. The escorting galleys, with their sixty-oar power, must needs go dead slow lest they outdistance her. Long, low and savage-looking, they seemed to fret like hounds on leash.

It took them until mid-afternoon to reach the vicinity of the southern end of Coll, which were the two anchorages. All the way they thought to see Alexander's galleys swarm out to challenge them — but none materialised. One or two dark shapes they did glimpse silhouetted against the sky or slipping away behind lesser isles, but nothing approached near. The Hebridean Sea appeared as innocent and peaceful as though no rival claimants to its lordship existed.

Down the east side of Coll they beat, a fairly low-lying and green island but with rocky shores. At the mile-deep inlet of Loch Eatharna, wherein lay Arinagour the chief township, they could discern only a few fishing-boats. But Loch Breachacha was six miles to the south, at the head of which rose the castle. Here was the likeliest place for Alexander's strength. The fiery young skipper of one of MacIan's galleys was instructed to go forward to inspect, to make enquiries. If Alexander was indeed on Coll, he was to come back for Marsala, to take her to him.

They did not have long to wait. The news was brought that Alexander, Lord of the Isles, had left the island four days previously, with a large force, heading north.

James pondered. This could mean little or much. Alexander could merely be putting himself discreetly further away from Ardnamurchan on the other hand, northwards lay his main territories of Skye, Knoydart, Glenelg and Lochalsh itself, where he could recruit his greatest strength.

Flower turned into the north.

Now the galleys ranged far in advance, seeking to discover what they might — for in that medley of islands, headlands, deep winding sounds and sea-lochs, a host of ships could lie hidden in a score of places before Skye was reached.

The sun was low in the sky, and purple shadows staining all the western sea, when one of the galleys came racing back to them, its tiered oars sending up boiling spray on either side. News of Alexander. He was not far away. A fishing-boat from Eigg had informed them that he was concentrating all his forces on the Isle of Rum. The great bight of Loch Scresort there was packed with his long-ships.

The towering and majestic peaks of Rum, most spectacular of all the Inner Hebrides, were rearing blue before them no more than four miles away.

"Good!" James cried. "We now put this matter to the test. Time, it is. Sail for Rum." He went below to give Marsala her instructions.

In the full flourish of the sunset they came to Rum, its pinnacles and summits ablaze with orange and violet, fissured with inky black, while away to the north the Cuillins, the black dog-toothed mountains of Skye, snarled at the conflagration. The approach to the island from the south gave no hint of any host thereon, even of any occupation by men, with nothing but mighty frowning cliffs and soaring peaks to be seen. But rounding the point that guarded the mouth of the deep loch of Scresort which penetrated into the very heart of Rum, even Sir Andrew Wood was moved to wonder, to alarm.

The inlet, cradled amongst fierce mountains, was full of ships. Never had the old admiral, experienced as he was, seen so many ships at one time — and fighting ships almost all of them. In disciplined serried ranks they lay moored on both sides of nearly a mile of waterway, leaving only a comparatively narrow central channel of open water. Although each had but a single mast, these rose like a forest. The high prows were like a legion of dragons' heads upraised to quest the evening air.

"Christ God!" Wood cried. "I knew not there were so many galleys in Christendom! This man Alexander may call himself Lord o' the Isles indeed — by yonder token!"

James said nothing.

"Sire," Rob Bruce exclaimed. "Here surely is madness! To confront this host. Naked and alone as we are." It was seldom indeed that Rob actively questioned the royal judgement. "Let us be off whilst we may. Turn and run before the wind."

"I flee from no subject of mine," James said, jaw set dourly. "Besides, even with the wind at our heels, these galleys would overtake us. Nothing faster sails the seas. And look yonder." He pointed.

Edged out just a little way from the long lines of moored galleys on either side, were two with oars poised, their bulwarks black with men.

"Bring me Marsala MacIan," he commanded.

"I am here, lord," she announced at his back. "You still seek Alexander?"

"I do. More than ever. Know you where I should seek him? On one of these ships? Or ashore? Is there a castle . . .?"

"No castle. But the house of Maclean of Rum. At the head of the loch."

He nodded. "Here, in fullest view of them, there is no virtue in sending you on before. We shall seek him together."

The two MacIan galleys were now noticeably holding back.

Sir Andrew and the shipmaster were concerned over shoals and soundings. The leadsmen were shouting constant measurements, but though the water was shallowing fast, there was still ample depth.

Up between the long lines of silent long-ships *Flower* slid, with sail reduced to a minimum to provide steerage-way, the master cursing sudden down-draughts from the hillsides. James counted eighty-seven galleys, and was by no means finished when Rob Bruce touched his arm and pointed sternwards. The two manned craft which had been waiting there had slipped out behind them and closed the channel, cutting them off from their Mingary escort.

No comment was made, nor necessary.

Loch Scresort, hidden from the west by high peaks, was now fairly deep in shadow, but the entire area nevertheless was illuminated by the rosy glow from hundreds of cooking-fires that spangled the lower hill slopes. There must have been many thousands of men concentrated on the island.

Four hundred yards from the head of the loch, Sir Andrew

would hazard his ship no further, with the tides to consider. The anchors were run out. They had run the gauntlet of those watchful ranks of ships, and even now prows reared dangerously close on either side. The black looks directed at the King were by no means all on the Islesmen's side.

The royal barge was lowered, and James aided Marsala down to it. With only Bruce and Glenarklet, and all unarmed, they were rowed ashore.

A crowd awaited their arrival, a fiercely warlike company, bristling with arms, all tartans, feathers, hide jerkins and chainmail. None spoke. Scanning the leader's stern and suspicious faces, James glanced at Marsala.

She shook her head.

"I greet you all," he called, raising a hand. "I am *Ard Righ*, your High King. I come to salute Alexander. Take me to him."

As they walked at the heels of the stiffly unbending and wary warriors, with the rest of the crowd more vociferously hostile at their backs, James mentioned to the young woman that he thought that the face of one of the chieftains who had awaited them was familiar.

"That is MacNeill of Gigha," the girl nodded. "He whose sword you used to knight John of Islay."

"Ha! So that way jumps the cat, does it! How many more of Sir John's faction have deserted him for Alexander, I wonder?"

"I would not say that they have deserted him," she answered. "I warned you not to trust John of Islay."

"But I may trust *Alexander's* honesty, you believe?"

"If you live long enough to test it!" she murmured, low-voiced. And then, in a different tone. "You are risking much here. All. Your life. Make no mistake. Why, I know not. But . . . be careful — oh, be careful what you say. All may hang on a single word. Be wise. Be not headstrong."

Sidelong he glanced at her. "You speak more kindly, I think, than you have yet done. Why?"

"I admire a brave man," she said, briefly. And then, lest that seem over-warm, "But never a fool!"

"I am neither, I believe," he told her. "Merely a king, with a broken realm to unite."

She seemed to be about to speak, but changed her mind. Silent, they followed their haughty guides.

Maclean of Rum's house lay no great distance back from the

head of the loch, embosomed in more luxuriant trees than were usual in the Isles. It was in fact a timber-built hall-house, with stone chimneys, long and low and sprawling, but more commodious than any stone castle, with a roof of reed thatch. All around clustered the cabins and cot-houses of his people, as chickens round a hen. The place tonight was stirring like an ant-hill disturbed.

The visitors and their escort had to thread it all as best they might.

In front of the great house not a few men lounged or paced about, by their feathers and bearing major chieftains all. But none seemed to be singled out above another. Only in one place did anybody stand alone, and that was on a mound some way to the right of the house, seventy yards perhaps, where a squat figure waited unmoving, as though graven in stone. It was not this man, however, who drew James's eye—but others less immobile above and behind. Four wind-blown Scots pines, gnarled and massive, crowned that knoll, and from their red branches, at various levels, men hung, and swung and birled in the breeze. At these the King stared. He counted eleven of them. It was towards this knowe that they were being led, indubitably, not to the house.

James dragged his glance away from that sight, to look at the girl at his side. Her face seemed a little more pale and her lips were tight, but when he looked enquiringly, unbelievingly, towards the mound, she nodded, wordless.

Well might he question what he saw—those hanging corpses or the man beneath. From what he had been told, he had pictured Alexander of Lochalsh as a man of fine appearance, tall, handsome, lordly, elderly, a nobler and less stern version of John of Islay, perhaps. This man was quite otherwise. Not so much short as so square that he appeared so at first glance, he was perhaps in his early forties, swarthy, with curling jet-black hair, undistinguished features, and so great a breadth of shoulder as to be all but deformed. Enormous strength undoubtedly lay in that barrel of a chest and in the long dangling arms which hung down hands level with his knees. His legs were slightly bowed, and muscular. Low-browed, thrusting jawed, clean-shaven, he looked almost ape-like as he stood there waiting, seeming to lean forward a little. Only the intensely live and startlingly blue eyes, so unusual against his colouring, gave a different impression.

James drew a long breath. Marsala's warning to be careful was

137

now scarcely necessary. That man, backed by those grisly reminders of total power, was his own warning. Moreover it was probably significant that they were being brought here, to what obviously was the judgement-seat, the mote-hill, of the island, rather than to the house with its complications of hospitality. He, the King, was being led into the presence of this extraordinary man on the knoll, as though their positions were reversed.

At the foot of the mound their escort drew aside, leaving the pair very much isolated. Rob and Glenarklet were halted some way behind. No word was spoken.

James cleared his throat. "Alexander, son of Gillespie, of Lochalsh, in peace and cousinly affection I greet you," he declared, louder-toned than he intended.

For long moments there was silence. Then the other nodded. "Marsala MacIan — I see you in strange company," he said in a voice strangely soft, gentle, to come from a man of such appearance.

The King bit his lip at the snub — until, hearing the girl reply, he realised that in his preoccupation he had spoken in his own tongue, not in the Gaelic.

"I come with James, our High King, Alastair Dubh, and out of my fondness for you. And that I might witness the meeting of two men."

That gave them both pause, especially her notable emphasis on the word men.

James spoke first, this time in Gaelic. "I had hoped that you would come to visit me at Mingary, my friend. But since you did not . . ."

"I have heard what was done at Mingary," Alexander said in his quiet voice. "I wanted none of it."

"But I wanted something, Cousin. So I sought you here."

"Rashly!" the squat man said briefly.

"Perhaps. But only you can give me what I seek. Help me in my quest."

"Your quest and mine are like to clash."

"I hope not. I believe not . . ."

"James Stewart," the other broke in commandingly, the more authoritative somehow for the very softness of his enunciation. "Spare me hypocrisy and lies. It will serve neither of us." He thrust his head forward, a picture of menace. "You are here to

138

pull me down. Do not deny it. If you can do it by soft words and conceits, you will. As you did at Mingary. If not, you have ships and cannon and many men for the task. But I will not be pulled down. You have said that there is no room for two kings in Scotland — and will assure it. I say that there is no room for two Lords of the Isles!"

Never had James been spoken to thus, even by his most arrogant nobles. But this man was not arrogant in his manner; utterly sure of himself, rather, confident in his power, personal and military.

"If you know all this, you know that I have left my ships and my cannon behind at Mingary," he said.

"I know it. Your every move is watched. I know how and where you sleep each night. With whom you company." His vivid glance flickered to Marsala. "The words that you speak. The men you deceive."

James mustered a smile. "Your interest in my affairs flatters me," he observed.

"Alastair Dubh," the young woman intervened. "This is not worthy of you. I told the Lord James that you were noble, generous, a true man. Yet you greet him thus — on this evil hill." She looked up, with a shudder, at the hanging men. "You keep far distant. You offer not even the civility due to the humblest guest. Is this Alexander of Lochalsh?"

Gravely he appeared to consider her accusation. "I regret that you think me uncivil, Marsala *a graidh*," he said. "And that these offend you." He gestured back at the corpses. "*They* were uncivil, now. Grievously. They shamefully assaulted some of Maclean's women here. My own men, from Lochalsh. A lesson they are . . . to all who doubt that I mean what I say!" He sighed. It was strange to hear such reasonable-seeming talk coming from such a man in such a place. "As to guests, would you have me take a snake into my bosom? *You*, Marsala MacIan? I believed you to be my friend . . ."

"I am your friend, always."

"Then you must know that if he is received under any roof of mine, tastes of my provision, then my hands are tied. I may nowise touch him. He well knows that likewise."

One of the chieftains behind the King raised an angry voice to advise Alexander to make a round dozen of danglers from the pine trees, and have done with it. The squat man ignored him.

"Knowing all that, why did you come, Marsala?" he persisted.

"I came that perhaps I might put myself between two obstinate, headstrong and foolish men," she answered, even-voiced. "A woman, I hoped, might shame you both out of the worst folly."

Alexander smiled—and when that man smiled he was transformed, his pugnacious heavy features lightened and irradiated, his blue eyes dancing. "The trouble we are to you, *a graidh*," he said. "Always the same Marsala, who would save us from ourselves. Ever on a mission, since you were a child . . ."

James seized his opportunity. "It is I who am on a mission," he asserted. "One that I have cherished since *my* childhood. In which only you can aid me."

"To cheat me of my patrimony, as Jacob did Esau?" Alexander threw back at him.

"No. Quite otherwise. To lead me to a shrine that I seek. A pilgrimage I must make. With you as guide. Only you."

He had the man's fullest attention now—and not only Alexander's. "What mean you?" the other jerked, seeming to thrust forward with his jaw.

"I seek Scotland's talisman. To see the Stone of Destiny. The Stone of Scone. As is my right and duty. Only you can show it to me. As is *your* right and duty."

For long moments there was silence, save for the creaking ropes of men who swung in the evening breeze. At last Alexander spoke. "What know you . . . of this?"

"What I know I would liefer not shout at you from so great a distance, Cousin," James answered, pleasantly enough.

The other considered that, nodded, and came striding down the bank to them. For so stockily built a man he moved remarkably lightly on his feet, his kilt swinging. His relenting went no further than this, however. Nearer Marsala than the King, he halted and waited.

"My ancestor, King Robert Bruce, when he lay dying, sent for your ancestor, his friend, Angus, Lord of the Isles," James went on. "He was anxious for the safety of the Stone, Scotland's most prized possession. Edward First of England, of ill memory, denied the true Stone, had quarried a lump of Scone sandstone and taken it south with him, to deceive his people, enthroning it in a chair in Westminster Abbey—where it remains, a graven lie. But his son and grandson knew that it was false, and their spies were ever seeking the rightful Stone. The Bruce feared greatly that once he was dead traitors might sell its secret hiding-place to the English. Or to Baliol. So he sent for Angus of the Isles. He gave him the Stone. Entrusted it to him as a sacred charge. To keep it safe, hidden and secure. Himself and his successors. Until such time as the rightful King of Scots should require it of them. Angus brought it here to his Isles. One hundred and sixty-six years ago. Secretly." He paused. "Is that a true account, or is it not, friend?"

Alexander examined the knuckles white in a clenched fist—as well he might. Deftly the King had put him into a cleft stick. Only the reigning Lord of the Isles and his next heir were privy to this secret. To deny knowledge of it was to admit himself no true heir of his uncle. But to acknowledge it, was to concede his duty to do as the King asked. Alexander was not the man to temporise, but time he had to have.

"That was long ago. In 1329. This is 1495. There have been many kings since then. Many Lords of the Isles . . ."

"Because these others forgot their duty, should I? Is a vow, a promise, any less so for the passing of years? Or does your ancestor's word mean nothing to you?"

"What do you wish of me?"

"That we go on this pilgrimage together, Cousin. You and I? To the Stone of Destiny."

"And then?"

"Then we shall decide what is best to be done. Perhaps the Stone itself will aid us in this? It is holy, the touchstone of my line for a thousand years."

"You would trust yourself to me? Your person? Alone? Here?"

"Why, yes. I do so now, do I not? Your uncle, the old Lord, told me that I might. In his monastery, before I sailed for the north. I went to see him. Moreover, Marsala here speaks for you. Her word I accept—and therefore yours." He smiled. "I believe that she might now even say a word for mine!"

The young woman inclined her head. "I trust the King's word," she said.

The other squared his huge shoulders. "Very well," he agreed. "But . . .. I, Alexander, am Lord of the Isles! None other!"

"Let us not quibble over a small word," James said. "Lord *in* the Isles, you may be. Indeed, it seems that undoubtedly you are! But Lord *of* the Isles is henceforth the King of Scots. As he is lord of all his realm of Scotland. By royal decree."

141

The other laughed shortly. "*My* lordship I hold by a different tenure. By right . . . and by the sword!" he said.

Their eyes met, and locked for a little. Then both shrugged, prepared to leave it at that.

"We shall talk of this another time, my lord," James said. "Meanwhile, I place myself in your hands. Your strong hands."

Alexander looked down at those hands, and bowed, if only slightly. "I shall require Maclean to offer you the hospitality of his house."

"I thank you. And the Stone . . .?"

"Tomorrow we sail north."

Marsala MacIan uttered a long quivering sigh of relief.

They turned their backs on the hanging men.

8

THE galley surged alone through the blue seas at an exhilarating speed, under a canopy of constant fine spray from windward, where thirty long oars smote the water with unending and rhythmic sweep and disciplined fury. One hundred and twenty men, two on each oar, bare torsoes streaming with perspiration above their short kilts, leaned and dipped and heaved, with bulging muscles, to a stirring, throbbing refrain which rose in waves and troughs more regular even than those they drove through, whilst harpers on the stern-platform thrummed the beat — the age-old galley-song of Clan Donald, catching the heart as the smell of strong men's sweat caught the nostrils. Above them bellied the great square-cut single sail, itself boldly and colourfully emblazoned with the tressured galley, emblem of the Lord of the Isles. No other craft accompanied that swift wolf-hound of the sea; *Flower*, and a disgruntled Sir Andrew Wood, had been left with all Alexander's great armada in the anchorage at Rum.

On the high prow platform under the beaked eagle figurehead, James revelled in the pace and vigour and atmosphere of it all, problems, policies and doubts for the moment forgotten. He had never before travelled so fast as this on water — indeed he wondered whether his fleetest horse could carry him at this speed. Beside him, Alexander swayed his muscular body to the beat of the oars and the harps, crooning the refrain, his huge fists opening and shutting as though they clenched an oar-shaft. Indeed he had done just that earlier when, emerging from the mouth of Loch Scresort into the open sea, he had jumped down into the well, pushed aside the inner oarsman on his bench at the stroke oar, and shouting his challenge, himself set the fierce pace which they now maintained, pulling so and singing lustily for fifteen minutes before yielding up the oar again.

Between them, now, Marsala stood, humming the tune, eyes sparkling, dark hair blowing free, every now and again grasping the arm of one of them, sometimes both, to steady herself against the roll of the cross-seas. Never had James known her so evidently happy, never so kind.

The stern platform Rob Bruce and Glenarklet shared with the harpers and a couple of chieftains.

When the King had asked whence they were bound, Alexander had briefly told him to Skye; with this he had to be content. Alexander was civil enough today, indeed in good spirits, but still wary. Neither man thought to spoil the bright forenoon with controversy.

Already they were running up the western flank of the long Skye peninsula of Sleat. Ahead soared the great horseshoe of the fiercely proud, pinnacled Cuillin Mountains, frowning darkly even on this morning of sunshine and colour. Towards the shadowy gulf at their rocky bases the galley seemed to be racing.

"Those mountains," James said, pointing. "I cannot like them, named after your hero Cuchulinn as they may be. They gloom. They growl."

"They keep watch," Alexander amended. "Aptly enough, named for one named after a dog."

"You know the story of Cuchulinn and the daughters of Skye?" Marsala wondered.

"I know it, yes. Of Uathach and Aoife and the rest. Of beauty and sorrow. I have shed foolish tears over it all, indeed."

Alexander looked at him curiously, but said nothing.

"*That* I would not call foolish," the girl said quietly.

Crossing the mouth of Loch Eishort, they rounded the tip of another peninsula, green against the prevailing black background, and there opening before them was an arrow-shaped loch which seemed to drive into the very heart of the scowling mountains. There could be no doubt now as to their destination.

Straight to the head of Loch Scavaig the galley sped, and now the beetling peaks and precipices almost seemed to be toppling in on them. Into a sort of tiny natural harbour amongst the dark rocks, Alexander himself guided his vessel. When it was securely moored, he threw off plaid and helmet and sword-belt, like a man stripping for the fray. He signed to James to do likewise.

"No road to be encumbered with gear," he said.

But when Marsala stepped forward also, he held up his hand.

"Wait you here, my dear," he commanded, though gently. "This is a matter between James Stewart and Alexander Mac-

Donald only. Your part is played. Moreover, it is a rough road for a woman."

"You know that I care not for that," she protested. "You know that I have climbed every cliff in Ardnamurchan. And did we not once watch the sun rise from the top of Sgurr nan Gillean, here?"

"You were little more than a child then, lass."

"I was seventeen – and happy!"

A cloud came over Alexander's face, and he looked away to those savage nightmare peaks. James glanced from one to the other, wonderingly.

"Even so, this king and I go alone, *a graidh*," the older man said, quietly.

Sir Rob Bruce had come up. "Where His Grace goes, I go," he announced flatly.

"Not so. We go alone, or not at all."

"Sir Robert is himself of the line of the Bruce. And leal. I trust him before all men," James declared. "And Marsala is . . . Marsala!"

Alexander shrugged. "They may come some way with us. Both. But that only. Then they must wait. And for some time. I swore my most sacred oath to it, once. As have all of my line. To none but the King would I reveal this thing."

With that they had to rest content. Marsala kilted up her skirts to just above the knee, and tied her girdle to hold them there. When Alexander stepped up on to the slippery seaweed-hung rock, turning to hold out his hands to her, she ignored them and leapt up and ashore, light as a hind of her own hills, with a gleam of long white legs. She was setting her own pattern.

James and Rob followed.

Over a ragged stony mound dotted with straggling heather, moraine of some glacier, they scrambled. Beyond, glooming inky black before them, separated by this mass of detritus from the sea, was an inner loch, narrow, still, stark, perhaps a mile long by only a quarter wide. Denied the sun it lay sullen, and sheerly down into its sombre depths the cliffs and screes and crags plunged, with nothing of verge or kindly strand to stop them. Jealously those savage peaks hemmed it in, and only their black barren majesty was mirrored on its ebony surface.

Alexander paused, and pointed not down towards it, but upwards, right-handed.

"A rough road, as I said. Drum nan Ramh, the Ridge of Oars. Do you all wish that I go on?"

It was an appalling prospect. A lofty mountain spine, fully three miles in length, soared almost two thousand feet above the loch and thrust back into the main mass of the Cuillin. Well named the Ridge of Oars, its slashed and riven sides resembled nothing so much as serried banks of oars striking down from a high galley. Only, these ribs and blades of rock were infinitely steeper than any oars could be held, innumerable buttresses and razor-edged spires and spurs, towering from black water right to the dizzy summit serrations, cleft with deep scars and funnels too sheer to be termed ravines, down which white streams cascaded, more spume than water. No path, nor possible route for such, showed on that daunting face.

"Up . . . there?" James swallowed.

The other nodded.

"I have climbed worse," Marsala commented, and moved on. After that, of course, no man could hold back.

The boulder-field, seamed with treacherous scree, though brief, took time to negotiate however eager certain climbers might be to show their mettle. Then it became sheer collar-work, requiring hands and toes and often knees, on bare, naked, nobbly rock, frequently running with moisture. Alexander led the way, and though no actual course or route seemed possible, he appeared nevertheless to be following some predetermined if notably erratic line, pausing often to scan landmarks, look back, and check positions, sometimes even retracing difficult steps for no evident reason. His followers had little breath to spare for questioning him. Marsala came close at his heels, a changed woman now, sure-footed, vigorous, and seemingly caring little for the restraint and modesty which hitherto she had worn like a garment. She had the tails of her skirt now tucked through between her thighs and tied to her girdle in front. Apart from the deep heaving of her bosom, she appeared to be fresher than any of them. James climbed with dash and flair, seeming joyfully to accept the challenge of the place — although he made more slips and mistakes than did the others. Rob Bruce brought up the rear a little way behind, dourly determined.

Only the King utilised breath on speech, and that not often,

146

frequent as were his gasping exclamations. On a dizzy ledge, however, perhaps one-third of their slantwise way up that beetling ascent, with the drop below so steep that they could not see the slope's meeting with the water, he panted out.

"Friend . . . I swear . . . no Stone . . . was ever brought . . . this way! You would not . . . cozen me?"

"It was lowered from above, I was told. From the high ridge. By ropes. Long ropes. To men who climbed as we do."

"Oh." James suppressed a groan. That meant that there was a vast deal of climbing to be done yet. Their destination could only be fairly near the top of this plaguey hill.

They continued on their zig-zag painful way.

It was almost half an hour later when Alexander halted. For a middle-aged man he was extraordinarily fit. His breathing was much the least disordered of the four, and undoubtedly he had been restricting his pace for the others' benefit. They had reached a sort of platform on the hill-face, between two waterfalls.

"Here you will wait, Marsala," he directed. "With Bruce. You will be well enough here."

"How much . . . further . . . do you go?" Rob jerked.

"Some way," the other answered cryptically. "Do not attempt to follow us."

For once Rob Bruce was disinclined to contest the matter.

Marsala sat down. "May your quest bring you what you desire," she said to James.

The two forged on. And now Alexander seemed to abandon all suggestion of holding back, of restraining his speed, as though it had only been for the woman's sake. He rushed ahead, climbing like a cat. James had almost to burst lungs, if not heart, even to keep near him. Some day, the King promised himself, he would make Alexander of Lochalsh pay for this — but meanwhile he must needs grit his teeth and struggle on.

After leading a comparatively short distance on approximately the same line as before, when well out of sight of the others, the Highlander quite suddenly changed direction altogether, turning about almost at right angles to climb east by north instead of north by west. They proceeded so for a few hundred more trying feet, and then began to level off, contouring the face rather than climbing higher. Undoubtedly they were well past the position where they had left their companions, back towards the ship, but considerably above them. Owing to the steepness of the slope, and all the intervening ribs and pinnacles of rock, they could not see them; nor could James tell how near they might be to the eventual summit.

His guide was now constantly glancing about him up and down, obviously seeking to establish landmarks and lines. The sharp pointed peak of a mountain directly across the gut of Loch Coruisk seemed to be important in this process. When James perceived the dark yawning mouth of a cave up a stone alleyway just above them, he exclaimed and pointed. But Alexander shook his head, and moved on.

Another smaller cave they passed. They seemed to have reached an area of faults in the hard dark rock. Then, with the noise of rushing water just ahead, Alexander quickened his pace. Rounding a knobbly buttress of gabbro, they looked into a narrow chimney cut in the rock by a waterfall. It was very steep, almost perpendicular, and down it, all but filling the funnel of it, the white water cascaded amidst the pale smoke of its spray.

Up the side of this they clambered a little way, wet from the splatter of it. Then, under the very lip where the cataract spouted outwards, Alexander edged into the fall itself, close against the stone, and disappeared behind the white curtain of water.

Stepping carefully on a wet and slippery ledge, James followed. Only a slight weight of water momentarily beat about him, and he was through.

There was another cave behind that cataract. A strange cool green light, unearthly and wavering, filled it, sunlight percolating through water. The noise of the fall was magnified and echoed into a hollow throbbing roar. The place was shaped like an arrow-head, the floor rising steadily, and the ceiling descending similarly from perhaps a dozen feet at the entrance, until they met at almost twice that distance in. Where he could go no further without stooping, Alexander stood waiting. He gestured, unspeaking.

Up near the apex of the cavern it stood, Scotland's palladium and most revered relic. Dark, almost black, a block of stone carved and peculiarly shaped, graven fate — the Stone of Destiny.

James hurried forward, and sank down on one knee before it, breathless as he was. At first, though his hands went out to touch it, they faltered and sank again to his sides. He devoured the thing with his eyes.

It was a strange stone, and nothing remotely like the shapeless lump of soft red sandstone which had been described to him by his envoys in London. It was taller, for one thing, of seat height, perhaps some eighteen inches high, by about the same width and half as long again, of some intensely hard and durable polished marble-type rock. Its top was not flat but hollowed in the centre in a shallow bowl-shaped depression. At each lateral end it was curved over in a roll, or volute, as though for lifting. The sides of it were intricately carved in elaborate interlacing ribbon design, with a sort of pleating pattern and dog-tooth bordering, notably Celtic in aspect. Vigorous and clear as when it was executed in the iron-hard material untold ages before, it seemed to be alive indeed, its involved ornamentation appearing to coil and twist and heave in that flickering green light.

As in a trance the King stared at it, the authentic symbol of his sovereignty, the Stone on which a hundred monarchs had sat to be crowned. He touched it now, his fingers running over the polished sculptured surfaces, tracing the patterns. At his shoulder Alexander had to shout to make himself heard above the echoing roar of the fall.

"Is it as you believed it?"

"Better!" the King cried. "Better. Finer. More handsome. Always I have dreamed of this day. At my Coronation I vowed that I would find this Stone. I should have sat on it then. Had my father done so . . .! My line has suffered much ill because of this Stone, I believe. Because we have not sought it out. Cherished it. Each King should at least have visited it. Sat upon it. As was decreed."

"Is that not superstition?"

"I think not. For a thousand years this has been part of our history. Woven into the very fabric of our dynasty. Did Kenneth MacAlpine carry it across the breadth of Scotland, to unite the Picts and the Scots, out of superstition? Did Edward of England desire it, out of superstition? Could Bruce not die easy for it, out of superstition?" James rose to his feet. "Will men die for superstition? Many men have died for this Stone."

"Men will die for strange things," Alexander averred. "I cannot believe this to be Jacob's pillow. Or any man's. I would not wish to rest my head on it!"

"No. That, I think, is but myth. And the carving is of the Celtic people. The Stone itself I think to be a thunderbolt. Such were esteemed holy. I have been told that it was Saint Columba's own altar. That he brought it from Ireland. A sacred relic of his princely house. This hollow a font from which he anointed the King Brude. But what matters it whence it came? For fifty generations and more our fathers have known its worth. I accept their testimony." Loudly, almost defiantly, James made that last declaration. Then turning, carefully he seated himself upon the Stone.

Alexander watched him, rubbing his chin.

James cleared his throat. "On this Stone, the true throne of my line," he said, "I, James, King of Scots, High King of Alba, do hereby renew the vows of my Coronation." Strong and clear his voice came now, even with something of intonation. "I swear to rule justly all sorts and degrees of my people. To honour and maintain Holy Church. To uphold the right, be it to my own hurt. And, God aiding me, to draw together my divided realm into one true unity. On my kingly oath, and in the sight of Almighty God, I swear it on this holy relic!"

The other stared down at the rock floor, and shuffled his hide brogans a little.

James jumped up abruptly. "By Saint Ninian — you would not smile and smirk at me, man?" he cried. "I' faith — you would not dare!"

Alexander smoothed a great hand over his features. "I would not, no," he agreed.

"No?"

"No. I, who made my own vow once. And kept it, bringing you here."

Closely the King scanned that craggy unprepossessing face. "If I thought . . . if I believed that I saw you smile . . .!" he began. And then, with a quick shake of the head, he brushed past the older man and stalked to the cave's entrance. Out behind the waterfall he went, caring nothing for the soaking, into the afternoon sunshine, to blink in its glare.

When Alexander joined him a few moments later, James had recovered his poise. "It will require many men, I fear, to win the Stone down to the sea. To the galley," he observed.

After a slight pause, the other shrugged. "No doubt," he said.

"Will it be best to take it up, or down, think you? Up, on ropes — as it was lowered here? Or down the hill?"

"I know not." Alexander answered heavily. And, after a moment. "Nor care."

Swiftly the King turned on him. "What mean you by that? You do not care . . .?"

"I mean that the matter does not concern me."

"But your men? I shall require them. To move it."

"No men of mine shall move the Stone," the older man declared. He tipped a loose stone with the toe of his brogan, edging it so that at length it fell over the brink of the cliff, and went bounding away — an act simple yet with nevertheless a strange finality. "Nor of yours," he added quietly.

James clenched tight fists. "But it is necessary," he jerked. "The Stone cannot remain here. Hidden."

"The Stone remains here, James Stewart. Secure."

"But . . . you cannot do this. Against your King's commands."

"None commands in the Isles, save the Lord thereof!"

"Not even the High King?"

"Not even such."

"Then . . . then your oath means nothing, after all?"

"I have fulfilled my oath. I swore to hold the Stone secure, even with my life. And to reveal it only to the King. Nothing more. I have revealed it. Now, I hold it secure."

James drew a long quivering breath as he sought to master his indignation. "But why?" he demanded. "It is mine. The King's Stone . . ."

"Which king?" the other questioned. "From Fergus onwards, to Kenneth MacAlpine and Malcolm Canmore — aye, down to the third Alexander — the kings were of my race, not yours. You are a Norman, from France. As was your Bruce before you."

"I have the blood of Malcolm in my veins!" James exclaimed. "As of Kenneth."

"Mightily watered, is it not? *I* have it somewhat thicker!"

"This is insufferable!" James burst out. "I am the anointed King. Bruce gave the Stone into your ancestor's keeping to hold it secure for the *King*. Not for himself. You break your trust . . ."

"Not so. I hold it secure for you here. For Scotland, your realm. I am the Keeper of the Stone. See you," Alexander brought a reasonable note into his voice, "the Stone is secure here. You will not deny it. More secure than with you in the south. Do the English never threaten now? Think you what they would do if they heard that the true Stone of Destiny was in

Stirling, or Edinburgh. And their own at Westminster Abbey a thing of no worth, false. Would they not make excuse to come for it? Is it so long since they last came ravaging over your border? You have traitors in your camp. Angus. Buchan, your own uncle. And others. Can you swear that none of these would not be glad to sell the Stone to Henry?"

"I shall guard it well, never fear."

"No." The other shook his head decisively. "You will leave it here with me. Why not, at all? How will it serve you better in Stirling? It is still in Scotland. You have seen it, touched it, sat upon it. Sworn your oath on it. What more do you require?"

"*It*, I require. The Stone itself!"

"Then, sir, you must needs take it. If you can! I have finished talking."

For long the two men considered each other, weighing, assessing. Then, without another word spoken, Alexander turned and led the way downhill.

No speech had been exchanged by the time that they reached the terrace on which the others waited.

"Did you find it? Your Stone? Your talisman?" Marsala cried, starting up and coming towards them. "Was it as you hoped?"

"Yes," James answered with unwonted curtness.

"You gained what you desired? Accomplished your . . . your pilgrimage?"

"In part."

Quickly she looked from one to the other. "All is not well?" she wondered.

"Well!" the King barked. "This noble and generous man, Alexander of Lochalsh, whom you esteem so highly, denies me what is most undeniably and justly mine."

"But . . . you mean . . .?"

"I expected no other," Rob Bruce declared from behind her. "Ah, no . . .!"

"It is the truth. Ask him. He cannot deny it."

"I deny nothing. But I counsel you all save your breath," Alexander advised tersely. "Climbing down is no less trying than climbing up. Come, you."

They reached Rum once more at sundown, after an uncomfortable voyage, with the King stiff and aloof, Alexander mockingly amused, and Marsala unsuccessfully seeking to mediate between them. At Loch Scresort James shortly refused further hospitality in Maclean's house, and transferred forthwith back to his own ship *Flower*. Indeed he would have ordered sail to be hoisted straight away and the return course set for Ardnamurchan and Mingary without delay, had not Sir Andrew Wood and most of his crew been ashore, and those left aboard in the main stupefied with Highland whisky. He sent Rob Bruce to recall the others to the ship, but it was long before that faithful envoy could get back with the noisy beneficiaries of Island hospitality.

Indeed Marsala returned before them. She had accompanied Alexander ashore, but as dusk was falling was rowed back to *Flower* again by a dashing young Highlander, richly appointed and handsome. James, pacing the poop deck in frustration and impatience, watched their arrival with jaundiced eye. He made no move to welcome either of them.

Nevertheless, Marsala brought the young man aft to him. "Lord James, this is Donald Gallda, Alexander's son," she announced. "He wishes to greet you."

Coolly the King looked him over, a young man of approximately his own age. "His greetings, if honest, I accept," he said sternly. "But from such a sire, that is by no means certain!"

The other stiffened visibly, and the young woman, biting her lip, went on hastily.

"Donald comes in goodwill. I have told him of you. Much. He thinks well of you."

James bowed ironically. "I thank you," he said. "Though I have no doubt his father will inform him much otherwise."

"I go back to him now, sir," Donald Gallda said, fair head held high. "I but came to bring the Lady Marsala to your ship. I bid you goodnight." He jerked a brief bow, and turning about strode away.

Marsala, after a moment's hesitation, elected to remain beside the King. "That was not well done, I think," she said quietly. "You could have made *him* your friend."

"To what end? I had rather have such as my enemies, I swear! Then there is no mistake. Safer so!"

"You are bitter," she sighed. "This is not like you. Does this Stone mean so much to you? More than all else? More than the unity of your realm that you have worked for?"

"No. Not that. But I can nowise abide bad faith."

"Are you sure that it was bad faith? Alexander does not esteem it so. He kept faith in taking you to the Stone. He conceives it to be his duty to hold it safe. Secure. Could he not be right?"

"Not against my wish and royal command."

"Perhaps, even so, he may consider his duty to his oath more binding?"

"Then he is no true subject of mine."

"True he is. But subject . . .? Do not forget his pride. He is proud. As proud as are you, I fear . . ."

"I am not proud. Not for myself. Only for my throne and realm."

"You are proud," she insisted. Sombrely she shook her dark head. "The pride of men! So hard a thing to fight. Unreasoning. Barren. In that, I vow, Alexander is no worse than you? And no better!"

James turned on her. "What is Alexander to you? A man who could be your father!"

"He is my friend."

"More than just friend, I think! Did you not say, this morning, that you had once watched the sun rise, together, on one of the Cuillin peaks? And had been happy!"

"Yes," she admitted slowly. "I said that." She drew a long breath. "But there was another there with us, on Sgurr nan Gillean. Malcolm. His son. Alexander's second son. That is why I was happy."

"Ah!" He paused. "And you were close? You and this Malcolm?"

"We were close. We were very close. Betrothed. Our hearts were as one."

"*Were*, you say . . .?"

"Were. He is dead. Drowned dead. Five years ago. Five long years. In his galley. Coming to see me, at Mingary. A storm, it was . . ."

James touched her arm, impulsively. "I am sorry," he said.

She nodded. "Malcolm was his father's son," she added, with a strange calm. "More so than is Donald Gallda."

He considered her thoughtfully now. "Just what you mean by that last I do not know. But much that I did not understand before is now clear. About you, Marsala. I . . . I esteem you the better for it."

"Then heed me. Now. With regard to Malcolm's father. Heed me, James." That was the first time that she had acceded to his request so to name him privately. "If you cannot forget your pride, remember his. He comes of a line of princes as long as yours. Leave him some of his pride, and you will not be the loser. I knew from the first that you were two men who would measure one against another. Men of the same stamp, though so different. You came here to him in peace and high purpose. Do not leave him in anger and pride."

"I came in peace, yes. But he flouts me to my face. Denies me what is mine. So I must leave him. And come again . . . otherwise!"

"You mean . . . in war? Ah, no! Not that. Never that. Not . . . not for a piece of dead stone!"

"It is the token and symbol of my rule. He knows it, and so withholds it. He would deny me what is part of the throne of my fathers. Why? He says that if I would have it, then I must take it. That I mean to do!"

"But that would mean battle!" she almost wailed. "After all that you have said, and done. For peace. For the unity of your realm. To bind the Highland folk to you. If you bring your men and ships and cannon here, to try to take the Stone, all these galleys and as many more again will confront you. Thousands upon thousands of men. Blood will flow. And even so, you will never gain your Stone . . ."

"Alexander may have a host of men and ships. But he has no cannon, I have noted! And swords are but feeble things against cannon, see you."

"Your cannon may kill and maim and sink and batter! But they will prevail nothing against the peaks of the Cuillin, and men amongst them determined that you shall not have the Stone. Could not a score of Alexander's fighters hold the hill above Loch Coruisk against all your strength? You know it."

James frowned. "That may be so. But I can teach your Alexander a lesson that may make him change his mind. That will make him glad to give me that Stone. If he lives so long!"

Horrified she searched his face. "Is this the man who said that he would bring peace to the Isles? Who declared that it takes two to make a fight?"

"I told you also, did I not, that I would bring you here with me, seeking Alexander, that you might learn who rules in Scotland?" He sighed a little, nevertheless. "Either I am King, and rule. Or I am nothing."

She moved away from him to the carved stern rail, to stare landward, where again the myriad cooking fires of the Highland host glowed and twinkled. "I had thought you nobler. Ungrudging. A man — not merely a king!"

"Am I the less a man that I will not be cheated out of my right?" He came over to her side again. "What sort of a man do you seek, Marsala?"

"I sought a man strong enough to be generous. True to his word. More merciful than proud. Thinking of others, not only of himself or his position."

"High standards, woman! Does Alexander of Lochalsh meet them?"

"Perhaps not. I had believed that he did. Now . . ."

"Now you have your doubts?"

"Perhaps. But must I also lose my belief in you, James? I thought you a man who sought love and esteem rather than just your rights." She paused, and when he answered nothing, added in something of a rush, "Was not that what you sought . . . even from me?"

He moistened his lips eyeing her sidelong. "That I sought — but did not attain!"

She leaned over, to look down at the water. "I had thought you less easily discouraged," she said quietly.

For a space there was silence between them, if nothing of peace. The high ululation of pipe music came sobbing across the loch to them.

When he did not speak, she went on slowly. "Does a man change his mind so readily? As . . . as may a woman!"

"Have you chánged your mind, then?" Thickly he spoke. "About me?"

"Say that I thought that I had. Until this talk of war and ships and cannon."

"And now?"

"Now I am not sure again. A foolish weak woman."

"I swear you are not that!" he said, almost grimly. He knew well what she was doing — but he did not leave her side. "You could be convinced, I think?"

"You, I believe, could convince me, James."

"Tonight?"

She inclined her head.

"You notably sacrifice yourself in the cause of duty, Marsala

MacIan!" he declared, frowning a little, a note of harshness in his voice. "As dutiful a friend to Alexander as you are daughter to MacIan!"

"No! Ah, no — not that! Never that!" she cried. She turned to him urgently. "Here is no duty. This I *seek*. I would indeed be . . . convinced!"

"You mean it? Of a truth?" He gripped her shoulders, forcing her round to face him directly. "This you desire?"

Looking up at him mutely, she nodded.

Releasing the grip of only one arm, he swept her bodily about and hurried her across the deck to the poop stairway.

Below, within her cabin doorway, he let her go, and halted. In the semi-darkness of it she went a few paces, and then turned to look back to him. She held out her arms.

MARSALA MACIAN was no coy maid or teasing miss. Her decision taken, there was no holding back. Murmuring, she aided the man's clumsy fumbling fingers to undo her simple clothing, and so slipped easily and without fuss out of the constriction of it, to stand before him frankly in the shadows, gleaming pale, slender, lissome.

"Woman—you are lovely!" James muttered, almost groaned, and sweeping her up in his arms, practically ran with her to the nearest bunk.

She coiled cool white arms around his neck. "James! Seumas!" she whispered. "Play the man now, if you will!"

She was passionate, demanding, skilful, no passive bedmate this. Even her kisses had a scorching quality. Practised lover as he was, the man perceived that he was on test, on trial. She made no mention of the chain about his loins.

Impetuous, headstrong always, in the first test he was aware that he gave less than satisfaction.

Almost as though he had been a wayward child, thereafter, she chided him, encouraged him, aroused him. At least, he did not fail to rise to her challenge.

Later, as he lay back and ran a trembling but appreciative hand over her loveliness, he spoke throatily but coherently.

"You are a very wonderful woman, Marsala my dear. Most beautiful. Accomplished. And kind. Few indeed are all these, I have discovered. The first all men can see. But the others you hid passing well!"

"You must have known many more beautiful. More accomplished. Aye, and kinder, I think."

"No."

"Some, surely, were better formed? More inviting?"

"No."

"I have heard it said that men prefer larger breasts than mine. More rounded limbs. Softer flesh. Hair less dark."

"Why do you doubt yourself? Men desire *women*—not parts of

women only! Whole women. Some I have known are but the parts. All breast. All loins. All belly. All buttocks. Aye, and some all flesh but no spirit. But you are all woman, indeed — of a piece. And match me admirably, do you not? See how your breast fits the cup of my hand. How your hip cherishes my groin. How your long thigh partners mine. We fit very well, you and I — do we not? I desire no better."

"Desire . . .!" she murmured. "Desire, yes. But have you ever yet met a woman, James, for whom you felt more than desire?"

He stirred a little at her side. "Why, yes. Certainly I have. To be sure. Many." He paused. "H'rr'mm. That is . . . why do you ask? Do you take me for a brute-beast? An animal? You, Marsala, I esteem most highly. From the first, I have seen you as one to whom I could be close. Most close. In love and affection . . ."

"In love and affection," she echoed. "In esteem. You also are kind, James. But . . . it is not of these that I speak. Have you ever known for any woman more even than these? That greater, fiercer passion that burns, that devours? That having, perceiving, knowing, fills you to overflowing, making all else as nothing? And lacking, losing, leaves you but an empty shell. Have you known such?"

He did not speak.

"I think not," she answered for him, after a moment or two. "Indeed, I know that you have not. Not yet. Although I believe that somewhere there is a woman who can light such a fire in you. Who has already kindled the first small flame of it, perhaps? I have sensed it in you, more than once. A woman to be envied, greatly. Or greatly pitied. I know not which."

He stared up at the shadowy timbers above them.

"Such a love only few may encompass, perhaps," she went on. "And fewer attain to. You, James Stewart, I think, are of that quality. One day, you may rise to it."

"As you did?"

"As I did. And paid the price. Always there is a price to pay. Pray that you may not grudge the price when the time comes."

"You conceive that I might?"

"The man would not, I believe. But the king might."

He frowned into the gloom.

Perhaps she sensed that frown, for she moved, turned in his arms, to raise her lovely body above his, and, propped on her forearms, to gaze down at him, the tips of her breasts gently stirring against his chest.

"Forgive me," she pleaded. "Here is no way to use a man. We Highland woman all think to be seers! But this is scarce the time for it. I must not tire you with my talk." She lowered herself, and brushed his mouth with her moist parted lips. "Do I tire my lord with aught else?" she whispered.

"I' faith, you do not!"

When, presently, the noise of shouting and singing heralded the belated return of the ship's company from Highland hospitality, the King neither commented nor cared.

Sometime during that hot July night, when quiet talk was again not inappropriate, the girl spoke of Alexander once more.

"Does he sleep, now, I wonder?" she mused. "I think not. I see him pacing, pacing alone. Always he is alone. He loves his people—but always he is alone. More alone even than you, the King, I think. He will be seeking to see where lies his duty. Always it is that—his duty."

"He seemed in few doubts about it, earlier!" James declared. "And it was not his duty towards his liege lord that worried him!"

"His duty he will conceive to be towards his people, rather—the people who look to him as chief and lord."

"Yet he hanged eleven of them but yesterday! His own men. For incivility, as he said! Is that the father of his people?"

"It would hurt him sorely to do it," she said slowly. "But he must have seen it as his duty, also. They had broken the law of hospitality—one of the first amongst our people. They repaid open-handed welcome by savagery and rape. That had to be punished. Maclean, here, as host, was entitled to such amends. The men would know what they did. My father would have acted as did Alexander. It is our law. Would you not have punished them?"

"I would not have hanged them—for that!"

"Perhaps it is that you think differently about women?"

"I think passing well of women!" he averred, strongly. His hand slid over her person assuredly, possessively. "Do you not perceive it?"

"You enjoy women. But do you honour them, I wonder?"

"I honour you . . ."

"Do you? Can you?" she demanded.

"To be sure. Why not? None but you would question it."

160

"Alexander would question it, I believe. If he could see me now, what would he think of me?"

"I care not what Alexander thinks, woman! Of what you do. Or what I do."

"But you should care, James — you should. For much depends on what Alexander thinks, and does in consequence. The future of the Isles, of all the Highlands perhaps. The peace of your realm. The lives of many. You care for these, do you not?"

When he was silent, she pursued her advantage.

"Thought for Alexander's pride. A generous gesture tomorrow. These could serve you well. So very well. At but little cost to your own pride, you could ensure his goodwill. Ensure peace. Return to your south, praised of all men. Not reviled. The death of none. The victor."

"How could this be? Alexander is firm set in his course, I swear."

"Firm set that you shall not take the Stone away. And in that resolve he must win. Accept it, James — for the sake of us all. For your realm's sake. Leave the Stone. Here, where it is secure. Tomorrow, go ashore — or summon Alexander to you here. I will fetch him for you. Confirm the Stone of Destiny in his care and keeping. Publicly do him this honour. Knight him, even, as you did John of Islay, who less deserves it. He resents John's knighthood, I think — he *must* resent it, since it seems to show your support for John's pretensions to the heirship of the Isles against his own true claim. In the eyes of all men make Alexander your friend, your lieutenant — not your foe. You will not regret it."

"You do not seek that I lick his shoes, also?"

"I ask you to do what only a strong man would do. The man I believe you to be. *You* would go from Rum the victor, not Alexander."

For a long space there was only the creak of timbers, the lap of wavelets, and the distant muffled sounds of revelry, to be heard in that cabin. Then James grunted, combed his fingers through her dark hair, and spoke.

"Never did I think to be taught statecraft by a woman, and in bed!" he said.

"I teach nothing," she averred. "I but learn. Learn to know the mind and the heart of a man."

"Then you have learned enough, woman, for one night! Speak no more of it."

161

"Yes. Forgive me. You have been very patient. Sleep now, James *a graidh*."

"Not so! A pox—that I will not! I may sleep any night, Marsala MacIan! Come . . .!"

In the morning, Marsala brought a wary, mistrustful Alexander, and some of his chieftains, out to the *Flower*. James welcomed them less than effusively, before a blear-eyed ship's-company. Lacking something of his usual gift for words he, without undue ceremony, announced to all and sundry that in respect of his cousin Alexander of Lochalsh's well-known and proved leal and faithful love and service towards himself, and in gratitude for his taking him to the secure hiding-place of the Stone of Destiny and witnessing the renewal of his sacred Coronation vows upon the said Stone, he, James Stewart of Scotland, High King of Alba, hereby nominated and appointed the said Alexander de Insulis MacDonald of Lochalsh to be Keeper and Guardian of the Stone of Destiny, as were his fathers before him, to hold it safe and sure in the King's name, until such time as the King might require it of him. In token whereof he now desired to mark and demonstrate his royal trust and confidence in the goodwill of the said Alexander by raising him before all men to the high honour and estate of knighthood.

If Alexander had been suspiciously cautious before, now he was most clearly astonished and at a loss. Not normally a man for hesitation in action, he looked from James to Marsala, to his colleagues, and back again, his whole bearing a question-mark.

The young woman stepped over to his side, and stood there, unspeaking but eloquent in her support, her wordless assurance.

The King scarcely paused—for rejection of his gesture by Alexander now would be disastrous. Quickly he took the sword which Rob Bruce held ready behind him, and moving forward, without even suggesting that the other should kneel, as was usual, brought the gleaming blade to the chief's plaided shoulder almost as swiftly as he might have done in more conventional swording.

"I dub you knight, Sir Alexander de Insulis MacDonald of Lochalsh," he jerked.

Unlike the knighting of John of Islay, no storm of exclamation or acclaim greeted this totally unexpected action. All men were silent, wondering—none more so than the new knight himself.

Again the young woman bridged the gap. She touched Alexander's arm. "No man is more worthy of the honour, I think," she said quietly. "Moreover it honours he that gives equally with he that receives. Does it not?"

Nobody actually answered that. Alexander searched her face, and then did the same for the King. Finally he bowed, very slightly. "So be it," he said. "The honour I accept, and shall seek to justify. The Stone I shall keep . . . secure!"

After a moment or two, James nodded. It was as much as he could expect; better much than might have been. The fewer words exchanged now, the safer, probably.

"I am assured that you will worthily keep faith, likewise," he observed. "I take leave of you now, confident that peace will prevail in the Isles."

"You go now? You leave us?"

"Forthwith. I sail for Mingary. My work here is done . . . meantime."

The other met his eye, and smiled faintly, but not mockingly nor yet unkindly. "Go, with my goodwill," he said.

An hour later *Flower* beat down Loch Scresort between the serried ranks of long-ships. At the mouth of it, the two MacIan galleys of their escort materialised from nowhere in particular, and distinctly sheepishly fell into place behind her as she turned southwards.

They were a bare half-way to Ardnamurchan when another craft bearing the blazon of MacIan on its great square sail came racing to them from the west, in a flurry of spray. It bore the Lord Drummond, seeking the King. A courier had arrived at Mingary the previous evening, from the Chancellor, he announced. He brought evil tidings. Treasonable correspondence had been intercepted between the Earls of Angus and Buchan and King Henry of England. The plot was to seize the kingdom, putting James's young brother the Duke of Ross on the throne, under the overlordship of Henry. It was thought that the attempt might well be made whilst James was thus occupied in the far north-west.

Grimly the King sent the galley ahead, back to Mingary with all speed, with request to the Lord High Admiral to have the royal fleet ready to sail at the first possible moment.

It seemed almost as though the Stone of Destiny had been safe enough in its cave in Skye, all along.

The bay of Mingary presented a scene of much activity when

they rounded its point. Small boats by the dozen scurried between the host of ships and the shore, ferrying water-casks and provisions. By and large, however, it looked as though most of the King's ships were almost ready for sea. No doubt Bothwell had anticipated the order. Without delay, James was rowed ashore, with Marsala, to take his leave of MacIan. He noted that John of Islay's galleys had disappeared from the anchorage.

MacIan and some of the other mainland chiefs, who had observed the *Flower*'s approach, hastened to meet them on the strand.

"Ill news, Lord James," he greeted. "You leave us? A poor parting this."

"It is. But I shall come back, never fear. And much has been achieved. My visit will bear rich fruit, I think." The prospect of action, even of danger, stimulated James, as ever, to brisk vigour.

"Yet still there is much to be done . . ."

"Yes. And done it will be. I shall leave my clerks and scribes with you. They will take note of all fiefs, charters and grants of lands, held formerly of the Lords of the Isles, for conversion into Crown charters, held direct of the King. You will form a council of chiefs to consider all debatable claims and disputes, and the clerks will write your judgements and recommendations to me, for decision. You I charge to see to this, MacIan."

"I am honoured. But some may not accept me, in such position."

"Then I hereby declare you, before all men, to have my royal authority to act on my behalf. For the weal of my realm. Here on the mainland."

"And Alexander? John of Islay?"

"Their's are the Isles. I think that they will counter one the other! I have knighted Alexander also. Your daughter bids me trust him."

"Aye." MacIan looked from the young man to Marsala, thoughtfully. "And you take her advice?"

"I do."

"Very well, so. Be it as you say, Sire—all as you say."

When they had all kissed his hand, James turned to the young woman, and taking her arm led her a little way apart, to the water's very edge.

"So swift a parting," he said.

"Yes."

164

"With so much left unsaid. Undone."

"Yes. Yet, I think that you have gained most of what you sought, have you not?"

Swiftly he glanced at her. "You mean . . .?" He compressed his lips. "You might have spared yourself last night, Marsala — had these tidings come but a day earlier!"

She looked away. "Would you leave me with that unworthy thought? I . . . I had looked for kinder."

"I am sorry," he told her. "I should not have said it."

"No, you should not. I would not wish to have been spared . . . anything that happened."

"Forgive me, then. As you have forgiven me much else."

She nodded.

"So short a time, we had," he went on. "And yet you have taught me much in it."

"Taught? I did not seek to teach you anything, James."

"What then did you seek? Other than peace between myself and Alexander?"

"Must a woman always be seeking something? May she not but follow her heart at times?"

"Your heart?" he said, and was silent.

"My heart, yes." She emitted something between a sigh and a brief laugh. "I . . . I had thought it broken. But never fear, my Lord James — the state of my poor heart need concern the King nothing. He has greatly more important matters to look to. Go look to them, with my . . . blessing."

He stared away across the loveliness of the Hebridean Sea. "I shall come back," he said.

She shook her dark head. "No. I think not. You may come back to Ardnamurchan, who knows? But not to Marsala MacIan. That tale is told. Seek you your princess, James *a graidh* . . . or that other whom you hide deep in *your* heart. And do not hesitate to pay the price I spoke of, if need be. As shall I."

He nibbled his lip, and said nothing.

"If I may counsel you, this last time? Let the man ever rule the king, where your heart is concerned. It will serve you better."

"Aye. Perhaps. And you? What of you and *your* heart, Marsala?"

"Me? Why, Alexander has another son. You remember?" she said, level-toned. "Donald Gallda. You saw him. Should I complain?"

165

When he found no answer, she touched his wrist. "Wish me well, James," she whispered, her voice breaking. "Then go. And quickly. For sweet Mary-Mother's sake! For I can bear it no longer."

Shaking his head, he looked beyond her to the group of chiefs around her father, who waited, seeming not to watch. Then, wordless still, he took her hand and raised it to his lips. For a moment or two he held it there, before turning it over and kissing the open palm, fiercely yet tenderly. He closed her fingers over it, and turned abruptly away. Without a backward glance he strode through the splashing shallows to the waiting boat.

The girl saw nothing as he was rowed out to the ship.

Down that beautiful and terrible seaboard, the most fearsome in all Europe, the royal squadron sailed for two days and two nights, skirting the islands and skerries, rounding points and headlands innumerable, threading the sounds and narrows. And all the way and all the time, save for the very few hours of darkness, the look-outs kept turning from these navigational hazards to gaze seawards where, hull-down against the dark bar of the horizon, the tips of innumerable square and raking sails kept them perpetual company. Nearer these never came, more identifiable they did not grow. Galleys they were, of course. But whose? And wherefore?

At the mouth of West Loch Tarbert, James, fretting and impatient, left his long slow train of galliots and transports to continue up-loch to his castle of Tarbert, there to re-provision and water – for they carried nearly four thousand men consuming notable quantities of provender. *Flower* with the six other tall galleons pressed on southwards down the lengthy fifty-mile coastline of the peninsula of Kintyre.

Darkness overtook them before they were much more than half-way down, and the ships stood well out to sea – for the Mull of Kintyre was no place to be near by night. And as they moved outwards, to the west and the sunset, so moved those shadowy accompanying sails on the horizon, keeping their distance. James frowned towards them in perplexity.

In the morning light, dimly they could see the mighty thrusting fist of the Mull due east of them, its base as ever lost in clouds of spray. The squadron turned to head at last for the mouth of the

Firth of Clyde, sheltered waters far up which lay the port of Dumbarton, their destination.

Passing a couple of miles from the very tip of the peninsula, they could perceive the castle of Dunaverty, perched astonishingly, like the eyrie of some sea-eagle, high on the summit of a curious pyramid of rock at the cliff-top, hundreds of feet above the smoking seas. From its highest tower the royal banner of Scotland flew — but at half-mast.

The King, eying that flag and debating its message, decided that he must investigate. He ordered his other ships to proceed on towards Dumbarton with all speed. *Flower*, the fastest of the fleet, would take him in to discover the reason of the keeper of Dunaverty's signal. He might well catch up with the others before Arran was passed.

Dunaverty Castle, most strategically situated, commanding the route to the Western Isles and also the narrows of the Irish Sea, indeed the nearest point of land to Ireland, had been the first of the Lord of the Isles' strongholds to be taken by James some three years before. Strengthening its already formidable defences and equipping it with heavy cannon and installing a governor and garrison, he had made it a sign and symbol for all the west to see of the power that ruled in Scotland.

There was a sheltered anchorage not far from the castle, wherein a single galley was moored, and down to this the governor Captain John Boyd, came hurrying at the sight of the Lion Rampant at *Flower*'s main masthead. Rowed out to the ship, his tidings were that for the past three days a dozen or more galleys had been lying off the castle's vicinity threateningly, drawing closer at night, receding further by day, seemingly waiting to pounce. He had directed much cannon-fire at them, but they had kept just out of range. Now he was running short of powder and shot, and moreover desired reinforcements in case of an attempt to take the castle. Young MacAlastair of The Loup, whose galley was anchored here, said that they were John of Islay's ships.

Annoyed at having been diverted and delayed unnecessarily for such a tale, James brusquely informed Boyd that he was a fool. John of Islay was now his friend and ally, and moreover knighted. No doubt his galleys were here in a protective role, in case rebels from the Buchan-Angus faction should attempt to capture this strategic stronghold from the King. No reinforcements could be spared from *Flower*'s complement, but a few barrels of powder and shot, to replace the wasted ammunition, were transferred to the shore. James hurried after his other galleons, intent on more serious business.

Flower had in fact rejoined the rest of the squadron, and they were well up the narrows of Clyde approaching Toward Point, when a single galley, surging after them at spectacular speed, caught up with the King's ship. It was young Angus MacAlastair of The Loup, son of the loyal chief of that name in Kintyre, with dire news. Swarming agilely up a rope ladder to the galleon's deck, he panted out his story.

Shortly after the King had left Dunaverty, the long-ships had appeared again — indeed *Flower* would have been still in sight had she not rounded the fist of the Mull. But now these were not any dozen galleys, but scores, with the blazon of the Isles on their sails. One flew the personal banner of Sir John of Islay. Assured now that these were friends and allies, Captain Boyd had met them not with cannon-fire but with welcoming signals and open doors, greeting them in the King's name. John Cathanach of Islay himself had come ashore, climbed to the castle, and entering it had rounded suddenly on the unsuspecting garrison, put them to the sword and hanged Boyd from the topmost battlements. He now dangled from the flagpole beneath the banner of the Isles, whilst the flag of Scotland was burnt to ashes. Thereafter Sir John had issued a proclamation declaring that Dunaverty, a castle of the Lordship of the Isles, had been retaken by himself as effective Lord of the Isles, let all men take note, as he would do to any other strength or house insolently usurped by James Stewart or other interloper. MacAlastair blurted this out in urgent Gaelic — but involuntarily took a pace or two backwards before he had somewhat falteringly finished, at sight of the other young man's contorted face.

Without a word James left the young chief where he stood, and the others who listened, and strode away to the ship's side. Gripping one of the shrouds fiercely, he stared back whence they had come, his features working convulsively, his comely good looks all but unrecognisable. For long minutes he stood thus, his back to all of them unspeaking, unapproachable. When at length he turned, his expression was almost blank, his lips stiff, his eyes narrowed.

"MacAlastair," he said in a level, grating voice. "I cannot turn back now. As I would. Before Christ God I would! I have other snakes to crush, first. Aye, first. But you. Go you back, with all haste. Not to Dunaverty. Go to Mingary. To MacIan. Tell him that the King requires the head of John of Islay. Aye, and of his four sons, also. Those shoulders that I knighted — they must be headless! Do you hear? Headless!"

"Yes, my lord . . ."

"MacIan must see to it. As my lieutenant. He must call the chiefs. Aye, call even Alexander. It may be that he will find it his duty . . . since he does not love John Cathanach." James ran a hand over his bare head. "I believed those ships that dogged us to be his. Alexander's. It seems that I misjudged him. Aye. See you Marsala MacIan, MacAlastair, as well as her father. Tell her from me that she was right. As ever. That I was wrong. And acknowledge it. Tell her . . . tell her . . ." James paused, and shrugged, and sighed. "No. Never heed. Go now, man — go. And at your fastest. And leave MacIan in no doubts as to my wishes! Begone."

All the way up the narrowing Firth of Clyde the King stood alone at the stern and gazed back to where the black mountains, gradually diminishing, rose out of the pewter plain of the sea. None sought to break in on his reverie there, not even Rob Bruce.

PART THREE
Chain of Destiny

10

ALL along the lengthy colourful line the banners and pennons flapped in the breeze, cracking like a continuous salvo of pistol-shots. There were many banners there, behind and flanking the Red Lion of Scotland, with many and notable devices and blazons — but not so many as there might have been, and with some equally notable absentees. The breeze, blowing strongly from the east, was chilly for August, and the bare open moorland above the twists of the Bannock Burn was exposed, so that James stamped to and fro, wearing a track for himself in the rough grass and reeds, his armour clanking. Others were doing the same behind him and up and down the long line — although more had retired to the tents and camp-fires in the rear, tired of waiting.

The host had been waiting there for hours, and now the tension and excitement had practically all faded out of it. Most of the men, indeed, had been encamped on the slantwise moorland, site of the original and ever-glorious Battle of Bannockburn, since the night before. Only the King himself seemed still to maintain his air of eagerness, his alert readiness. Lesser men had long since been satisfied that there would be no fighting that day. It was now an hour past noon, and the challenge had been for mid-day.

James halted his restless pacing, to watch the approach of a single horseman who galloped an obviously weary beast diagonally across the open ground in front from a north-easterly direction, an armed man wearing the Drummond colours. He rode for the royal pavilion pitched directly in the centre of the mile-long front, before which James and his Standard-Bearer and Sword-Bearer stood, and throwing himself from his lathered and sweating mount, bowed jerkily to one knee.

"The Lord Gray has halted his host, Sire," he panted. "He lies at the other side of Forth, at Boat of Cambus . . . but has not moved these two hours. I reckon he comes no further."

"A-a-ah!" The King's breath escaped in a long sigh, part relief, part regret. "The fox has second thoughts! A pity, perhaps."

At his back, Bothwell snorted. "Pity you call it? I call it a God's mercy, Sire! Gray's a bonny fighter, and can field three hundred men of his own, and a thousand from his sheriffdom of Forfar."

"Aye. But would they all draw sword against their king?"

"Deil knows!"

That was indeed one of the two great questionmarks which had hung over all this day's proceedings, a question to which James had gambled impetuously that he might not have to discover the answer. Some, many, called his gamble more than impetuous – reckless, headstrong, crazy, however typical. A bare week earlier, reaching Stirling from his Highland adventures, he had found himself to be just in time to forestall a more or less bloodless coup, the taking over of his kingdom by the Angus-Buchan-Gray faction, and the placing of his young brother the Duke of Ross on the throne as puppet to Henry of England. It seemed that only the English monarch's notorious stinginess had held matters up, for spies asserted that the conspirators had been awaiting only further promised consignments of gold from London, and the moving of Henry's North of England levies over the Border. All else was in train, and the plot ripe to burst.

James had acted swiftly, however, much against the advice of his ministers. He had immediately issued a nationwide summons, to all his lords, barons and freeholders, to attend him six days hence, before noontide, on the celebrated field of Bannockburn, armed, accoutred, with their retinues and retainers. He had used the ancient custom, calling them all to a traditional wapinschaw or demonstration of arms, rebel and loyal alike, friend and foe. It was a dramatic, challenging and dangerous gesture, a spectacular throwing down of the gauntlet, positively requesting his enemies to assemble against him in force for a trial of strength – with no certainty as to how many of his own supporters would choose to rally to his side. He had sent couriers with the summons to every corner of his kingdom reachable within a couple of days from Stirling, and in especial to Bell-the-Cat Angus, to his great-uncles Buchan and Atholl, to Lennox and Lyle and Andrew, Lord Gray.

Thereafter, all over the land the King's scouts and informants had watched, to send him word as to the results. Many bodies of men had made and were still making the journey to Bannockburn, undoubtedly – and how many of them would elect to fight on the royal side if the opposition was sufficiently numerous was a matter for debate. But no great forces were reported from the chief conspirators' strongholds, from the Douglas territories, from Atholl and Buchan—save only this Gray contingent from the Carse of Gowrie and Forfar. Lennox had not stirred, save to send his younger son with a tiny token force. Lyle in fact had come in the day before with two hundred men, professing all loyalty to his liege lord James. Unless the King's spies had been consistently hoodwinked and there were hidden hosts on their way somewhere, it seemed certain that the plotters were not prepared to put their cause to the test. Apparently Lord Gray had come to this conclusion likewise, and had halted his advance.

There was no holding the already broken and wilting long lines of wearily waiting knights, men-at-arms and moss-troopers, any longer. Since daybreak they had stood there, more or less patiently, girt and armed and horsed, some six thousand men in all, mainly Bothwell's and Home's Borderers, and the levies of Lords Drummond, Graham, Ruthven and Kennedy, and of sundry bishops and abbots. Now, as the word ran down the ranks that the only large body of possible foes within twenty miles of them had halted, everywhere men relinquished their vigil and broke away, loosening cramping armour, removing heavy helmets, laying down arms. A general move was made towards the rear, to the tents and cooking-fires.

James made up his mind with characteristic speed and whole-heartedness. "Tell my Lord Lyon King of Arms to have his heralds sound the respite from arms," he ordered Sir Rob Bruce. "We shall not waste all this good day. Lists to be set up on yonder level, at the Bloody Fold. We shall have jousting instead of battle, a true wapinschaw. Send to Stirling for meats and wines and ale. For all. Much victual. Squeeze Stirling dry, Rob! And fetch the women. All you may find—ladies, wenches, trulls, gammers! By royal command! Fiddlers and singers and harpers, too. Jesters. Tumblers. Bears to bait. Today the realm is saved once more. 'Fore God, all men shall know it! Even Henry of England. Aye—bring also that fox the English envoy. Dig him out of his den in St. Mary's Wynd—if he is not already with Andrew Gray! We shall give him something to write to his master!"

When Rob had gone to carry out these large instructions as best he might, the King, eyes gleaming, recalled the Drummond courier. "A fresh horse, man," he cried. "And back to my Lord

of Gray, at Boat of Cambus. Take one of my heralds. You, Hay
— go you with him. Tell Gray that I look to see him at my
wapinschaw. At his earliest. Tell him that I bid him come to
break a lance with the King's champion. Aye, tell him that."

"He will not come, Sire . . ."

"You think not? Then tell him that I expect him. I await him,
command him. Tell him that he has naught to fear from his liege
lord if he is a leal subject!"

"Still he will not come, Sire, I swear," John Hay, Slains
Pursuivant, asserted.

"We shall see. Go you and tell him." James unbuckled his
cuirass of richly engraved steel and tossed it to his Armour-
Bearer. "And now, my lords — to work!"

Stirling was less than three miles away, and by late afternoon
the high ground above the Bannock Burn was transformed. On
the level greensward known as the Bloody Fold, where two
hundred years before a party of fleeing English archers were
caught and fought to the death after the rout of battle, a jousting
ground had been roped off, lined and enclosed by the colourful
pavilions of the nobles and knights, with a royal box and reserved
area on the mound immediately to the west, seated with rows of
hastily improvised benches for the gentry. Banners fluttered
everywhere in the breeze, tentage flapped, and music, singing and
laughter resounded. All around were booths and stalls, tables
laden with food and drink which harassed servitors guarded less
than successfully, and great casks of ale set up for all who wished
to partake. Hucksters, pedlars and beggars, like children and dogs,
had materialised in extraordinary numbers, seemingly out of the
very ground itself. All of Stirling appeared to have flocked there,
to mingle with the army. Wandering priests and friars did
excellent business, men-at-arms strutted, quarrelled and came
to constant blows, and the more discreet whores plied their trade
behind every tent and booth.

More orderly contests of arms and skill and brawn went on in
the enclosed tourney-ground, announced by successive flourishes
of trumpets — jousting between mail-clad knights, tilting at
marks, sword-play on horse and afoot, archery, single-stick duels
and wrestling. It was the sort of occasion which James dearly
loved to organise, and to take part in. Today he was personally
donating handsome and extravagant prizes for almost every event,

handed over by the ladies of his Court — some of whom added a favour or two of their own when the occasion seemed to warrant it.

The King, at his gayest, was to be seen everywhere, far from confining himself to the enclosure, mixing with all and sundry, laughing and joking with the merry, sampling his own hospitality, stealing kisses, applauding feats of skill in others, demonstrating his own. His high spirits were infectious, and there were few gloomy, sour or anxious faces to be seen, even amongst those who might well have started the day prepared to support the conspiracy. It was to be noted, however, how frequently the King paused in his gallantries to gaze away north-eastwards towards the low plain of Forth.

Another who glanced in that direction, though less obviously, was the handsome Robert, Lord Lyle of Duchal — who was, of course, nephew to the Lord Gray. If he was a little strained, less easy and carefree than most of those around him, this could be accounted for by the fact that it was not always simple for a man who had been in armed rebellion against his king on previous occasions, to appear as though such was quite impossible today. Rob Bruce, suspicious by nature perhaps, and more than doubtful of James's forgiving propensities and policies, kept a keen eye on him.

Indeed, he declared his misgivings to the Lady Margaret Drummond. They had become great friends, these two, seeming to understand each other instinctively, to be at ease together in a fashion that was apt to set the King twitting and railing at them, sometimes even casting hot aspersions in jealous ire, although he knew any such suspicions to be groundless. That Bruce, no ladies' man, should have such evident success with the one woman whom James appeared to be unable to impress, who kept him consistently at a distance, undoubtedly rankled.

Today, however, in the matter of Lord Lyle, these two saw less than eye to eye. Lyle, during one of James's many sallies from the royal box, had been talking to Margaret, very attentive and gallant despite those occasional preoccupied glances across Forth. As he moved away a little, Rob came close.

"I wonder that you can find it in you to speak fair with that man," he declared. "A traitor he was and a traitor he is yet, I swear — for all his smiles and graces! He and his two hundred scoundrels would be at our throats today, I warrant, had Angus and Buchan met the King's challenge."

"Perhaps not," she demurred. "He came to the King's summons yesterday, after all, before he could know that the others would or would not. Why should not he have come in loyalty, his lesson learned?"

"I do not trust him. And what lesson did he have to learn? He suffered nothing for his last treason. James forgave him all. Even sent him as envoy to England. As he forgave the others. No lesson there — save that if another treason failed, he might be as fortunate!"

Margaret Drummond shook her fair head. "I think you misjudge, Rob. Mercy, kindness, trust — these are seeds which can bear a bountiful harvest. James is right, and wise, to seek his enemies' love rather than their fear and hatred. He takes risks by forgiving, to be sure — but he would risk much more by binding together the forces against him in revenge and malice. He inherited a sorely divided kingdom, with little might of his own to bind it to him. Might he still lacks — but love and admiration and the trust of his people, may serve him instead."

"Yet only a fool trusts and forgives an adder that once has stung his heel!"

"Men are not adders, Rob — men with souls and hearts."

The young man frowned. "I still think overmuch forgiveness is unwise . . ." He paused. The King, readily identifiable in his red-and-gold striped doublet and vivid shoulder-length auburn hair, had come into view amongst the crowd, making his way back to the enclosure, laughing, clapping men on the back, slipping his arm around women, teasing children. Even as they waited, he tossed a coin that gleamed silver in the sunlight to a lame man bent over a crutch — and when the cripple failed to catch it, started forward himself, stooped to pick it up, and handed it to the man with a smile.

"See you that?" Margaret said, with something of a tremor in her voice. "There is something that no one has seen in Scotland ere this! No King of Scots has ever done the like, been so close to his people. There is where James will find his might — in the hearts of his people."

"The people, may be — the common folk. But what can they do for him? It is the lords, hungry for power and land and riches, on whom all depends. And this means naught to them. I' faith, it could mean weakness, not strength. Look yonder and see how much this all pleases my lords!"

Lyle had moved over to chat with Bothwell and Drummond. All were watching the King's progress. Lyle's lips were curled in evident distaste at what he saw. Bothwell was grinning in red-faced mockery, and even Margaret's father looked unimpressed by a monarch who could so demean himself with the rabble.

The girl bit her lip. "They are wrong," she declared. "*He* is right. James has the rights of it. He is good, true, with a warm heart." She said it tensely, as much to herself as to Rob. It was not often that that young woman allowed herself to show so much emotion. "He seeks, I think, not only to be king to his people, but father."

"Aye!" For Rob Bruce, who did not lack fondness for James, that was something like a snort. "Father! You are right." And again he pointed.

James, laughingly waving away a supplicant friar, was hurrying forward, hands out in evident welcome and greeting. Before him, coming indeed from the vicinity of the enclosure, was a woman, a lady, leading by the hand a child, a little boy. As the King approached, the boy ran forward to meet him, a ruddy-headed sturdy child. James swept him up high, and set him sitting on his shoulder, and came on to greet the lady, slipping an arm around her waist and turning her about to return with him to the waiting courtiers. A pleasing, natural picture they made, despite Rob Bruce's tightened lips and Margaret Drummond's sudden lack of expression. The woman was Mistress Mariot Boyd, plumper than formerly but still sonsy. The child was her three-year-old son Alexander.

"He dotes on that boy," Rob said.

"He is fond of all children."

"And their mothers!"

"Perhaps. He is capable of . . . much affection."

"Aye." Sidelong he glanced at her. "And gives sure proofs of it! But he . . . he loves not all alike."

"No?"

"You, now, he regards differently."

"No doubt."

"Differently from any and all others, I think."

She said nothing.

"Always he returns to you. Other women he pursues, enjoys. You he comes back to."

"He comes back to her also, does he not? To Mistress Boyd."

"Differently."

"Differently, yes—because *I* ensure it so! Because I act differently from Mariot Boyd. Only that, perhaps."

"No . . ." Unhappily Rob shook his head. "It is more than that . . ."

There was no time for further exchange. James, with the child and Mariot, had reached the royal box.

"Ha, Margaret!" the King called out. "See whom we have here. Does he not, like his father, grow ever more handsome?"

"He is a fine boy, Your Grace. Mistress Boyd is to be congratulated." The girl managed to keep her voice steady.

James grinned. "She chose a good sire, see you!" He set down little Alexander. "One day this one will serve the realm bravely, I warrant. No sign of Gray, my lords."

"What do you expect, Sire?"

"I expect Andrew Gray! He is no friend of mine—but at least he is no craven. Like some others!"

"No fool either, Highness!" Drummond added.

James came over to Rob, who still stood with Margaret. "I am minded to show these good folk some of the ploys we learned in the Highlands, Rob. At Mingary," he declared. "Let us have a young tree cut down, and trimmed. A caber, they named it. To toss. Let us show skill outdoing brute strength. A stone to cast, also—find us stones of the right weight, to pitch. Then we might have some swording, Highland fashion. We learned many new things up there in the Isles, Margaret."

"So I have heard, Sire. And some things that are not so new, I think?"

He met her glance. "Aye. Perhaps. They are a notable people, different from ourselves, but nothing inferior. I gained much from them."

"And lost something also, did you not?" She lowered her voice to a mere murmur. "Some say that you lost your heart."

He considered her for a moment, and his glance slid over to Rob Bruce before he replied. "Not so," he said, shaking his head. "That was not possible. For my heart was already lost." There was no lowering of voice there.

Again their eyes met.

Muttering something, Rob went in search of stones and saplings.

Margaret moved to reach out and lightly touch the red head of the little boy as he ran past. "Mistress Boyd," she called out.

"You have a fine son. Guard him well . . . lest I steal him from you!"

James looked at her very thoughtfully.

A noise of shouting, more purposeful than the generality of the noise, chatter and laughter, drew all eyes away towards the northeast. Then a trumpet neighed its haughty challenge. Above the heads of the crowd, coming up from the lower ground in the direction of the Forth, appeared the helmets and nodding plumes of a body of mounted men, a banner flying above them. It did not seem to be a very large group, but it had a tight-knit and purposeful appearance. The banner showed a white rampant lion on a blood-red background.

James drew a long breath. "My Lord of Gray, at last!" he murmured, to no one in particular. "Here is . . . a reckoning!"

Gray, superbly mounted and clad in full armour inset and chased with gold, his plumes of red and white rising above the crest that surmounted his great helm, reined up his heavy white war-horse and bowed slowly, formally, from the saddle. He did not dismount, and briefly waved back the esquire who jumped down to assist him. Behind him, led by his standard-bearer and trumpeter-herald, some twenty steel-clad horsemen, armed to the teeth, pressed sweating mounts close, watchful, unsmiling. Thousands of eyes considered them intently.

"I came at your royal summons, Sire," Gray announced, with his twisted smile on lips that showed so strangely red against his black beard.

"I rejoice to see it, my lord," James answered affably. "Although with fewer men than I had looked to see!"

"Men are costly, Sire. I believe that I have brought a sufficiency. For a wapinschaw."

"M'mmm. Perhaps. Yet did I not hear that you had four hundred, at Boat of Cambus there?"

"You did? Boat of Cambus is too far, I swear, to see such things clearly, Your Grace! My modest company was . . . much thronged by all the countryside flocking to your wapinschaw. It was such base rabble that was seen, no doubt."

"Aye. No doubt," the King accepted dryly. "But it is of no matter. It is yourself, my lord, whose presence I sought – not your men, whatever their number. I am right well pleased to have you here, sir."

Gray's steel-gauntleted hand stroked at his beard. "Your Grace is too kind," he said, but without conviction. "My leal service is ever yours, of course. But ... how else may I serve you?"

"Did my courier not tell you?" It was James's turn to smile. "You can serve us all, my friend, now that you are here — entertain us all, this fine day. You are namely as a fighter, a warrior, not least at the tourney. With a lance, they say, few are your equal. You must let us see your knightly prowess, my lord."

Gray normally had excellent control of his features. But now as he glanced from the King over to where Bothwell and Drummond stood, and more especially on to Lyle, there was momentary doubt, question, indecision on his dark long-chinned face. "You flatter me," he said.

"That remains to be seen. I have a champion here. A knight who shall be nameless, but of renown sufficient to meet the Lord of Gray. Will you break a lance my lord, with this, the King's champion? For our ... delectation?"

Gray's eyes narrowed. "This is ... all?" he demanded.

"To be sure. From so doughty a fighter it will be sufficient, I warrant."

"And this knight, Sire? You say he is of sufficient renown to meet me. But is he sufficiently skilled? I will not be mocked with any fumbler. He who fights Andrew Gray must be a proven master." That was harshly stated.

"You have the King's word," James said shortly.

The other inclined his head. "Very well, Your Grace. And the prize?"

"Never fear. The prize will be as adequate. That I assure you also."

"So be it. When is this contest to be run?"

"So soon as you are rested and refreshed, my lord. There is no call for haste. Of time there is plenty. Food and drink, likewise. Your nephew, my Lord Lyle, has his pavilion pitched. It will serve you, no doubt. Aught that you require, command it."

Nodding, Gray consented to be aided down from his great war-horse, heavy armour clanking.

Within minutes the entire concourse was humming with the news, with exclamation and speculation. My Lord of Gray, the most notable jouster in the land, was to fight with some unknown knight. A bold knight indeed, for not only was Gray a most skilful and seasoned champion whom no one could recollect having lost a fight in recent times — he was a savage, almost vicious fighter also, his worsted opponents by no means always escaping with their lives, only games as these tourneys were supposed to be. Gray, his passions roused, was a killer. The tension and excitement mounted, in consequence.

Who was this bold fellow that the King had found? The question swept all that breezy upland place. An Englishman, perhaps? Some foreigner anyway, unaware of Gray's reputation? Was it someone whom the King hated, and would destroy? Although was not Gray himself thought to be the King's enemy, hand-in-glove with Bell-the-Cat? It was all most strange. Could the King hope that both would kill the other? Or was this champion some paladin indeed . . .?

James was at his gayest — and very busy. He personally arranged everything in the lists to his own satisfaction. He selected and tested lances, surveyed the ground, placed heralds, stewards and markers. Deliberately or otherwise he did not go near the royal box until Gray's esquire came to announce that his lord was ready and awaited the King's command. Then, summoning trumpeters to sound a prolonged flourish, he mounted the master of ceremonies' dais and in ringing tones himself declared the details of the contest. All knew the Lord Gray's fame, he said, but none save himself knew the identity of the knight who would ride against him. He was satisfied that he would give a good account of himself, however — so much so that he was content to call him the King's champion. The Lady Margaret Drummond would be queen of this tourney, and would he hoped, reward the victor suitably. Let the best man win!

Amidst the clamour of the crowd, James hurried to the royal box, Rob Bruce as ever at his heels. All questions as to the identity of his champion and his chances against Gray he turned aside. Only to Margaret did he address himself.

"I have waited long for this day," he said. His voice was low-pitched, but there was no hiding the excitement behind it. "You, I think, love the Lord Gray little more than I do? Do not pray for him, at the least! If he should win, there is a golden-tipped lance at Stirling for his prize. I have sent for it."

"And if your champion wins?"

"I beseech you to be . . . kinder."

Searchingly she looked at him. "What strange game is this you play, James?" she asked. "Who is this paladin?"

"A man having a score to settle with Andrew Gray — an old score. It is my hope that my lord will find his match, at last!"

"But . . ."

"See you, I must go speak with him. There are matters to discuss. I shall observe the contest from closer at hand. From the lists. It may be that I can aid my champion . . ."

"James — you will not be foolish? Unwise?"

"What is wisdom, but to grasp opportunity when it offers? To choose the right course, before not afterwards? And who may surely judge? Wisdom, I swear, is a craven business. I distrust wisdom and wise men." He lightly touched her hand. "I trust God, and Saint Ninian. Adieu, my dear."

With only Rob in attendance, James hurried down through the press to the rows of colourful pitched tents and canopies of his lords, knights and captains. Without pausing or any exchange, he strode straight to his own great red-and-gold pavilion under the streaming tressured Lion of Scotland.

"None enters here — of any sort. None, you understand?" he jerked to the double guards at the doorway.

Within was only the Armour-Bearer, waiting.

"You have all ready?" the King demanded.

"Aye, Sire. But I have neither crest nor plume for the helm . . ."

"None is required, man. Such are for display, for recognition. I seek neither — only victory. I have tested the lances. What of the battle-axe? The sword?"

"Here, Your Grace. The best and truest. Right for weight and for your reach."

"Good." James took the long-handled battle-axe to try the feel of it, swinging it this way and that. "I pray Saint Ninian this may be little required," he muttered. "I never liked this butcher's tool!" Then he picked up the great two-handed sword. It was entirely plain and not quite so large as Bruce's famous brand which Rob was wont to carry for the King. "Aye, this will serve. It balances well. Now — aid me into this harness."

A suit of jet black armour lay there on a trestle, severely plain, untouched by emblem, chasing or inlay. Strangely menacing, almost ominous, it seemed, in that colourful place — helm, gorget, cuirass, gauntlets, greaves and sabbatons, all sable, sombre, stark.

As James was being aided and buckled into it all, Rob Bruce spoke, slowly.

"I know well, Sire, that no words of mine will halt you in this undertaking. But if not for your own sake, then for the sake of your realm and your friends, remember that you are King — that if you fall, war and death will assuredly stalk this land. Your friends will suffer . . ."

"I do not forget it, Rob."

"Then if Gray seems to be besting you, Sire — as God knows he may! — yield you, reveal yourself, while there is yet time. The man is a devil. He would kill as he has killed before."

"You rate my prowess but modestly, man!"

"I rate your life, Sire, above all!"

"Aye, Rob — no doubt. I shall not forget. But there are occasions when a man must act the man — even though he be a king!" James sought to adjust the chain round his loins so that the metal taces of the armour did not press it too sorely. "This gorget, see you — it sits but awkwardly," he added, stretching his neck. "Can you ease it . . .?"

Presently as the great jousting helm was being fitted, totally enclosing the King in black steel, a loud shout arose from the crowd. One of the guards at the door called in that the Lord Gray had appeared, mounted and ready, at the entry to the lists, with his attendants. A flourish of his bugle-horn amplified this announcement with its strident challenge.

"We shall not keep him long waiting," James boomed, through his visor. "Is my mount ready?"

"Aye, Sire. Your own war-horse Sirius, stands armoured behind the tent, here."

"No, no — not Sirius. All know Sirius as the King's horse. Some other. But a stout beast . . ."

"Mine, Sire — use my roan," Bruce suggested. "He will carry you well."

"Your beast is well known also. Some other less kenspeckle brute. Quickly, Rob . . ."

So presently, led by an ordinary man-at-arms, the King of Scots rode out into the sight of his people, mounted on a heavy bay charger of no particular merit, wholly enclosed in black and nondescript armour, with no banner nor blazon nor crest to identify him, nor so much as a trumpeter to herald his appearance. No shouts of acclaim greeted his entry on the scene, but rather an excited buzzing as of a hive of bees disturbed, as folk stared and debated and wondered.

Since Gray, under his banner and supported by his attendants, had taken up his stance at the near end of the lists, James must needs pace his way the entire length of the tilting-ground, the target of all eyes. Stiffly upright in his saddle, turning neither to left nor right, nor even glancing towards the royal box, he rode. A notable silence gradually settled upon the whole great concourse.

The starter's bugle-horn blew loud and clear. Raising their lances, the two contestants trotted their cumbrous mounts out from opposite ends of the lists, to pull up in the centre, a few yards apart, and bow stiffly towards each and then towards the royal box and thronged galleries. Lord Gray looked magnificent. Over his richly chased armour he wore a surcoat of his white rampant lion on red. His shield was similarly emblazoned, as were the trappings of his great white war-horse. His helm, gleaming with gold inlay and circled by a coronet, was surmounted by his brilliantly-painted anchor crest, and above tossed horse-hair plumes of red and white. In contrast, his anonymous opponent, dark, sober, wholly unadorned even to the horse-armour, seemed grim and forbidding indeed.

If the black knight's sternly functional appearance had a marked effect on the crowd, it assuredly made no daunting impression on Andrew Gray. Sounding hollowly from his visored helm, his voice was mocking, haughty.

"How rash a man are you, sirrah?" he demanded. "I would not soil my lance and steel on you, save for the King's word – and he is rash enough, in truth!"

"You think so, my lord?" James had no need to disguise his voice; the enclosing steel did that for him. "Crow not too soon, lest you prove the rash man!"

"Insolent!" Gray snapped. "You shall pay for those words."

"We shall see who pays, my lord – and for what!"

Wheeling their mounts around, without further exchange they trotted back to their respective ends of the lists. Each raised his lance arm high.

In the royal box, Margaret Drummond lifted a hand to wave a kerchief. And again the bugle-horn sounded.

As though jerked down by the same hand the two lances dropped to the couching position. Two pairs of spurs dug fiercely into the horses' flanks. Stooping low over their lance-butts, the contestants hurtled to the onset.

185

They made an impressive charge of it. Admittedly they did not gallop. No horses which could carry that weight of steel, in addition to their riders, could have risen to a gallop. But their massive lumbering canter had its own impressiveness. The entire arena seemed to shake and quiver under the beat of huge hooves. Sods flying, necks arched, nostrils flaring, trappings streaming, they pounded straight for each other.

Through the slit in his visor, teeth gritted, James eyed his oncoming adversary. The initial impact was of vital importance, whatever its immediate results. Even though the contest might not end there and then, that first blow might grievously shake, even part-stun, one of the riders, as well as have a bad effect on a horse, making it less manageable thereafter. Success here depended on adroit horsemanship, exact timing, resilient carriage, and the most skilful use of both lance and shield.

In those all-important few seconds, James never for a moment let his gaze leave Gray's bent right arm and the gauntlet that gripped the lance. Rigid as it seemed, that arm's least movement could change all, demanding split-second reaction from himself. Gray had chosen well, of course; he had the westering sun behind him, and its glare was no help to the younger man.

At the very last instant, with only a few yards separating them, Gray took the expected initiative – but not as anticipated. His left hand jerked across in front of him, to twitch the reins hard right, so that instead of brushing the King's mount close on its right, as had seemed to be inevitable, his white charger swung directly into James's path, even momentarily across it. At the same instant, his lance-arm extended rightwards, driving his point not upwards or downwards as might have been anticipated, but inwards in a sweeping arc from that side.

With perhaps the greatest exercise of will-power of his life, James somehow kept himself from making the automatic reaction and pulling his horse over to his own right to try to avoid the otherwise inescapable collision. Not by a fraction did he change course – with his left arm, however, he twisted his shield over to that side, to meet the lunging lance-tip.

It might have been all over in that brief first encounter. Failing to turn his opponent's course, Gray himself had fiercely to try to swing back again, to save being ridden down, part sideways-on, and bowled right over. His lance wavered somewhat in consequence. James's shield caught its tip in a jarring upward deflecting sweep — and its top quarter snapped off like a broken twig. Then the King's bay smashed into the white, with the clangour of metal, James's lance scraping a glancing blow along Gray's side and over this mount's back. The younger man himself was almost unseated by the impact. As for the other, only superb horsemanship and balance averted complete disaster. His beast staggering, and down on one foreleg, he managed somehow to save both of them. Round and away he scrabbled, however undignified he looked, keeping the horse on its feet and himself in the saddle.

James swept on. It was forty yards before he could pull up. Only then did he become aware of the excited cheering of the crowd. As far as it went, the first onset was undoubtedly his.

He made no acknowledgement of the acclaim. He knew that this first success had been negative rather than positive, Gray over-reaching himself. Here was no test of his own prowess. His opponent would not make the same mistake again.

Gray required a new lance. His esquire could fetch it out to him, or he could ride back to his starting-base to collect it. But the latter course would be something in the nature of public acknowledgement of defeat in the first course instead of a mere mishap — and Andrew Gray was not the man to concede anything of the sort. He waved imperiously for his esquire.

James sat his mount, without changing his present position. From here, at least, he had the sun in his favour and in the other's eyes.

Grabbing his new lance, Gray began to sidle round to the left. Perceiving his manœuvre, to regain the sun's advantage, James moved to counter him.

Recognising that nothing was to be gained thus, without warning Gray lowered his lance and charged, from no more than thirty yards.

The King had three choices of action. He could ride to meet him — but would attain no speed and impetus before the clash and so would be handicapped; he could seek to sidestep and evade the onset — though such would appear a feeble course; or he could stand still and meet the assault head-on. In the bare moment allowed for decision, he chose the last.

There was little time to wait. Like a thunderbolt Gray was upon him. Eschewing last-moment tricks on this occasion, the older man sought to overwhelm by sheer weight, force and momentum. With a resounding crash they met. Both lances struck squarely on shrewdly held shields with such headlong shock as to shatter each in splintering ruin half-way up their long shafts. James's arm felt as though jerked right out of joint.

That was the least of it. The white horse crashed into the King's bay. With the weight and pace behind it, inevitably it forced the stationary beast right back on its haunches. Although reeling with the impact of the lance-breaking, Gray spurred straight on, pressing his advantage. Over went the bay, toppling backwards and sideways. Desperately kicking away heavy square-toed sabbatons from stirrups, James sought to throw himself clear both of his own falling mount and of the trampling white, casting the useless lance stump from him.

Heavily he landed on all fours, overbalancing with the weight of the awkward shield still attached to his left arm. Over he rolled, jarred and bruised by the unyielding armour, away from the path of those great pounding hooves.

In the event it was not the hooves that most nearly menaced him, but Gray himself, Gray's person. His manoeuvre of over-throwing the other horse had been just too successful, for his own mount, plunging straight over the fallen beast, was caught in the latter's flailing legs. It stumbled and fell in turn, arching neck under, hurling its rider right over its head. Lord Gray crashed down almost on top of the King.

Both men knew how to fall in armour, and automatically minimised the effect. Nevertheless, both were much shaken, and for moments made little movement. Attendants began to run out towards them from the bases.

James, who had fallen much the least heavily, found his breath and his wits first, getting to his knees, staggering to his feet. Swaying, he stood above his fallen adversary. Again he did not hear the cheers of the crowd.

Both horses struggled up, seeming little or nothing the worse. Each went careering away in a different direction, with a great clanking of armour, men hurrying out to catch them. Gray got up unsteadily.

It was difficult to know with whom lay the advantage now, or who might claim this second round. But James, though his head swam, had wits enough to perceive where advantage might be gained. Since he had been first on his feet, he could presume to exercise the winner's right of choice. He waved away the attendants with the recaptured horses, making the sign that he would use the sword, and on foot. The battle-axes were still secured at the horses' saddles. He had never liked those lethal and cumbrous weapons.

Gray presumably did not object, as one of the finest swordsmen in the land. He could have sought a breathing-space, by a return to his end of the lists, but did not do so. No exchange took place between the two heavily-breathing contestants before the massive two-handed swords were brought to them, and their shields removed.

Although a sword-fight between fully armoured knights might be thought to be little more than the merest banging match, there was in fact a deal more to it than that. Hard knocks admittedly were important, but skill and knowledge had a vital part to play. While finesse would but doubtfully describe any play with a two-handed sword nearly five feet long, expertise was entirely necessary.

Gray took the initiative as always, driving in with an unlooked-for upwards thrusting stroke to James's throat almost before his esquire had stepped back after delivering the sword. The King parried it only clumsily and just in time, and caught off balance, barely recovered himself before a great swinging swipe from the left struck cuirass and gorget, shaking him grievously and forcing him down on one stiff knee. Only by awkwardly thrusting his sword's length between the legs of his advancing foe did he save himself from the vicious following forward stab to the joining between helm and gorget, which could have ended the matter there and then. Gray tripped and stumbled, and only kept his feet by driving his sword-tip into the ground and using it as prop.

Panting, the duellists faced one another like angry dogs. But tired dogs now, for the weight of steel they carried was wearing indeed.

Starting approximately even again, they attacked and defended now in more or less conventional sword-play, lunging, feinting, parrying, swinging, smiting, circling round each other seeking an opening, rushing in, jumping back – but all in slow motion, burdened as they were and handling weapons almost as long as themselves. Soon James was soaked with sweat, trembling with fatigue, muscles wearying and slowing in their responses, head dizzy and throbbing with the violent jarring impact and clangour of the blows. No doubt his opponent was in little better state.

In such contests, the winner was most frequently merely he who could remain longest on his feet in the struggle with vertigo and exhaustion. James, the younger man by nearly thirty years, almost certainly here had the advantage.

James perceived the dagger suddenly in his opponent's left hand. That Gray had just drawn it from his belt no doubt had its own significance – although the other was not greatly concerned, for fighting as they were with these long swords, they were unlikely to come close enough to use such short blades. Nevertheless, he snatched out his own dagger from its belt-sheath.

Wielding the great sword with one hand was scarcely practicable, save for brief thrusts. The drawn daggers therefore were a distinct nuisance. James was still searching in his mind for Gray's purpose in this when all too clearly and abruptly it was made evident. Suddenly, as he parried a slashing one-handed stroke, he found his own blade gripped as in a vice of iron. A vice-grip indeed fairly described the situation, The weapon in Gray's left hand was no ordinary dagger. It was much stouter, stronger, than usual, and near its haft a deep slot opened half-way across the blade, slantwise, reinforced with thicker steel. In this slot James's sword had been skilfully caught and held. Even as he stared, confounded, the other pushed in closer, running the clamp of his strange dagger down the long sword-blade. Then, two-thirds of the way down, Gray jerked his wrist with a powerful snatching motion. With a crack like a whip-lash the sword blade snapped cleanly in two. Abruptly released from the fierce grip, the King lurched backwards, the handle and a mere useless foot of broken sword in his hand.

He had heard of these sword-breakers, developed for warfare in France and the Low Countries, but never had he seen one – nor looked for such to be used at a jousting.

Gray wasted no second of his advantage. Dropping the dagger, he drove in with a sideways swipe to James's head with all his force. Caught unready, the young man could only partly parry it with his arm. The stunning blow of it on his helm all but took away his wits, and sent him reeling. Down on his knees he sank, head drooping.

That droop of head and shoulders possibly saved his life. A jabbing thrust upwards between the joints of his armour, beneath one of the overlapping flanges could have been the end of James

Stewart. And Andrew Gray was the man to make that vicious thrust. But because he was using such a lengthy sword, because his victim was down on his knees and momentarily leaning forward, the lunge could not have the required upward deflection. Instead of the vital stab under the gorget, therefore, Gray drove downwards, below the tiny steel skirt of the cuirass. Then a skilful upwards twist ran the sword-tip in behind the flange of armour and along the line of groin and hip. James knew a searing red-hot hurt, and the harsh, tearing rasp of metal on metal.

Although dazed, faint and racked with pain, the King was fully aware of what had happened. The sword's point had struck the chain which for so long he had worn round his loins, and run on along its links. He was wounded, undoubtedly — but not vitally, he thought.

In the selfsame instant he was aware of something else also. Gray's sword was now at his mercy. Throwing himself bodily forward, pain or none, he bore down suddenly with all his weight and strength on the remaining length of it, tearing it out of the wielder's grasp. Down it crashed. Awkwardly he clasped it to him as tightly as its transfixing position would allow.

Gray, himself staggering, stooped to try to retrieve his weapon. Finding this impossible he side-stepped, and swiftly looked around for the sword-breaking dagger which he had dropped. It lay on the trampled grass only a yard from the King's side. Stiffly he bent to pick it up.

James's arm reached out to encircle the other's legs. He wrenched, and down the top-heavy lord toppled like a felled tree, in the heaviest fall of the day. It was not chivalry — but James was far beyond such niceties. Little of that duel had been in the chivalric tradition, whatever the King's original intention.

Gray lay on face and stomach groaning, probably part-stunned by his own armour. The younger man found himself to be clutching in his left hand the only free weapon left in the encounter, his own dagger. Raising it high, he smashed it down, heavy hilt first, on the base of his enemy's helm where the steel lay against the nape of the neck. With a choking snort, Gray ceased his groaning, and even within his iron casing most obviously went limp.

Slowly, painfully, the world reeling and rocking around him, James got to his knees. Somehow, inch by inch, he eased and jerked the long sword out from under his cuirass, gritting his teeth at the hurt of it. Using it then as prop and support, he gradually levered his aching body on to unsteady feet. With the weary deliberation of an old man he lifted one black sabbaton, to place it heavily on the torn surcoat and rich armour of his fallen foe's back. Then he raised one arm to hold waveringly but on high the captured brand, and so stand, swaying, for dizzy moments. He was not aware, through the red mist which was all that he saw, that he was not even looking in the direction of the royal box.

In that box Margaret Drummond was on her feet, one hand convulsively clutching her breast.

James slowly let the great weapon drop. It fell from his gauntlet's relaxing grasp. Wide-legged, he took a few jerky, erratic paces, in no particular direction, and then, buckling at the knees, pitched all his length on the grass and lay still.

From the royal gallery, amidst all the clamour and exclamation, a single high wail arose, as Margaret Drummond, brushing all aside, came running down to the lists towards the prostrate victor.

11

JAMES was only vaguely aware, some time thereafter, of move-ment, jolting, and of voices which seemed to come thinly to him as through a veil and without meaning. When true consciousness returned, however, nothing of this any longer plagued him. All was quiet, and he lay still. Racked with pain and his head splitting, he nevertheless perceived at once that he was in his own chamber in Stirling Castle, the paintings on the timber ceiling familiar even though they jigged and danced somewhat. Naked he lay on his back on the great bed with its gold-fringed canopy. But he was not alone. Someone gently but persistently touched and aggra-vated the burning pain at his groin and hip, would not leave it alone. Moistening dry lips, and with a major effort of will, he turned his heavy aching head, to protest.

Margaret Drummond sat beside his bed. On a table was a bowl of steaming water and a tray of simples and medicaments. She was lightly dabbing at his wounded side, anointing it with some preparation on a cloth. Despite the scorching smart of it, the protest died on his lips.

"Margaret!" he said. At least he meant to say it, but at first no sound came. His second attempt in consequence jerked more loudly than was necessary.

The girl started, and turned to him, eyes wide with anxiety. "James! Oh . . . hush you!" A hand came to soothe his brow. "Hush you. Fear nothing. Lie still, now. All is well . . ."

"Aye," he said thickly. "I . . . you . . . well indeed." He sought to raise himself, but sank back with an ill-suppressed groan.

"Still, now — for sweet Mary's sake!" she urged him. "Care for nothing, James — but to lie still. Do I hurt you? Is it cruel pain?"

"It is my head. It opens and shuts. Like a book, I swear." Gritting his teeth, and despite her restraining hand, he sought to sit up again. He achieved only a partial rise, resting on a bruised and stiff elbow. All his body felt bruised and stiff. "How grievous is it? The wound?"

"Not deep, God be thanked. A glancing gash. But you have

lost blood. This chain saved you, the saints be praised. But there is much earth in it. In the wound. The sword must have been in the earth. It must be cleansed. It could have been . . . it could have been otherwise. A dire wound. The death of you . . ."

"Aye." Grimly James mustered the caricature of a smile. Despite the state of his head, he was fully in command of his wits, suffering no hazy transitional stage. He stared wryly at the angry red slash which slanted upwards from crutch to hip-bone. "My manhood escaped, indeed, but by a hair's breadth! The chain . . . how strange!" Again the twisted smile, at his present helpless nakedness. "'Fore God — my manhood is . . . is but a puny thing now, on any score!"

She flushed a little, and busied herself with the sponging process.

"It took this to get you to my naked bed!" he added, gasping as he lowered himself again to his pillow. "I' faith, 'tis not how . . . I would have had it!"

"Hush!" she ordered once more, this time in a different tone of voice.

"Gray?" he asked suddenly, after a moment. "What of Gray?"

"He lives," she told him briefly.

"Aye. I did but seek to stun him, at the last. But where is he? How fares he?"

"He is taken to my Lord Lyle's lodging. Sore, but with his wits recovered." She paused. "Would that he was not. Would that you had slain him!"

This was so unlike Margaret Drummond that the King raised his throbbing head again to gaze at her. "This, my dear — from you?" he exclaimed wonderingly.

"He tried to kill you. From the first. He fought like a savage and no knight. It was no fair fight. The work of an assassin, rather!"

"He fights to win, does Gray, I grant you. He near had me, more than once. It is the nature of the man."

"He would have killed you, if he could. I know it."

"Perhaps. Think you that he knew it was the King that he fought?"

"I do not know. But you were the King's Champion. That would have sufficed."

"Did any other know? Who I was?"

"*I* knew. The moment that you entered the lists."

"How did you know?"

"I cannot tell. But I did know. Something told me. And . . . I would have stopped your folly if I could!"

James lay back. "I had a bone to pick with Andrew Gray," he said slowly. "An old bone, which only I could pick. I have picked it now, and am satisfied. I believe that I bested him, there before all men. Only just, I grant you – but sufficient." He paused. "Do all now know? That it was the King who fought, and no strange knight?"

"Yes. At the end, when you fell, when I reached you. Rob Bruce also. And others. When we took off your helm, there was a great cry that it was the King. So all learned it."

"And they said . . .?"

"What matters it what they said? Hush you, James. You are talking too much. Rest. Sleep. I shall soon be done with this."

He did not sleep, of course. He did not even shut his eyes, content to watch her there, ministering to his need. He cherished even the pain that her gentle fingers caused him, glad even of his helpless nakedness beneath her eyes, unembarrassed and believing her to be no longer embarrassed. More than once a knock sounded at the door of the bed-chamber, and each time the young woman herself went to open it, and held quiet converse there before closing it again without admitting others to the bed-chamber. Margaret Drummond, it seemed, was at the moment in full command of the kingdom.

It was nearly dusk of a dull and sultry August evening that might presage thunder, the breezes of the day having died away quite. Before Margaret was satisfied that the wound was clean and its dressing adequate, the light was all but gone from the dark, small-windowed, arras-hung chamber. From the circular tower dressing-room which opened off it, she brought James a tray bearing a light meal of chicken and curds and honey, helping him to eat it in the half-dark. She even aided him with other natural requirements. Then, when she would have left him, standing over him and again bidding him sleep, he gripped her hand and held her fast.

"No, Margaret my dear – do not leave me," he pleaded. "Not now. I need you here. Stay with me. I shall not sleep, with you gone. I know it."

"You will sleep better lacking me . . ."

"No. Do not go. I shall but fret for you, I swear. Fret and toss. Your place is here. By my side. I need you."

"My place . . .!" she murmured, sighing a little. Then she nodded. "Very well. For a short while, perhaps. But you must be quiet. Do not talk."

"Yes, yes . . ."

She sat again, and he took her hand. For long they sat, fingers intertwined, silent, while the night deepened around them in that great fortress on top of its towering rock. Out beyond the small west-facing window, the black line of the Highland hills faded into the gloom.

At length he spoke. "I owe much gratitude to Andrew Gray, I think. He only has achieved this, for me!"

She did not answer.

"For long years I have awaited this night," he went on. "I have dreamed of it, a thousand times. But never dreamed that it would be thus — come about so, and myself little better than a helpless babe!"

"For all your dreams you have not lacked other partners for your bed-chamber," she reminded him quietly.

"That is true. I . . . I have a great need of women. But my need for you is different. You I have needed not just because you are a woman. Margaret Drummond I have needed, longed for, so much more deeply than for all the others."

"Because, unlike the others, she has not given herself to you. Has not fulfilled your dreams.",

"No, it is not that. Or only a little, perhaps. You, Margaret, my heart has wanted. Not merely my mind and body. Can you not understand? My dreams of you have been sweet pain, not just desire. Sore, fruitless dreams. So often I have asked myself why? Why?"

"Perhaps it is because I also have my dreams," she said slowly.

Swiftly he took her up. "You do? Dreams in which . . . in which James Stewart, even, figures?"

"Sometimes," she admitted. "I will not lie to you."

He gripped her hand more tightly. "Margaret! What is *your* dream?"

"My dreams are my own, James. Do not grudge me them." She rose. "Lie back, now. You must rest. I shall go, for you but excite yourself."

"Do not go, Margaret. Not now. You must not go. Why should you go? I promise not to talk if you will but stay."

"Better that I go, James . . ."

"Why?" he persisted, with almost fevered urgency. "Is it for your good name that you think? Surely this night at least it is safe, with me stricken and helpless?"

"My good name!" Almost there was a smile of sorts in her voice. "No — not that. My good name is long gone. Most of your Court, I swear, believe me to have been your paramour these many years!"

"Dear God — you say so? *You*, who have always denied me! You cannot be right in this, Margaret!"

"It is true. Long have I known it. But it is not important."

"I think it is," he said, staring away. "But . . . why must you go now, then?"

"It is best for both of us, I think."

"No. I need you tonight. As never before. Does that mean nothing? And my love for you. Does that likewise count for nothing?"

"You . . . you love me, James? Of a truth?"

"You, and you only, my dear. Now, and always. I have loved, truly loved, only you. Let Ninian and all the saints be witness."

"And the Highland girl? Marsala MacIan?"

"We were close, yes. In spirit. We understood each other . . ."

"There was more than that between you, was there not? Mariot Boyd and the others I can make myself accept. But this other was different, was she not? This talk of spirit, of closeness. You are not the man to let spirit suffice, in a woman, James!"

"Aye. We lay together, Margaret. Once. That last night. Why deny it? We learned much from each other, Marsala MacIan and I. But not love. Her love, you see, was for a dead man! Mine for . . . another."

There was silence for long moments. Then the girl spoke. "For you, then, loving and bedding are things wholly apart? For me they are one."

He swallowed. "What . . . what do you know of love?" he demanded, tensely.

"Sufficient. Sufficient to know that it is more sorrow than joy, more pain than laughter."

He moistened his lips. "What man taught you that?"

"Who but James Stewart?" she answered, almost wearily, as though laying down a burden long carried.

"God . . . be . . . thanked!" he breathed. "God in His heaven be praised!" Somehow he was sitting up, his arms outstretched to her.

Murmuring she pressed him back to his pillow. He did not loosen his grasp of her, but held her leaning over him.

"You love me, then?" he panted. "After all? We are one, you and I, despite . . . despite . . ."

"Hush, my dear — oh, hush you! I am a fool. I should not have said it. You are sick, fevered. This is folly."

"But it is truth? Your heart truly is mine?"

"Yes. Oh, yes. I have loved you for long. From the first. Since we were children, I think. But . . . let that suffice, I beseech you. No more of it now, my heart. You must let me go. Lest you do yourself further hurt, a lasting hurt . . ."

"You cannot go now, woman! Now that we have found each other. At last. There could be no hurt, no pain, to equal that. Can you not see it?" He was trembling now, shaking with the strength of his emotion that was fighting his bodily weakness.

The young woman perceived that there was probably truth in what he said; that she would do more harm by going than by staying. "As you will," she said. "I shall stay. But if you love me, lie quiet. Have mercy on your poor head. Do not further rouse yourself. It is to your ill . . ."

"What matters a sore pate when my heart is bursting for joy?" James demanded. "Would you have me lie like a felled tree when the gates of paradise itself are opening wide for me? Would you?"

She smiled. Low but warmly she said it. "I would have my lover a man, a whole man, as soon as may be . . . and no felled tree! That is what I would have, James Stewart!"

"Aye," he agreed, with a sigh. "So be it. God willing, you shall. And quickly!"

She sat down again beside him. Only for a few minutes was he content to lie silent. Soon he was turned urgently to her again.

"Margaret, my heart — was ever a man so plagued and bedevilled? To have, after years, won the woman he has loved and longed for, to his bed. And then to be unable to . . . to . . ."

"Do you complain? When it was your inability, your weakness, that alone brought me here? Be content, James. You have achieved enough . . . for one night."

"Content!" For an injured, fevered man his snort had considerable power. "How can you so much as name the word! To lie here helpless, with you so close . . ."

"Yet you will not let me go."

"No, by God! That were worse! How can I make you understand? I am a man. Your every part and particle and member cries out to me. To have and hold you. To possess you. Knowing you now to be mine. For you, a woman, no doubt it is otherwise. You cannot know the hurt of it . . ."

"You think, James, that women are so different? That we know nothing of desire and need? That men alone know passion?"

"No. But it is not the same, I think. Women are more gently made . . ."

"Are you sure? Perhaps we but better control ourselves? Think you that now I, who have found my love equally with you, should be so free of the same strife that besets you? With you lying there before me so . . . and, and myself neither sick nor enfeebled!" This last was little more than a whisper.

He drew a long quivering breath, but did not dare trust himself to answer her.

The quiet resumed, although there was little of peace to it.

Presently Margaret went over to open the door and speak at some length to whoever guarded it. When she came back, James questioned her almost suspiciously.

"I but sent for my bed, my clothing, to be put into the dressing-room here," she told him. "From my father's lodging in the Mar Tower."

He sighed with something nearer to satisfaction, but made no other comment.

"Rob Bruce sees to all," she went on. "Dear Rob Bruce."

"Do not find him too dear, I counsel you!" the King warned her. "You are mine — and I can be jealous!"

"I am not yours . . . yet!" she asserted, but a little wearily rather than tartly.

"I shall make you so, then. Once and for always. We shall be wed."

The young woman did not offer any remark upon that statement. Indeed she turned away from him and moved over to the pale void of the window.

"We shall be wed," the King repeated. "Just as soon as I may contrive it. You shall be Queen Margaret. The fourth such in

Scotland. And none, I vow, more worthy. Even my mother! Even Margaret the Saint—who was not all saintly, as I have heard!"

"James," she said from the window, her back to him. "Why deceive yourself? Since *I* am not deceived. You know that you cannot marry me, make me Queen. It is not possible."

"If it is the King's will, it is more than possible. It shall be."

"Your will is not enough, my heart, in this. You know it. The realm must be served. The realm requires that you wed a princess, a king's daughter, not Lord Drummond's daughter. The Queen must be . . . very different from Margaret Drummond."

"The Queen *shall* be Margaret Drummond—if the Queen is to be wife to James Stewart!"

She shook her head, sighing. "I fear not, James. The crown is not for such as me."

"It was for your ancestress. For Annabel Drummond, wife to my great-great-grandsire, King Robert the Third."

"A weak king, and a queen whom none respected. None would wish to see the like again." She turned and came back to his bedside. "It will not serve, my dear. Folly to shut our eyes to it. The nobles, the Council, would never countenance our marriage. Even now your ambassadors are in Spain to treat for a marriage with a princess there, an Infanta, are they not . . .?"

"It is but a move in the game of statecraft. To threaten the English with a Spanish alliance, so that Henry may be more cautious, less bold against my borders."

"Perhaps. But marry Margaret Drummond and you can make no more such moves in the realm's game. When you marry it will be to ally some other realm to Scotland. You know it. The Privy Council will insist upon it."

"And you, *you* would have me wed some unknown woman for that! You would advocate such travesty of marriage! For me?"

She sat down abruptly at his side. "God knows I do not! But . . . such is the marriage of kings, the saints pity them! It is ever so."

"Not this king . . ."

"James—as you love me, do not be blind! You know even better than do I the forces which will mass against a marriage with such as me. The Council will demand a royal match, to a king's daughter. And the lords will not accept a daughter of Drummond, as Queen. Of all the lords, my father is one of the least. He was but a simple laird whom your father raised up. Against the wishes of his Council. Of ancient lineage but little standing—John, first Lord Drummond! Think you that all Scotland's proud earls will bend the knee to his daughter, as Queen?"

"They shall bend their stiff knees to my wife, whatsoever her name, by the Mass!" he swore hotly.

It was the very violence of his assertion that brought the girl to her senses, reminded her of his state. "Oh, I am sorry, James—sorry!" she cried, leaning close, to peer down into his face in the gloom. "Fool that I am to be talking so. Upsetting you. Forgive me! There shall be no more of it, I promise . . ."

Her assurances were choked off as the man's arm encircled her neck. He pulled her down to him. His strength was sufficient for that, at any rate—and she did not struggle overmuch in resistance. Their lips met.

At least she kept her promise about further talk. Words, apart from murmured incoherences, were suddenly unnecessary, unimportant.

Exhausted, in time James lay back, the girl on her knees at his bedside. For long they remained thus, each with a strange mixture of emotional frustration and contentment. Presently the man was shivering, with great uncontrollable shudders.

Alarmed, Margaret covered him up with bed-clothes. "Sweet Mary—it is as I feared! Now your are truly fevered, worsened. Oh, James—I should not have stayed."

When the trembling spasms not only continued but grew worse, she hurried through to the dressing-room and brought her own bed-coverings to heap over him. But still he was racked by great shakings, so that even his teeth chattered.

At last, her heart wrung for him, she stood up. With quick fingers she loosened the fastenings of her high collar and the lacing at the back of her gown. The heavy embroidered velvet fell to her feet, and she stepped out of its folds. She kicked away her shoes, and peeled off the woven hose that she wore. Then, clad only in her brief linen shift, she turned back the bedding, and climbed in beside the shivering man. In her strong rounded arms she took him, to hold him close, pressing her warm vital body against his, stroking his damp hair, crooning over him.

"Bless you . . . heart of . . . my heart," he got out, from between clenched teeth. "Is this . . . heaven? Or hell?"

"Hush, hush, my sweeting," she whispered. "No talk. No words, any more. Lie still. In my arms. I shall be your warmth. Your strength. Lie still, now. Rest. Shut those eyes. Not a word . . ."

"If . . . you will promise . . . not to leave me . . . this night?"

"I shall not leave you," she agreed. Gently she felt for and re-arranged the lie of the chain at his groin, so that it did not press too grievously into either of them. "There, my love — rest."

Seldom can any man have less desired sleep with his mind. But James's weakened weary body was otherwise inclined. Gradually the shuddering convulsions lessened, dwindled in intensity and frequency, and presently died away. His breathing deepened, and though he twitched intermittently, the young woman could feel his tensed body relaxing. When his hands sought to wander, she took them in her own and held them, stroking, soothing.

In time, then, he slept — if time had any relevance or substance that strange night.

For long thereafter Margaret lay, eyes wide but unseeing. She did not sleep before dawn was lightening that small fortress window.

12

It was nearly noon next day before James awakened — to find himself alone in his room, and wondering how much of the excitements of the previous night had been dream, how much actuality? His fever had quite gone, but he was still weak and limp — although not so limp that he was not quickly shouting for the Lady Margaret. Rob Bruce answered his summons. Brushing aside his friend's solicitous enquiries for his health, the King demanded querulously to know the young woman's whereabouts and to have her sent to him forthwith. Rob informed him that she had in fact been up betimes, had had her bedding removed from the dressing-room back to her father's quarters in the Mar Tower, and had been seen passing down from the castle to the town on foot, with her maid — no doubt about the necessary domestic business of providing for her father's table.

Appalled at such swift and unsuitable descent to humdrum and prosaic matters from the romantic and dramatic heights which they had shared, James exclaimed over the inconsistency of women, their lack of sensibility and judgement. He ordered the lady to be brought back to her monarch's side the moment she returned from her ridiculous merchandising. Rob expressionlessly agreed to transmit the royal command, but pointed out that if His Grace was sufficiently rested and recovered to receive callers of any sort, certain matters of state were urgently requiring consideration. He would humbly advise that the regal toilet be attended to — since this was most patently called for — and thereafter, for instance, of the many who awaited audience outside, the Chancellor, the Earl of Bothwell, and the Bishop of Aberdeen be admitted. To say nothing of the physicians.

Frowning, even groaning, at the thought of such interviews, James, after an initial irascible refusal to see any of them, agreed that perhaps in the circumstances he ought to have just a word with Chancellor Home. Also with Patrick Bothwell. As for the good Bishop Elphinstone, he suppose that he could not deny him audience — though it must be short. And there was to be no wearisome and presumptuous reproach and chiding on the subject of his yesterday's jousting – he would not have it. That must be understood before any of them were allowed in. As for the physicians, they could betake themselves off; he would have none of their old wives' nonsense. Partly as a reaction to his late father's morbid preoccupation with the whole tribe of leeches and apothecaries, James, like many another young man accustomed to rude good health, had the utmost scorn for both those who practised the healing arts and those who sought their ministrations.

So presently the stiff and reserved Lord Home, who had succeeded the late Argyll as acting Chancellor and grown the more severe in consequence, the hearty Bothwell, and the gently shrewd Elphinstone, now Lord Privy Seal, were admitted to the chamber, to be received by their liege lord propped up on pillows and wrapped in a furred bedrobe. James gave them neither time nor opportunity to even obliquely deliver the reproofs which he was well aware must be on the tips of their tongues, but dismissing all courteous queries as to his wellbeing, plunged straight into his own enquiries regarding the prevailing political situation. Was there any word of Angus and Buchan? Had Angus still his young brother Ross in his hands? Had Henry of England's levies crossed the Border? What of that fox Lennox?

Bothwell, as ever, did most of the talking. Angus had not stirred from Tantallon Castle, where he still entertained the Duke of Ross. Buchan was said to have retired across the Border near Berwick. The English host had not moved northwards. Lennox was on his way to Stirling, no doubt to congratulate his King on having returned just in time to preserve the peace of the realm. Gray was lying in the Lord Lyle's lodging here in the town, a sick and angry man – but still dangerous. He would be safer lacking his head, in Bothwell's opinion. And the opportunity was notably convenient.

Home made concurring noises.

The Bishop mildly suggested that less drastic courses could be adequate to the occasion.

James began to nod his own head vigorously – and hastily desisted at the hurt of the process. "If I had desired Gray's death, I could have achieved it yesterday in the lists," he declared. Which was not strictly true perhaps, although it sounded well. "His death now could be more dangerous to my throne than his life, I do believe. He has over many powerful relatives and friends. Moreover, since yesterday, my ill-will at my lord of Gray is much assuaged — my bone picked. Perhaps kindness, my lords, would serve us better at this juncture — and hurt him more!"

"As well be kind to a viper!" Bothwell grunted.

"Or to Angus! Or Buchan!" Home added, frowning. "They as much merit it."

"Ha! You are right!" James agreed, deliberately taking the other up wrongly. "These two, perhaps, also. This, I swear, is a time for kindness, for goodwill towards all. The realm is saved, the Highlands much pacified, the people know who rules in Scotland . . . and I, gentlemen, have found me a wife! Is it not an auspicious occasion?"

All three stared at him, with varying expressions.

"I have decided to wed the Lady Margaret Drummond," he told them swiftly. "To emulate my forebear, Robert the Third. She is a true and lovely lady. She will make a noble Queen."

"But, Sire — this is impossible!"

"Your Grace — what folly is this? You cannot be serious . . .?"

"Rest assured that I am serious, my lords. It is my will, my royal will and decision."

"But . . . but . . ."

"Margaret Drummond is fair. And, and a good lass, no doubt," Bothwell exclaimed. "All know your devotion to her. But she cannot be Queen."

"Cannot", James cried, jerking forward, and then gasping and closing his eyes with the pain of it. He sank back — but his voice was still strong. "Cannot is not a word to use to princes, my lord of Bothwell! I shall wed whom I choose."

"But your choice, Sire, must be amongst princesses. A king's daughter. That is meet. And necessary. For the realm's sake. You know it."

"I know that I shall wed the woman of my heart. Margaret Drummond."

"Your Grace — even now we treat with the King of Spain, for one of his daughters . . ."

"A mere device. Pantomime. For Henry of England's benefit. We do not even know if Ferdinand has such a daughter, unwed! I marry no such spectres!"

"The Emperor Maximilian's daughter . . ." Home put in.

"A mere child—and promised to Spain's son."

"There have been younger queens. And the Prince of Spain is weakly. Elphinstone, here, says that she is both clever and comely."

"I tell you, I'll have none of them! I wed Margaret Drummond."

"Your Highness," William Elphinstone intervened quietly, his first remark in this sudden controversy. "Your royal decision must prevail. None may gainsay you. And your weal and felicity, in marriage as in all else, must be all our wish. But you must be informed of all the circumstances, that your decision be right, justified . . ."

"I know my own mind. Aye, and heart, my Lord Bishop."

"Very well, my son. I counsel that we leave this issue meantime, while we consider the other more urgent matter of the embassy. Which indeed may affect the other also . . ."

"Embassy? Which embassy? You mean, to Spain? Bishop Blackadder's mission? You yourself, who advised it, know the worth of that!"

"Not so, Sire. Much otherwise. A new embassy. To you, here. Which but arrived this morning. You have not yet been told of it? It is from Margaret of Burgundy. She has sent The O'Donnell, Prince and Earl of Tyrconnel in Ireland, to Your Grace. To solicit your aid."

"She has? The Duchess Dowager of Burgundy—the late Edward of England's sister? What is this?" James, head or none, was leaning forward again. "Why have I not been told?"

"The Lady Margaret said that you were not to be disturbed!" Bothwell pointed out, grinning.

"They have been but a few hours here," Home said. "O'Donnell talks of a treaty. With the Emperor. Maximilian is the Duchess of Burgundy's stepson. They do say that she leads him like any child. O'Donnell says that the Emperor would reconsider the matter of his daughter and the Infanta of Spain, to wed yourself."

"A treaty? Between the Emperor and Scotland?" James broke in. "Such could only be aimed against England. I'll wager the Duchess's fine Fleming is in this! The man whom she calls her nephew—and who is either the base-born foundling Perkin Warbeck, or the Prince Richard of York, who should be King of England."

206

"Aye," Elphinstone sighed. "That is the way of it. She desires your recognition of him she calls the Prince of England. And more than that. She has sent him to Ireland where he gathers support — or so says The O'Donnell — and but awaits your permission for him to come to Scotland."

"He would come here?"

"For reasons most patent. Here he would raise his standard against Henry. The standard of ancient York against usurping Tudor. He would bring a sword, to be pointed at England's heart — but to be wielded by *you*, my son. A heavy price to pay for even an Emperor's daughter!"

It was James's turn to stare at them all, wordless.

"O'Donnell says that the Irish will rise for him," Bothwell went on. "And France is in the alliance — King Charles has given the man a prince's guard-of-honour, commanded by our Scots Lord Monypenny. The Emperor speaks with a powerful voice."

"But it is not from France, nor yet Burgundy or the Empire that the blow is to be struck!" the Bishop pointed out. "It is from here, Scotland."

"Any other attempt must run the gauntlet of Henry's ships," Bothwell reminded.

"It could be the downfall of the treacherous Tudor," Home declared.

James said nothing for a few moments, and then sank back on his pillow. "I must think on this," he said slowly. "Think deep. Here is food for thought indeed. My lords — I thank you. Leave me now. I am tired. Convey my greetings to The O'Donnell. Show him all courtesies. As befits a descendant of the High Kings of Ireland. I shall see him, and you, anon."

"There is the matter of Lennox, when he reaches Stirling, Your Grace?" Home asked. "Shall I ward him, for trial. On treason again. We have his letters to Angus, intercepted . . ."

"Indeed no, my lord. Mercy, did I not say? Kindness. Such will serve us best. And for greater rogues than poor bumbling Lennox. But, God ha' mercy — can all such not await tomorrow at least, when I shall be myself again? A truce now, for sweet Ninian's sake!"

As the three Privy Councillors moved to the door, the King raised his voice again.

"My Lord Bishop — one word with you, if you please. On a, a matter of the spirit."

William Elphinstone sat down on the chair which Margaret had used, and his keen blue eyes considered the young man quizzically and yet fondly, sympathetically. "Be at peace, my son," he said. "Lie still. There is naught that calls for haste. I am an old done man, with all the time in the world for my small activities . . ."

"You are the busiest man in my whole realm, my Lord Privy Seal, I do believe. And the wisest," James gave back. "Would there were a dozen of you in Scotland. Or even two!" He frowned. "This Warbeck? Is he what he claims, or what the Duchess claims? Or is he false?"

"If I could answer that I were the wisest man in your realm indeed! Or in Christendom, I think! God, and perhaps some woman in Tournay, alone knows whether he is the young Duke of York whom Richard Crookback thought to have smothered twelve years ago in London Tower, or someone less loftily conceived but of great ambitions."

"The Duchess Margaret believes him to be her brother's son. And Charles of France has accepted him, it seems."

"The Duchess is a woman of great passion, with few scruples. Like other Plantagenets. Her hatred of Henry Tudor is great enough, I think, to affect her judgement. Or her policies! She also supported Lambert Simnel, as the other of the poor murdered princes – who was proved an impostor. He was but a rod with which to beat Henry. I fear that you cannot wholly trust the Duchess Margaret. Such was my estimate of her, you'll mind, when two years ago you sent me to her Court."

James nodded, rubbing his chin. In one of his first attempts in his search for allies with whom to counter the intrigues of England's Henry Seventh, he had sent the Bishop on a tour of certain European capitals, ostensibly looking for a bride for the King of Scots. Now, it seemed, the position was reversed. The Princess Margaret of England, sister of the murdered Edward Fourth, of Richard Third his evil brother, and aunt of the two unfortunate princes believed to have been smothered in the Tower of London, had married the Duke of Burgundy and was now Governess of the Low Countries for her stepson, the Emperor Maximilian. That she lived for revenge on the usurping Tudors, and the restoration of the House of Plantagenet to the English throne, there could be no doubt. But she was a proud, shrewd and effective woman, and if she declared herself as satisfied that this Perkin was indeed her nephew, the Duke of York, younger of the two supposedly murdered princes, her friends and allies were hardly in a position to say that they doubted it. And it was said that the youth had a notably Plantagenet look to him, and a royal charm of manner.

"Charles of France must believe her."

"Charles of France is at perpetual war with Henry, who claims so much of his realm," Elphinstone mentioned. "His support of any rival to Henry need not imply his . . . too great credulity!"

James fiddled with his bed-clothes. "You would have me reject this man, then, as imposter? Forbid him my realm?"

"Not so. That would be folly also, since we require allies and must needs keep Henry uncertain, fearful. He is well served with spies at this Court, never forget. No — receive this young man, my son, but with caution. Commit yourself to no adventures. Be not hasty. Let time show you how you must act. Time — and prayer."

"Time and prayer!" the younger man repeated. "Henry Tudor, I think, does but little deal in these commodities! He bribes my subjects, threatens my border, seeks to steal my throne. Had I not returned from the Highlands betimes, he might even now have had my young brother sitting in this castle as his viceroy!"

"Aye. Henry is a fox. But it will take another fox to outwit him. Not a lion! Nor yet a boar. A fox." The prelate smiled a little. "I fear that you are but an unlikely fox, my young friend and lord! So heed you the advice of a foxy churchman . . . God forgive him!"

James did not commit himself. "I will consider it," he said, and shrugged. "Now, what of this other, kinder matter? Of the schools. The grammar-schools. What have you done since I went into the Highlands?"

"Sire — should we talk of this now? While you are weak? Sick?"

"My head is sore — but that it will be anyway. And my heart is in this matter. Tell me."

"The work is slow. It is not a thing that may be managed overnight, Your Grace. But it progresses. Aye, it progresses. Three schools are already opened. One in my own Aberdeen. One in Strathearn, where the good Bishop of Dunblane is sympathetic. And one in Gray's sheriffdom of Forfar."

"Gray! But this is scarce believable. Gray, of all men!"

"Is it so strange? My Lord of Gray may not be your friend. A man of violence. Godless. But that he is also an able man, none will deny, with wits above most. He perceives the worth of these schools that we seek to establish. Recognises that the men who administer the realm's laws and justice should have the knowledge to do so in proper fashion. For their own sake, as well as the realm's. His own son and heir, the Master of Gray, was the first to be enrolled in the Forfar school."

"I' faith — I had not expected this!"

"Not all your lords and lairds are so far-seeing, more's the pity. Most, I fear, are well content with ignorance, so long as they have power. They laugh at the notion that they need schooling."

"Then we shall make them laugh on a different note, my friend! If they will not learn willingly, they must learn otherwise. I shall make it a royal decree. That the sons of every freeholder of land, of every baron, lord or laird who has hereditable jurisdiction, shall attend at a grammar-school to be established in every sheriffdom of my realm, to learn to read and write and understand the laws of this land — on penalty of forfeiting that jurisdiction. That will serve our cause, will it not?"

"Aye, Sire — if the Council will pass it."

"The Council will pass it. Rest assured. I will not be denied this. I will not have the good laws of Scotland mocked and made of none effect by ignorant fools administering it! Since the baron-courts of this land sit in my name, they must mock neither me nor my subjects. See you to it, my Lord Bishop."

"It shall be as you say, Sire." The older man paused and considered the glitter of his sole adornment, his episcopal ring, before he spoke again. "This may not be the time — when you are in pain, weary. But I so seldom see Your Highness alone. I have a favour to ask."

"It is granted," James said simply.

Elphinstone lifted that ringed hand, partly in protest, partly in gratitude. "My Lord James! The good God bless your warm heart! But . . . how shall we ever make a wise ruler out of a young man who acts so?"

"Is it not a wise ruler who knows the men that he can trust — and trusts them?"

"Perhaps. And for that word I thank you, likewise. But to

grant any man's request before hearing what it is—this is too much."

"To yourself. Or to Rob Bruce. Or to Margaret Drummond. No. To all others, yes. These three will ask for naught that hurts me. Or my realm. What then is your favour, my friend?"

"It is also to do with education, with bringing learning to more of your subjects. I crave your licence and charter, Sire, to found a new university college. In my see of Aberdeen. A new great seat of learning."

"By Saint Ninian—you ask a favour indeed! A university college! Would you oust St. Andrews? Or Glasgow? Do you seek to become Archbishop?"

"No, no, my son. I seek to build, not to pull down. To light a new torch of learning. Scotland needs a deal more of the light. St. Andrews is overcrowded—both colleges. Glasgow is as yet small, with but twenty-five students. Archbishop Shivas is grown old, and smiles not on innovation, as well we know. Holy Church suffers. She needs many more men with scholarship. The new grammar-schools will need masters. The land—aye, and the Church too—lies steeped in ignorance and superstition. Few can afford to go to Paris or Padua or Bologna . . ."

"Aye. But Aberdeen! So far in the north . . ."

"The more reason for lighting the torch there! Your realm is wide, Sire. The light of St. Andrews scarce reaches the north. And there is this great matter of the Highlands. You wish to bring the peoples of those parts into the life of the country, to make the Scots one people, under one king. Here you may greatly assist such dream. A university in the north, so much nearer to the Highlands, where the sons of the clans may come to learn, and from which light can shine out to the farthest glens . . ."

For a little both were silent, contemplating the vision the older man's words conjured up, of a land enlightened and united by knowledge and scholarship. Both men's eyes glowed.

"It will require money, much money. And labour," the King declared. "Men of courage and skill, as well as knowledge."

"All these, with your help, I think I can find."

"And the Pope? Universities are in the Pope's care, are they not?"

"It would require a papal bull, Sire. But at your request he will grant it, I have no fear. Why should he refuse?"

"It is a great thought—a noble thought. If it were possible. It would much help to bring the Highlands into union with us. What subjects will you have taught?"

"Theology, first and foremost—for there the need is greatest. I weep for the low estate of Christ's church. How may the flock prosper when so many of the shepherds are ignorant, misguided and uninformed? Then the law must be taught, canon and civil. My greatest difficulty, with the grammar-schools, after the hostility of the nobles, is to find teachers versed in law. Medicine also as in Paris—for there is no sound teaching of the science in these islands. The arts, should be expounded. And literature. On these foundations the college should be raised."

"What of logic? And philosophy? These are taught at Glasgow, are they not? Also at St. Andrews. And metaphysics . . ."

"First things first, Your Grace. You will make approach to the Pope?"

"To be sure. Did I not give my word that your favour was granted?" James smiled. "It occurs to me that this business will but little commend itself to Henry Tudor. He has but two universities in England. It is suitable, I think, that Scotland should have three! Have me a letter written to the Pope, my Lord Bishop."

James's smile had ended in a grimace, as he twisted round in his bed. The older man leaned forward anxiously.

"You are in pain, Sire? Your wound troubles you . . .?"

"It is my chain. It galls my hurt at times."

"You still wear it, lad? After all these years. I had believed rumour to lie . . ."

"Aye—and shall, to my dying day. So I vowed, and so I will fulfil."

"Your father's death is sufficiently atoned for now, I think," the other said gently.

"Is it? Can it ever be?"

"There is a greater Atoner than you, or any man. Place your burden on His shoulders, my son. You have borne this one long enough."

"A vow is a vow, my lord. Besides, had I not worn this chain yesterday, I would have been a dead man today. It took and turned Gray's sword-point, under my armour. Is it not singular?"

"I thank God for it, then. But . . . no need to wear it in your bed, at least."

"Now you talk like all the ladies!" James paused, blinking a little at that significant all that had slipped out. "H'rr'mm." He cleared his throat.

Elphinstone nodded. "Perhaps I should advise the Lady Margaret Drummond, then, to ask a favour . . . for herself?" he suggested mildly.

James opened his lips to speak — and then closed them again.

"Meanwhile, until this matter of the visit of the possible Prince Richard of York is overpast," the Bishop went on, "it would be advisable, would it not, to say naught of any other marriage, my friend?"

The King knit his brows, but did not speak.

Giving him a blessing, the Lord Privy Seal withdrew.

13

KING JAMES seldom did anything by halves. Having decided to receive Master Warbeck as prince and rightful claimant to the English throne, he did so in princely style. It was November before the Duchess of Burgundy's protégé arrived in the Clyde from Ireland, with an unconscionably large train of Irishmen under O'Donnell and the Earl of Desmond. They were met by a royal salute of gunfire from Dumbarton Castle, where the Earl of Bothwell, as Lord High Admiral of Scotland, with Lord Home, acting Chancellor, greeted the young man and conducted him and his retinue towards Stirling, looking somewhat askance at the vast number of Irishmen, who obviously considered the entire expedition to be a sort of bloodless and successful invasion.

James himself awaited his guest at a specially erected encampment in the flat-bottomed grassy valley just below the rock of Stirling Castle to the north-east, where tournaments and sports were wont to be held. Here amidst gay pavilions and hoardings painted to represent the London gates which it was the visitor's ambition triumphantly to enter, with even the Tower thereof rising somewhat precariously in the background despite its presumed unhappy memories, the King paced about impatiently before his assembled Court, anxiously dividing his attention between the approaches from the west and the lowering leaden clouds over the Highland hills, which threatened to ruin all by cascading their contents upon the elaborately devised scene.

"Where a pox has the fellow got to?" he demanded, not for the first time, of Rob Bruce who waited near by. "We heard an hour ago that he was well past Kippen. Bothwell should have had him here ere this. If that rain comes, all this that I have prepared will be destroyed, perished. A havoc!" James himself had conceived the imaginative background of London Town on painted canvas and the like, even with his own hand assisted with the artistic effects; the possibility of it all being washed away in a rainstorm before the object of the demonstration arrived to behold it, was preying on his mind.

"He will be here shortly, Sire, for certain," Rob soothed. "They will have halted for refreshment, no doubt. At Gargunnock, perhaps. Or Touch. It is a long ride from Dumbarton . . ."

"I have done it in three hours, man!"

"But few ride as does Your Grace! And this is a progress. In state." His eyes followed his monarch's glance north-westwards. "The wind is from the south-west. It will blow those clouds elsewhere, I think."

"There are more clouds, yonder." Frowning, James stared around him. "Margaret? Where is the Lady Margaret?" he demanded. "Did I not tell you to send for her? Is she not here yet? I' faith — does *she* flout my wishes, now . . .!"

"I did send your message, Sir. To the Mar Tower. But I think that I saw her a short while back. Here. With her sisters . . ."

"She should be with me. Here, by my side. I told her Not with those babbling sisters of hers!"

"There she is!" Rob pointed. "Amongst those women. By yonder thorn tree, on the bank."

"I do not see her."

Since James was looking straight at the girl, amidst a small group only fifty yards away, and his eyes were as good as Rob's own, the latter slid a quick glance at his liege lord, but said nothing.

"Well — bring her to me, man!"

When Bruce escorted Margaret to the still-pacing King, and when she dipped in curtsy before him, James had shed nothing of his frown.

"Why are you dressed so?" he all but barked at her. "In that . . . that . . ."

"That what, Sire?"

Margaret wore a fairly simple gown of grey and silver that well suited her fair loveliness, with a fur-trimmed high-collared cloak at present thrown open to hang at her back, a winged and veiled coif framing her piled-up flaxen hair.

James glared at it all. "Where is the gown I had especially made for you? The fine gown to partner my own apparel? It was made for today. Why do you not wear it?"

"I prefer this, Sire. It is not new. And humble perhaps. But my own."

"I have seen this worn a score of times! Today is a notable occasion. You know that I had this most handsome gown especially made. For today. For you to wear at my side. To welcome this prince. I have been awaiting you. All this you know."

"All this I know," she echoed quietly, slowly. "I am sorry. But ' . . . we see the matter differently, Your Grace. I sought to tell you. Yesterday. And before. But you would not heed me."

"Is it not enough that I, the King, gave my command? In this matter of the reception. My royal command?"

She shook her head, wordlessly.

Biting his lip, James plucked at one of the gold-encrusted tassles which held his short tabard-like over-tunic in position. Today he was a magnificent figure, dressed wholly in cloth-of-gold and scarlet, the colour of his realm, the red Lion Rampant of Scotland outlined in gleaming rubies on breast and back. One muscular leg was moulded in scarlet hose, the other in gold. His brief silken trunks were slashed in the same colours. A heavy belt of solid gold encircled his waist, to support a jewelled dagger. His long auburn hair fell sheerly to wide padded shoulders from under a red velvet cap, glittering with gems, and from which curled down a handsome gold-dyed ostrich feather, its myriad points tipped with tiny rubies.

In the Mar Tower of the castle, completed and delivered only the previous night, lay a gown equally magnificent, identically coloured, as richly gemmed, the companion and complement of the King's finery.

Man and woman stared at each other, unhappily, he angrily, she sorrowfully — but never remorsefully.

"Is this how you love me?" he grated, low-voiced.

"Yes," she whispered. "It is. Cannot you understand, James? Dressed so, at your side, you would make of me a strumpet and a gazing-stock, for all the world to point at."

"I would make of you a partner, rather! For the world to esteem and honour. As I do. Whom I would have my queen."

Her expression softened. "There speaks a warm heart — but no clear head, I fear! Do you not see? Partner of your bed only, I would seem. The latest mistress. All would esteem me but that. You cannot make me queen, James — and all know it. It is proved. Even now, this man you wait to greet, sees you as wedding the Emperor's daughter."

"It is but a ruse, an expedient. When we have ousted Henry Tudor, I shall have no need of the Emperor's daughter."

"But until then you cannot have a queen. Or seem to favour other as queen. It is part of the project, is it not? Part of this alliance?"

Stubbornly he set his jaw. "*I* will decide how I shall behave. Not others. I am the King. It shall be as I say."

"Not in this, Sire. I shall not wear your golden gown, your finery and jewels. I shall not stand at your side before all, as though I sought to be your consort, presuming advancement by my body, seeming to ape your dress, to play the proud jezebel. I will not. I am my own woman yet!"

Flushing, the King glanced around him. Although Rob Bruce had discreetly moved away a little and turned his back, few others in that great throng were so nice. Hundreds of eyes watched with undisguised interest this most evident controversy between the monarch and his presumed mistress.

Margaret had spoken the literal truth. She was indeed still her own woman. After the night succeeding the jousting, she had never again slept with James, despite consistent and vigorous pressure. She had been kind to him, closer than formerly by far, allowing him favours and lesser intimacies, as well as a deal of her time and company, now that love was declared between them. But on the vital matter of sharing the King's bed she was gently adamant. In the weeks that had passèd, with James making a speedy return to virile health, his siege of her had inevitably been intense, by turns beseeching, cunning and purely authoritative. Yet despite the undoubted belief of most of the Court, she was not his concubine. For a man of James's impetuous temperament, it was a trying situation.

Since their avowal of love, therefore, there had been more emotional upheaval, quarrels and explosions than ever before. For one with so gentle and seemingly serene a nature, the young woman could be extraordinarily stubborn and unfeeling, James felt – and declared. He found it impossible, in fact, to understand her attitude, and made the fact clear with frequent and characteristic vehemence. It was not that she was cold – he had proof of that. Nor was she foolishly prudish – she indeed allowed him familiarities and small liberties now which quite disproved anything of the sort. Nor was she a tease, being far too essentially honest. But she did not appear to be able to accept the idea of his marriage to her as practicable – and admittedly the circumstances prevailing ever since he had announced it as his desire had been such as to make any public intimation next to impossible; and it seemed that she was not prepared to give herself wholly to him outside of marriage. All of which, to the masculine mind, seemed quite unreasonable, ridiculous . . . and notably bad for the temper.

"You are also my subject — and for once will do as I say!" he jerked. Obviously there was no time for her to be sent back to don the disputed costume. "You will stand here, close to me, even dressed as you are! And you will aid me welcome this prince . . ."

A shout from a vantage point on higher ground interrupted him, announcing the appearance of the expected cavalcade between the Raploch and the cliff of the castle rock. All eyes turned in that direction. A single drop of rain fell on the King's face.

Margaret, curtsying again, fell back and to the side a little, biting her lip, beside Sir Rob Bruce. At the other side of the King a group of notables made their way forward, including Bishop Elphinstone, Sir John Lundie, the Treasurer, the Earl of Huntly, and the Lords Drummond, Kennedy and Gray. The latter was still at Court, a wary and undoubtedly perplexed man. Instead of being made to suffer for his behaviour and his injury of the royal person, since his recovery — rather more slow than that of the King — he had been treated with unwonted consideration, reproached not at all, and almost smiled upon by his late adversary. Undoubtedly he was not alone in wondering the whys and the wherefors.

A flourish of trumpets announced the arrival of the travellers at the reception area. The gaily dressed crowd parted right and left, and the Lord Lyon King of Arms and his heralds, in their gorgeous tabards, paced out to meet the realm's guest and bring him to the monarch. Almost, the eager throng held its breath. The numbers of the following entourage did not fail in its effect.

There was a great dismounting of horses, and from the confused press, led by Lyon, five men came walking forward across the hundred yards of greensward to the waiting King — Bothwell and Home, a tawny giant in gaudy clothing and a long saffron cloak, a small dark older man in antique armour, and a well-built handsome youngster, of darkly intelligent features and graceful carriage, dressed in half-armour and rich but quietly toned apparel of mulberry and blue.

James glanced briefly behind him. "Come closer," he said. None doubted but that he spoke to Margaret.

She moved only a foot or two forward, and even so signed for Rob to come with her. Uncomfortably, he did so.

The walkers came to within a few yards of where James stood. Lyon halted then, with upraised baton of office.

"The Prince Richard of England, Duke of York!" he announced. "To greet James, King of Scots, Duke of Rothesay, Earl of Carrick and Lord of the Isles."

The young man bowed low. "Your Grace's humble servant and true admirer," he said in excellent English if with a strange but attractive accent.

The King inclined his head. "Welcome to my Court and realm . . . Cousin," he said.

There were breaths caught all around—especially that of Bishop Elphinstone. The visitor, younger than James himself by two years, looked up quickly, his eyes widening, lighting up. By that single word cousin, his host had conceded full recognition of his claims and pretensions without waiting for the explanations, assurances and negotiations.

"Highness," he got out. "I . . . I thank you. From the bottom of my heart. You are most good, most kind."

Impulsively James stepped forward, to reach and grasp the other's mail-clad shoulder. "Friend," he cried, "it is my privilege. I rejoice to see you here. This is a 'great day, an auspicious day."

"I have waited long for it," the newcomer nodded.

Lyon coughed. "His Highness of York's most illustrious companions," he intoned. "The high and mighty O'Donnell, Prince of Ireland and Earl of Tyrconnel. And the most noble Fitzgerald, Earl of Desmond."

"O'Donnell and I are old friends," the King smiled, greeting the giant. "My house is his. And I have heard the fame of Fitzgerald, and rejoice to receive him." He turned and looked at Margaret. "Here, now, is the Lady Margaret Drummond who, since I have as yet no queen, will play your hostess, my lords."

Margaret, flushing a little, dipped low in curtsy, but kept her eyes down.

The Duke looked quickly from the young woman to the King and back again. "Enchanting . . .! " he murmured.

O'Donnell, who knew Margaret from his previous visit, chuckled. "Fairest flower of all Scotland!" he said in his rich Irish brogue. "Generous His Grace is—but his generosity will have limits, I do swear!"

James frowned a little. He moved on. "And here is the good Bishop Elphinstone, my Lord Privy Seal. And the Treasurer, Sir John Lundie . . ."

Two or three large spots of rain fell as the introductions were being made. The King hastily cut the civilities short, taking the Duke's arm to turn him to face the elaborate backcloth of painted scenery and pavilions.

"See yonder, Cousin," he said. "A prospect for you. An augury, and a foretaste, I hope and believe, of things to come."

The other considered the canvas city, dominated by the great square representation of the Tower of London, which swayed and flapped a little in the breeze. "A fair picture," he acknowledged. "A notable scene."

James indicated the Plantagenet flag flying over the Tower.

"You are most generous, most kind," the Duke went on. "Does this depict your capital city of Edinburgh? And its great citadel, of which I have heard?"

James stared at him. And not only James. "That . . . that is London. Your own city. And the Tower. Where they . . . where you. . . " He cleared his throat. "The Tower of London."

"Ah, yes." The other acceded, quite calmly. "It is so long since I have seen it. Twelve years, and I but a child. I do not picture it so in my mind, I fear. I see all so much larger, higher, more fearsome. A child's frightened fancies. And no one but yourself, Sire, has sought to paint it for me, since."

"Ah. H'mmm. To be sure," The King nodded. "No doubt. Come, then. Let us inspect closer. Refreshment is here. And . . ."

He got no further. Without added warning, and like a grey curtain dropping on the scene, the rain came down, sudden, cold, heavy and continuous, a deluge of great drops.

In only a few moments chaos reigned. The orderly, richly dressed crowd broke its ranks in every direction, men shouting, women screeching. Most rushed for the doubtful shelter of the tentage. Others, realising that, already drenched, they would find but little comfort there, hurried off for the town or the castle itself. James, leading the royal party hot-foot for the pavilion set aside for their refreshment, swiftly perceived this also.

"To the horses!" he cried aloud, changing direction, "The horses. Mount – and back to the castle. No profit here. To the castle."

In the scrambling confusion that followed, it might have been noticed that the King paid a deal more attention to the task of getting Margaret Drummond to shelter and safety than he did to any of his honoured guests.

The painted London Town dissolved and disappeared.

That night, in the great Banqueting Hall of Stirling Castle, Richard of York charmed everyone – or nearly so. He was friendly and sociable, talented and witty, genial with the men and modestly gallant with the ladies – yet with it all never forgetting his dignity nor bearing himself with less than a royal graciousness. Perceptive, sensitive, he was an excellent talker and knowledgeable in a great variety of subjects – a man after James's own mind and heart. The King was captivated quite – and forgot the debacle of the afternoon.

The Duke was much interested in Margaret Drummond, obviously, seated, during the feasting, in the next place of honour to himself, at the other side of the King at the high table. Later, when the trestles and food had been cleared away for music and dancing and entertainment, the young woman more than once found him at her elbow – during the brief intervals when James was not dancing with her or otherwise monopolising her company.

"His Grace is greatly fond of the dance, I perceive," he mentioned, on one of these occasions. "He dances with much vigour, much enthusiasm."

"Most things that he does, my Lord Duke, he does with vigour and enthusiasm." She smiled a little.

"Ah, yes. A quality most admirable. And with your beauty and grace to inspire him, Lady Margaret, most understandable."

"Not all his enthusiasms would I inspire," she said.

Sidelong he glanced at her. "No? But he tells me that he greatly trusts your judgement, madame."

"He greatly trusts . . . everyone! Trust is noble, a virtue. But therein lie certain dangers, do they not?"

The Duke stroked his beardless chin. "You believe him *over* trusting? That he may be deceived?"

"I do, sir. At times. He is of men the most honest. And cannot conceive that others are frequently less so."

"H'rr'mmm. And you? You warn him against such? You believe that you scent dishonesty where His Grace does not? And he heeds your warning?"

She looked at him levelly, directly. "No, my lord. He does not.

Frequently. Nor do I frequently presume to offer such warning. I am but one of His Grace's humbler subjects. I am not one of his advisers."

"Yet he seats you at his left hand, above all. He names you hostess of this great citadel. He keeps you close at his side — very close."

"Today he does, my lord. But not tonight!"

He inclined his dark head without change of expression. "For a prince of such enthusiasm, His Grace has much . . . restraint! I had not heard it quite so."

She said nothing.

He nodded towards the King, who was now dancing with Mariot Boyd, with undiminished wholeheartedness, clasping her generously voluptuous person with frank and laughing enjoyment. "Yonder is the prince I have heard tell of. This lady he keeps close also — but not as he keeps you, I think."

"That is Mistress Boyd. Mother of the King's son. The child Alexander . . ."

"Ah, yes. She, then, may be held close this night?"

"Perhaps, my Lord Duke. Who knows? His Grace is . . . catholic in his affections. Of vigour, as you observed."

"But this lady does not sit at his left hand at table, nevertheless. Nor did she stand behind the King to greet me, today. She is not named chatelaine here. The Lady Margaret Drummond I conceive to be differently thought on. Destined for higher place?"

Margaret bit her lip. This man had a shrewd, probing mind, which she could by no means outmatch. "You mistake, my lord," she said shortly. Not far off, William Elphinstone stood talking to the Earl of Desmond. Urgently she caught his eye, beckoning him to her aid. The older man came over in but a few moments.

"The Duke, my lord Bishop, believes me closer to His Grace than I am," she declared, less calmly, more hurriedly, than was her usual. "Tell him how we were childhood companions, reared together in this castle. How our fathers were friends. To me the King turns when he requires the aid of a woman. In matters of his household, and . . . and . . ."

The Bishop looked from one to the other. "That is so," he agreed gravely. "Always they have been almost as brother and sister."

Margaret was honest enough to have to look down at the floor, to hide the slight flush that rose to her cheeks.

"Indeed?" The Duke bowed. "Would I had almost such a sister!"

Looking up, she was too late to see whether there was mockery in his dark eyes.

Elphinstone nodded, smiling gently. "The King is fortunate indeed." Still smiling, he went on. "You, sir, will likewise have happy childhood memories, no doubt? It is said, I think truly, that such do remain clearer in the mind than all others. Is it not so?"

"No doubt," the other acceded, after the briefest pause. "That is, I believe, when the memories are happy. Where they are unhappy, is it not that the child will shut them out of his mind, lock them away to be forgotten?"

The older man stroked his beard. "That may be so. There is point in it. But all *your* child's memories are not thus blighted, I hope, my Lord Duke?"

"Why, no, sir. I have many that please me well enough."

"To be sure. Your lady mother, Queen Elizabeth, loved you well. I had the honour to attend her once."

"You did?" The Duke traced a pattern on the floor-boards with the toe of his shoe. "When was this?"

That was not answered directly. "She was a notable woman. I can see her yet. So fair . . ."

"Dark as *I* am, Sir Bishop," the other amended. "As indeed are all of her house of Woodville."

"To be sure. I meant of course fair as to feature, not in colour. Of great beauty . . ."

"Save only for the birth-mark."

"Ah, yes – the birth-mark! But it by no means impaired her beauty."

"As you say."

Neither man pressed the matter further.

The jig over, the King came back to them, gay, a little breathless, hitching his hidden chain back into less discomfort, a movement which had now become as second nature to him. "I' faith," he cried, laughing, "either I am wearing old, or yonder Mariot grows heavier by the month! You are not dancing, Cousin? Do our Scots cantrips alarm you? They are perhaps more hearty than you are used to? But the Lady Margaret here would have tutored you gently, I think."

"I was well content to have the Lady Margaret instruct me in

223

other matters, Your Grace," the Duke observed. "And was well rewarded."

Quickly James glanced at him. "Indeed? In what matters?"

"Of your brotherly regard, no less . . ."

"Of childhood memories, and the like?" Elphinstone intervened smoothly. "Of what is remembered and what forgotten."

James looked at Margaret, mystified. "Sober fare, I swear, for such a time! Here is music, wine, fair women. And you talk thus? Shrive me – I must find you better employment!"

"Do not concern yourself, Sire . . ."

James was staring around him, searching with his eyes. "I'll find some fair head that is stuffed less soberly full!" He laughed. "There are a-plenty of such, I vow! But not all meet to tread a measure with England's rightful king. I would not have you . . . ha – there is one, now! Kate Gordon." He gestured towards a group of three young men who clustered round a single girl, young, slender, and of a wistful beauty, dark as the Duke himself. "A cousin of sorts of my own – the Lady Katherine Gordon, daughter to the Earl of Huntly."

"Most comely, to be sure," the other acknowledged politely. "And of a notable house. But she is fully occupied. And I do not so greatly seek to dance . . ."

"At my Court, Cousin, you must dance," James insisted. "Kate will teach you the way we do it. She is kindly made, is Kate. And her head is not yet full of sober memories! Come!" Taking his guest's arm, he led him away.

Margaret turned to the Bishop. "You do not believe in him? That he is the true prince?" she demanded quickly, low-voiced.

The other pursed his lips, and shrugged.

"You questioned him so, to test him? About his mother, the Queen. Her colour. Her beauty. This birth-mark . . .?"

"I did, my dear," the cleric nodded. "I was doubtful, I confess."

"And now?"

"Who knows? Who can tell? You heard him. Is he true – or exceeding well-versed?"

"Could he have learned about the Queen Elizabeth Woodville so well, so closely, if he had not seen her?"

"The Duchess of Burgundy, his patron, could have taught him. Closely. She knew her good-sister all too well. And did not love her."

"He seems so sure of himself."

"That is true. But it was passing strange that he did not recognise the Tower of London, yonder. Of all places, he should have known that. Where all his hopes spring from. And it was painted fair enough. As was Whitehall Palace and London Bridge. I would know them always, although only once seen. Here was something, perchance, which the Duchess did not, could not, teach him!"

"Yes. I thought it strange also. But . . . perhaps he could have forgotten."

"Aye. Who am I to say that it is not possible . . .?"

James returned to them, alone. "Now, my two fine friends," he said. "Those heads are too close together, by far! For my comfort. What treasons do you hatch against your liege lord? For his good, of course — always for his good! And what fell ploy have you been up to with yonder Richard of York? I smell a plot, I swear!"

"No plot, Your Grace. We but spoke to him of his lady mother," Elphinstone said, mildly.

"To what purpose?"

"To ascertain, Sire, whether he perchance remembered her more clearly than he did the Tower of London!"

James paused for a moment. "And did he?"

"He did. Or knew his lesson better."

The King frowned. "My Lord Bishop — I'll thank you to spare my guest such inquisition! He was but a child of eight years when he was removed from England."

"Were you, my son, not a child of only six or seven when last you saw your uncle, the Earl of Mar? He died in the eightieth year of this century."

"My Uncle Mar was kind to me. Gave me gifts. A child remembers such well."

"A year earlier you were taken on a pilgrimage, with the King your father, to the shrine of Saint Mungo at Glasgow. I was then Vicar of that great church. It was our first meeting, Your Grace. You remember it?"

"Aye. But . . . see you, this is profitless. A beating of the air. Do not men vary in their memories? Are we all made the same? This prince has more than memory to commend him. He wears Edward his father's ring. He has notable warrantors. He is of truly royal grace and manner. He looks every inch a Plantagenet."

225

"Nevertheless, Sire, I cannot think you wise to have so swiftly and certainly named him cousin. To have given all away, so soon. The young man is personable, gifted, and may be all that he claims — or that Duchess Margaret claims. But to grant him fullest recognition before ever you come to bargain with him . . .!"

"Bargain!" James almost barked. "There you have it. I am no huckster, no packman in affairs of state, to chaffer and bargain and ply trade. Such may be Henry Tudor — but not James Stewart! I am King of Scots, my friend — not the realm's chief merchant!"

"Then Your Grace might have permitted a humbler man — myself, for instance — to chaffer and bargain for you. Or for Scotland. There are times when a lowly huckster may serve more profitably than a proud monarch." Though gently, moderately said, there was most patent reproof in that.

The younger man glared at the elder, eyes blazing. "My Lord Bishop — you presume!" he exclaimed.

"Perhaps I do," Elphinstone admitted, "But it is out of love for you, my son. And for this realm of yours. I would not see you deceived and made use of by an impostor. When so much may hang on it. Your support for this man could cost Scotland dear."

"So could my failure to support him! Can you not see it?" James said urgently. "What is the great threat and danger to my realm? Henry of England. Always it has been England that menaced us, yes — but this Henry Tudor is different, more cunning than the others, who sought to conquer us by the might of arms. He intrigues with my subjects against me, bribing and corrupting my nobles. Gold, the dagger, the poison cup — these are his weapons. Not the clean sword and honest lance! Am I to go all my days in fear of them?"

Almost the other smiled. "I have not perceived Your Grace's so great trembling!" he mentioned. Then he nodded. "He is an ill neighbour, Sire, truly. But you have taken his measure. When you challenged him, three months back, Henry did not move. He lay low. His levies did not cross the Border. Angus and your uncles dared not move without him."

"Henry was not ready. He did not expect me back from the Isles until the winter. We know that he assembles men, ever more men, from all his kingdom. He intends to have my throne. By intrigue and treachery if he may — but by arms, if not. *You* know it. So I must take better steps against him than by protests and challenges. Against both his arms and his treacheries and plots. Two steps I shall take—and this Richard of York represents one of them. Whether he be true or false."

"You would support him, even if false?"

"Say that I support him even though there are doubts. There will be no proving the issue either true or false, I think. But if France and the Low Countries and the Emperor support him against Henry, then I were fool to hedge and haggle. Here at last is rod to beat Henry, to my hand."

"Aye. But who wields this rod to beat Henry? France? Or the Emperor? Or only Scotland? Only you, Sire?"

"Why, all of us. Together. With the Irish. And those English who hate the Tudors. And they are many."

"You mean . . . war?" Margaret put in, her voice strained. "Invasion of England?"

"I mean deeds, not words. Action in place of waiting. An end to protests and complaints. Call it what you will."

"War," she said, "is war—under any name."

"As is treachery, bribery, double-dealing . . ."

"Your Grace mentioned two steps," Elphinstone said. "Against Henry. One you have told us. May we hear the other?"

"To be sure. This of Richard of York is to counter Henry's arms. To counter his bribes and perfidy, I have other plans. Perchance I shall out-bribe the Tudor! I shall out-favour his favourites. Angus and my dear uncles, Buchan and Atholl. Instead of banishing them the realm or warding them in their castles, I shall keep them close to me, notably close. Give them high appointments. Make them officers of state. That I may hold them under my eye. I shall honour Henry's treasonable friends — and watch them like a hawk!"

Wondering, the others eyed him.

"You think to ween them from Henry by mercy and forgiveness?" The Bishop shook his grey head. "As a priest, I should commend your heart and Christian charity, my son. But as one who has long meddled in affairs of state, I must not encourage you . . ."

"That is not my intention. I have forgiven these men many times ere this, and gained no thanks for betterment. Now, rather, I seek to draw their teeth. To confuse them. To have them wonder whom it will pay best to serve—since they are men with a price. If they are under my eye at all times, they will less successfully plot my hurt, I think. I have been unwise in keeping them far from me. Their levies, all the Douglas host in especial, mixed with the men of my own more leal lords, will lose much of their threat. Is it not so?"

Elphinstone plucked his lower lip. "Here is shrewd policy, Your Grace. But dangerous."

"Being a king is dangerous, is it not? And doing nothing, more dangerous!"

"Perhaps. Is this, then, why you have been so generous to the Lord Gray? I wondered. All wondered."

"Partly so," James admitted. "Partly also that I have bested him before all, and no longer see him as the same dire bogle. Moreover, you yourself assured me that he is an able man, and supports our grammar-schools. That he sees further than do most. I do not trust him — I shall never trust him. But I shall seek to use him. For the good of the realm. Also, to drive a wedge between him and Angus, I shall favour him first. Since he perceives, you say, that judges should know their trade, and that learning is not only for clerks, I am minded to make him the chiefest judge. Andrew Gray is now Sheriff of Forfar. I will make him Justiciar of all Scotland, I think. And keep him busy. And Angus envious!"

"My Lord James," the older man murmured. "I had not judged you so deep, so cunning. Nor so much the cynic. On my soul, I do not know whether to rejoice . . . or weep!"

"*I* know," Margaret Drummond put in quietly.

Swiftly James turned to her, not for a moment doubting her meaning. "And yet, woman, you it was who would ever have me forgive. Forbear. Bind your enemies to you with bands of mercy, you said, did you not?"

"I said it, yes. But this is not true forgiveness. This is the milk of mercy curdled, gone sour. Here speaks no warm heart. For the warm heart that was, I would weep!" Without even a pretence at a curtsy, she turned and hurried away, making for the door to the castle courtyard.

"Would she have me ever a child? An innocent wide-eyed bairn, believing all, forgiving all?" he demanded, frowning after her retreating back.

The Bishop rested his hand on the King's arm, but said nothing.

CHAPTER

14

STOOPING yet disdainful, like some elderly bird of prey, the Earl of Angus thrust through the throng, ignoring every greeting, careful, obsequious or grudging. In his old-fashioned garb, inevitable half-armour, with furred cloak flapping behind him, he glared straight ahead of him, lip curling, alone, a man sufficient unto himself, old in more than years. The gay fashionable crowd might not have been there.

This time King James had been fortunate with the weather. Although still only March, it was like a day borrowed from summer, the pale blue of the heaven only flecked with white, the turf of the North Inch already glowing green, and only the streaked snows, stark against the purple of the Highland peaks, reminding that winter might not yet be over.

Throughout the long, cold, wet months, James had been fretting to organise one of his favourite entertainments and demonstrations, a jousting and wapinschaw. Ostensibly this was in honour of his illustrious guest – for the Duke of York was still very much present; but more truly it was to work up martial ardour and display the Scots people's readiness for war, a gesture not only towards English Henry but to the Emperor and France. And Spain also, where Ferdinando was dragging his feet. All the ambassadors were summoned here today. Moreover, there was the distinctly trying matter of the Duke's large and ever-growing Irish following, which might be very useful in military operations but was a major embarrassment to the entire countryside meantime; it was calculated that there were now fourteen hundred of these ebullient warriors and their relatives and hangers-on, and Scotland groaned under their cheerful rascality. An assembly and demonstration of Scots arms, therefore, might well prove beneficial to all concerned.

St. John's Town of Perth had been chosen for the venue, as convenient for a large Highland contingent to take part for the first time in what the King intended should be an exposition of his policy of a united Scotland – for Highland manpower might well prove a most important factor in future operations; also, it fell to be admitted that, while Perth was used to Highlanders, any sizeable invasion of clansmen further south would undoubtedly meet with the hostility of a population as yet less sympathetic than their peculiar monarch towards the northern barbarians.

The wide grassy levels of the North Inch, flanked by the silver Tay, were alive therefore with movement and colour and clamour as Archibald Bell-the-Cat pushed his way after the royal party as it made a circuit of the ground before the contests began. He caught up with it as the King was introducing a spectacularly-clad young Highland chief to the Duke of York.

"Ha, my lord Chancellor," James greeted him affably. "You will have ridden from Stirling this fine morning? Here is Ewan Allanson, Captain of Clan Cameron, son to Lochiel."

Angus barely glanced at the others' magnificence. "Aye. No doubt," he grunted. "A word in your ear if you please, my Lord James."

The King sought to keep his features expressionless. "Ewan Allanson has come far to grace our wapinschaw," he observed. And added, significantly, "Clan Cameron can field almost as many good broadswords, my lord, as Douglas can lances!"

The Red Douglas snorted. "May be — but of different quality, by God! Sire — my tidings are important."

"To be sure. But they will keep for a few moments, will they not? Ewan Allanson was telling me of my friend MacIan of Ardnamurchan. How he has pursued and slain the treacherous John of Islay and his sons, who rose in rebellion against me. How with the aid of Alexander of Lochalsh he trapped him. There has been a great battle. Is not this excellent tidings?"

"Mine are of greater moment. Come, Sire . . ."

Nettled, James strove to control his hot temper. "The affairs and well-being of half my realm are moment enough, my lord Chancellor," he jerked. "In this great battle, amongst the Isles, many died . . ."

"The death of a few more or less of these barbarians matters not at all," the Earl of Angus growled, shrugging. "Whereas my tidings may shake all your realm." Scornfully the older man turned his fierce predator's eyes in the direction of the watching and interested Duke of York. "Aye, and mayhap shake some upstart popinjays off their perches in the by-going!" he added.

The King passed hand over mouth, as though to school his lips.

Eyes narrowed, he considered this fierce and arrogant Douglas whom he had recently appointed to the highest office of Chancellor of the kingdom, to the affront of many and against the counsel of all his advisers, thereby setting all Scotland by the ears. He was assuredly having to pay, in strained patience and much else, for this appointment – but he still believed that it had been wise; that Angus was a safer subject in the Chancellor's seat than in Tantallon Castle hatching treasons. That the old Earl had ridden the thirty miles from Stirling after all, when previously he had derided this Perth gathering as bairns' play and a waste of time and good money, indicated that something must have much moved him. James courteously besought the Duke and young Lochiel to excuse him for a few moments therefore, and paced aside a little way with Archibald Bell-the-Cat.

"I would ask you to show more respect to my guests, Uncle," he mentioned, mildly enough.

Angus snapped clawlike fingers. "That for your guests, James!" he declared, without any lowering of voice. "A bare-kneed savage out of the hills, and a mountebank from some Flemish kennel! Douglas does not respect such as these, foul fall them! Nor should the King of Scots."

"Watch your words, my lord! To me, if not to them. Your mountebank may yet be King of England!"

The other hooted rudely. "In that day, Douglas will watch his words, perhaps. Not before! Yonder puppy will no more oust Henry Tudor than will a pig fly!"

James had actually to take a pace or two away from his Chancellor, before, set-faced he could look at him again. "Your tidings, sir?" he got out, stiff-lipped.

"Aye – time for them, by the Rood! The new Spanish envoy is rode into Stirling this morning. A dark carle with a quick eye, and worth the watching. What word he brings from his donnart swithering master I know not nor care. But the word he brings from Henry of England is notable." Angus actually lowered his fleering, raucous voice. "He offers you his daughter, no less – the Princess Margaret!"

James was so astonished that he was for the moment bereft of words. He stared at the Earl.

"Well may you gawp, lad! I jaloused you should hear o' this first, before the Spaniard brought you the word himself. More fool him, he said he would ride here to Perth to see you so soon as he was rested. So must I ride earlier and faster — a plague on him!"

If the King was expected to proclaim his gratitude, the Douglas was disappointed. "Henry says that? His daughter? To me? Henry would have me marry her? I' faith — he mocks! Me, for his goodson? Henry of England?"

"Aye, the same. So says this Don."

"But it is scarce possible! England wedding Scotland . . .!"

"It has been done before."

"Not the King's daughter. Besides, this Margaret is but a child."

"Near eight years. Princesses have been married younger."

"God pity them! But . . . why? Why this? And why by the hand of a Spaniard?"

"Not the hand, lad — the mouth! This is too subtle a business for writing in letters. Too much under the tongue for committing to the English ambassador. Henry must feel the way. He would be as great a fool to risk you openly refusing her, as would yourself be to do so! This new Spanish envoy comes to Scotland by way of London. Henry sees him, and uses him — and can deny the thing, should need arise. A Spanish plot, it would be then, no more."

James wrinkled his brows. "It could be that now, indeed."

"No. It is honest. True. Henry sent a message to *me*." Unblushingly the other admitted it, admitted that he and the English King were close enough for such confidences. "He would have it so — for the good of both realms. Here is no trick."

Urgently, biting his lip, James considered the man before him and what he revealed. If Henry suddenly wished to marry his only daughter to the King of Scots, it must be for some very good reason. Hitherto his only concern for the King of Scots had been to have him deposed, assassinated or otherwise slain. Henry, like all the English monarchs, wanted Scotland — he had not changed in that, James would swear. He had intended to gain Scotland by treachery, bribery and invasion only a few months ago. What had altered, that he now sought a son-in-law instead? Only one circumstance. It must be Richard of York, the coming of Perkin Warbeck. Henry was afraid, then? He feared an alliance between Scotland and the Emperor and France. He feared a successful invasion of England, from Scotland, with Charles of France and the Emperor Maximilian threatening from across the Channel. So he would buy off Scotland with his daughter, keep his northern flank safe. It must be that.

"He would have it so," James repeated. "And you also, my lord Chancellor?"

"Why, yes. To be sure. Here would be a great blessing to your realm, James. Peace with England, assured, continuing. And at so small a price."

So small a price . . .! To be wed to Henry's daughter, a child of seven. Or was she eight? Instead of Margaret Drummond! A red mist rose before the young man's eyes, hot words surged up to choke his throat. But somehow he controlled himself, forcing himself to be the king and not just the man. He would not marry Margaret Tudor — that went without saying; but he need not say so here and now, outright. There was bound to be more in this than met the eye. Angus would have it so — therefore it behoved him to walk carefully. Angus must see gain in it for himself, to come thus hot-foot, to be so keen. Many said that Angus was Henry's man — but that was probably a mistake. Angus was his own man, and none other's, loyal to no one but himself. He would love Henry no more than his own king — but would use him, or James, or both, to increase his own power and wealth. If Angus desired and saw profit in this marriage, rather than in the support of Richard of York, then it was as well for his monarch to be aware of it and take precautions accordingly.

"I shall consider well what you have told me, my lord," he said, then. "I thank you for your diligence in thus warning me. When the Spanish envoy comes, bring him to me. His name . . .?"

"Ayala. Don Pedro de Ayala. A perky blade, I'd say — one for the women to watch for! Quick with more than his eye, if I know aught!"

"Ah — say you so?" The King nodded. "I shall look forward to meeting Don Pedro. Now, I must return to my guests — the bare-kneed and the mountebank, you'll mind! Do you come . . .? Ah, no — a pity. But watch, presently, the fighting of my Highland-men, Uncle — and assess, if you may, how many of their broad-swords will equal one of your Douglas lances! A task that will interest you, I vow!"

The individual contests of the first part of the day, in sword-play, jousting, tilting, archery, single-stick and so on, went well enough – although on the few occasions when Highlanders took part, it was usually against a background of laughter and catcalls from the Lowlanders; and should, by any chance, the former seem to be winning, the boos and jeers were apt to develop almost into active interference with the competitors, so at odds were the majority of his civilised subjects with their liege lord's extraordinary attitude of association with and pandering to the tartan-clad barbarians of the north. In the parades of armed strength, too, despite the colourful garb, bristling arms and squealing bagpipes, the various clan contingents made scarcely so brave a showing as the vastly more numerous retinues of the southern lords' and lairds', mounted men-at-arms on decorated horses, in gleaming steel, riding under fluttering banners and lance-pennons, their masters' coats-of-arms painted on breastplates, led by the said masters in the full panoply of polished armour, heraldic surcoats and plumed helmets. Nevertheless, few would deny, at the finish, that the true highlight of the day undoubtedly was the massed battle of the Highlanders themselves, when great masses of the kilted warriors hurled themselves at each other, from opposite sides of the Inch, with vast enthusiasm and every appearance of warlike ardour. This had been James's *tour de force*, intended not only to be a major spectacle but an eye-opener to the Lowlanders as to the military prowess of the clansmen. It succeeded almost too well.

Long ago, almost a century before, in the reign of Robert the Third, there had been just such an arranged clan battle in this very place, the North Inch of Perth, before the King and his nobles. But that had been a very different affair, with only thirty men on either side, and a fight to the death, between just the two clans, of Chattan and Kay. James had this very much in mind, of course – but desired today's event to be infinitely more impressive and not so much a gladiatorial combat as a demonstration. Three hundred men of the western clans, under Young Lochiel, therefore, were ranged against a similar number from the Central Highlands under MacGregor of Glenarklet, with instructions to fight it out with fullest Gaelic fervour – but no bloodshed. This was perhaps an essay in the impossible, like not a few of James's notions, but the King was vehement on the subject of the penalties he would exact if a single man was killed.

Despite this grievous handicap, the onset went with such dash and realism that many of the spectators took to their heels. The long lines of massed clansmen formed up fully a quarter-of-a-mile apart, and stripping off all encumbering clothing, plaids and gear, stood like hounds held on leash, broadswords in one hand, dirks in the other, targes or round shields slung on their left arms, whilst their chiefs, no different-seeming from the rest now save for eagles' feathers in their bonnets, harangued them, and pipers paced up and down before them blowing lustily. At this stage the vast majority of the onlookers were still hooting, laughing and making pleasantries about naked savages. But when, at the King's signal, the pipes were suddenly drowned in a wild high-pitched yelling that went on and on, seeming to rend the very air, and like two great waves the Highlanders moved forward to the attack, all others fell silent. There was something altogether too deliberate and elementally menacing about those advancing warriors for even the most brash laughter or witticisms.

At first the serried ranks on either side came forward, behind their chiefs and perhaps a dozen pipers each, not in anything so pedestrian as a march but with a swift lithe step. But in only a score or two of yards it had changed to a trot. The pipers trotting likewise, still blew, and still kept their places ahead of the others. Then the trot heightened and increased to a loping run. How the musicians managed their awkward instruments and yet ran also, was beyond comprehension. But now, though they still blew, however erratically, their stirring battle-tunes were swallowed up in the terrible slogan-crying of the clans—"Cruachan! Cruachan!; Loch Moy! Loch Moy!; Gregalach! Gregalach!" and so on. The uproar was deafening, frightening, but purposeful and in its own way disciplined.

Now the men were bounding towards each other in great leaps, seeking who might be first at the clash, swords upraised, dirks flashing in the sun, some fighters actually casting off their kilts and hurling themselves forward mother-naked that they might be the less impeded in the fury of their attack. If this disgusted the Lowlanders, it was only in retrospect, for all were much too affected by the fierce violence and essential drama of the scene to question parts of it. Some few ladies, about to swoon away at the noise and passion, changed their minds.

The collision, when it occurred, was shocking, like the concussion of elemental forces rather than mere men. In play it might be, but nobody remembered that there and then, either spectators or participants. A Highland charge has down the ages been considered to be the most frightening attack for men to face. This was James's purpose in demonstrating it before his proud lords. But two Highland charges, meeting headlong, was almost too much even for him. Gripping Rob Bruce's shoulder, he all but dislocated it in his emotional reaction, shouting incoherences the while.

It is to be presumed that the great mass of fighting, heaving, shouting men now recollected that this was a demonstration not a true battle – but if so no impression of the sort reached the watchers. The ringing clash of steel on steel, of targe on targe, the noise of six hundred straining men, yelling, cursing, grunting, sobbing, the strange high squealing of the bagpipes which still sounded wildly, crazedly, intermittently, above the clangour – all this never for a moment indicated less than the bloodiest stramash.

It was when struggling groups began to burst out from the main conflict and came battling amongst the spectators, that folk commenced to run. Hand-to-hand fighting, be it in earnest or only in excellent imitation, demands space for manoeuvre, and, as though by centrifugal force that furiously straining mass spread outwards and outwards. Soon the entire North Inch was a scene of widespread struggle and chaos, with booths and stalls and tents being overturned, barriers broken down, horses stampeding, and men and women scurrying for safety in loud-tongued alarm.

Perhaps it was an unfortunate moment for Don Pedro de Ayala, the new Spanish envoy, to arrive. Any other Chancellor, in the circumstances, would probably have quietly escorted him from the scene to await a more apt opportunity for presentation; but Angus almost gleefully brought him forward to James at the height of the furore, just as the Earl Marischal came up hastily to urge that the levies of mounted men-at-arms of the various lords be summoned to assemble, to impose order and discipline on this unruly rabble, if necessary with their swords. His demand was strongly supported by many of those surrounding the King.

James rose to the occasion. "One moment, my lord," he told the Marischal, calmly, and turned to Angus and the Spaniard. "I rejoice to see the new representative of His Most Catholic Majesty of Spain," he said courteously. "I only regret that you have had this further journey from Stirling to add to your long travelling, sir. But at least you are in time to witness a most

236

notable occasion — a combat of arms between some of the keenest fighters of my realm. Forgive me, Don Pedro, if I seem to neglect you for the moment. I must show my appreciation of the spectacle to these clansmen who have so nobly diverted us."

The foppishly dressed but darkly handsome youngish man with Angus bowed low — but his lively and eloquent eyes darted in most evident astonishment and question between the grinning Angus, the apparently unperturbed monarch, the agitated lords and the scene of noisy chaos below and around.

"I most admiringly await Your Majesty's convenience," he murmured, in excellent English, with the slightest lisp.

James swung back on the Earl Marischal. "My lord," he said. "You mistake. Not swords — trumpets! Rob — have my trumpeters sound a flourish. A continuing flourish. The Summons — aye, the Royal Summons. Quickly. They are to keep sounding it. My lords — have each your trumpeters to join in. See to it, each and all. Many trumpets."

"Trumpets!" the Marischal protested. "How will trumpets serve, Your Grace? Cold steel alone these heathenish bogtrotters understand . . .!"

"Not so. Lowland swords out against Highland claymores now would turn play-acting into earnest indeed. It is not to be, hear you! It would be folly. Worse. Where are your wits, my lord? Trumpets, I say . . ."

Rob Bruce had not waited for arguments. The royal trumpeters, like the lords' own, were ever near their master on such occasions, when announcements had to be made and identities impressed. Now, the first tentative blasts blared out, raggedly at first but soon coalescing into the challenging and well-known Royal Summons, ringing high and clear. One by one the bugle-horns of the nearby lords joined in.

It took a little while for any effects to become apparent, but once they did it was remarkable how quickly the neighing haughty dominance of the trumpets imposed their indisputable authority on the crowds, alike on the struggling Highlanders, the agitated and fleeing onlookers and the angry men-at-arms. All around movement, clash and panic eased off, fighters drew apart, however reluctantly, and the rush away towards the town gates ebbed. As the trumpeting continued, and men stared around them doubtfully, the King strode to the nearest horse, vaulted on to its back, and beckoning to his Standard-Bearer and the royal trumpeters to accompany him, rode slowly down into the thickest of the Highland mass, smiling, bowing and waving his hand towards the still panting contestants. Purple-faced, his buglers continued to blow, if unevenly now, while James weaved his way amongst the clansmen beneath the great Lion Banner of Scotland. Tempers cooled, glazed eyes became clear again, grins replaced scowls, and the day was saved.

Judiciously the royal announcement was made that after this magnificent display of martial prowess, no further events were to be contemplated; that the King thanked all concerned from the bottom of his heart; and that all present were invited to be his honoured guests down at the haughs of Tay near by, where meat and drink in plenty would be laid out.

Cheers for the King's Grace resounded from innumerable hoarse throats. If a number of limp bodies were quickly and discreetly spirited away from the scene and disposed of in the useful Tay, at least the royal patron perceived none of it.

Not a few powerful lords made their way back through the gates of Perth that afternoon thoughtful of mein.

Later that evening, in the great hall of the Monastery of Black-friars, possibly the most palatial monastic establishment in all Scotland, which a succession of Stewart kings had used as their residence when in Perth, James gave a banquet in honour of the Duke of York. At his high table on the royal dais were seated, besides the Duke, a strange selection of guests. This included no fewer than four Highland chiefs — some of them looking slightly battered despite their tartan finery. Such a thing was as un-precedented as it was unsuitable — especially when it meant that noble lords of high degree and station had thereby to be dis-placed. That the new Spanish ambassador should have been so honoured might be accepted as a mere mark of welcome; but why was the Earl of Huntly, with his daughter, thus exalted — Huntly, the Cock o' the North, a swithering weathercock of a man indeed, all pride, vainglory and wind, no use to any faction by his inconstancy and turkey-cock folly? The two Irish earls that called themselves princes, with a sprinkling of ladies, suitable or unsuitable according to taste, completed this topmost table — thus forcing into lower places the rightful occupants of such honourable positions, the true supports of the throne, such as the Lords Bothwell, Home, St. John, Ruthven and the like, the

Archbishops of St. Andrews and Glasgow, and the Abbots of Scone and Inchaffray. The only consolation was that also excluded were the wretched new men whom the King, unaccountably and ungratefully, had put into many of the high offices of state of late, known treason-mongers and creatures of Angus and Gray. Angus the Chancellor indeed himself had to sit in a comparatively lowly place.

Margaret Drummond, on the King's immediate left, as always now, mentioned the sour faces and disgruntlement all over the hall. "Think you it is wise, so to offend so many of those who have long supported you?" she murmured, low-voiced. "Wise, or just? Do your friends not deserve better?"

"Friends?" James repeated. "May a king have friends? I esteem myself to have but three true friends in all this realm. Rob Bruce, William Elphinstone, and yourself. And perhaps Mariot Boyd. But she is different . . ."

"And Marsala MacIan?"

He nodded unsmiling, slowly. "Marsala also. But her friendship is as from a far time and a great distance. She might be a friend that is dead, indeed."

Thoughtfully Margaret considered him, and his words. She alone ever spoke to him of Marsala MacIan, and always he was thus strange in his reaction. She could not understand what this Highlandwoman had meant to him – but perversely she could not help bringing up the image of her, even though it was to her own hurt. She made no comment now.

James went on. "My friends, if they are true friends, care not where they sit. Do Rob and the good Bishop scowl and glower at me? These others will play my friends for so long as it is to their advantage to do so – and no longer! Scowl now as they will. So it is the advantage I must well consider – not the sitting nor the scowling!"

Troubled, she shook her head. "It may be so. But . . . I cannot be happy that you should see it so. That you should judge men and women thus. You have much changed of late, James." Margaret spoke in little more than a murmur, that none should overhear. "You are become harsh in judgement, seeing little of good in men, believing the worst. You act now as though almost all men were to be bought and sold . . ."

"And are they not?"

"No! No, surely they are not! Most are not so, I do believe."

239

"Most, perhaps, amongst the lowly and the poor. But amongst those who surround a king? I wonder? Power and wealth are notable corrupters of honesty, Margaret, I swear. How many of my nobles, would you say, are honest?"

"I do not know. Who can tell? But . . . can *you*, James? Are you not in danger of judging wrongly, of condemning the true along with the false, in this new harshness? Can you see into men's hearts . . .?"

"Let me see into their pockets, and I see most of their hearts, my dear!" he answered, with a twisted smile.

She sighed, sinking her lovely head. "This is not the James I used to know. And . . . and love! The James who prayed at every shrine. Who loved honour and gallant deeds and high endeavours. Who . . . who bound a chain around his loins lest he forget his faithful oath . . ."

"That chain is still there!" he jerked, low-voiced but grating.

"I know it. But does the same faith hold it there now? I think perhaps that now you are proud of your chain — where once it was worn to humble you."

"God's curse, Margaret Drummond . . .!" Voice suddenly raised, James swung on her, his fist beating down on the table so that silver platters and goblets jumped. "I'll thank you to watch your words! How know you my mind? What is in my closest heart? You, who keep me from you . . . distant . . . hold me off? You say I can see into men's hearts. Can *you* see into mine? Can you — and yet reject that heart, spurn it, as you do . . .?"

"Oh, I am sorry! Sorry!" the girl breathed. But nevertheless her hand went out to his wrist to grip it tightly, her nails to dig fiercely into his flesh, warningly. "James! Sire! Your Grace!" she urged in a tense whisper. "Not here. Not thus . . ."

With a major effort, the King controlled himself. Not a few eyes were upon him, notably those of Richard of York at his other side, and the dark speculative ones of the new Spanish envoy beyond. Biting his lip, for a moment he frowned, and then suddenly smiled, laughed even, however abrupt was the transformation. He leaned over the other, way, to the Duke.

"Cousin," he declared. "I have been neglecting you, leaving you to His Excellency of Spain. Now, you shall have no complaint on that score!" Without warning, James pushed his great chair back, and rose to his feet. Perforce all in that hall must rise with him. He waved them down.

"My lords and ladies, my friends all," he cried, "It is my pleasure to announce to you a matter of rejoicing for us all. My dear cousin, Prince Richard, Duke of York, honours this realm with his presence and us all with his friendship – preparatory, we pray God, to bringing the realm of England closer to us in a like loving spirit in due course. To that end we prepare."

The King paused, and men all but held their breaths. This was as near a declaration of war on King Henry as had yet been heard publicly – and after the day's emphasis on armed strength, was doubly significant. On one side of him, the Duke's carefully controlled features lighted and his eyes gleamed for a moment; at the other, Margaret's blue eyes closed. Down near the head of the central table below, the English ambassador, sitting beside Angus, tugged at his pointed beard.

"To further our happiness, therefore, . . . and, we are assured, his own," James went on, "I now declare to you all that it is my royal pleasure to ally my cousin of York even more closely to myself and my realm, by conferring on him in marriage the hand of another relative of my own, the Lady Katherine Gordon, daughter to my friend and cousin Alexander, Earl of Huntly, whose mother the Princess Annabel was aunt to my father. I believe that they will be well matched, beauty to . . ."

The rest was lost in the excited outbreak of exclamation, question and comment which rose high in every hand. All eyes turned to where the comely young Lady Katherine sat, flushed and nervous, beside her swelling pouter-pigeon of a father, and back to the calmly self-possessed but obviously gratified Duke. The latter rose to his feet, bowed low to the King, then, stepping back, moved with a nice mixture of dignity and enthusiasm to where the lady sat near the end of the royal table, bowed again, and catching her hand raised it gracefully to his lips. Then, still holding her fingers, he made a skilfully calculated lesser bow to her father, suitable for a prince who ought one day to be a king to make to his future father-in-law who was, after all, only an earl. Considering that it was entirely unrehearsed, it was all most dexterously done.

The great company undoubtedly perceived dexterity in more than the Duke. Those who were for his cause equally with those who were against it – and the country was probably fairly evenly divided on the question – saw this as a highly shrewd move on the part of the King. On the one hand, he greatly aided the Duke by this bestowal of a relative of his own upon him, and at the same time undoubtedly saved the royal treasury a considerable and constant drain – for his guest and protégé was practically penniless, and, with ambitious tastes and a growing retinue, was a serious expense to his host; James, with his typical impetuous generosity, had indeed already conferred on him a pension of £1,344 a year. But Huntly was wealthy, one of the wealthiest men in the realm, and his son-in-law-to-be might reasonably anticipate being able to draw substantially on the great Gordon revenues. Moreover, should the Duke's efforts prevail, James would be in the strong position, not only of having aided him to his throne, but of having presented England with her Queen. On the other hand, should the cause flag, fail, or fall to be abandoned for one reason or another, the Lady Katherine was insufficiently close to the Scots royal house to cost the King much in the way of esteem or create serious embarrassment. As a gesture it could scarcely have been bettered from almost every point of view. Huntly, who had blown hot and cold in the King's favour, as in all else, would now be bound to James's support – but could be jettisoned, of course, if the Duke turned out to be, after all, but Perkin Warbeck, an impostor.

Aspects of all this kept the company busily chattering until the banquet was finished – and Margaret Drummond silent by the King's side. As ever with James, feasting must be worked off with vigorous dancing. On this occasion, as a compliment to his High-land guests, when the trestles and benches were cleared, he decided to commence the gaiety with a dance which he had learned at Mingary, a reel-of-eight, danced to the jigging music of Highland fiddlers – something new and far from admirable for most of those present. Since there were no ladies present com-petent to trip this rude and uncouth caper, the two sets of eight were formed wholly of clan chieftains save for James himself and Rob Bruce whom he dragged in. Margaret, in consequence, found herself momentarily free. As was becoming almost habitual with her these days, she sought out for guidance and comfort Bishop Elphinstone, the Lord Privy Seal, who had retired to occupy one of the stone seats of a deep window embrasure of the hall, watching the colourful scene. She seated herself beside him, and for a little they sat in silence.

At length the Bishop patted her rounded arm. "It grieves me to see that fair face troubled," he said. "Need it be so, lass?"

"I did not know that I showed my feelings so clearly, my lord. But . . . is there not much to trouble me, to trouble all of us who love the King? In this room tonight."

"Loving a king must inevitably result in trouble, I fear, my dear," he told her slowly. "In especial, such a king as this. Kings are born to trouble; it is their lot. Those close to them cannot escape its touch."

She made no comment on that. Her eyes never left the King at his gracefully wild Highland dancing.

"What in especial troubles you this night, child?"

She sighed. "Oh, everything! All is wrong, at odds. I have hurt and angered him. Again. So often I do. God knows I do not wish it! But . . . he is changing. Has changed. *You* know it. How now he is suspicious of all, believes in no man, acts coldly, craftily — he who is so hot by nature. He plays faction against faction, lord against lord, the Church against the burghs, Highlands against Lowlands. And now this of Katherine Gordon and the Duke!"

It was the Bishop's turn to sigh. "That is statecraft, I fear. God forgive me, I have played that game myself — must still play it. Only so may a king rule a divided realm . . ."

"Oh, I know, I know!" For Margaret Drummond that was almost impatient, exasperated. "Always he has had to do that. But before, it was as something outside of him, a tool that he must use. Now — oh now, it is becoming part of himself! I can feel it. He is coming to live a lie — he who was more honest than the day. He has built a palace of lies for himself — call it statecraft if you will! He has brought in these wicked men, the Earl of Angus and the Lord Gray, and their friends. He keeps them about him so that he may watch their every move — but it is costing him dear. He is beginning, I fear, not to know the lie from the truth!"

Elphinstone shook his grizzled head. "I think, perhaps, you fear too greatly in this, lass. James will not readily outgrow his own warm nature. Curb it he must, if he is to continue to sit this realm's uneasy throne. He must live with deceit and scheming, yes — but I do not believe that these will best the true James. He endeavours great things, do not forget. He does, or seeks to do, what no king in Scotland has ever yet attempted. He seeks the love of the people — and has in a large measure won it, I think. None have sought that before him. He seeks at least the respect of his lords, their wary respect — since he can by no means have the love of all of *them*. He would provide justice for all, not only for the rich and powerful. He would light the torch of learning, for the greater glory of God and the well-being of Holy Church as well as the realm. He would unite the Highlands and the Lowlands, a task that no man ere this has thought or cared to do. If, to build this fine vessel of a Scotland that he dreams of, he soils his hands a little with tarry pitch, are we — you and I who love him — to decry and deny him, my dear? Look at him now, throwing himself into yonder strange dance like a loon new loosed from schooling! Sparing nothing of himself in whate'er he does. Is there a man in this great hall so alive as is the King? You know that there is not. He will not deny that life, child, I verily believe, until he lays it down. Nor must you, whom he loves. No, nor I either, old and feeble prop to his strength as I am."

Moistening her lips and blinking a little, Margaret Drummond reached out to grip the Bishop's fingers for a moment, saying nothing but nodding her head.

He nodded, also, but in another direction — possibly to aid her to master her emotion. "Yonder, now, is the man we must watch, you and I. Archibald Douglas." His shrewd glance was now trained on the Earl of Angus, whose tall, stooping, vulturine figure could be observed moving about the hall, speaking briefly with this lord and that. "A man older even than myself — old in violence and treason. Our Lord James believes that he has the measure of the Douglas, so long as he keeps him under his eye. I would that I could deem it true. It is so much more easy to pull down than to build up. James builds — but Bell-the-Cat has been pulling down all his life."

"You believe that he still intends harm to James? That even as Chancellor he will betray the King?"

"I fear that it is his nature so to do. He may no more deny his true nature than will James — save of course in God's good providence." Elphinstone sighed. "Sinner that I am, I do grievously tend to overlook God's providence — an unworthy shepherd of his sheep. But . . . the King and I see Angus differently. He considers that it is power that the Douglas seeks; give him power and he will not be ever seeking to gain it. I believe that the very core of the man is rotten — that it is not the will for power but the need to betray that consumes him. That he will betray, whatever the power he is given. And the greater the power, the greater the ability to betray."

The girl shivered a little, eyes widened.

Noting it, the cleric changed his tone, even smiled slightly. "But probably I talk foolishly. An old man's havers, out of his fears and maunderings. James may have the right of it, and be more than a match for the ageing Douglas." He shrugged. "The strangest part of it is that, at this moment, Angus is on what I — and I think you also — consider to be the side of the angels! Working against this project of the Duke of York. Though, no doubt, for very different reasons."

"He is against it also?"

"Aye. But not for the King or the realm's sake. Angus is King Henry's pensioner still, I believe. He will play King Henry's game for so long as it pays him to do so. He will betray Henry, no doubt, as he has betrayed James — but that time is not yet. Meantime, he works for the Tudor. As now."

"Now? How can you know that, my lord Bishop? How can you be so sure?"

"See how he speaks in the ear of each lord. He does not normally so unbend and condescend, does the mighty Douglas. He whispers to them what he has already whispered to me — secret of secrets as it is. That Henry has offered his daughter, the young Princess Margaret, to James as bride and queen."

Margaret's breath was sharply indrawn, and she stiffened on that stone seat. "The Princess? The Princess of England? To marry!" she whispered.

"Aye." Compassionately the Bishop took her hand, stroking it. "That is Henry's offer. By the lips of the new Spanish envoy."

For a little the young woman stared away and away, seeing nothing of that crowded chamber. The old man gave her time, still holding her hand.

"And . . . and James?" she got out, after a few moments.

"Angus declares that the King will refuse the offer. To the danger of the realm. Unless he is prevailed upon to change his mind."

"I . . . see," she said, low voiced.

The eightsome reel had come to its boisterous end, and James, laughing, breathless and mopping his brow, was apparently arranging for some other Highland dance to be demonstrated, requiring crossed swords to be laid on the floor. Fixedly she watched him.

"She is but a child, is she not? This princess?" she asked.

"A child, yes. Seven years, I think."

"But it is shameful! James would never marry such."

"Not of his choice, certainly. But . . ."

"But, my lord? But what?"

"He might be persuaded to consent to a betrothal."

Out of another pause, she asked. "And you . . .? Would so you advise? That he takes that course? A betrothal to this princess?"

Gravely he looked at her. "I might, Margaret. I think that I might. For the realm's sake. But I much doubt if he would take *my* advice." There was a distinct emphasis on the personal pronoun.

She made no comment.

"Henry must be much afraid, to make this offer. He fears that James means war. Faced with the Emperor and France threatening him across the narrow seas, and with unrest and conspiracy in his own realm, he dreads a Scots attack, with perhaps many in England rising for this Duke who claims his throne. Henry Tudor is a schemer, a plotter, rather than a warrior. He must see war as near."

"War!" Margaret drew a long quivering breath. "No! Not that! *You* do not believe war is near?"

"Not near, perhaps — but possible. Very possible. I believe James does contemplate it. This last attempt against him, while he was in the Highlands, has grievously angered him, disturbed him. He would remove the threat to his throne — and sees in this Duke his opportunity."

"But, before there could be war, there must be preparation? Much preparation. Surely this is so? This realm is not ready for war . . ."

"No. Therein, I deem, lies the danger. James may have decided on war — but he cannot mount an invasion of England for many months. I fear that, if he rejects this proposal of the princess, Henry will take it as a sign that war is intended, and that he will move first. Invade Scotland, to forestall James. He has armies in being, where James has not. In England the King has soldiers of his own, many soldiers. And can hire more. He does not depend, as here, on the levies of his lords. He could move much the faster . . . if he was assured that the Emperor and France were not ready to move against him. And that, I believe, is the case. I had a word with this new Spaniard. He journeyed here by France and the Low Countries. Then London. He holds that these cannot take the field before the summer. Moreover, they doubt James. No doubt so Don Pedro told Henry. So the English have time – if Henry's marriage proposal is rejected."

"But . . . what of the Emperor's daughter? The proposal that James should wed her? Is that now to be forgotten?"

"The King seems hardly to take that seriously. The Duke's faction press him to do so – but he holds off. As you, my dear, know well." Elphinstone sighed. "The Duke, I think, believes that he has no intention of such a marriage. So across the seas they doubt him. James will lose on both sides. He loses the confidence of the Emperor, and at the same time will force Henry to action against him."

"Because . . . because he will not take a wife!"

The other nodded. "Because he seems not to *consider* either of these princesses. The taking need not be yet – but the considera-tion, the negotiations, are vital in this game of kings and alliances. James, however, looks . . . elsewhere."

Slowly, deliberately now, she said it. "You mean, my lord Bishop, that he looks at me?"

"I mean that he has said, on many an occasion, that his desire is to marry you, Margaret."

"And this is . . . impossible?"

"Not impossible, my child – but scarcely to the realm's benefit."

She twisted her fingers together. "I have told him so, myself. Often I have said it. I have held him off . . ." Her voice broke.

"I know it. Deeply I grieve for you. Both of you, who love each other. Was he any other man than the King of Scots . . .! So much hangs on his choice, lassie."

"What . . . what do you wish me to do, my lord?" That was little more than a whisper, but said with a slight raising of her fair head, almost the suggestion of squaring of shoulders.

He looked down. "Who am I to tell you?" he said huskily. "Spare me that, of your charity! And . . . forgive an old man who loves you both. As I pray God will, also."

Without another word she rose and moved away, down from that window embrasure, into the brilliant throng.

Strangely enough, for the remainder of that evening, Margaret Drummond was gay – never more so. She was seldom far from the King's side, smiling, rallying him, dancing with him with a vivacity and enthusiasm, almost an abandon, which was markedly not her usual. James was swift to respond, and the pair were the life and soul of the jollity, leading the measures, egging on others, tireless, sparkling, a most handsome and exhilarating couple, the magnet for all eyes. Certain eyebrows were raised, of course, but the gaiety was infectious and the general atmosphere was one of carefree hilarity. The Duke of York and the Lady Katherine, whose especial evening this ought to have been, were quite eclipsed, but seemed well enough content. From his perch in the window, William Elphinstone looked on, sombre-eyed.

Nevertheless, despite all this merriment, and the undoubted success of the evening, it was Margaret who brought it all to a close, earlier rather than later than was usual. After one of the essential intervals for refreshment and the recovery of breath, wherein one of The O'Donnell's Irishmen entertained them with broadly humorous miming, as James, acting as his own master of ceremonies, was about to announce another dance, the young woman laughingly raised her silvery voice into the brief anticipatory hush.

"A truce, Sire — a truce!" she called out. "Would you weary us all, quite? The night is made for more than dancing, it is not? Reserve some small strength I prithee!"

There was an astounded silence, before titters rose from here and there.

James stared at her, so near, so flushed and lovely and desirable, all breathless ardour, so strangely altered from her normal serenity of poise. "Why, Margaret — have I so greatly tired you?" he demanded. "You show it not, I swear!"

"Not yet, Sire — not yet!" she told him, still smiling, and loudly enough for all to hear. "Perhaps you shall, before the night is out. But not, I beseech you, all with your dancing!"

Again the snicker of laughter, less inhibited this time and more widespread. The King, perplexed yet excited, roused, at the same time, drew hand over mouth and chin, eyeing her closely, all the warm invitation of her person, so much more subtle than her words.

"You would be gone, sweeting?" he murmured. "Other-where?"

She answered him in no murmur. "Would not you, Lord James?" That was simple, frank, shameless indeed. She moved up close to him, and reached up to run a finger-tip down the line of his jaw, flicking away the heavy auburn locks of hair that hung to his shoulders. "Where we may be alone!" she breathed into the ear thus uncovered.

His manhood rose to her challenge in a hot surge. "'Fore God —if that is your wish!" he exclaimed thickly, fiercely gripping her arm.

She trilled high laughter, and turned, leaning bodily against him, to look around on all that crowded, watching room. "I see that my Lord Duke is gone," she said. "The Lady Katherine also. It ill becomes the King's Grace, does it not, to keep others from . . . their couches? Shall we retire, Sire?"

Flushing now himself, James turned abruptly away, towards the door at the head of the hall, still holding Margaret's arm. Perforce he turned her with him. "Come, you!" he jerked, almost grimly.

With a sudden twist of her wrist, the young woman broke free, and with more high laughter, kilted up her long satin skirts and ran before him to the doorway. With expressionless face a guard there, in the royal scarlet and gold livery, opened it for her. She passed through, the King long-strided after her, and the door was closed on the noisy and unrestrained commentary of the crowd.

On his window-seat, the Bishop of Aberdeen bowed his lined face down into his cupped hands and so crouched, silent amidst the clamour.

The royal apartments were situated at the other end, from the hall, of an open cloister flanking a paved court in which a fountain played. The young woman had ceased her running before she was half-way along this, and James caught up with her easily enough. She was no longer laughing. He grasped her by the shoulders, somewhat roughly, and jerked her round to confront him. "Margaret!" he cried. "This is . . . this is . . .!" He shook his head, and her person also, at a loss for words, in bewilderment, excitement and roused desire. Holding her, he thrust his face close to hers, peering into her eyes in darkness illumined only feebly by a lantern or two and the light from windows. "What does it mean?" he demanded. "God be good—what means it all?" But even as he asked, he was stooping, pulling her bodily to him, his eager lips crushing down on her own.

She did not seek to draw away, but she slipped her fingers up between their mouths, twisting her head a little. "Not here—not here, James!" she panted. "The guard! Wait, you!" Her glance darted to where another of the royal bodyguard stood, with his halberd, on duty before the door of the King's own chambers at the end of the cloister.

"A pox on the guard!" James growled. But he raised his head, straightening up. "Do not think to balk me now, with the guard, woman! I swear I'll not have it . . .!"

"No, no. Only wait." She turned, within his arms, and he loosed her. Firmly she walked away, over the flag-stones, towards the man-at-arms, who, watching warily their approach, opened the door for them.

Within was an ante-room, littered with armour, trappings, weapons, clothing. At a long table a man sat alone, writing a letter — Sir Rob Bruce. He started up as the pair entered, his startled gaze on Margaret Drummond. He did not speak.

She was not prepared for this. She had not perceived, in all the stir of that hectic evening, that Rob had left the hall early, contrary to his usual habit of closest attendance on the King. Meeting his eyes now, she faltered, opened her mouth to speak, but found nothing to say. He stared down at the floor, and strangely, a red flood flushed his face to the very ears.

James frowned, and bit his lip, looking from one to the other. Then he forced a laugh. "Sobersides, Rob!" he exclaimed. "Writing letters? On such a night! Where's your spirit, man?"

"Your Grace has spirit enough for two, and to spare!" the other answered, not looking up. "I . . . ah . . . congratulate you!" As neither James nor Margaret commented on that, he abruptly turned and stalked over to one of the two doors across the untidy room. This he threw open. The mellow glow of only a pair of candles and the ruddy firelight showed beyond, flickering over rich carpeting and the hangings of a wide four-poster bed.

Taking the girl's arm almost fiercely, the King propelled her forward. As they passed close to him, Rob bowed.

"Shall I inform Mistress Boyd, Sire, that she is not required?" he asked, level-voiced. "Or do you still wish that she holds herself in readiness?"

"A curse on you, Rob Bruce . . .!" James blazed, and swinging round, slammed the door shut in the other's face.

Margaret paced into the middle of the warm and handsome room, and reaching out a hand grasped one of the uprights of the great bed, there to stand, staring set-faced at the fine hangings of the wall beyond.

"A plague on him and his ill tongue!" James exclaimed. "Does he dare to mock me — *me*, the King! I'll . . . I'll . . .!"

"Not you, but me," the young woman interrupted evenly, wearily. "You are as ever you are. It is I who offend Rob tonight. It seems that I may not please your one friend without hurting the other!"

He stared at her back. "What do you mean by that? One friend? The other? What mean you?"

She shook her head. "It is nothing, Sire. A foolish woman's thought — that is all. Your Grace must bear with me . . ."

"Devil burn me, I shall not! You Sire me, still!" he cried. "Here, in my very chamber is it still to be Sire! Your Grace! I' faith, woman — is it all a play, then? A deceit? Do *you* mock me, now? For if you do, by the Mass I'll show you otherwise . . .!" He strode forward, to take her by the shoulders.

She turned to him swiftly. "I am sorry, James — sorry! It is not so. No deceit. I . . . I am yours, now. All yours. In truth. Here is no play. Take me now, as you have so long wanted. Take me, James."

Faced with that strange invitation, almost demand, the man yet paused in his angry urgency. Perplexedly he searched her lovely troubled features. "Margaret," he charged her, a pleading note coming into his voice. "What is it? What a God's name's here? What has come to you? Tell me what it means. It is not wine? Overmuch wine . . .?"

"No. Not that." And at the folly of this, she wagged her head helplessly. "Oh, James — what matters it how or why? I am here. As you have always desired. Is it not enough?"

"No, it is not!" Almost he shook her. "Why, woman — why? Why now? Tonight? Tell me."

"I am here because . . . because it was time. High time. We have waited overlong. I was foolish, unkind, unfair. At last I have seen it — and I am here!"

Still he stared, unconvinced. "You *wanted* to come? This is your desire?"

"Yes. Yes. I wanted it." With something almost like desperation she grasped the slashed sleeve of his velvet doublet. "Wanted, do you hear? Long have I wanted this. Can you not understand? It was against my own desire that I held you off. I am a woman — no gutless child!"

"Yet you *have* held me off. For years. What has changed you, Margaret, to, to this?"

"I was mistaken. Is that not enough? Mistaken, I tell you!" She threw back her head. "James—is this the man I have believed you? Hot? Smoking? Or is your ardour all but words? Questions?" Releasing her grasp of him, she flung up a swift hand to her throat, to wrench at the fastenings there and jerk open her gown, pulling it down over one white shoulder, displaying the swelling, rounded bosom. "Must I do your work for you . . .?" Her voice broke.

At the enchantment, enticement, thus revealed, offered, thrust at him, so close, so inviting, so desirable, James could by no means hold in his passion longer. Stooping, he swept the young woman up bodily off her feet, in his arms, burying his face in that delectable fairness, exclaiming, kissing. He staggered the few paces to fall with her upon the great bed.

He was wrenching now at the awkwardly placed chain. "Margaret! Margaret! Margaret!" he cried, chokingly, as he drowned in a sea of passion and liberation.

After a while, with the violence of his need and desire spent for the moment, the King raised himself slowly on one elbow and gazed down at all the warm and disarrayed loveliness beneath him, and as slowly shook his sweat-damp head.

"Marry, girl—can you forgive me? Forgive a furious, bungling oaf? A rampant clown? Foul fall me—I might yet be a raw, callow youth, unfledged, after all these years! I thought, I believed, that I had learned better, learned control of my frantic flesh, But *you* . . . you make of me the merest botching boy again. Good lack— can you forgive me it? A—a rape, no less?"

She did not answer. But her bruised lips were parted, nevertheless, in a small and secret smile. She gazed up, not so much at him as past him to the tapestry-roof of the four-poster bed whereon the embroidery seemed to weave and dance in the firelight, and her eyes were melted in a lambent glow.

Peering at her, he drew a long breath. "Precious soul of God —you are beautiful!" he whispered. He ran a slightly trembling hand over her smooth and shapely breast, lingering over its heart-breaking delight. "Margaret—you are beauty incarnate! And I treated you like . . . like . . ."

"Like a master, James," she murmured. "A master, yes. You

252

mastered me. I think that was . . . necessary. Do not blame yourself, my dear – do not."

"But I do," he declared strongly. "Not that your are here, that I took you – since that was your doing. But that I took you so! Like any selfish boor . . ."

She shook her head. "Like a master," she repeated. "So that I am now your mistress indeed. Am I not? As I sought to be."

He frowned down at her. "Mistress . . .? Why do you say that? What folly is this? Mistress – that you never wished to be. Nor should. Wife, not mistress . . ."

"Mistress," she asserted. "That I am now, am I not? Margaret Drummond, mistress to James, King of Scots! Long I have been named that – now it is true. And all men yonder know it."

"Why do you say that? What is here?"

"I say it because it had to be. I shut my eyes to it for long – too long. But now there is no denying it. This is my place . . ."

"No!" Vehemently he said it. "Wife I said I would make you – and I shall. Mistress, no! Not you."

"Not wife, James – that cannot be." Earnestly she besought him now. "Your wife must be . . . other. The Princess of England, perhaps."

"A pox! How heard you that?" He started up from her. "What are you saying?"

"That the Margaret you must marry is Margaret Tudor, James – not Margaret Drummond. For the realm's sake. For both realms' sake. That there may be peace, not war . . ."

"Henry's brat! A child, a mere child of seven! To buy me off with a chit of a bairn!"

"To keep Scotland and England from each others' throats, rather. To end this long and senseless strife. To save lives, many lives, James . . ."

"You, lying there, say that I should marry a child of seven years! You that love me?"

She looked away. "You could be betrothed. Until she is older . . ."

"No! And desert the Duke's cause? I have said that I will aid him gain his throne."

"Does that course not mean marriage likewise? To the Emperor's daughter? You cannot marry either of these – and me!"

"Then I marry neither!" Impetuously, James twisted round,

flung his legs over the side of the bed, rose, and began roughly to re-arrange his clothing. "Get up, Margaret. Quickly," he ordered, abruptly brisk again, his physical lassitude forgotten.

Astonished, she watched him.

"Come, lass," he urged. "You would not have Rob Bruce see you so?"

That roused her. She sat up, biting her lip but hastily pulling her gown up over her breasts and seeking to close its ravaged fastenings.

The King gave her little enough time. Still only approximately decent as to his own dress, he strode over to the door and threw it open. "Rob!" he cried. "Here. To me, man."

Sir Rob, in shirt and trunk hose only, emerged from the second inner doorway of the ante-room. Obviously he had been preparing to bed down himself.

"The guard, Rob. Get the guard. From the door. Bring him in."

"The guard? Your Grace desires the guard?" the other wondered. "For some errand . . .?"

"No, no. Bring him to me. Here." James turned back into the bedroom, where Margaret was now on her feet, smoothing down the satin folds of her skirts, disarrayed still but covered at least. Perplexed, confused, even a little indignant, she eyed him.

"That will serve. No need to do more," he told her.

"What means this, James?" she asked, breathlessly, "I had not believed . . . I had not thought that, so soon . . .!"

He was not listening. "You are beautiful!" he said, staring at all her dishevelled comeliness. "I' faith, Margaret — you are most beautiful!" Perhaps in that she had answer enough to reassure her misgivings.

Rob appeared within the doorway, ill at ease and as perplexed as the young woman. "Here is the guard, Sire . . ."

"Aye. Come in here." He glanced at the bewildered man-at-arms, a middle-aged soldier in the royal livery, morion and half-armour. "Your name, my friend?" he asked. "And where are you from?"

"Lindsay, may it please Your Highness — Pate Lindsay," the other stammered. "Frae . . . frae Anster, in Fife, lord."

"You could be honest, nevertheless!" James told him, with a smile. "Wait you, Rob — both of you I need." He turned to Margaret. "Come, my dear — your hand."

254

Doubtfully, brows raised enquiringly, she came to him, and he grasped her hand. "Here is what I should have done long ere this," he declared. "But better now than not at all. Rob Bruce, my good friend, and you Pate Lindsay — see here. Before you both as witnesses, and before God in Heaven who sees us all, according to an age-old custom and lawful usage of this my realm, I, James Stewart, take this woman Margaret Drummond, to be my true wedded wife and I to be her true wedded husband, we both being unwed and of full age. To the truth and certainty of this marriage, you are both to adduce and depose, if called upon to do so. In your presence, I now declare that we, James and Margaret, are man and wife till God do us part."

His words were succeeded by utter silence, save for the quiet hiss and splutter of the logs on the fire. Margaret was clutching his hand with a grip so tight that her knuckles stood out white — as white as her face, as she stared blindly straight ahead of her at the arras-hung walling. The two watching men were speechless also, Rob almost as overcome, the guard mystified, dumbfounded.

James broke the spell by stooping to kiss the girl's suddenly stiff and cold lips, with gusto and vigour. "So there's you wed, Margaret Drummond!" he cried gaily. "A maid, forsooth, no longer! So simple a matter, was it not? Come, my love — a kiss for your husband! Do I not deserve that, at the least?"

She searched his smiling face now, eyes wide, lips no longer stiff but trembling. "Oh, James," she faltered. "What . . . what have you done? Here is folly! Folly!"

"Folly to marry the woman that I love — instead of a seven-year-old bairn? Or a woman across the sea whom I have never seen? No, no — here is wisdom, not folly. Joy also — aye, joy my dear. Does it bring you no joy?"

"Ah, yes. But . . ."

"No buts, Margaret, my love. No buts on our wedding night! God knows that it is not how I would have had us marry! But kings, it seems, may not always choose as may more fortunate mortals." He turned to the two men. "See you, now — here is a very privy, secret matter. None are to know of this night's work. Not yet. None at all. Is it understood? The Lady Margaret is now my wife. We know it, and you know it. The time for others to know it will come — but not yet. Too much of weal or ill for this realm may hang on the talk of my marriage to this princess or that, to my sorrow! Until the road is clear before us, such base trading and chaffering may serve the realm. It is not how I would have it – but such is the lot of princes. You understand, Pate Lindsay? No word of this to any – or I will have your head! Rob, see that he is well rewarded. And you yourself, man – do not stare at me so! As though you saw some spectre! Do you not congratulate me, rather? Is not that usual, to the happy Benedick?"

"Aye. To be sure, Sire. That I do. I rejoice. I . . . I . . ." He shook his head, and swinging round to Margaret he took her free hand and raised it jerkily to his lips. "I am glad!" he said. "Glad! This is good. So much better . . ." He left the rest unsaid.

Misty-eyed she smiled at him. "Thank you, Rob – thank you. It is better, yes – so much better."

Nodding, they eyed each other.

The King clapped him heartily on the shoulder, and laughed. "Now, begone! This is a bridal chamber, I'd have you to remember! I'll not have you making eyes at my wife in it! Off with you both, for sweet Mary's sake, and leave me to my bride! And, Lindsay – mind you my royal command."

As the door closed again behind the two men, James turned to the girl, and held out his arms. After only a moment's hesitation she came running to him, to throw herself against him, burying her face in his chest.

"James! James!" she sobbed. "Hold me! Hold me close. Hold me – always!"

He stroked her fair hair, kissing it. "Do not weep, my heart. Here's no time for weeping."

"I weep . . . for happiness," she mumbled into his doublet. "It has been so long."

"You are happy then, to be my bride – even so? With only myself and Rob and one poor soldier knowing it?"

"Yes. Happy."

"I curse myself, nevertheless, that I should do no better than this, Margaret. But . . ."

"No buts on our wedding-night!" she repeated, raising her head and smiling through her tears. "This is how I would have it. To you, and to God, I am your wife. To the world, I am your mistress. I am content."

"I do not much like the name of mistress, Margaret. Not for you . . ."

"Yes, for me, James. Your mistress I shall be, in men's eyes –

I must be. I shall be proud to be it—for your realm's sake. Not only you may serve the realm. And now . . . and now . . ."

"Aye—and now!" Looking down at her, he was suddenly all man again, all urgent masculinity, his hands already busy at her gown. "Is it wife or mistress that you are to be now, woman?" he demanded thickly.

"Both, James, my love—both!" she whispered.

15

THE long line of armed and mounted men came to a wavering halt all along the low grassy ridge of Oxenrig, in the Merse, to gaze southwards from under the forest of standards, banners and lance-tip pennons. For almost a mile that host extended, many men deep, and the steam from thousands of sweating horses rose like a cloud over all, to dim the glitter of armour, the flash of steel, and the heady colours of helmet-plumes, painted shields and breastplates, heraldic surcoats and flapping ensigns. A strange sound, something between a growl and a roar, rose and fell on the gusty south-westerly breeze from one end to another of the lengthy ranked array, a savage sound full of anticipation, menace, triumph; for ninety-nine out of every hundred men on that ridge, it was their first glimpse of England.

Before them, the ground sloped gently down over green pastureland dotted with wood and brush, to the gleaming, winding links of wide Tweed, the great river which formed the Border, where the little grey town of Coldstream crouched on guard over the first fordable crossing, fourteen miles up-river from the estuary at Berwick. Beyond, the land, so similar in aspect but so different, so foreign, so hostile, in the eyes of this army, rose and rose in long slow undulations to the series of rounded heights, diminishing all the way from towering Cheviot in the west to the blue sea itself on the east – the Northumbrian escarpments of Monylaws, Branxton, Flodden, Barmoor, Etal and Duddo, defended by their castles and towers. Fierce eyes ranged over that fair wide prospect, and many lips were licked in anticipation.

Near the centre of the line the banners were thickest and largest, the press of men deepest. Highest and proudest of all, no fewer than four great standards streamed out in the wind, presenting a sight never seen before, or since, on that Border, age-old scene of invasion and battle as it was – for side by side flew the flags of Scotland and England both, and only a little behind, those of France and Burgundy. A stirring picture they presented –

whatever the tortuous political manœuvrings that had effected to bring them there.

King James, splendidly arrayed in gold-inlaid black armour, but with his head bare as usual, his long thick auburn hair held in place by a slender gold circlet, turned smiling to his companion, who sat under the rippling leopards of England.

"Yonder, then, is your realm, my Lord Duke," he said, waving an arm. "All yours . . . for the taking! May it welcome you fittingly." Despite the smile, that was grimly said.

The other did not smile. There had been but little of smiling between these two for months past now—and none since last night's camp at Ellemford in the Lammermuirs, twenty miles to the north. The Duke of York was clad and mounted even more magnificently than was James—albeit at James's expense—in chased and bejewelled armour polished like silver, his great charger caparisoned in the Plantagenet colours. But his face was grave, sober, strained, as he stared out at his promised land.

"May it so, indeed," he said levelly. "But until we are certain of it, I still say that we should content ourselves with Berwick, Cousin. Once we hold Berwick, the Northumbrians will quickly discover their loyalty to my house, I think!"

"No, my lord!" James's fist beat down on his saddle-bow. It might have been noticed that these days it was usually the Duke who named the other cousin, and not *vice versa*. "We made our decision last night. Berwick is strong. It could withstand our siege for many days. Even weeks. In despite of my cannon. But let us take these English lands down to the Tyne, and I warrant it will fall of its own accord, like a ripe plum." The King waved his arm round and backwards, northwards. "Think you I brought all this host thus far to sit around Berwick-on-Tweed?"

Looking back, all the great plain of the Merse, the March of Scotland, stretching far and wide up to the purple and green heather slopes of the Lammermuirs, seemed to move and crawl in the fitful sunlight and shadow of that showery late September day. The movement, seen from this Oxenrig, looked slow. But it was deliberate, steady. Companies of marching men headed southwards along every road and lane and track; long baggage trains and packhorse columns followed them; great lumbering teams of oxen dragging the heavy artillery that was the King's pride, plodded in their wake; and hordes of camp-followers, grooms, smiths, armourers, cooks, friars, minstrels, servants, and their women, spread like locusts over the land. Only the chivalry and the cavalry had reached this last ridge before Tweed — although the tireless and agile Highland contingents were close behind, almost as mobile as mounted troops; the infantry, as ever, took their own time, burdened with armour, weapons and gear — and added to that gear as they went along, whatever their orders. Small wonder that Alexander, Lord Home, near by, glared back at the sight with less pride and satisfaction than his liege lord — for this was Home territory, and most of his strength in fierce moss-troopers were here, with the cavalry, and not protecting their vulnerable homesteads and cattle, back yonder, from the rest of the army.

The Duke did not answer. Although this invasion was on his behalf, to set him on the throne which he claimed was his, he was in no position to argue with James as to strategy. Of the fifteen or sixteen thousand men involved, not one in ten was of his own furnishing. The fourteen hundred Irish gallowglasses under the Earls of Tyrconnel and Thomond he might claim — but they were the least popular folk in Scotland by this time, having long outstayed their grudging welcome. The sixty German mercenaries sent by the Duchess of Burgudy at the last moment, were scarcely a force to which he would wish to draw attention, however proudly the banner of Burgundy flew in consequence; and as for the lilies of France, under them rode but one man as representing King Charles — and he a Franco-Scot, the veteran William Monypenny, Sieur de Concressault, former Captain of the Guard. All the rest, save for a few Englishmen, were the King of Scots' providing. Bishop Elphinstone's prophecy of so many months earlier had been fulfilled all too exactly. The rod to beat Henry Tudor, though forged in the chancellories of the Empire and France, was being wielded almost solely by James of Scotland.

Patrick Hepburn, Earl of Bothwell, spoke up, a heavy, puffing, purple-faced man now, but still as forthright and headlong a fighter as ever. "What ails us, Sire, that we should not ford the Tweed without more ado? If I see no great host of English waiting there to welcome their rightful king, neither do I see any waiting to contest our crossing! Moreover, by the Rude, since when have Scots had to wait on English invitation to cross Tweed? Not so was I reared, i' faith!" And the Earl shot a fleering glance at the small company of Northumbrian squires and younger sons who rode in an uneasy cluster behind the Duke.

"Aye, Patrick—but this, you'll mind, is more than one of your marchmen's moonlight rievings!" James pointed out. He too turned to the Englishmen. "My friends—look you there. All Northumberland and Cumberland knows that we come, that Prince Richard approaches to claim his inheritance—for we have made no secret of it. I have sent out my heralds and couriers. No town or castle from the Tyne to the Eden but knows that we are here. Yet, despite all professions, where is your strength? Where the hand of welcome? I see yonder not even a single flag flying, not a beacon ablaze, not a tented camp. There, if I mistake not, lies Wark Castle. Is it held for us or against us?"

None answered the King. Who was there to answer? And what? This was but a resumption of last night's angry scene at Ellemford, when it had become crystal-clear that the promised and counted-on English support was in fact a chimera, a mirage. Envoys and representatives of the North Country lords and leaders favourable to the Plantagenet cause had been summoned there, twenty miles inside Scotland, to meet the advancing army —the Cliffords, Nevilles, Stanleys, Herons, Skeltons, Thwaites, Dacres, and the rest. But who had appeared? Only this miserable band of petty squirelings. No single lord or knight, nor even the emissary of one; not a bishop or abbot or even prior; not the spokesman of the meanest town.

Lord Drummond backed Bothwell. "Sire—what matters it whether the English join us or no?" he cried. "Here you have the finest array Scotland has ever sent to cross the Border. We need wait on no laggard aid from such as these. Across, I say, and let our steel persuade these doubters!"

The shout of agreement from almost all who could hear him left no doubts as to the feelings and spirit of the Scots leadership —even though this entire campaign was by no means uniformly popular in Scotland. Only the one voice was raised counter to the general clamour; the strong, ever mocking voice of Andrew, Lord Gray.

"That were well enough, my lord, were the prize a castle or two, a few prisoners to ransom or a creagh of cattle. It is a throne at stake, I'd remind you. And a throne calls for subjects as well as swords!"

James considered keenly the man whom, to the astonishment of all his kingdom, he had made Justiciar of Scotland, the man whom he still believed had murdered his father. Gray had proved a success as Justiciar, bearing down a stern and heavy hand on all the barons who would pervert their hereditary jurisdictions to their own advantage and profit. Nevertheless, the King had not dared to leave him behind, on this expedition, though Gray had been against the project from the start, as of course were all of Angus's faction; James had insisted that he come along, however sceptical – for left in Scotland with Angus the Chancellor and hearty Uncle John of Buchan, who could tell what might have been the result? Buchan, therefore, was despatched on a special embassy to King Henry himself – actually still chaffering about the hand of the Princess Margaret – and Gray was here on the Borders, although with precious little of his manpower at his back.

The King nodded. "There speaks sound sense," he acceded. "Our object, my lords, is to gain the Crown of England for Prince Richard, not to win battles. To that end, we require the support of many of the English people. My lord Duke believes that to be his – and pray God that he is right, despite what we see here!" He shrugged, under his gleaming armour. "But we have not come so far to turn back at Tweed, I grant you. Nor yet to sit idly around Berwick. We cross the river, my lords – but we do so not as invaders but as liberators, as friends not as enemies. Mind you that, I say – mind you!"

The murmur that met his warning might have meant anything or nothing – and none knew it better than James Stewart.

He changed his tone, judiciously. "My Lord Home – this is your bailiwick. Be so good as to prospect the fords for us. We follow you down."

In the surge of acclaim and gratification that greeted this decision, Home and his moss-troopers galloped off towards Coldstream and the Tweed. Cheering, the long line moved onward again.

Tweed was less high than sometimes, and the crossing of the cavalry at least was effected without incident. It would take the remainder of the day, and more, for the foot, the baggage, the cannon and the hangers-on, to get over – but that was the responsibility of Sir Andrew Wood, in command of the rearward, and Borthwick the Master of Ordnance. All the town of Coldstream was assembled at the riverside to watch, but on the far side only two or three cottagers and salmon netters silently eyed the spectacle.

Before proceeding southwards, King James sent off small detachments, each with a herald or spokesman, to the nearby castles of Wark, Cornhill, Twizel, Norham and Tillmouth, to inform their keepers of the situation, declare his goodwill, and invite co-operation and support for the Duke of York.

Five miles ahead, the deep and swift-running Till had to be crossed, a lesser stream than Tweed but more readily defendable in its steeper channel, with each of its few bridges or fords guarded by strong castles. Scouts sent ahead to reconnoitre returned to the King with the news that the crossings at both Ford and Etal appeared to be undefended, with no sign of any especial activity at the castles thereof. Wrinkling his brows, James sent a small force under Drummond to secure and hold Etal, whilst he led his main strength to the crossing at Ford, two miles to the south.

The army rode through a pleasant but seemingly empty and silent land. No cattle lowed from the fine pastures, no sheep grazed on the green slopes, no poultry scratched around the farmsteads, no smoke rose from cottage chimneys. Yet houses were standing fully furnished and but imperfectly shuttered and barred, middens still steamed in the yards, horse and cattle droppings were comparatively fresh on tracks and meadows. The deeper James rode into England, eyes busy, the more silent he grew. At his side the Duke had even less to say.

At Ford, the Scots advance-guard held the river crossing under the very ramparts and towers of the castle, a goodly fortalice of some size, though not a major strength. No challenge had met them therefrom, Sir Patrick Home of Fastcastle, uncle of Lord Home and forward commander, announced. The place was barred and shut, its drawbridge up, and no flag flying from its keep; but it was not empty, Sir Patrick asserted. He and his men had seen movement at windows and along its seemingly deserted battlements. He awaited the King's orders. Attack now, or wait until the cannon came up?

"Neither!" James cried. "Have I not told you? We come not here as foes and conquerors – even though these English hide from us as though we were the pestilence itself! The lord of yonder castle is rightfully a subject of the Duke. If he does not welcome us, at least he does not dispute our crossing. Have you spoken with him?"

"I shouted from the knowe, Your Grace. Across the river. And received no answer."

James frowned. "We shall see if he shows more civility to the King of Scots. My Lord Duke," he jerked, "do you care to come talk with your first subject on English soil? Heron is the name, they tell me. Sir William Heron, a knight of some worth."

"If so you intend, Cousin. But I . . ."

"Your Grace! Sire — you do not *yourself* mean to go? To go parley in front of that strength?" the steel-clad Abbot of Jedburgh, another Home, exclaimed.

"I do, Sir Abbot."

"But . . . this is madness, surely? A single arrow, shot from those battlements, could end all!"

"Aye, Sire," Bothwell agreed. "Here's no work for a king. A herald, any pursuivant in the King's name, will serve — and cost less if this Heron is fool enough to show fight."

"Why send a herald in the King's name when the King is here to speak for himself, Patrick? Because the King dare not face an arrow?"

"By the Mass — none doubts Your Grace's courage! But here's no call for it. For some paltry English knight cowering in his castle . . .!"

"Yes, Cousin — it would be unwise, I think," the Duke intervened. "Naught is to be gained by hazarding yourself here . . ."

"There you are wrong, all of you," James declared. "I see it otherwise. Much may hang on this. Here is our first encounter on your English ground. How we act here may well echo through this realm. The land is none so empty as it seems, I swear. Hiding eyes watch us everywhere. I feel it. I know it. We do not wish to leave at our backs dread and malice. But if the King of Scots himself, with Prince Richard, speaks this first castle fair, great good may come of it."

"No doubt, Sire — but that can come after the herald has tested this Heron's temper," Bothwell argued. "We can spare a herald better than we can our liege lord!"

"You think they may well shoot at our herald? Well, then — so much more reason that I speak to them myself. Once arrows start to fly and men to fall, it is war. We must then bring down this Ford Castle. The sword is unsheathed. That way we may win Northumbria — but never win the Northumbrians for the Duke. No — I go. They will not shoot at the King, I believe."

Nothing would alter James's resolve. He led the way across the ford, the water up to the horses' bellies. Few men's eyes left the frowning battlements of that castle, rearing so high above them, from whence a shower of arrows, a single cannon's fire, or even slung stones, could wreak havoc indeed amongst them. No sign of life showed from the towers or parapets.

On the far side, they rode up the steep ramp, keeping as far as they might from the high moss-grown walls of the outer bailey. Some distance from the twin drum-towers of the gatehouse they halted, and the King dismounted.

"My Standard-Bearer. And one trumpeter," he ordered. "You, my Lord Duke — do you accompany me?"

"I do, Cousin — wise or not."

"At the least, wear your helmet, Sire," the Bishop of Dunkeld pleaded.

He was ignored. "Sound a summons," James commanded the other trumpeters. At the ringing challenge of it, he strode forward without further ado, the Duke only a little way behind, with the Royal Standard raised high above them. Automatically, unasked, Sir Rob Bruce, with the great sword, fell in at their backs.

There was perhaps one hundred yards to walk over a bare open forecourt, to the deep dry ditch above which the gatehouse towered, its drawbridge pulled up. Armour clanking hollowly, the five men paced on, and once the trumpet-notes died away, their clanking was almost all the sound to be heard. No faces appeared at the gatehouse windows, nor between the crenellations of the towers. Ford Castle might have been a fortress of the dead.

Unfalteringly, steady paced, James marched on. Now they were nearer to the beetling walls than to the armoured ranks that they had left. Fifty yards, forty, thirty. Any shooting now from those long keyhole-shaped arrow-slit windows, and the marksmen could scarcely fail to hit even the smallest mark.

At about twenty-five yards the King halted, and raised one hand. The silence now seemed almost to throb, to pulse. He waited, and thought of that other castle, Mingary in Ardnamurchan, which he had once approached in just such naked doubt.

After perhaps half-a-minute, turning his head, he jerked a word to the trumpeter, who raised his instrument and blew a single high searing note, demanding and long-sustained. As it died away, James lifted up his voice.

"I, James Stewart, King of Scots, greet all in this house," he called. "I come in friendship, in peace. With me I bring Richard Plantagenet, Duke of York. Does your door open to us?"

Seconds passed without answer or acknowledgment. Then, as he drew breath to shout again, more loudly, a voice replied, a thin, high-pitched, strained, and seemingly disembodied voice.

"I hear you," it said. "If . . . if you are the King of Scots, how come you in peace? With all these at your back? I do not believe you, that you come in friendship. As to Richard of Plantagenet, I know him not."

For moments on end James did not reply, so great was his surprise; not at the words so much as at the fact that it was a woman who spoke. He stared at the massive, harsh frontage of stern stone, the drum-towers with their iron-barred windows, the portcullis gate, the up-ended drawbridge and flanking bartizans, so utterly at odds with the slight and silvery tones which emanated from somewhere therein.

"I . . . I regret . . . I assure you, it is not so," he called back, at a loss. "That is a woman, is it not? Who speaks? Is Sir William Heron not lord of Ford Castle?"

"He is. I am wife to Sir William. He is . . . from home. I pray that you go away, sir. And leave me and mine in peace. If peace brings you across Tweed."

"H'mmm." James stroked his chin. "Peace, yes. But friendship also, lady, I said. Is there naught of that in Ford Castle?"

There was a pause, for long enough to make him fear that she had said all that she was going to say. Then suddenly she appeared at the open parapet which crowned one of the drum-towers flanking the portcullis, an unmartial figure as slight and slender as her voice. The King's surprise was heightened. She was young, much younger than he had visualised, and handsome, little more than a girl — and her hair was as red as his own.

James bowed as deeply as was possible in restricting armour. "Lady Heron — I congratulate your husband!" he exclaimed.

"I shall inform Sir William," she gave back. "What does Your Majesty require of me ? Of Ford Castle?"

"Your benevolence, lady — no more. Permit that I pay my respects at something closer as to range! That we both may be spared more of this unseemly shouting." Hastily he corrected himself. "Though, I vow, *you* shout most sweetly!"

She ignored that. "To the end that you may gain entry to this hold at no greater cost than a few honeyed words?" she charged him, "I think not, Sir King!"

"That is unworthy!" he protested. "Your house I do not seek. Only your goodwill."

"You are gallant, Sire. But . . . my goodwill you will best gain by passing on, by going from hence and leaving me and mine in peace. I ask no more of you than to be gone."

At the King's back Rob Bruce drew a long breath. How little this young woman knew of James Stewart! No surer method could she have devised to detain that impressionable prince than to speak him so. Not that Rob deplored such eventuality. He had no enthusiasm whatever for this English venture, and envisaged any possible delay or entanglement with a young woman, at this stage, only a mile or two over the Border, as probably advantageous in that it might serve to postpone and prevent more drastic and dangerous activities.

James reacted as could have been prophesied. Frowning a little, he inclined his head. "I regret that you find my presence so little to your taste," he said. "Perhaps I may occasion you to judge otherwise, on closer inspection, Lady Heron. And at the least, you might honour your rightful king, the Prince Richard of York here, by some small attention." He glanced around him. "You will yet have the opportunity to do both, however – for it is near to evening, and I see that you have a goodly park. We have travelled far enough for this day. With your permission, we shall encamp here for the night." Before the other could protest, he turned to Bruce. "Rob – return to my Lord of Bothwell, and tell him that we pitch yonder in the park. It will serve very well, with wood and water. Do you not agree, my Lord Duke?"

His companion could scarcely do otherwise.

The young Lady Heron perceived that her position was as untenable diplomatically as it was militarily. She stood for a few moments hesitant, and then called something to unseen persons below and behind her. With a creaking and a clanking of chains, the heavy drawbridge began to descend.

James sat, irritable and impatient, at the head of the great table in the hall of Ford Castle that night, drumming fingers on the board. Around him his lords, prelates and captains lounged replete, at ease and relaxed after the long day in the saddle, drinking their wine – such as were not already asleep or fallen forward drunken over the table. Only the King looked fretful, restless — although on his immediate right, the Duke of York sat silent and preoccupied.

James had more reasons than one for his ill humour. He had just had to rebuke Bothwell for his cheerful boasting as to the lesson he looked forward to teaching these unwelcoming English on the morrow — and had been left in no doubt that the sympathies of the vast majority of his commanders were with the Earl's pugnacious attitude rather than with his own. In the interests of unity, too, he had had to put up with a series of typically mocking slights from the Lord Gray. Again, no English lord or knight of any consequence had repaired to the Scots camp to the support of the Plantagenet cause — and it is to be feared that the King had not spared his ducal protégé's feelings as a result, for this was ominous indeed for the entire campaign. Moreover, and perhaps most galling of all, the Lady Heron was not present, had quite refused to grace her own table with her presence — and James was not only disappointed but wounded as to self-esteem in the important matter of his success with the opposite sex, certain sniggered comments which he had not failed to overhear by no means helping.

Thus it was that Rob Bruce found him as he came to his shoulder, to whisper.

"Sire — the Lady Heron would speak with you. She, h'mm, craves audience. She asks that she may be spared attendance on you here, before all these, praying that Your Grace will honour her . . . elsewhere."

James started up, smiling. "You are but a poor liar, Rob!" he said. "I do not believe all this humble craving and respect, from that one! But at least she would see me, you say? Which is something. Where is she?"

"Her chamber is directly above, Sire."

"Ha!" Waving down into their seats those of his companions able and sufficiently sober to rise to their feet when their monarch rose, James jerked a brief word to the Duke, and strode to the inner door of the hall.

Up on the floor above however, where Rob conducted him, disappointingly he found the young woman standing waiting for him in the lamp-lit hallway, not in her own chamber. She dipped him the sketchiest of curtsies in response to his bow, and made still less acknowledgement of his smile.

"I regret to disturb Your Majesty at meat," she said coldly.

"In your house, lady, you are mistress. Moreover, I am ever the delighted servant of beauty!"

"Your speeches are fairer than your actions, Sire."

He pulled a face. She was very good to look upon, despite her air of proud reserve, and the flickering lamplight seemed to strike glowing sparks amongst her vivid auburn hair, notably to belie her chill of manner. James assessed her as not yet twenty, but lacking nothing in physical maturity and capable of vehement responsive passion if suitably aroused.

"Give me but a little of opportunity, and my actions will be fair enough, I promise!" he assured her.

"There is opportunity and to spare, God knows!" she answered shortly. "Come."

She turned, and taking up the lamp, moved, not back to her chamber door but on towards a small winding turnpike stairway in a tower close by. James followed, but when Rob Bruce began to bring up the rear, he waved him back, away.

Intrigued, James climbed the narrow corkscrew ascent in the wake of those rustling skirts, up and up, tripping now and again over the shadowy steps. One landing they passed, and then another, but still the girl went on. That was the fourth floor of the castle keep, he reckoned.

His guide did not halt until, panting just a little, she emerged through a narrow doorway out of the stair caphouse into the September night itself, on to the topmost flat platform roof of the keep of Ford Castle.

Surprised, he gazed about him. It could scarcely be for dalliance that she had brought him up here, he feared — besides, unfortunately, there was an armed watchman pacing round the battlements.

She moved over to the crenellated breast-high parapet, at the north-east corner, to lean out, pointing. "I believed you to say that you came in peace!" she threw back at him.

He walked over to her side. Before them and below, the blue evening was ablaze with fires. The great park in front and the river-banks to right and left were studded with scores, hundreds, of small winking points of red and orange light — the camp-fires of an army. But it was not towards these that the girl looked, but above and beyond them. Her out-thrown arm described most of a circle, her finger stabbing at other fires, larger by far if more distant, if not by the score by little less, staining all the night sky a murky scarlet. The man's eyes widened, but he did not speak.

"Yonder, on the hill, can be none other than Duddo Tower," she said. "It blazes like its own beacon. And fire all around it — the village too!" Her finger moved further north. "That will be Tindal, I think." Round a little more. "Etal burns also. That is only the castle that we see. There is a village in the hollow of the river — we can only see the glow of that. Look beyond, Sir King — that must be either Castle Heaton or Tillmouth. Aye, Tillmouth probably, the fair house where I was born!" Level-voiced she went on. "We cannot see Cornhill from here, for it is in the valley of Tweed. But we can see the glare of its fires. Nearer is Branxton, there — at the foot of Flodden Hill. You burn churches also then, Majesty? As well as castles and manors and villages . . ."

Hoarsely he interrupted her. "By Ninian and all the blessed saints — I knew naught of this! God's death — the fools! The purblind fools!"

"Aye — foolish! Foolish indeed. I could name it otherwise. Look there, the other side of Flodden Hill, Highness — Milfield, huddled round its church," she went on inexorably in that flat voice. "It burns still brighter than Branxton. Why should that be, think you? Doddington we cannot see, beyond that ridge — but we can see the colour of its sky, can we not? Yonder pale flickering must be Lowick . . ."

"Fiend seize me — enough! Enough, I say!" James cried. "God be good — it is wrong! All wrong. Damnable! I did not know — believe me, I did not know! I commanded quite otherwise. That we came as friends, not foes."

"Scots?" she asked. "Friends?"

The simplicity of that silenced him. But only for a moment. Then, swearing a great oath, he turned and left her standing there. Hurrying to the caphouse doorway he thrust inside, and went running, stumbling, down the dark winding stairway.

Rob Bruce awaited him patiently in the hallway they had left. "Did you know of this, man?" he demanded hotly. "By the Mass, did you know of it?" He did not pause in his running.

Hurrying after him down the main stairs, Rob, at a loss, sought to discover what was amiss, but without success. At the foot, the King, in front still, burst open the hall door, and baredly slowing from a run, went long-strided across to his place at the head of the table. The Duke had gone, as had some few others. Of those who were left some were getting to their feet once more when the crash of metal and breaking pottery startled everyone, save the hopelessly drunk, into shocked attention. James had picked up his great silver drinking goblet and hurled it down the length of the littered table.

"Hear me!" he shouted. "Hear me, all of you! Against my royal commands, a great evil is being wrought, here in this country. All round us castles and houses and townships are being sacked and burned! I said that we came as friends, liberators – those were my sure orders. Who commanded otherwise? God's Passion – who saw fit to cross me in this? Who was fool enough, who had the effrontery, to command differently from the King?"

In silence the company stared at him.

"Answer me! Speak!" Dramatically he pointed. "Out there, the night is aflame. Not one burning castle or village, not two, but a dozen, a score! Who is responsible? Tell me – who did this thing?"

Still none answered him. Never had anyone present seen the King so angry.

James's pointing hand changed direction. "You, my Lord of Bothwell, High Admiral, commander of the middle guard – is this your doing?"

"No, Sire. I know naught of it. But . . . do not concern yourself so greatly, over a few burning thatches . . ."

"Silence! Alexander Home! You, my lord, command the fore-guard. You are Warden of the East March. Did you order this? Contrary to my royal word?"

"Not so," the thin-faced Home declared. "I ordered as Your Grace did. But this is war, Sire – and in war such things happen. Be not so hot against . . ."

The King's fist smashed down on the table. "War it is not!" he cried. "Are you all witless, as well as deaf to my commands? We crossed the Border to gain a crown and subjects for the Duke. Not by killing and burning, but by friendship and goodwill. These fires will burn more than English houses – they will burn the English throne for Richard Plantagenet!"

"Your Grace brought two score of cannon across the Border in friendship and goodwill?" That was Andrew, Lord Gray, mocking as ever. "Sixteen thousand men to speak peace and love!"

271

"Strength we must show — but not savagery," James returned. "We bear the sword for the Duke, but seek not to use it. Now, all is wasted, ruined. By folly and disobedience — if not by treason!"

"Sire, you make overmuch of it," Bothwell protested. "A few houses burned in Northumberland — by the Rude, on any rieving foray our moss-troopers do as much and more! When Hepburns and Homes, Scotts and Kerrs, cross Tweed, they seldom fail to light such a beacon or two! As with the English themselves. When Dacres and Riddells and the other Tynemen ride north, do they spare our roofs?"

The rumble of agreement with that from the company was more of a growl than a murmur, leaving no question as to the feelings of at least the great majority.

Diplomatically the Bishop of Dunkeld spoke up. "Moreover, Sire, laudable and worthy as are your scruples, noble as is your object — is it not too much, perhaps, to expect a like royal understanding of statecraft from all these lesser men? Your Grace has brought a great host across Tweed. I fear that they see themselves more clearly as an army at war than as missionaries for a gospel of friendship and understanding. Be not too hard on them, Sire . . ."

"They have my royal command. That should be sufficient for them."

The prelate spread out his hands. "Should be, perhaps, Your Grace. But men . . ." he began, when he was interrupted by Lord Gray's grating voice.

"Perhaps the King forgets whose commands these thousands of men see fit to obey!" he declared. "Whose men are they, after all? The King's men? Ask them, I say. They are Bothwell's men. Home's men. Seton's men. Drummond's men. The good Bishop's men. Some bare-kneed Highland robber's men. Even some few of my own men. Your Grace's royal commands are perhaps . . . insufficient for these, lacking their lords' closer word!"

For moments no man ventured to speak into the shocked hush. What Gray said was absolutely and painfully true, of course — but never had it been put so baldly, so starkly, in the presence of the monarch. Embarrassed, the very lords of whose men he was speaking looked down and away. None looked at the King.

Strangely enough this brutal frankness had the effect, not of increasing James's wrath but of cooling it down. Gripping the edge of the table, he leaned forward, eyes narrowed, willing himself to calm consideration, to clear-headed judgement in this crisis which had burst unheralded upon him. Much, he was aware, now and in the future, depended upon how he comported himself in the next few minutes.

"I thank my Lord of Gray for his most true and timely words," he said slowly, carefully. "They are apt for the occasion—as is perhaps to be expected from the man whom I appointed Justice-General of my realm!" He paused for a little, and at that even Andrew Gray looked down. "It is true that the King of Scots directly commands no host of armed men—save only his palace guard," he went on. "Such has ever been our Scottish custom. "The King is esteemed to be the father of his people rather than their master. My Highland friends have the best name for it. *Ard Righ*, they call me—the High King. If there is a high king, there must be lower kings. I am the prince of princes, therefore —as well as the father of my people. And you, my lords, are those second princes. Each and all with the powers of such. Aye—and each and all with princely responsibilities, towards my realm and yours."

Again the pause and the silence.

"The King of Scots, then, must seek to rule his people by love and understanding. Through his lords. That I have ever sought to do. Not as Henry Tudor does, by might and tax-levying, the cell and the block. We have no Tower of London in Scotland! Nor as Charles of France does, by edict, the secret council and the torture-chamber. Is ours the feebler course, my lords? Should we change it? Tell me."

None answered him.

"Does the King rule in Scotland, or does anarchy rule?" James demanded, his voice rising a little: "It is for you to say, my lords. You are not my Privy Council, but many of you are of that Council. Say now if every lord is for himself alone, every baron his own master, sufficient unto himself! If such be then Scotland is not a realm, it is a rabble! You are lords, my lords — of what? Of a hundred of your fellow-men? Two hundred? Five hundred? Lords of so many acres of your native soil? Of this castle and that? Is such what you are lords of? 'Fore God, I say otherwise! You are Lords of the Parliament of Scotland, called to that estate by your King. Aye, and your King can un-call you! Your baronies are fiefs of the Crown. And by a scratch of the

273

Crown's pen they are forfeit, reduced, transferred, gone! For the land, my good lords, unlike your men-at-arms, is not yours — it is the King's. In law, every stick and stone, every sod and turf, is in the Crown's grant, however long you and your fathers may have sat thereupon. Do I interpret the law aright, my lord Justiciar?"

Grim-faced, Andrew Gray inclined his head.

James smiled then, not a smile of triumph but the sudden warm and friendly smile which was one of his greatest assets. "So, my friends, you see that there is a balance — a balance that has endured all down the long centuries of our realm. We need each the other. You need my land to feed your men. I need your men to keep my land. My royal command is given, not to your men but to you, my lords — from the High King to lesser kings. It is for you to command the others. Will you do so?"

For seconds no man moved, spoke, or even seemed to breathe. Then the Earl of Bothwell suddenly strode forward and dropped on one knee at the King's feet, taking a hand and raising it to his lips. "Hepburn is yours to command, my lord King!" he exclaimed.

There was a great cry, an uproar indeed, as almost all the other lords pressed close, stumbling over stools and benches, shouldering each other to reach the King's side. One after another they knelt and kissed the royal fingers, some even taking James's hand between their own two palms in the oath-of-allegiance gesture of the Coronation. What they said could by no means be heard in the general clamour.

Over the heads of kneeling men, James's glance found and held that of Andrew Gray. Sombrely they eyed each other.

When the last lord had risen, the King raised his well-kissed hand. "My friends — out there Scotland is shamed. While we talked, Scotland's fair name burned as truly as these English roofs. Go, I prithee, and halt this folly — each and all of you. In my name and your own. No more burning and slaying. Perhaps it is not too late, even yet. Ride fast, my lords, before more ill is done."

When he was alone in that hall, save for Rob Bruce and a couple of hopelessly drunk figures sprawled over the table, James emitted a long breath. He turned to his friend. "Is the fault mine, Rob?" he asked, a little wearily now. "Should I never have brought this host over Tweed? Should I have foreseen this? Was it myself who was the purblind fool?"

274

The other had been against this venture from the start, conceiving it as mistaken. With the Lady Margaret and Bishop Elphinstone, he had done what little he could to dissuade his headstrong monarch. But now he could utter nothing of this to the man he loved in his ineloquent, undemonstrative fashion. His eyes still shining with the admiration and emotion engendered by the King's dramatic and masterly turning of the tables on Gray, he shook his head, wordless.

"I have a great talent, Rob, for believing what I wish to believe!" James went on. "Hating Henry Tudor and all his works, his plots, his treacheries, I desired that this Richard should hurl him from his throne and sit thereon in his place. I desired that the English people should think likewise, hating an oppressor and a deceiver, and so should greatly welcome a prince who comes of the old Plantagenet stock. And so desiring it, I believed it. And am proved wrong. I have brought war and hurt to England — but have I brought her her new king?"

"My knowledge of such matters is small, Sire — but I never thought so," Rob admitted, low-voiced.

"Well, we shall know all too soon. If in a day or two more, there is no support appeared for the Duke, then we shall have the answer for certain!"

"And then, Sire?"

James sighed. "I cannot put the crown of England on Richard's head by force of arms, even if I would. Sixteen thousand men I may have, but this is not sufficient to march on London, or even York, if there is no English rising in our favour. So . . ." He left the rest unsaid. "Meantime, I must save what I can." He changed his tone. "Time that I was in the saddle also, Rob. See — go you to the Lady Heron, with my respects. Tell her that the King of Scots greatly regrets what is done. That is it against his wishes and orders. That he gives her his word that what ill may be undone shall be. Aye, and tell her that he will present himself to her again when he may look her in her fair face without shame! Say that, Rob — then follow me."

16

WEARY in mind and body, yet with no desire for his couch, King James paced to and fro over the dew-damp grass before his handsome royal pavilion, pitched under a tall tree of the park beneath the pale September stars, a solitary, restless figure at odds with the night and his fellows. Around him the great camp slept, save for the sentries — and save also for Sir Rob Bruce who sat just within the door of the nearby tent he shared with the Lord Lyon King of Arms and the Standard-Bearer, watching his liege lord. The last drunken singing of roystering men-at-arms, the last screeching of women camp-followers and possible local prizes, had died away; the lamp in the Duke's great tent, near to the King's own, was at last extinguished; the ominous glow of fires, near and far, had largely faded, although not entirely — indeed the King feared that one or two increased points of brightness might represent new though distant conflagrations rather than revived old ones. It lacked only an hour or two till dawn.

His triumph of eloquence before his lords, earlier in the night, had long turned sour in the King's mouth. Words, words, so soon to be mocked by actions that spoke vastly otherwise. It was one matter to talk about royal commands, or even lords' commands, and altogether another to impose such upon thousands of armed and undisciplined men thirsting for blood, booty and women in what they looked upon as the hated territory of the Auld Enemy. The race memories of centuries of English raiding and oppression and menace, especially amongst the Scots Borderers, were much more potent than any disquisitions on statecraft, woolly talk of goodwill, pleas for forbearance, or even threats of punishment to follow. Besides, it was physically impossible to find and control all the small roving bands into which much of the infantry in especial had split up, across Tweed, once it was clear that no large armed force opposed them, demanding a united front. If the Homes' own Merse in Scotland had suffered, what hope was there for defenceless Northumbria?

James himself had spent three or four fruitless, enfuriating hours, riding angrily around that benighted and terror-stricken countryside, seeking to stay fierce hands, commanding, explaining, pleading, threatening – to little effect. Most of his lords had given up much more quickly their attempts to counter the age-old instincts of fighting-men let loose in a foreign land. It was indeed a custom hallowed by long acceptance, not only in Scotland, that men-at-arms, being unpaid in money and giving their service in return for plots of land, rights of grazing and the like, from their masters, should recoup themselves where they could by the spoils of war. It was part of the system. No kingly talk about calling the English friends was going to alter that.

James had seen some grievous sights. He had been correct in believing that the country was less empty than it seemed. The rich and powerful had largely betaken themselves out of the way, removing themselves from the threat of the Scots invasion; but the poorer folk had only gone to ground, hidden away in concealed refuges, deans and hollows, even churches. It had not taken the expert rievers and moss-troopers long to find them, their women and their small livestock. The King, whose conception of war was romantic and chivalrous, was as appalled as he was wrathful. The knowledge that it was he and he alone who had unleashed this horror on this land, kept him from his couch.

And not only that. What of the morrow? If the English had failed to rally to the Plantagenet banner before, what hope was there now? He had urged the Duke to issue a proclamation for his hoped-for subjects – indeed he had himself largely compiled it – branding Henry Tudor as a miscreant and usurper, accusing him of the murder of Sir William Stanley, Sir Simon Montford and other of the ancient nobility, of having invaded the liberties and privileges of Holy Church, and of pillaging the common people by heavy and unjust taxation, the Duke himself pledging his word to remove these impositions, to maintain the privileges of Church and nobles, the charters of corporations and the rights of the burghs and of individuals; even offering a reward of one thousand pounds for Henry's head, as though he were a common malefactor. All this had been most carefully aimed at mobilising the known grievances of all classes in England, and the terms of it sent well in advance of the army. Yet it had resulted in no support. If none materialised in the next day or two . . .

So James paced and fretted, flogging his tired mind, beneath the proud flapping Lion Rampant of Scotland, and only Rob Bruce watched his uneasy vigil and guessed at his extremity of feeling, grieving for him.

It was a strange circumstance indeed which put an end to the King's unquiet perambulations eventually. At the turning-point of the track which he was so grimly beating out on the greensward he suddenly paused, peering. Something had caught his preoccupied eye, something which could only be movement, unlooked-for movement. Halting, he stared.

Yes, movement it was — furtive, secret, careful. Two shadowy figures, three, four, were converging on one of the tented pavilions, even in the darkness their aspect stealthy, inimical. It was another of the great tents that they approached — that of the Duke of York.

Quick as thought the King drew back into the deeper shadow between his own pavilion and the next to it, the lesser tent in which Rob Bruce sat watching. Behind this he slipped, silently. Whoever approached thus, at such an hour, was up to no good, for certain.

The Duke's tent was pitched less than thirty yards from his own. James moved swiftly along behind three others until he was level with it. Keeping himself hidden, carefully he peered round, narrowing his eyes in the gloom.

The newcomers were still there, motionless now, huddled in a tight group near the closed flap, menace in every line of them. Even as one moved forward to that tent-flap, James heard a tiny sound, but evil — the thin screak of steel, as dirks and daggers were whipped from sheaths.

Without a thought for his own unarmed state, he acted. Leaping forward, he raised his voice. "To me! To me! The King!" he shouted. "Treachery! The Guard! To me — the guard! Treason . . .!" Tripping over one of the ropes pegged into the ground to support a tent, he fell all his length on the damp grass.

There were hurried abrupt exclamations, questions, curses, in front, as uncertainly the four men paused. One of them turned, and came running back towards the fallen King, followed by another. James was struggling to his feet.

Then another shout changed all, just in time. "Sire! Sire! God's name — where are you?" That was Rob Bruce, coming at the run, tugging out his poniard. "What's to do . . .?"

At sight and sound of such swift response to the King's cry, the assailants took swift further thought to their situation. One of them jerked commands, and then they were running also, off down the lane of tents.

But running in the darkness amongst closely pitched tentage is a hazardous proceeding, and first one of the fugitives slipped and stumbled over a guy-rope, and then another. The first recovered himself, but the second crashed headlong. His companions did not pause to aid him. James, without waiting for Rob, was fairly close at their heels. Just as the fallen man was rising, he hurled himself bodily upon him, grappling him, seeking to pinion his arms to his sides, lest he attempted to use his dagger.

Rob came pounding up, and though James breathlessly directed him after the other three, Rob's concern was for his monarch's wellbeing. He dropped on his knees beside the two struggling men.

"Sire! Your Grace – are you hurt? Sweet Mary – who . . . what is this?"

"Hold him! He has a dirk!" James gasped. "The others! A pox – we'll be too late! Fiend take them – there were four! After them, Rob . . ."

But by the time that they had got themselves and their prisoner to their feet, it was obvious that it would be fruitless to go chasing the others. All around men were emerging from tents, guards and sentries were coming at the run, shouts and questions were filling the night. In the confusion, the runaways would be unfortunate indeed not to escape.

Rob had disarmed their single captive, and now held his poniard's point at the man's throat. He seemed to be one of the men-at-arms, of the better sort, a stocky bearded man in breast-plate and leather, who had lost his morion in the fall. He was part-winded and showing no fight.

"Take him to your tent, Rob," the King ordered, low-voiced. "Quickly. There is strange work here which may be best kept close. Hold him fast. I would question this dastard. But . . . let not others have word with him meantime. You understand? Off with him, now."

James soothed and put off the lords and leaders who now came thronging around him, asserting that it probably was but a drunken escapade of some of the out-of-hand soldiery. When he could get rid of them, he went to the Duke of York's tent. It was still in darkness, and when a startled esquire admitted the King, it was to find his master still asleep. After a moment's thought, James left him to his heavy slumbers, and crossed over to Rob's tent.

The captive would not talk, at first. But in the King's present mood of anger and frustration, it did not take long for him to convince the man that he meant what he said when he threatened rack and thumbscrews as a means of loosening reluctant tongues. Rob Bruce's fingering of his naked poniard, too, had its effect. The fellow capitulated.

It had been a plot to seize the Duke of York, the man confessed. It was not to kill him, only to seize him. To carry him away. To end this war and invasion. By all the saints, he swore that it was not to have been murder. Only a seizing . . .

"Who is your master?" James interrupted curtly. "Whose man are you?"

"My Lord o' Gray, Sire. But he kens naught o' this. I swear it. This isna his ploy."

"I do not believe you."

"It is God's ain truth, Highness! It wasna him . . ."

"Who, then? Out with it, man—or I'll hang you by your thumbs until you tell me! Whose plot is this?"

"I canna say for sure, Sire," the captive whined. "I'm but a pair man o' nane account. They dinna confide in such as me."

"Fool! Four of you, there were. Do not tell me that you knew not the others. Or that you did not talk of them that sent you, paid you. Out with it. And quickly. Who were the other three?"

"One was callit The Friar, Highness. They say he is a broken priest, and a man o' my Lord o' Buchan."

"Buchan! Ah, yes. And the others?"

"One was a black deil o' the name o' Douglas—Will Douglas. An ill man to cross, Sire. He made me dae it, see you . . ."

"And the third?"

"An Englishman. A serving man to the English envoy—him they ca' Wyat . . ."

"So! There we have it! The same sorry coven! My hearty Uncle John of Buchan. Will Douglas—a creature of Angus, my Chancellor. And a servant of Henry's ambassador, Wyat. And you—Gray's man. Dear God—when shall I be free of them and their plots? What was to happen to the Duke of York, wretch—when you had seized him?"

"Naught o' harm, Sire—naught o' harm. We were to carry him to Berwick. Near to Berwick. To a bit they ca' the Ord. House o' Ord."

"To whom? Who was to receive him at this Ord?"

"I heard them say it was Ramsay. Sir John Ramsay. Him that yince was Earl o' Bothwell."

"Aye. Likely." Ramsay had been one of his father's favourites, created Earl of Bothwell, who had fled Scotland after Sauchieburn and had been in Henry's pay ever since, an associate of Angus and Buchan, whose earldom James had taken from him and given to Patrick Hepburn, Lord Hailes. "Ramsay, too! Ramsay is a friend of your master, the Lord Gray, fellow. Do you still say that he knows nothing of this?"

"I swear it, Sire. Leastways, he's no' been named by them. And he doesna ken I'm here. It was yon Will Douglas and The Friar who came to me."

"I think probably you lie. But . . . no matter. I have learned enough, to discover the rest. I have learned that my enemies spurn my forbearance, take all, and are my enemies still. Away with him, Rob. It will serve."

"Aye, Sire. But what shall I do with him?"

"I care not . . ."

"Hang him!" Lyon advised, succinctly.

James frowned. "That is too much, I think. He is but a cat's-paw, who achieved nothing."

"What, then? We cannot let him go free."

"Sire! Highness! Majesty! Forgie me this, an' I'll be your man, your true man. I'll dae aught you say. Spare me, Sire, o' your royal mercy . . .!"

"Quiet, rascal! Come, you," Rob commanded.

"Wait!" the King said. "I have a notion. Your name, fellow?"

"Moncur, Sire—Tom Moncur. I'm but a pair man . . ."

"Aye, Moncur, you are but a poor creature indeed—but it may be we shall yet have some worth out of your worthless life. I give you your freedom—at a price. Go back to your service with my Lord of Gray. Be his man as before. But be *my* man, also. For your neck's sake, if not for your King! Use your eyes and your ears. In my lord's service I warrant you may hear much that I would do well to know! Aught that you hear that is against me and my realm, come to tell me. Or, not me—come to Sir Rob Bruce here. Secretly. You understand? Anything of importance

281

plotted against the King, or the realm, come and tell Sir Robert. Do not fail me, or forget – or you pay for this night's doings. Begone now, Tom Moncur – and keep your eyes and ears wide, and your mouth close!"

Cutting short the spate of the man's babbled gratitude, Rob hurried him outside.

"I have ever hated plots and spies and informers," James declared, after a moment or two, looking at the others almost defiantly. "I have scorned to use such, as unbecoming in a prince. But . . . must I ever tie my hands against these Judases, these vipers? Must I never use their own weapons against them? By the Mass – who, in God's name, would be King of Scots!" And he flung out of that tent.

Sorrowfully Rob Bruce looked after him, as he entered his own pavilion.

James threw himself on his couch, fully clad as he was. It was almost light before he slept.

The great camp, in consequence, had been long astir before the King was awake. Even so, Rob Bruce was loth to rouse him, and delayed as long as he might. But the Duke of York was urgent, insistent. Reluctantly Rob acquiesced.

So, sitting hunched and heavy-eyed on his couch, and in no very receptive frame of mind, James was confronted with an agitated and anxious prince before ever he had sustained himself with breakfast.

"Your Grace – here are grievous tidings! I am sorely distressed. Something must be done forthwith. Surely you must see it? I have learned this morning of this evil thing . . ."

"To be sure, Cousin – to be sure," the King nodded. "These are the methods of our enemies. But there is little harm done, and we may yet profit . . ."

"There is much harm done, Sire! Do you not see it? Last night's work could be the end of all."

"But it was not. They failed. Now we are warned. In tilting for a throne, my friend, you must look for answering blows. And since it is Henry Tudor's throne, the blows are like to be underhand . . ."

"*Parbleu* – I say that this is like to have *lost* me that throne!" the other exclaimed.

James frowned, drawing a weary hand over his head. "What

282

mean you? Since they failed in their attempt on you, and now we are warned . . .?"

"Not that." The Duke dismissed the night's attempt with a wave of his hand. "It is of the shameful attacks on my people that I speak."

"Ah. I mistook you."

"I fear that I mistook you also, Sire! I believed that you were a prince of enlightenment and honour." The Duke's normally calm and carefully modulated voice quivered now with an emotion that he had hitherto managed to disguise. "It seems otherwise. This morning, certain gentlemen of this country, this unhappy country, Sir John Appleby and Master Horton of Akeld, have waited upon me. They told me of terrible things — of men slain, houses and villages burned, women ravished, gear and cattle stolen. The entire land given over to sword and flame. *Mon Dieu* — is this your friendship?"

"I am sorry, Cousin," James began, with a sigh. "It is regrettable . . ."

"It is barbarism! Worthy only of robbers, savages! I came to deliver my people, and you . . . you . . ." Indignation choked him.

James jumped to his feet. "Have a care for your words, sir!" he cried. "No man speaks the King of Scots so! Some roofs have been burned, yes — some blood shed. But in war such things happen . . ."

"This is not war! This is massacre, rapine, pillage. My people have not drawn sword against you. *Ma foi* — you and your Scots have but used my cause and claim to come and wreak your cruel wills on these my folk! To harry and rob and slaughter, as has ever been your savage wont. So you deprive me of my throne! Who in England, now, will receive me? My cause is like to be lost — because I put my trust in the Scots!"

"Have a care how you speak, I say, Sir Duke!" James's voice was hoarse. "You presume! If ever you sit on Henry's throne, it will be because the Scots put you there! And only the Scots. What does the Emperor for you? Save speak fair words? And Charles of France? Do they move? Do they venture a single man? Do they threaten England's southern shore, as they promised? Even your Duchess. What is Burgundy's contribution? Sixty men — sixty! Only the Scots, the barbarous Scots, draw sword for Plantagenet! If that sword spills a little blood, precious soul of

God, must you therefore berate them, condemn them? Is your princely thought only for these spineless English who hide and skulk and make complaint . . .?"

"If I am their prince, would I not be iron-hearted not to be moved by the sufferings of my own people?" the other asked, more quietly, simply.

The unanswerable truth of that, with its dignity, had more effect on James than had the earlier railing. But he was in a cleft stick on this entire issue, and he hardened his heart. "You talk much of your people, your own folk," he charged. "But do they so think of you? I believed you when you said that they would — or I would not be here. You seem now to worry yourself over what does not concern you — for you have called these English your subjects. Yet not one of them has offered to help in a war waged on your behalf."

"The war, Sire, was to be waged against Henry Tudor — not against these my people," the Duke answered. "I would sooner renounce the crown altogether than gain it through the misery of my subjects."

"Noble words!" James declared bitterly, mockingly.

"They are true words, nevertheless. I will be no party to this sackage and butchery. I crave Your Grace's leave to return to Scotland. Forthwith."

"You do?" James gulped a breath. "Then go, sir — go! Your crave is granted! Aye, go back — and take your Burgundians and your Irish with you. For you serve no good purpose here — your own, or mine!" The King flung round, to stride back and forth in his tent, like a caged lion. "Begone — for you will make no King of this England!"

"Must kings live with blood and fire and tears, then, Sire?"

Tortured-eyed, King James halted, to stare at him. "Aye, they must," he said, almost groaned. Gripping the chain at his loins, he jerked at it savagely. "God's pity on them — but indeed they must!"

Without another word the Duke bowed briefly, and head high walked from the tent.

In the doorway, Rob Bruce sorrowfully watched the anguish of his monarch and friend until, unable to bear it longer, he left him alone.

That 21st of September 1496 was probably the worst, the most unhappy day of James Stewart's entire life. Certainly none had ever seen him in so ill a humour. At odds with the world, none who crossed his path escaped his ire, his hurt, his spleen.

The Duke of York, true to his word, rode off northwards, back to Scotland, after a notably stiff and formal parting, with the Burgundians, the two Irish earls and their people, and sundry other non-Scottish adherents. There was considerable heart-burning and even confusion about this exodus, not only on the Scots' part, for the Irish had been just as active in the process of showing Northumbria who was master, and most of the departing warriors were heavily laden with booty.

There was much anger in the camp.

Morale was not improved when, almost as soon as the prince was gone, James gave orders that five men-at-arms caught that same morning in the act of killing, raping and looting near by, were to be hanged out of hand, on the mound directly under the windows of Ford Castle. Despite pleas by the Lord Seton, whose men they were, and others, and representations that though this might be apt justice it was bad for the army as a whole, the King was implacable. Let these men be a lesson and example, he declared grimly, to others who disobeyed the royal commands. He would not hesitate to hang others caught in similar shameful activity. Perhaps he recollected Alexander of Lochalsh's corre-sponding discipline on the Isle of Rum. The host murmured its resentment. Only some few noted that the King had held his hand until the Duke of York had left.

The Lady Heron's plea, thereafter, that the unfortunate examples of royal wrath should not be left to dangle in close vicinity to her windows, was curtly refused.

James announced to his commanders that the advance south-wards would not continue meantime, and that the camp would remain at Ford. But he sent out strong mounted columns in various directions, over into Cumberland and as far south as Newcastle, to show the flag, spy out the land, and discover what support there might be, in less typical Borderland country, for the Plantagenet pretender. The King himself, the need for violent action of some sort strong upon him, set out on a hard-riding angry tour of the immediate area, to investigate the scale of depredations and damage done by his marauders, only a small escort in attendance.

It was on the return from this depressing inspection, angrier than ever over what he had seen, that James found his camp in a state of uproar, almost of mutiny. The Earl of Bothwell, left in command, explained the situation to his black-browed monarch in an attitude of grim I-told-you-so. It seemed that the only major castle in the area which had not fallen to the invaders was Castle Heaton, a very strongly sited eagle's-nest of a place set high above the Till some five miles downstream from Ford. Because of its position, and the fact that the Scots artillery could not be brought to bear on its walls, this stronghold still held out. Indeed, James had given orders for it to be left alone. Growing bold, therefore, no doubt informed of the King of Scots' instructions and deeming them abject weakness—possibly having heard of the hangings likewise—the garrison had demonstrated their contempt by actually making a sally, attacked a party of Lord Home's moss-troopers who were occupying Heaton Mill near by, surprised them, and after a bloody struggle had carried off no fewer than fifteen of the Homes as prisoners. Those fifteen now hung in a row, in chains and by the heels, from the topmost tower of Castle Heaton—all save one, who was hanged the right way up, so that he could wear a mock crown and be draped with a red and yellow robe as King of Scots.

James grew ominously still as he listened, whatever the outraged comments of those around him. Rageful as he was within, he perceived so much more in this final piece of ferocious folly than the mere insulting challenge that had set his camp by the ears. He saw it as the last and unanswerable publication of his own failure, his misjudgement, the slamming of the door on any possibility of retrieving a grievous situation. All too clearly he saw what this must mean, must entail. He could not ignore it, or pooh-pooh it. By publicly mocking the King, all Scotland's pride and reputation was at stake. If he, the King, did not wipe out this insult, he would no longer have an army to lead or lords to command. Well he knew it. On top of his own hangings, this shameful deed demanded immediate retribution if his Scottish host was not to degenerate forthwith into a rage-maddened horde. Moreover, it could hardly have been worse, in that the victims were Home's men. Lord Home was Warden of the East March, the King's appointed lieutenant for the maintenance of law, order and defence on this section of the Border. Not to proceed with all vigour against the perpetrators of this outrage was to undermine fatally the morale on which the continued defence of the Border rested. Only six or seven miles away was the Home territory, across Tweed.

Something of all this flashed through the King's unhappy mind as he listened to his commanders' expressed fury. But something else also, he perceived. Castle Heaton, although immensely strong in situation, was a comparatively small place, no great fortress. For the King of Scots, with his whole army, to concentrate on the reduction of such a minor establishment might well turn him into a laughing-stock if the matter was unduly prolonged. That had to be considered likewise.

James held up his hand for silence. "My lords," he grated. "This is insupportable? A provocation not to be borne. We shall teach these miscreants a lesson! But . . . why did they do it?"

"Why, but that Your Grace has shown yourself over-soft! Too mild and gentle!" someone cried. "The hand that draws the sword dare not be palsied!"

"Aye—you are right! There's the truth o' it."

"They see Your Grace as weak, fearing to offend . . ."

James cut his hand down as though to slice through that critical talk. "Silence!" he barked. "Use your wits, my lords. Even though these English may mistakenly esteem the King of Scots as feeble as you say, they know that *you* are here also, do they not? Whom none would dare to label as soft or over-mild!" That was finely scornful. "They know that there are fifteen thousand Scots at their gate. Yet still they do this. How is it that they dare?"

"They have seen the Duke of York march away . . ."

"They believe us divided. Hanging our own kind . . ."

"Tush! That would not make them thus bold. I think, my lords, that they must believe that they will be relieved, and quickly. And to relieve yonder hold, this army must first be defeated. Which, since all the world knows your lordships' well-tried valour, would require a larger host than this! Close at hand."

There was no more raillery and baiting now. Of a sudden the group around the King fell silent, eyeing each other.

"Our outposts and spies report nothing such," James went on. "But these in Castle Heaton may have truer word. It may be that we are but poorly informed. There is much land beyond these hills where a great host might approach. And there is more than that. You'll mind, my lord of Bothwell, and you, Sir Andrew

—when MacIan of Ardnamurchan thought himself safe in Mingary Castle because for hundreds of miles the land was secure, he yet woke one morning to find an army under his walls! In ships. Berwick haven, which is held against us, lies not ten miles on our flank—and King Henry has many ships."

"By sea! You think . . .?"

"Is it possible, Sire? An army? To bring even ten thousand by ship?"

"Not all by ships. But some thousands, as we did at Ardnamurchan. With cannon. Others to come by land. From the south and west. The people here to rally to them. Such could close upon us to our great danger. It may not be so. All may be only in my mind. But something has given these English great boldness. We must discover it. Many more scouts and spies must go out. They must probe the land. We must watch the coast. Get men into Berwick town, somehow. As pedlars or friars or beggars, so that we be not caught unawares. See you to it, my lords."

"And Castle Heaton, Sire?" Bothwell demanded.

"I go there now," James declared.

The deep, dark but fast-running Till wound its way northwards through a steep tree-lined channel from the Cheviot Hills to the Tweed, creating a major natural barrier. Since crossing Tweed lower down than Coldstream presented a much more ambitious and dangerous operation, practically all Scots raiders and invaders had to face this barrier soon after entering Northumbria; and its crossings, by Twizel Bridge and the various fords, were all defended by strong castles. Of these, Castle Heaton, the first above Twizel Bridge and only two miles from Tweed, though not the largest, presented probably the most awkward military problem. King James, when he arrived there to inspect the situation, late that afternoon, was left in no doubts as to the difficulties, either by his companions or by his own eyes.

Perched on a ridge of high ground on the west side of the Till, the castle was defended on three sides by steep banks to the river itself, and on the fourth or west side by a flooded area of mere and marsh, of wide extent, through which twisted a tributary stream. Only a narrow causeway crossed this, as approach, and the causeway itself was gapped by two drawbridges. The outer of these, over the winding stream, was a long way out from the castle walls, and remained raised except when in use, guarded by a strong squat tower and having a covered way from the main battlemented gatehouse which protected the second and inner drawbridge over a moat. Behind this, high thick curtain walls rose sheer, crowned by a parapet and with strong flanking towers at the angles, and all this masonry was pushed forward to use every available inch of the high ground, so that there was no least toehold to be had beneath, even if such position could be reached. Within the enclosure, the high square central keep crowned all. It was from the caphouse which covered the stairhead to this keep's battlements that the fifteen grim corpses of the captured Homes now swung in chains, the lowermost hung of all representing the King of Scots. Sir John Swinburne, lord of this strength, perhaps had reason to consider himself fairly safe to indulge his individual sense of humour.

James curtly cut short all the efforts and attempts to demonstrate to him the problems facing any attackers of this place; he saw them all too clearly. On the three sides bounded by the river, the slopes rising straight from the water were almost steep enough to be termed cliffs, providing no access for even the most agile assaulters. Individuals might climb up there in the darkness, but the sheer frowning walls of the castle soaring straight out of the rock above, offered no gathering point or base for scaling-ladders. Nor was there scope for breaching the walls by artillery fire. Cannon could not be brought to bear effectively; there was no space for them at the foot of the cliffs, and even floated on the river in rafts the angle of fire would be too steep — while across on the east bank, which sloped up at a somewhat less steep pitch, the range would be too great.

On the remaining west side, conditions were almost worse. The marshland spread out for over a quarter of a mile. If it had been real water, a lake, it might have been possible to float the guns close; but this quaking morass precluded anything of the sort. The causeway itself was so narrow that only one cannon could be mounted thereon at a time. Any attempt to fill up the bog with brushwood or the like, to make it sufficiently substantial to bear the weight of heavy guns, would be a labour of Hercules — and before it became of any valuable effect would have to be carried out well within bow-shot of the castle. It might be possible to get a cannon near enough to demolish the tower guarding the outer drawbridge — but that, on the face of it, seemed as much as might be hoped for.

After making his circuit of inspection, James withdrew to a

hillock at the side of the marsh, rejecting even Rob Bruce's company. Well aware that his own ill-humour was no help in any aspect of this trying situation, yet unable to banish the anger, frustration, disappointment and actual shame that clouded his mind, he yet flogged his tired brain to make a reasoned and comprehensive consideration of what was possible and advisable. His inclination, now, was to cut his losses, to take the obvious course of winding up this ill-fated and unhappy expedition forthwith, and march back to Scotland in the wake of the Duke. This would be interpreted, almost certainly, as arrant weakness by friend and foe alike. But would it in fact be weakness, if it was the wise and right decision, however unpopular?

He never seriously considered the notion, of course. His reputation with his own people would never recover from such an apparently pusillanimous gesture — and the Scots people were not gentle with weak kings, as his father had discovered to his cost. On the other hand, to fruitlessly besiege this strong but unimportant private castle would redound almost as little to his renown — although to leave it unpunished was equally dangerous for his own credit with his army. Some middle course there must be, surely?

He must at least seem determined to reduce this wretched stronghold — but not as any major effort, using any large proportion of his army. It would be as well if he himself could be seen to take some brief but spectacular part. What to do with the remainder of his host, then — since to leave them idle would be highly dangerous, leading to more foraging and pillage; and any general advance southwards, without English support, would be risky in the extreme should Henry send a force by sea to Berwick. Berwick — might that not serve? A feint towards Berwick? The place itself was the most secure fortress in the two kingdoms, not to be won without great cost and a long siege; but a feint towards it meantime, whilst he awaited news of Henry's moves, and took steps against this Castle Heaton, was possibly his best hope. What steps here, then? Long James pondered, cudgelling his brain — until he perceived that in his preoccupation he had been poking at a mole-hill at his feet, ripping up its run with a stick. A mole! Of course! Perhaps a mole might get him out of his difficulty? His ancestor, The Bruce, had once gained instruction from a spider. Might not a humble mole do him a like service?

Jumping up, the King strode back to where his lords gloomily conferred. "Send a herald in my name to that arrogant Englishman." he cried. "Order him to surrender his hold forthwith. To come out barefooted and without arms, he and all his men — or else I shall topple his castle about his ears. Give him until tomorrow morning. Meantime, bring my good Mons Meg to this causeway, and pound yonder first drawbridge tower to dust. Maintain the cannonade throughout the night. While Mons barks, the mole will dig!"

They stared at him, as though he had taken leave of his senses.

"See to it," he commanded, shortly, conceding nothing. "I slept little last night — and shall not this. I return to my couch until darkness. My horse, Rob."

That night many besides the King did not sleep. For one thing, the great Mons Meg, largest of all the Scots cannon and James's pride, thundered her great roar at intervals throughout, hurling balls at the squat tower which guarded the outer drawbridge of the causeway. For a mile or so around Castle Heaton it would have demanded singular powers to sleep through that. At the other side, in the channel of the Till itself, there was a different sort of distraction. Just across from the castle a lesser camp was established, fires were lit well back from the river's edge, and much noise was made. Under cover of this activity and racket, men floated silently down the river on rafts to just below the castle, the King himself on the first raft, peering intently in the darkness for the exact point at which to make the awkward landing. Personally he quietly led the small group of tough Borderers, armed with picks, mattocks and lamps, in the difficult climb up the steep face of the cliff to a spot only a few feet below the foundations of the keep's walling. He had chosen the place carefully earlier, in daylight, before returning to Ford, prospecting it necessarily at a distance from across the river — a section of the cliff where there was more raw earth than naked stone, under a slight overhanging shelf of rock. Undoubtedly in wet weather water would ooze out and flow down there — which indicated flaws in the rock and rotted stone. Here, on their precarious stance, with as little noise as possible, he set his men to gouge out the beginnings of a cavity.

It was anxious work at first. Once they had excavated something of a cave, they would be comparatively safe, but until then stones, boiling oil or other missiles could be hurled down upon them from the castle above. Fortunately the very height of the keep walls was something of a help, for the parapet—where presumably watchmen paced—was fully eighty feet higher. Even so, James cursed his men on the other side of the river for not making more noise—since that was all they were there to do. Mons Meg's bangings helped, of course—but the loading and priming of that impressive piece of ordnance took a considerable time between shots, and its functions were rather to keep the garrison's attention fixed on that side of the castle, than to cover the sounds of picks and rolling stones.

Only a very few men could work at one time without getting in each others' way. Anyway, there was no room for numbers to stand on that precarious sloping ledge. Those not wielding mattock and pick were employed in taking away the spoil and loosened rock in their hands, to bestow it somewhere so that it would not roll noisily down the bank. This was no work for a king, but James toiled at it with the rest, bent double, seeking to keep his feet on the slantwise ground, swearing when a stone escaped them to go bouncing downhill—but preferring this to standing by inactive, waiting for the feared challenge from above.

Fortunately the distractions of percussion, firelight, noise and movement, seemed to serve their purpose. At least, nothing came down upon the busy group digging directly beneath the castle walls, no indication was given that they had been discovered. It was a cloudy night of thin, intermittent rain.

After the first heartening progress, through soft earth and loose rock, headway was painfully slow as they were confronted with ever more solid rock. It was too soon to risk lighting lamps, and the men had to feel with their fingers for cracks and seams in the greywacke barred with conglomerate strata, in which to insert the points of their picks and spikes. Panting, crouching, they proved and levered and heaved.

After a while, the King sent this party down for a rest, with orders to send up their reliefs who waited at the waterside, he himself remaining above.

All night the work went on, with relays of diggers, to the accompaniment of recurring roaring from Mons Meg and distinctly disappointing noise from the camp across the river. The cavity, roughly circular and about six feet in diameter, did grow and deepen, but very gradually, and a vast amount of spoil and rubble seemed to have to be disposed of for so small a hole. It was well into the small hours of the morning before they had penetrated deeply enough to risk lighting lamps. Thereafter, with the hewers able to see what they were doing, to trace flaws and seams in the greywacke, progress was considerably better. James himself occasionally took turns with pick and spike— but not for long at a time and for reasons of morale only, for he very soon recognised that he was quite the least effective of the quarriers, his muscles not being accustomed to manual labour. Quickly he was apt to revert to soil disposal.

With the first traces of a rosy flush beginning to stain the eastern sky, men waiting below climbed up with sods of grass, pulled undergrowth and pieces of brushwood, to cover up and disguise the scattered spoil and traces of the work, as far as might be. Soon thereafter, however reluctantly, James called off the labour, and led his toilers discreetly down to the rafts, on which they were drawn away upstream by ropes while it was still dark enough for them to escape notice from high above. They had been most fortunate to have remained unobserved all night, and while work on the tunnel itself could now proceed safe from attack from the castle, the only access thereto, up the cliff face, was so exposed and dangerous that it was obviously wise to keep the mining secret for as long as possible. Despite the delay, therefore, the work would proceed only by night meantime.

So tired that even the fretting, nagging anxieties and qualms of the past two days were for the moment almost banished from his mind, the King returned to his pavilion at Ford, hurled some orders at Rob Bruce, ever in faithful attendance, and was asleep almost as soon as he threw himself upon his couch.

James was up betimes in the morning, nevertheless. The main mass of his army was assembling ready for the march towards Berwick. There was much surprise and even some reproof amongst his lords when the King declared that he was not going to accompany them, and placed Bothwell in over-all command. Protests that a king's duty was to lead his host, and not to dig holes in the earth like any menial serf were expressed in voices less than discreetly lowered, the royal temper being thereby improved nothing. A further cause for disquiet were the reports from many of the baronial contingents of desertions during the night—parties and small groups of men-at-arms having quietly departed for home, laden with Northumbrian booty and driving captured cattle before them. This, of course, was something of a time-honoured custom in Border warfare, but galling indeed to commanders. Many an army had evaporated before its leaders' eyes ere this; lack of sustained action and major opposition seldom failed to breed such a situation. The King cursed, ordered drastic punishment for any caught thus absconding, but could force no more effective action on the men's masters.

Without waiting to watch his unenthusiastic legions depart in the direction of Berwick, James set out for Castle Heaton once more. Mons Meg had ceased her long bombardment with daylight. The drawbridge tower was nothing more than a mass of rubble, and the bridge itself smashed to pieces. No great advancement was achieved by this, however, for though it meant that the cannon could now be moved forward along the causeway across the marsh, to batter away at the main gatehouse and bridge, this section would be under the fire of the defenders, making any advance costly.

That Sir John Swinburne and his garrison were not unduly depressed by the loss of their outer defences was made amply clear, not only by the fact that the surrender summons had been rejected out-of-hand, but that the hanging man who represented the King now hung upside-down, with his tinsel crown firmly attached to his bottom, while all the other unfortunates had been turned right way up in their chains. All were now barefooted. There was no mistaking the message.

Undoubtedly the advance along the causeway ought to be postponed until darkness, when the castle's bowmen would be at a disadvantage; but James was in no mood for further inaction and delay this morning. Great shields must be constructed, of wood and hides, he declared, to protect Borthwick's gunners from arrows and slings. Behind these they would advance along the causeway, to teach these Englishmen the lesson they so dearly required.

Despite all James's fretting impatience, it was mid-afternoon before the shields were contrived, great ungainly canopies, heavy and cumbersome to move. They had to be strong enough to withstand stones and bolts hurled by slings and catapults, as well as sufficiently tough to keep arrows from penetrating. Casemates were provided for the cannon muzzles to thrust through. Each required at least a dozen men to carry it forward.

Under cover of these, the King led a group of men forward to bridge the gap in the causeway in front of the now ruined first drawbridge, using materials assembled while the screens were being made. Immediately they came under a hail of arrows, shot from the covered way between the demolished outlying tower and the main gatehouse, which had been but little damaged by the bombardment. The screens proved themselves at once, most arrows falling off the double hide surfaces like dead flies, although some that struck timber supports remained sticking out like hedgehog quills. None penetrated within, however. The shields would have been ineffective against cannon-fire, but Castle Heaton did not seem to be provided with such artillery – as was not to be expected in a private house; few, if any, Scottish castles, could have produced a cannon at this time.

Behind the screens, the work of putting a bridge across the stream went on with reasonable speed and success – even though not fast enough for King James. Once they had got a framework across, they were able to use some of the materials of the shattered drawbridge and tower. In prospecting and extricating such materials, James himself was probably the least careful to keep well behind the screens, taking many risks – although he was clad in full armour, of course, save for a helmet. This much upset Rob Bruce, whose protests were ignored or dismissed. One arrow, he pointed out, could make of Scotland an English dependency – for the heir to the throne, the young Duke of Ross, the King's brother, was weak and much under Angus's sway; Angus would make of him a vassal king to Henry Tudor, undoubtedly.

Once a serviceable bridge had been constructed, one of Mons Meg's lesser sisters was brought up, one of the shields having to be sent back for her, since arrows could still be dropped on to the causeway behind the busy builders. Indeed two or three men had been transfixed when risking dashes forward with bridging gear.

The covered way along this further section was a nuisance. It consisted of two drystone walls, set close together, with roofing of boarding and turfs, with gaps and embrasures, at intervals, for archers to shoot through. This had to be demolished in the path of the cannon, since it took up much of the causeway, and such demolition was very hard to effect behind a screen. The shields had to be raised just high enough to allow men to work from below, pulling out the stones and undermining the walls – and certain expert archers of the defence were not backward in attempting to shoot their shafts into the gap thus left open, difficult as it was. Two men were skewered through the calf before James ordered his workers back to collect and don leg-armour from such of the knights and gentlemen as watched proceedings at the marsh-side, out of range of the bowmen.

Slowly but surely the shields and the cannon advanced. Stones and missiles hurled by catapults and slings from the gatehouse towers began to fly towards them as they drew near. At about seventy yards range, James halted his sweating shield-carriers, cannon-pushers and demolishers, and called up the gunners. Opening the casemate, he himself fired the first ball at the gatehouse.

Artillery fire, as has been indicated, was a slow process at this time, so much having to be done between each shot. Nor was accuracy of aim possible, since the impellent charge inevitably varied, as did the weight of ball. A high proportion of the shots were wasted – but this was compensated for by the impressive effect on stone and lime of such fire as registered, dramatic indeed to men used to fighting with swords, spears and arrows. Impatient as ever, therefore, James commenced the construction of emplacements for two more cannon, one on either side of the narrow causeway, a task requiring much labour in the depositing of great quantities of bottom material, such as timber, brushwood, turf and stones, to give a solid foundation in the swamp. This was dangerous work, since it could not be given full protection from the shields, and Swinburne's archers took their toll of the labourers. The King himself worked harder than any, exposing himself with a reckless disregard for the enemy marksmen, and once all but foundering in the bog, into which the weight of his armour sucked him down. It was after this that, as he panted behind a shield, while Rob Bruce and his other rescuers sought to remove mud and slime from his person, a new protesting voice was raised – a pleasant if foreign-sounding voice.

It was Don Pedro de Ayala, the new Spanish envoy, a man of manners, humour and nimble wits, indeed a man after James's own heart, and to whom, in these three months he had grown somewhat attached. "Highness," he said, panting himself after having run the gauntlet of the causeway. "I come as ambassador twice over! From many of your nobles and gentlemen yonder. They pray that you will heed me, that you will cease to hazard your royal person so. All are much concerned, and I am appointed their poor spokesman. Be less bold, Sire, I pray you."

"Would you have me less bold than these subjects of mine who do my bidding, Don Pedro?"

"Your boldness should be of a different order, Highness."

"In the face of flying arrows there is but one order, sir."

"*Caramba* — but an arrow in the King is a different matter from an arrow in one of these!"

"Is it, my friend?"

"This I have been telling His Grace," Rob Bruce put in, level-voiced. "I pray he heeds you, sir, as he heeds not me."

"I speak for many besides myself," the Spaniard went on. "All esteem Your Majesty's courage and great heart. But your duty, they say, lies not here, amongst the arrows . . ."

"A captain's duty lies where his men are endangered."

"But you are no captain, Sire! You are the King. It is no general's part to play the captain — or why have a general? If a captain falls, he may be replaced. If the general falls, the battle may be lost. And if the King falls, the kingdom also may fall."

"You would have me sit in safety and order my subjects into danger? Such is not my notion of kingship, Don Pedro. Is it so in Spain? A king must lead, or be no king."

"But lead in mind, rather than in body, Sire, is it not? Any man may labour with pick and axe, any man may carry a sword or serve a cannon. But the King must devise and plan and command. He must see all the battle, as from a height — not see only one point, as does the captain. If he tires himself with such toil as this, can he scheme and devise as he ought?"

"I think you go too far, Don Pedro," James said, but wearily rather than angrily.

"No doubt I do, Your Majesty — to my great regret. But this I was sent as envoy to say, by those others. All are agreed. I beg of you to heed them — and myself, your humble servant."

"Aye, sir. I hear and heed. I shall consider what you say. But you must let me be my own judge as to my kingly duty."

James, of course, did not allow this eloquent plea to effect his actions to any noticeable extent — although perhaps, since Don Pedro elected to remain forward himself and even begged to be allowed to fire the cannon once or twice, the King refrained from exposing himself quite so frequently. Anyway, the light was failing fast, and archery becoming less accurate.

By nightfall those gatehouse towers were barely recognisable as such, resembling rather mounds of rubble and quarried stone.

The second drawbridge itself was but a mass of splintered timber, and the portcullis smashed in ruin. Nevertheless, as a defensive unit the position held out. The defenders were indeed bold enough to light fires on top of their broken and pounded walls, so that no approach to bridge the intervening moat might remain unobserved in the darkness. Into the illuminated target the cannon continued to hurl balls with ponderous regularity.

With orders that the bombardment should be maintained throughout the night, James at last left the causeway — but only to move over and lead the miners and sappers to work on the tunnel beneath the castle walls above the riverside, snatching a few mouthfuls of simple food as he went.

But now, with the labour safely underground, and the only danger the climbing up and down to the tunnel-mouth, the King found the business dull and palling in the extreme. He allowed Rob to persuade him to leave the miners to their task meantime — especially when he heard that the Lady Heron was asking for him. He returned to Ford Castle.

The young woman was not in the Hall to greet him and, despite weariness and frustration, the essential and vigorous male in him knew an accession of hope as he was once again conducted upstairs towards the lady's own apartments. This time at least he got beyond the lamp-lit hallway, and was ushered through the doorway which he had eyed on the former occasion. It opened not into a bedroom, but into a pleasant boudoir or bower. The door of a sleeping chamber stood open beyond.

Any hope that his involuntary hostess might be more kindly disposed towards him than heretofore was quickly dashed, however. "Your Highness assails Castle Heaton," she declared without preamble and without any return of his courtly greeting. It was a charge, an accusation.

"I do," he agreed, mildly enough. "I can do no less."

"You told me that you came in friendship, not war. That the burnings and the killings were against your will, your commands. Yet now you attack and slay, at Castle Heaton. Your words to me meant nothing."

"Ask those five men who hang on your dule-tree yonder, whether my words meant nothing, lady!" James told her grimly. "They died as a warning that I meant what I said. As for Castle Heaton, it was no wish of mine to bring it low. But Sir John Swinburne has fifteen of my people hanging from his battlements, and one he mocks as the King of Scots. Can I shut my eyes to that? I offered him surrender, but he but scorned me further. Would you have me suffer his insolence?"

"Is it insolence for a man to fight for his own, sir?"

"To fight, no. But to challenge me so. That, I cannot ignore. Swinburne must pay the price of his folly and vaunting."

The girl bit her lip. She was less sternly assured than she seemed. "It was foolish, yes. Wrong," she admitted. "But can you not have mercy? A king need not heed the foolishness of a mere knight? Sir John is a hasty man . . ."

"And means much to you?"

"No. Though he is cousin to my husband. But . . . must all in his house die, for what he has done? Is that just?"

"When a castle defies an army, lady, all within are endangered, not just its lord. But I shall endeavour that no hurt comes to the innocent, to women and children . . ."

"How can you say that, when you intended death to all?" she cried. "By exploding all the castle with your gunpowder! You dig beneath its rock. That is what you intend for Castle Heaton, is it not? And all shall die."

"You are well informed, lady," the King murmured. "Some of my people have over-long tongues, I fear."

"All Northumberland knows what you do there," she said wearily. She took a pace or two away, to move the sconce which flickered in a draught in a window embrasure, and then came back to him. Indeed her hand actually reached out to touch his sleeve. "Do not explode Castle Heaton, Sire," she urged, pleaded. "My husband is there."

"I' faith — you say so? Heron — Sir William? In yonder hold?"

"Yes. I thought him in Berwick. But hearing that you . . . that the Scots came this way, he hastened back. To take me hence. He came near, but finding that he was too late, that you were here at Ford, he went to Sir John at Castle Heaton instead. That first night."

James frowned. "Why? He could have come here, to his own house and his own wife. To greet me, at the least. But he chose to go to one who defied me . . ."

"No doubt he saw half of Northumberland ablaze, and doubted your greeting and welcome!"

"But . . . with *you* here!" He considered her young comeliness with all the appreciation of a connoisseur. "Madam, *I* would have come to you, hot-foot, had Beelzebub himself been your guest! None could have kept me away!"

She stiffened at the frankness both of his words and his admiring looks. But, with an obvious effort she countered the equally evident impulse to draw back from him. Indeed the hand which had jerked away from him for a moment hovered and then returned to his sleeve. She forced herself to meet his assessing regard. She said nothing.

"Sir William, I think, lacks judgement," he declared. "Ardour, at the least! Perhaps he is old? To have so young and fair a wife . . ."

She shook her head. "Not old, but . . . older than I. We, we are most devoted, Sire."

"M'mmm. I would more believe it if he had come here to you, rather than to yonder hold, lassie!"

"It is truth! I swear it." There was a quick-breathing urgency about her now, an excitement which verged on desperation. "Your Majesty—spare Castle Heaton," she besought him.

His hand came down on hers that clutched his arm, to stroke her slender fingers. "I could allow Sir William to come forth unharmed, beforehand," he suggested.

"He would not come," she declared, positively enough.

"Why, I wonder?"

She did not answer that directly. "How long?" she asked, instead, breathlessly. "How long before you . . . you do it? Blow up the castle?"

He shrugged. "Cutting through the rock is slow work. It will not be ready this night. Tomorrow, perhaps. Or tomorrow night."

She blinked a little, seeming almost to be calculating. "So soon?" Then, sighing, "No—he would not come out. Not before tomorrow night, I fear."

James looked at her curiously, now. "Tonight, tomorrow, or the next day—what is the difference? For him?"

She did not answer that either. "You might do it tomorrow?"

"If it is ready, yes."

The young woman took a deep breath. "I beg of you, do not do this thing," she whispered. "Have mercy. I will do much, if you will stay your hand. Much."

James cocked his head. "*You* will?"

"Yes."

"So-o-o! Much you say? How much, I wonder?"

"I will do a great deal. More . . . more than it is to my honour to do." That was levelly said.

"So much! For me?"

"For you, yes."

"And all to save your husband?"

"Yes."

"You . . . surprise . . . me," he said slowly. "I' faith, you do! Women do ever surprise me. That you, so young, so well favoured, would give yourself, all your loveliness, for this man who does not even come to your side in your need! That you would offer me your body in exchange for his wretched life . . ."

Great eyes wide she stared at him, her lips seeking words which at first would not come. "Sir! How . . . how dare you!" she cried. "Shame on you! That you should speak so . . . to me! In my own husband's house! Is this a king who speaks, or some scullion, some base knave?"

"But . . . a God's name—what is this?" he floundered. "By the Rude—did you not just offer me your body, your honour? You said . . ."

"Not that! Never! Never—do you hear me! Are you crazy, mad?" She had backed away from him now, right to the wall, against which she pressed herself. "That I should give you my body . . .!"

"'Fore God, if that was not your meaning—what was it? You said . . . you said that you would give me much, more than your honour."

"But not *that*! Do you esteem me some light wanton, sir, to give myself to any man? To bed with such as you . . .!"

"A pox! Am I any man? Am I so abject? So ill-favoured. Others have not thought me so, I swear!"

"Then your others are less delicate than I am, sir!" Her eyes flashed, as she looked him up and down. "I would not lie with you were it to save my life!"

"No?" He clenched his fists. "Nor your husband's either, it seems. So be it, Madam—so be it! I am abhorrent. You have nothing to give me—and need look for naught from me! I leave you now—not force you, as I have no doubt you anticipate from one of the barbarous Scots! A goodnight to you, Lady Heron!"

He was almost at the doorway before she found her voice again—and a different voice indeed. "Sire—stay! Your Majesty—wait.

I pray you, wait. I . . . I am sorry. I should not have spoken so. It was not my intention — I swear it was not. Of your mercy, wait."

"You seek mercy from such as me, Madam?" He paused, but did not return to her. "You mistake, do you not?"

"I do not ask your mercy . . . for nothing," she reminded.

"Ah, no. Much you would give, in exchange! Forgive me that I forget it! Put to the test, I scarce feel hopeful of a profitful trade, lady — for Castle Heaton or your husband's life!"

"Hear me, and you may think differently," she told him, speaking flatly now. "For that house and my husband, I can do you a great service, I believe."

"At the cost of your honour!"

"Yes. Can a woman's honour not be of more than one sort? May she not betray other than her husband?"

Doubtfully he eyed her.

"Here is my price for Castle Heaton," she went on. "The saving of your army. Of many lives in place of just a few. King Henry's host is moving against you — a great host. Three great hosts. Of many more than your Scots numbers. One is not far off. In the hills behind Cheviot. Under my lord of Dacre. He but awaits the other two, to strike."

James had moved slowly back to her, staring. "*Three* hosts?" he said. "Three? How know you this?"

"A messenger came here. Last night. Secretly. From my husband. In Castle Heaton. He had come to him from Lord Dacre, and is now there returned. He told me. Castle Heaton is to keep you here, Sire, occupied, until these three hosts can join in battle against you. Two days hence."

He stood very still, a man transformed. "Two days? Three of them. And one is near by. This is the truth you tell me, woman?"

"The truth, yes. Dacre is Warden of the West March. He moved out from Carlisle two days past, with many thousands. Up the South Tyne, to Rede. They wait now in the hills at the head of Redesdale, and can descend upon you down the Bowmont and College Waters. The Percy, Earl of Northumberland, leads the main array — the messenger said, of over a score of thousands — from Newcastle and Durham. But not by the low country. Through the hills they come, by Corbridge and the North Tyne to Rothbury and the Coquet. He will descend on you down Wooler Water."

"And the third?" That was harsh.

"Sailed in ships. Many ships. By sea from Newcastle also. Two days ago. With much cannon. They wait behind Lindisfarne, assembling more, while the Percy marches north. Under Lord Daubeny."

"A-a-aye!" James's long exhalation of breath was eloquent indeed.

"The numbers are great, the messenger said. Twice your Scots array, at the least. My Lords Dacre and Daubeny will meet behind you, along Tweed. In two days. You will be trapped, Sire — trapped!"

"That we shall see. But . . . why do you tell me all this?"

"That you and yours may go. Back to Scotland. While there is yet time. And leave Castle Heaton unblown." She bit her lip. "Sweet Mary Mother — has there not been enough bloodshed? If I had not spoken, must not thousands more die? To what purpose? God forgive me for this betrayal — but by making it, may I not save many more than my husband? Is it not so. Tell me — is it not so?"

"Perchance you are right," James jerked. "We shall see." He bowed briefly. "I thank you." Turning, he strode without another word out of her bower, to the stairs.

In the Hall below he found the patient Rob Bruce awaiting him, half-asleep across the great table.

"Up, man! Quickly!" he cried. "I want men. Summon me men for scouts, for spies. But Borderers, see you — the best that we have left. Moss-troopers, who can ride the hills. Homes, Turnbulls, Scotts, Kerrs. A dozen, a score. What you can find, quickly. I must have news. From deep in these hills. Quickly, I say — there is no time to lose. Bring them to my own tent . . ."

Alone King James paced up and down the forecourt of Ford Castle the following evening, as he had paced for well over an hour, while the sun sank behind the long rolling Cheviot ridges to the west. Every now and again he raised his eyes towards those ridges, and frowned blackly.

It had been a trying, nerve-racking day. If formerly men had kept their distance because of the King's ill-humour, today they avoided his proximity with still greater cause. Never had any seen him so consistently rageful, bitter, irascible. Even Bothwell and Drummond, recalled in urgent advance of the main force's return from the Berwick vicinity, held off as much and as far as they might. Only Sir Rob Bruce dared act as link between the wrathful monarch and those who must approach him, patiently but not really humbly enduring the verbal assault that was his lot on each occasion.

The great park at Ford presented a markedly different appearance from that of the last three or four days. All the pavilions and tents were struck, the camp-fires out, the horses saddled, the men armed and accoutred. All was ready for a move, and had been since midday.

The King awaited the return of the half-dozen hard-riding moss-troopers whom he had sent south by west last night, to the foothill area of Rothbury, Wansbeck and the Roman Wall, to seek to ascertain whether the Lady Heron's revelations regarding the English main force under the Earl of Northumberland were accurate. Theirs had been the longest ride and most difficult task. The other two pickets sent out had both been back by noon. One reported a large force of possibly as many as ten thousand men lying hidden in the lonely mosses of the Cheviots between Redesdale and the head of College Waters, a mere fifteen miles away as the crow flies, having used the old Roman road of Dere Street to bring them north. Their outposts were on every height and pass between, and the scouts had had some narrow escapes; indeed a shepherd had told them that there was still another division further to the west, near the head of Kale Water – a great host, he had said, although they had not had time to verify this. The second party had made eastwards for the coast, and returned to tell of a forest of tall mast-tops appearing above and beyond the long island of Lindisfarne, two or three miles off-shore, seen from the little hills of Kyloe, together with much activity in small boats from the mainland. From Lindisfarne a fleet could sail into the mouth of the Tweed at Berwick in two or three hours.

If all this were not enough, Bothwell and Drummond had to report that the Scots army had melted away further during the night. Dispersed and inactive, more and more had slipped quietly off. There had been more sacking and pillage, in the Unthank, Ancroft and Cheswick areas, and many fine herds of cattle were now on their way back to the Tweed and Scotland. They, and other lords, had done what they could, made an example of some – but the thing was too general, the rot too widespread, and too many of the lairds and captains themselves were involved.

So James stamped and stormed at his impatient waiting, his irate thoughts punctuated at regular intervals by the booming of the cannon which still maintained the bombardment of Castle Heaton. More than once he had almost given orders that the cannonade should cease; but each time, glancing up at the windows of Ford Castle, he had withheld. Let Elizabeth Heron listen and wince and drink her bitter anxious cup, he decided, as he had to drink his own! That was the frame of mind James Stewart was in, that 25th of September 1496.

At length, almost with the last light, the men they had been awaiting appeared riding weary foam-lathered mounts down the slope of Ford Hill. But only three, where six had set out. Tired men, reeling after nearly twenty hours in the saddle, dismounted before the frowning King.

"They are there, Your Grace," the spokesman said thickly. "Nearer than you said. All the valley o' Coquet is full o' them. Their foreguard is on the Breamish. We were nigh catched there, at Ingram. We lost three lads in a sharp tuilzie. Had to run for it. Up Breamish and over the hills to Harthope . . ."

"How many, man?" the King jerked. "A large host?"

"Aye, Sire—larger by far than crossed Tweed. All England riding north! Every valley filled wi' men. All in the hills—nane in the plain. Hidden . . ."

"Fiend seize me—so be it, then!" James's clenched fist smashed down on his open palm. "Make an end! We'll have done with this course that has brought us only grief and dishonour. My lords!" He raised his angry voice, to those who had gathered near. "You hear? We make an end. Northumberland's foreguard is at the Breamish but twenty miles away. His main strength on the Coquet, but little further. Dacre is on our right, in the hills. Daubeny on our left, in ships. Twice, thrice, our numbers. I cannot face these with a rabble of cattle-thieves and pillagers and marauders! So I turn, my lords—God pity me, I turn! Back to the Tweed, to the Scotland we have shamed. To horse, I say, and be done with it!"

Nowhere did men meet his blazing glance.

"Patrick," he went on. "My Lord of Bothwell—send to Home, with the main array. Tell him not to come here. To make for Twizel Bridge. We shall meet him at Coldstream—if any men remain to him! Off with you, my friends—and see who may be first back at Stirling, to proclaim our noble victory!"

In silence men turned away from the bitter, mocking figure of their monarch, to transmit his orders. No single voice was raised in opposition or protest.

James swung on Rob Bruce. "My compliments to the Lady Heron," he said. "Tell her . . . tell her that perchance her judgement was right. Thank her for her so great hospitality! Tell her that the barbarian is gone, leaving her undefiled! Tell her . . . oh, tell her what you will, man!"

"You will not see her yourself, Sire? Just a word . . .?"

"No, I will not, by the Rude! Go you. I ride to Castle Heaton. My horse . . ."

Rob caught up with the King as he drew rein at the riverside near the other castle. Beacons blazed again on its walls, to provide illumination against any attempted assault. The camp-fires and the noise still maintained down across the river, but the bombardment had just stopped, as Master-Gunner Borthwick began to withdraw his cannon for the retreat.

"Well?" James demanded.

The other shrugged, and said nothing.

"Out with it, man! What says she now?"

"She deems Your Grace less than faithful. Or kind. She . . . weeps."

"She does? But not for me! It may be that a little weeping will do that one no hurt!"

The King rode on to where the night's miners for the tunnel were preparing to go to work, with the darkness. The brawny man in charge touched his forehead, and grinned.

"No' that much to do now, Sire," he reported. "We're under the corner o' the keep now, I reckon. We can blow her afore the morn, if you say. We'll hae yon vaunty castle a rickle o' stanes doon in this river, if you'll gie us enough o' gunpowder! A bonny sight it will be, I warrant!"

James looked up at the lofty black ramparts of the square keep, outlined against the beacons' blaze, where the corpses still dangled, the one in effigy of himself lowermost of all – and even though he could not see them in the gloom, his eyes narrowed and the knuckles which gripped his reins shone white. He drew a deep breath. "I think not," he said.

"Eh . . .?"

"I think not," he repeated slowly. "We shall leave Castle Heaton where it is, this time. The mole turns."

"Mole . . .," The man stared. "But, Sire—all is near ready. After all our toil! It but needs the gunpowder . . .!"

"I said no, man! No! Leave it. Leave all. Get your men away. Like the rest. Forthwith. We ride for Scotland. Away with you. You shall be recompensed for your toil, never fear. My thanks. Your work here is done."

"But, Sire—what of your name, your honour!" Bothwell, at the King's back, protested. "You cannot leave it thus. Yonder carrion hanging there, mocking you! This insult we can wipe out before we leave, at the least, by the Mass!"

"We can, yes—but we shall not, Patrick! Perhaps yonder carrion speaks the truth! My honour is better served, I think, thus," He turned to glance over at Rob Bruce. "She will have an ill night—but a brighter morn than shall I! Come—on to the Tweed!"

All night the Scots were crossing the great river at Coldstream, by the light of many fires and torches, the black waters and the lurid flames well reflecting the King's own black and burning state of mind, as he watched from a knoll above the haugh till the last laden pack-horse, the last sullen weary footman, the last lumbering cannon, were forded or ferried across, and only the Lord Home's moss-troopers, as rearguards now, remained on Northumbrian soil. At length, heavily, silently, he mounted, and his close attendants sighed with relief—but none spoke, for those who had ventured a word in the last hour or two had had cause to regret it.

At the long grassy ridge of Oxenrig, where the advancing host had halted, five days before, for the first sight of England, James presently drew rein again, and turned in his saddle to stare back into the night. Wordless, tense, he gazed. Then he raised his arm high, his fist clenched, and shook it.

"I will be back!" he cried, in a voice almost unrecognisable as his own. "As God is my witness—I will be back! And it shall be . . . otherwise!"

Savagely he dug spurs into his horse's flanks.

PART FOUR
Chain of Destiny

IT took Margaret Drummond a long time, months indeed, fully to win James Stewart out of his black temper and ill-humour. None had ever known him to be like this, his normally friendly, cheerful and sanguine nature blighted and weighed down. It was his first, his only great failure, a multiple and comprehensive failure and defeat, and he took it hard. He seemed to have failed on so many fronts, and so obviously so, for all men to see.

First, it was evident that his championship of the Duke of York — or Perkin Warbeck, as more and more people were daring to call him — was a grave mistake. The fact that Margaret, William Elphinstone, and even Rob Bruce had been so much against it, made the outcome no easier to bear. The Duke was now a changed man, withdrawn, wary, hiding himself almost, his bubble pricked. Whether genuine or not, his only hope of success had lain in the acceptance of his claims by some substantial proportion of the English people. James recognised now, too late, that he ought to have made thorough and extensive enquiries on this point, sent spies into England to test and ascertain opinion in all areas and amongst all classes, before venturing all. Then he ought to have had a clear understanding with the Emperor and the King of France that the Scots did not move until these powers had actually taken steps against Henry. He had trusted them to act militarily, as proposed, and they had not done so; but he should not have accepted that they would, without proofs of their trustworthiness. Here again Bishop Elphinstone had warned him.

But these political mistakes, though humiliating, were not what hurt him most. It was his failure as a leader, the inadequacy of his demonstration of kingship, which struck deepest. He had taken a great host over the Border — and failed utterly to control it. The Scots army had behaved like a band of cut-throat mercenaries, let loose on an undefended territory, to its shame and his own. That this was against his orders and wishes, he who had always looked on the resort to arms from the romantic and chivalrous stand-point, only served to underline his inability to command and control. The fact that it was not really an army at all, but merely an assembly of the bands of his jealous and undisciplined lords, and so was not his to control, was scant comfort to him, and would be understood by few. By skilfully playing his lords, barons and churchmen one against another during the eight years of his reign, he had managed to keep the ship of state on an even keel and to sail it into calmer waters, and in the direction he desired. But clearly this was not enough, where war and external adventure was concerned. He would have to rethink, on this score, radically. Meantime, he had stained his name abroad, endangered his borders, and lowered his credit at home.

Lastly, important on a totally different level, was his complete failure with the young Lady Heron. Most men would have shrugged this off with scarcely another thought – but not James Stewart. Women held an importance for him that far exceeded the mere physical demands of a lusty, virile and impressionable man. It was not that he must make a conquest of every woman who took his fancy; it was important to him that women should like him, and that those who attracted him should in some measure be attracted in return – not to be mastered as by a king, but to be appreciative of him as a man. Undoubtedly this was part of the essential need of a friendly and companionable as well as vital nature to escape from the loneliness of the throne; his position precluded the normal close relationship with other men – his father's failure in this respect was ever before him; but he could and did relax in the company of women, and before them seek to be the basic man and not the monarch. Elizabeth Heron had spurned and rejected both the man and the monarch – and this cut to the quick.

The dark months of that winter would have been black indeed had it not been for Margaret Drummond. James now lived with her openly and freely, and though she did not bear the title of queen or even wife, she was accepted by all as the mistress of the King's house as well as his bed, the recipient of the royal confidence, the monarch's comfort and inspiration. None could deny that she played her difficult role in this with a winsome modesty, a delicate judgement, and an unqualified success.

Margaret's qualities were severely taxed, nevertheless. James had the failings of his virtues, and could plunge as deep as he could soar. Having lost faith in himself, to a large extent, he seemed to lose faith in everyone else. Where previously he had been apt to act on swift impulse and warm-hearted instinct, now he brooded, put off, and hedged. Inevitably the young woman bore the brunt of his spleen and gloom, since the façade which he must keep up before others he could discard with her. It was the measure of their mutual love that they grew the closer together during this testing period, and for this the major credit undoubtedly went to Margaret's patience, understanding and unfailing serenity.

If an unaccustomed harshness was to be noted in the King's actions over this period, it would no doubt have been more so but for Margaret's restraining and gentle influence. Although the Duke of York's many followers were packed off back to Ireland and elsewhere within a month, and with scant courtesy, the Duke himself was not treated with any indignity. It was not until the following July that Scotland eventually got rid of the unfortunate young man, and throughout the interim his handsome pension was paid regularly—despite the fact that the entire adventure had sorely depleted James's never-overflowing treasury, so that in fact he had to melt down much of his personal gold plate and chains. Even so the visitor was sent away in some style, in a specially chartered ship, furnished fit for any king, and equipped with much clothing and travelling gear. The parting, at the port of Ayr, was cool but not acrimonious, James being affected by the loyalty of the Lady Katherine Gordon, who evidently had come to love her strange husband dearly, and who in fact did not leave him until two years later he suffered the death of a self-confessed and treasonable impostor on the Tyburn gallows in London.

James, of course, could not afford to mope and gloom at Stirling. He had raised the devil, in the form of Henry Tudor, and was faced with the problem of laying him, or at least seeking to contain him within his own borders. The large English army sent up to deal with the Scots hovered in a menacing fashion in Northumberland, and James spent much of an anxious and unhappy winter going from one Border castle to another, strengthening defences, blowing up bridges, rendering fords unusable, and preparing for the worst. It was typical of the man that he saw to this himself; he it was who had brought this danger upon his land, and stubbornly he insisted that he and not deputies, must seek to mitigate the consequencies. Margaret Drummond accompanied him frequently on these uncomfortable exercises, and spent many a weary day and chilly night on Border hillsides and in draughty peel-towers.

The fact that the English army did not invade Scotland after all, save for a few small-scale probing raids, could not be credited to these efforts of James, however, but to the fortunate accident of an armed revolt in Cornwall against Henry's taxations and tyrannies. This had been rumoured for some time, and no doubt accounted for the delay in Northumberland; when the Cornishmen actually started on their march on London, the northern army was hurriedly recalled southwards, leaving only the local levies and garrisons to face the Scots. James's relief was profound —but he still had spirit enough to lay token siege to Norham Castle, on the south bank of Tweed near Coldstream, partly to salve his own pride, partly to give Henry cause to dread renewed Scottish invasion. The gesture, along with others, had its effect, and soon after the Duke of York's departure English ambassadors came to Ayton, on the Border, and a seven years' truce was concluded, Don Pedro de Ayala being the energetic and trusted go-between. The terms, for Scotland, were better than might have been expected—for Henry, though he had crushed the Cornishmen, was very worried about other parts of his uneasy realm. James had to give up his cherished hope of the return of the town and port of Berwick to Scotland—one of his main objects in his support of Warbeck. He in fact sent a challenge to Howard, Earl of Surrey, Henry's chief representative, to a personal combat, to decide the ownership of the town in chivalric fashion, but the common-sensible Englishman made cynical refusal. Once again talk of the Princess Margaret Tudor, as bride for King James, was renewed.

So Scotland won out of the imbroglio into which the King's impetuous support of Warbeck had plunged her, and James could return to Stirling and a more normal life, though the hurt to his pride and spirit still rankled. Even so, things were not as they had been. The Court was noticeably less gay, for not only was the King in little temper for gaiety, but the royal coffers were empty. Moreover, in his grim mood, James had little appetite for maintaining a façade of civil relationship with his Chancellor, Angus, and the other nobles who supported the Douglas. Angus, always Henry's man, was now in a stronger position than ever —

which meant that more of the lords were prepared to gravitate to his side. James was forced to recognise that in this respect also he had weakened his position, and that he must hold his hand meantime and put up with his powerful internal enemies as best he might. Fortunately the Lord Gray seemed to have fallen out with Angus, for reasons unknown. It was James's concern to keep them so.

Although Angus was Chancellor and first minister of the realm, in fact more and more of the duties of that office fell to Bishop Elphinstone, the Lord Privy Seal. James, of course, preferred it this way, and might have risked appointing him Chancellor in Angus's place had the Bishop agreed. Angus himself, being lazy as well as proud, allowed the situation to develop, and the Bishop to do most of the work, while he spent his time at Tantallon in Lothian or in Douglasdale in the west. Elphinstone, grieving for his young friend and monarch, sought to lift him out of his depression by dint of much work. And there was much to be done. The state of the revenue had become an ever-present preoccupation, and on Elphinstone's advice James now began to devote much attention to improving the state of trade, to encourage manufactures, and to increase the prosperity of the townsfolk, merchants and burghs. There was more in this than just the need for increased revenue from these sources, however. One of the lessons learned in Northumberland was that until the King could be less dependent on the military forces of his lords his hands were tied. He now looked to the burghs to redress the balance. If the towns, under their provosts, bailies and guilds, could raise and equip town guards of some strength, and armed bands of citizens, then here was an alternative source of manpower for use in an emergency, to counter the nobles – provided that the townsfolk were sufficiently in sympathy with their monarch. Accordingly James paid more and more attention to the well-being of the burghs, affording them a greater degree of independence from the lords, giving them trading privileges, encouraging industries. Never before had the ordinary people been the recipients of such royal interest and policy. All over the land their appreciation was not long in taking tangible form.

Elphinstone also involved James in the progress of his new university at Aberdeen, although this was at the stage of only a modest beginning.

As the months passed amidst such valuable but humdrum activities, the King's essential restlessness began to re-assert itself. Hard useful work, and Margaret's unfailing love, might serve to keep his mind occupied and his ill-humours soothed, but something more vigorous and dramatic was required to re-instate himself in his own estimation. Curiously enough an occasion for such action was provided by none other than Sir Alexander MacDonald of Lochalsh. Since he and MacIan of Ardnamurchan had between them brought low Sir John of Islay, to the royal satisfaction, James had heard little of moment from the Isles, although whilst the Northumbrian affair was in progress, Bute had been devastated by an invasion of Islesmen, said to be Alexander's people, and it was clear that he was yielding nothing of his claim to the Lordship of the Isles. Now, in the autumn of 1497, Alexander moved again. In pursuance of a further claim to the Earldom of Ross, forfeited by his uncle to the Crown, he invaded the mainland of Ross itself, penetrating in strength from the mountainous west coast deep into the fertile lands of Easter Ross, his fierce warriors burning and slaying in traditional style. It was thought that he was making for Inverness, which had been sacked at one time or another by almost every one of the long line of Lords of the Isles.

James was torn by a conflict of emotions. He had learned a grudging admiration for that strange, strong, ugly, soft-spoken man with the intensely alive eyes – but he had not forgiven him over the matter of the Stone of Destiny. Now he was hurt that Alexander should have chosen to break out in frank rebellion, making a mock of his, the King's, assumption of the Lordship. At the same time he was sorry that it had come to this, to open conflict between them – if only for Marsala MacIan's sake, who would be unhappy indeed. But also he almost rejoiced that the man had thus offered him the challenge, the opportunity for action, for vigorous exertion and contest, that he had been craving for months. He did not hesitate for long. He sent urgent commands to MacIan, to gather the loyal clans and sail north, to cut off Alexander's communications with the Isles; he ordered Huntly, at Aberdeen, Lieutenant of the North, to make for Easter Ross with all speed and as many men as he could muster; and he himself set out with only a few companions for Inverness, hot-foot. How hot the foot may be gauged by the fact that he rode almost one hundred miles before drawing bridle on the banks of Spey — by which time Rob Bruce alone remained in attendance. It was almost like old times.

Despite all this haste and vigour, however, he was too late. Awaiting Huntly at Inverness, word reached him that Alexander was already defeated. A combination of the mainland clans, mainly MacKenzies and Munroes had surprised him at a place called Drumchatt, while much of his strength was dispersed, and the invaders had been roundly beaten. Alexander was said to be hurrying back to the Isles to raise a new host.

This news should have much cheered the King, for it was a demonstration of the success of his policy. He had been seeking to do in the Highlands what had been so effective amongst his Lowland lords — play off clan against clan, encourage rivalries, break up confederations, strengthen the weak and small at the expense of the rich and powerful, all that the central royal authority might be established and the King's justice prevail. This defeat of Alexander was the major first-fruits of this policy, since he had won the adherence of MacIan of Ardnamurchan, for it represented the defection from the Lordship of the great Clan Kenneth or MacKenzie. This, though not an actual part of the Clan Donald federation, occupied much mainland territory on the north-western seaboard contiguous with that of the Mac-Donalds, and though frequently at odds with the Lordship in minor matters, had always supported it in major issues. That the MacKenzies, whose chief's mother was a daughter of John of the Isles, and so a cousin of Alexander's, should not only have taken the field against him but joined up with the despised east-country Munroes to do so, was a feather in James's cap indeed.

Nevertheless, he was disappointed; first, that he was thus personally denied the opportunity for action, for the clash of arms which his mood craved; secondly, that it should have fallen to such as these to defeat the great Alexander of Lochalsh, and not the King himself. That day in Skye he had promised himself a reckoning with the man; it would have well suited his present temper to have had that reckoning now. Alexander was a foeman worthy of a king's steel.

James did not neglect, however, to send word to MacIan of his opportunity to catch the retreating Islesmen on the flank. Then, calling a meeting of Central Highland chiefs for his return, he went on a pilgrimage to the shrine of St. Duthac at Tain, Duthac being a vigorous and manly sort of saint very much after his own heart.

He held his conference with the chiefs at Inverness thereafter, continuing his process of granting them royal charters of their lands and so giving them the privileges of feudal barons but binding their allegiance to himself. Then he set out southwards, with Huntly, for Aberdeen. Half-way there a courier caught up with them, from MacIan. Alexander of Lochalsh was dead.

James was shocked. MacIan's message said that Alexander, smarting from his unexpected reverse, had ordered a great assembly of his forces in Skye. He had sent envoys to all the scores of chiefs of the Isles federation, and he himself had elected to go to the territories of the late John of Islay, to seek to raise men from amongst his former rival's supporters. A disaffected petty chieftain had sent word to MacIan as to his whereabouts, and they had traced him to the island of Oronsay, near Islay. Though accompanied by a mere handful of followers, Alexander had shown fight. In the struggle, he had been fatally wounded, possibly by one of the resentful Islay men themselves. He had died before MacIan's galley could bring him back to Mingary.

James was strangely upset by these tidings, regretting the death more than that of many close to him, despite the fact that it was bound greatly to ease his own problems with regard to the Highlands. The man had been so intensely, so essentially alive. Although during their brief association they had clashed on every score, some deep underlying sense of mutual respect, a sort of unacknowledged sympathy, had been generated between them, with Marsala MacIan acting as catalyst. He sent messages to MacIan and his daughter, the former to declare the King's forgiveness and goodwill to all in his Lordship of the Isles if they would forthwith return peaceably to their homes; the latter to seek to prevail on Alexander's eldest son and heir, Donald Galda, to come south to Court where he was promised a kindly welcome, and further to declare that the young children of the family should become his own royal wards. His memory of Donald Galda was of a somewhat weak but pleasant young man, and his generosity was tempered with shrewdness. He hoped that he could now quench further efforts to assert the independence of the Isles. He also hoped that Marsala, who seemed to feel herself linked with the young man, might also elect to come south to Court.

Abandoning the intended visit to Aberdeen to inspect the new university buildings, James returned directly to Stirling, troubled in mind but at least less preoccupied with failure and self-criticism. The news awaiting him there served further to banish his low spirits.

It was Margaret Drummond herself who informed him. He found her in the little terrace garden part-way down the face of the castle rock – indeed he heard her trilling laughter mingling with that of a child, and went almost at a run down the zig-zag path to this secluded eyrie that hung between the soaring battlements of the fortress and the wide spreading plain of Forth. She made a lovely, vital picture, at play with the little boy, Alexander, James's son by Mariot Boyd. With Margaret installed as mistress and unofficial wife at Stirling Castle, Mariot could not longer remain on the premises, and she was now married off to a worthy husband in far Galloway, leaving her four-year-old son with his father whilst taking her younger baby with her. Margaret was devoted to the sturdy little boy, and delighted to mother him.

The King swept woman and child into his arms with a hearty affection that was more like the authentic, uninhibited James Stewart than either of them had seen for almost a year.

"Bless you!" he cried. "Sweet Ninian bless you both! Here's joy! You bloom, my dear – you bloom! The fairest flower of my realm. Or any realm! Ever fairer – aye, and by the Rude, larger too, I swear! Eh, Alexander, my mannie? You must have been looking after her well indeed, while I have been gone. Is she not fat?"

"She was sick," the small boy announced importantly. "I saw her. Sick."

James cocked his head. "You do not look sick, my sweeting," he declared. "Sick at heart, perhaps, for your Jamie . . ."

"Sick *because* of my Jamie," she told him, smiling. "Yes, Sire of my heart – you have sired more than love within me!"

He stared. "You mean . . . you mean . . . a child? Margaret – a child?"

Softly she laughed. "What else, my potent prince? Are you surprised? As I am not. Are you happy? As I am."

She did not require to ask that. James loved children.

For a while he was all incoherent joy, concern, anticipation, waltzing her round the little grass plot one moment, extravagantly urgent for her care the next, declaring that she must rest, not exert herself, not catch a chill from the breeze off the hills. When would he be born, he demanded? Did she know when it had been? When they had conceived him? Was it that time . . .? Or that day amongst the broomie knowes at Torwood . . .?"

She closed his lips with a finger.

"We shall call him James, of course," he mumbled through it.

"You are so sure that it will be a son?"

"Why, yes. Never doubt it. A son. James Stewart. James, Duke of Rothesay, heir to all this realm of Scotland!" And he waved his arm in a sweep to include all the splendid panorama spread out below that high eagle's nest of a garden.

Margaret shook her head slowly, but still she smiled. "You go too fast, my dear — and too far," she said. "James it may be — but not James Stewart. And not Duke of Rothesay. Just James Drummond . . . heir to our love, and not to Scotland!"

"No!" He threw up his head. "James *Stewart*, I say! My son and heir. Duke of Rothesay, Earl of Carrick, Lord of Renfrew, Prince of Scotland! We are man and wife, are we not? Shall we then deny the child his birthright?"

Troubled now, she faced him. "James," she pleaded. "See clearly, my love. Think well. We are man and wife in óur own eyes. And, it may be, in God's. But not in the eyes of others, of your realm, of the world. To all but ourselves and God, this child will be illegitimate, born out of wedlock. You cannot, if it is a boy, name him James Stewart and heir to the throne without proclaiming our marriage to all. And that, as you know well, must not be."

"It must be, shall be. Now."

"No. More than ever it is necessary that none know of this thing. Your treaty with King Henry — peace with England. That is all important. It must endure. You have seen enough of war. Henry would have you wed his daughter. You have agreed to consider the match. Would you now proclaim that when you signed yonder treaty at Ayton it was false, not possible? That you were wed already? Make liar of yourself and fool of Henry? Dare you do that, James — knowing Henry Tudor's pride? Would not your realm pay the price, in blood? You know that you cannot do it. No — our compact must stand. Our marriage was for ourselves alone. To the world I am your mistress only — and must remain so. This we agreed that night . . ."

"But all is changed, Margaret, now that there is to be a child."

319

"Nothing is changed, my heart. You are the King, but I am not the Queen. For the realm's sake you must be free to marry this princess. Or another . . ."

"I shall never marry other than you, woman!"

"No? Then at least you must *seem* free to marry Henry's daughter. Or some other. So long as Scotland is weaker than England, or until King Henry changes his mind, none must learn of our marriage. You know it, James—you *must* know it!"

Lowering his head, he drew a long breath, saying nothing.

She laid her head against his shoulder, arms encircling him. "Now my prince, speak no more of it, I pray. Be happy, as I am. Here is our joy, together. We have made a child. Is it not a wonder? Part you, part me. Oh, James—I am well content! Be you so, also."

CHAPTER

18

"You have a fair patrimony, my lord," James said, turning in his saddle to gaze all around him at the rolling green landscape which sank in gentle folds barred with woodland, where the coils of the River Doon gleamed silver on its way to the blue plain of the Firth of Clyde, beyond which the purple mountains of Arran dreamed hazily in the afternoon sunlight. "I think, perhaps, to be King of Carrick is a better fate than to be King of Scots! How say you?"

John, second Lord Kennedy, grunted. He was having difficulty with his breathing, for he was a heavily-built, middle-aged man, fond of his table and not used to riding at James's breakneck pace. He had only kept up with the three younger men with difficulty in the ridiculous and unnecessary gallop round Martnaham Loch and up to the long crest of this Coylton Hill—and only done so because he was the King's host for the moment as he passed through his lands, and so in duty bound to escort him. "Fair enough . . . Sire," he panted. "I am . . . well content."

"I' faith—then you are the only lord in my realm to be so, I swear!" the King laughed, clapping his broad shoulder. "And well you may be—for though I am Earl of Carrick, you are King thereof! Heigho—to think that all this bonny land might have been mine, but for a spider!"

"Eh . . .?" The older man's bristling brows rose. "*Yours* . . .?"

"Aye, mine. I am Robert Bruce's heir, am I not? This was his land once. He was Earl of Carrick. Had he not so furiously sought a throne, I might have been born in Turnberry Castle over yonder hill with never a Kennedy in Carrick!"

"And Scotland a shire of England for two hundred years!" the Bruce's namesake put in, from behind him, heavily.

"True, Rob. Perhaps it was best so." James shaded hand over eyes against the south-westerly sun. "Can we see your house of Cassillis from here, my lord?"

"No' the house, but its park, Your Grace. Five miles it is, to Cassillis, yet. By the river, under Brown Carrick Hill. If we ride

321

down this bit valley, Sire, we can meet your train again at Dalrymple and cross the Doon there." Kennedy looked back, north-westwards, to the low ground at the foot of Martnaham Loch, where the long snaking cavalcade of the royal train wound its decent way. "There's nae need for haste," he added, pointedly.

James was not listening. In his admiring survey of that noble prospect his keen eye had been caught by movement, swift movement. Down there, in the opposite direction on the long southern flank of this Coylton Hill, less than a mile away, two horsemen were riding fast, crouched down over their mounts. Something about the foremost rider made the King narrow his eyes. Even as he gazed, more large-scale movement still developed, as out from woodland behind, half-a-mile behind perhaps, eastwards, more horsemen streamed. There were many of these, straggled out, and they rode fully as hard as the first pair.

MacGregor of Glenarklet had even keener eyes than his monarch, used to searching his Highland hills for the shadowy deer. "A woman, Highness," he observed quietly, at James's elbow.

"Aye – and riding at such a pace, a young one! A chase, eh? Hard riding and far, by the look of it. Many chasing two, and one a woman! Here's a matter we might look into, with profit. Eh, my lord?" Without waiting for Kennedy's comment, the King pointed. "Down here. Through the whins. Round the knoll, there – and we can head them off. If they hold to the line they ride now. Come!"

Spurring hard, James led the way downhill, caring nothing for burns, outcropping rock, gorse-bushes, or the wet and slippery slopes on which his great bay's hooves scored long red weals. Rob and the MacGregor kept close, but Lord Kennedy was quickly left behind, growling at the folly of men old enough to know better.

Cutting across on an intercepting course, the three young men swiftly closed the gap between themselves and what appeared to be two fugitives. As they drew nearer, it became clear that the others' horses, though of excellent quality, were very weary, covered in mud and their own foam. The foremost rider was indeed a young woman, riding superbly, and the strangeness of her appearance that had impressed itself upon the King at a distance proved to be her hair streaming out loose behind her, much hair and of the most vivid red that James had ever seen. The man behind was obviously a servant, a groom, a dark gypsy-like fellow.

The pursuers might number anything up to fifty, it could be seen, well strung out but with three or four of the leaders gaining fast.

The young woman had pulled away a little to the left, south-wards, at sight of the newcomers, but clearly the royal horses were much more fresh than hers. The King had ridden only from his castle of Dundonald, north of Ayr, and halted at midday to eat at Stair. There was no doubt that James would catch up with her – but she flogged her tired spume-lathered black savagely, increasingly, with a whip nevertheless.

As with thundering hooves scattering turfs, the King gradually crept up on the pair, he perceived that the serving-man had drawn a short sword. Looking back, he gestured to Rob Bruce to attend to the fellow, and pressed on.

At last James and the girl were riding almost neck and neck. She was richly dressed, and despite her dishevelment, of a striking and vivid beauty, notably well-made however crouching her present posture.

"Mistress!" James panted. "Need you . . . hurry so?"

She stared straight ahead of her, still lashing her beast, and answered nothing.

"Fear nothing . . . now," he went on. "No hurt . . . will come to you, now."

"Be off!" That was snapped out like one of her whip-cracks.

"Who are these? Behind?"

She looked at him then, and her great eyes flashed scorn, defiance, anger. "Go ask them!" she cried, and her whip lashed out, not at her horse this time but at the King himself.

James swore, as he twisted aside in the saddle to avoid the blow, and then, swift as thought, leaned over and reached out and grabbed her reins. She shouted, almost screamed at him, as he dragged her black's head round – and this time he could by no means avoid the whip, which cut viciously across his neck and shoulder. Furiously he dropped her bridle, and leaning far over, threw his arm round her slender waist instead, and with a violent effort heaved her right out of her saddle. Her mount veered off, uncontrolled, and he was left with the young woman's no light weight struggling on his single arm. It took him all his strength and horsemanship to remain mounted, and to get her hoisted somehow bodily in front of him.

She was like a wild-cat in his arms, snarling, spitting, striking out. "Fool! Scullion! Whore's-get! Take your vile hands off me!" she yelled. "Christ God's blood – unhand me, knave! Curse you! Curse you! Foul fiend destroy you . . .!" She beat at his chest with one hand clenched, and clawed at his face with the other.

James clamped his arms tightly round her elbows, crushing her unmercifully. Convulsively she continued to struggle in his vice-like grip — and even as he fought with her he knew a fierce satisfaction at the heaving vehemence of that magnificent body against his own. His satisfaction was short-lived however, for he had to jerk back his head abruptly to prevent her from biting him. Even so, as he strained away from her, she spat in his face.

Glenarklet rode close, to grasp the King's bridle and bring the bay to a dancing halt. Rob had the groom disarmed, and pulled up likewise. Alarmed, both men circled round the King's horse.

"Shall I take her, Sire?" Rob exclaimed. "She is crazed — a mad thing! Throw her down, and I will take her."

"No. *I* will tame her, by Ninian . . .!" James began — but was proved mistaken there and then, for somehow the girl wriggled and twisted out of the saddle and slipped, to hang suspended half-way to the ground, still struggling and all but dragging him with her. He let go of her, with an oath, only just managing to keep his seat. She ran a few paces, to whirl round and face them, arms akimbo, head up, tossing her hair from her flushed face, eyes blazing, deep bosom heaving. A cataract of abuse poured from her red lips, of a quality to make even a hardened man-at-arms blush. The three young men gazed at her at a loss, James wiping his face as he sought to recover both his breath and his composure.

Thus the Lord Kennedy found them as he drew up his heavy mount almost to its haunches. "Janet!" he cried. "A God's name — what is this? Waesucks — what's to do, girl? What now?"

Narrowing her fine eyes, she looked from him to the others, and then beyond them to the first of the pursuers who were now only a short distance off. She shrugged, and folded her arms over her breast. "Who is this man who dares to handle me so?" she demanded.

"He is your liege lord, Janet — the King's Grace himsel'!"

If her father, or any other, expected the young woman to display shock, dismay or contrition at this revelation, they were disappointed. She looked James up and down, without any noticeable alteration of expression, and said nothing.

"You, then, are the Lady Janet!" the King got out, with some difficulty. "Janet Kennedy, Flaming Janet!"

A twitch of one shoulder was all the answer he received. She spoke to her father. "I'd have outridden them. To Cassillis. They would not have caught me, by God!"

That was all there was time for, before the first of the pursuit came pounding up. These proved to be armed men, well mounted enough, wearing a livery of blue and red, with a crowned red heart painted on every breastplate. There was no mistaking that symbol. These were Douglases. Hands on sword-hilts, they drew up their almost foundered sweating beasts, in a menacing semi-circle round the five men and the girl, heavy-breathing, scowling, unspeaking.

"Nolt! Brute-beasts! Cattle!" the young woman flung at them. "Where is your lord? Are his aged bones cracked quite? Have you left him in some ditch, his stiff neck broke? Tell him to mount you on horses, not stirks, if you would catch Janet Kennedy!"

None answered her. None met her wrathful glare. Indeed, despite all their glowering it appeared as though they knew and feared her lashing tongue.

Others were coming up all the time. One arrived more finely dressed than the others, a long-faced, sallow youngish man with a haughty look. His glance flickered from the young woman, over the newcomers, to Lord Kennedy whom he seemed to know, and he fingered his straggling black beard. "My lord . . ." he began.

Before he could say further, Janet Kennedy interrupted. "Too late, Black Davy—as always!" she mocked him. "When you presume to chase a woman, choose some slow slut . . ."

"What's this, sirrah!" Kennedy demanded, but wearily rather than hotly. "Out with it, man. How come you to course Kennedy's daughter across Carrick?"

"We but sought to catch up with her—to give her a message from my lord. He sent us with word, after her . . ."

The girl's high skirl of laughter stopped him. "He'd have *you* drag me back to him, since he cannot do it himself! He shivers in his ancient bed, lacking blood . . ."

"My lord follows us. Not far behind. He was but something delayed."

It was a new experience for the King to be thus ignored in any company. He spoke up, now. "Since you, sir, are a Douglas, and this is the Lady Janet Kennedy, I take it that you speak of my Lord Chancellor, the Earl of Angus? Is he here, in this country? Is this . . . this folly, of his making?" And when the other did not deign a reply. "Answer, fellow! I am the King."

Startled, the dark man stared, and gulped. "Aye, sir. My lord. Sire. To be sure. Your pardon, Highness. Aye — from my Lord of Angus. We come . . . we come from Douglas Castle. My lord follows . . ."

"And must needs follow further! And faster!" the young woman finished for him. "And with open hands and purse-strings a deal less tight! Go tell him so, Davy. Tell him that I bed with no skinflint! No aged skinflint, in especial!"

James looked from one to the other of the speakers. "Douglas Castle, did you say? Douglasdale is thirty miles away! More. You have ridden, hunted her, from Douglas? Across those bogs and moors . . .?"

"Nor would have reached me — but for you!" Janet Kennedy hurled at him. "I should have been at Cassillis by this. Where I would be now, by the Mass! My lord," she said curtly to her father. "Must we all stand gawping here? Take me up on your beast. My own is done, anyway." She strode over to his side. There she turned. "And you, Davy — back to the man who whelped you! Was he a miser then, likewise? Or did your dam bear you behind some bush, and at no cost? Back to him, and tell him that he must think again, and think deep, if he would have Janet Kennedy back!"

The King of Carrick emitted something between a sigh and a groan, as he hoisted his daughter up before him. "God pity me — how did I come to sire such as you, girl?" he demanded of the world at large.

None answered him.

None contested the young woman's orders, either. As her father pulled his horse's head round, to head westwards for Cassillis House, the man Davy looked doubtfully at the King, sketched a bow, and then gestured to his men to turn back, eastwards. While the groom went to collect the girl's trembling mount, standing some distance off, James spurred after the Kennedys, his two friends at his back. There was no more formal parting.

For once, James Stewart was at a loss for words as he rode beside his host, eyeing the young woman sidelong, and occasionally raising a hand to touch the stinging weal at his neck where her whip had struck. She ignored him, ignored them all.

He had heard about her, of course — all Scotland had heard of Flaming Janet, Angus's new mistress, the tempestuous fiery-haired beauty who, it was said, was twisting the veteran Bell-the-

Cat around her little finger. Already she was known to have wormed substantial lands and manors out of him. Apparently she wanted more, a young woman with no doubts as to her own worth.

After a while, she caught his eye as he was considering her, and held his glance with insolent assurance and no sort of embarrassment. "You have red hair also," she mentioned, almost casually.

"Yes."

"I have heard that you have a way with women, sire. You should have known better than to lay hands on me so!"

He inclined his head, but did not take his eyes off her. She was extraordinarily, challengingly beautiful.

"You come to Cassillis? To our house?"

"For this night only," James was stiff. "I make a pilgrimage to the shrine of Saint Ninian, at Whithorn in Galloway."

"Ah, yes. To give thanks for the birth of a daughter, is it not? The daughter is well? And the mother?"

"I thank you, yes."

She tipped her lips with a pink tongue. "They tell me that Your Grace wears ever an iron chain about your loins. Always. At all times. Does it not, on occasion, incommode you greatly? And others?"

"Janet!" her father exploded. "Hold your vixen's tongue, in the fiend's name!"

"Does it not, Sire?" she insisted — and when James did not answer, laughed high and clear.

As they rode on, speechless, Janet Kennedy began to sing softly to herself.

The crowded Great Hall of Cassillis House presented something of a comedy that night to a most appreciative audience — and for once the fool and butt was the normally most feared and dangerous man in the kingdom, the Earl of Angus, head of the great house of Douglas. Travel-stained, weary and in a vile temper, Angus had reached Cassillis just after the royal train had arrived — and made no secret of the fact that finding it there by no means increased his satisfaction. His ill-humour was extended to all, even to his host, and he was barely civil to the King. Though not to Janet Kennedy. Towards her he was so amiable, so eager to please that it was laughable — and at the same time pathetic; to see this proud eagle of a man, elderly, great, vastly experienced, Chancellor of the kingdom, at whose word thousands trembled, behaving like any love-sick callow youth, was perhaps instructive without being edifying.

The young woman spared him nothing. She alternatively ignored him, lashed him with her tongue, or made a fool of him before all. Not that she was respectful towards any, even James — but to others her insolence was casual, general, while to Angus it was pointed and particular.

She made no secret of what was behind the situation. She had been Angus's mistress for some six months, and believed him insufficiently appreciative of her worth, in deed, however much he might grovel to her in word and manner. The Douglas lands were vast; next to the Church he was the greatest land-owner in Scotland, far outshining the King in wealth. Janet Kennedy had a shrewd and practical eye, however lovely. She knew what she wanted, and believed that she could get it. At the moment she wanted the rich lands of Kilspindie, on the Lothian coast, with its fine castle — why this in especial, she did not bother to explain. Angus had sought to fob her off with jewellery and lesser properties, on the inadequate excuse that Kilspindie was already occupied by one of his many illegitimate sons. Flaming Janet's reaction to that had been succinct if barely repeatable. And when he continued to refuse her, she had bolted for home.

James, after his initial sense of shock and offence at the young woman's behaviour, gradually grew as interested and amused at the by-play as any. He had no cause to love Angus, and once he was able to stomach his masculine sense of fitness at the sight of an elderly and important noble made public mock of by a slip of a girl, he found himself beginning to savour the process. Indeed, little by little, he began to do more than that. He commenced to join in the sport.

It was not intentional, at first — for he was concerned to teach this lamentable beauty a lesson, since no one else seemed capable of so doing. Clearly her parents had long ago given up the hopeless task of seeking to control her, and nobody other, least of all her elderly lover, had any authority over her — for even Robert Blackadder, Archbishop of Glasgow, who was participating in the royal pilgrimage to Whithorn, was cozened, flyted at and made eyes to, with no complaint. It was time that the King's authority was demonstrated.

It was less easy than he could have expected, however. James would undoubtedly have managed it most suitably had she remained in the same deplorable frame of mind in which she had first burst upon him. But when she deigned to show herself in the Hall, for the feast her father provided in the King's honour, she had changed more than her costume and appearance. She was still Flaming Janet, of course, to be handled with extreme care — but she was now disposed to captivate and enthrall men rather than to reject them, in her own inverted and shamelessly provocative way. She was all dazzling smiles, however wicked, her hair piled above her head in a vivid wonder, her gown so low-cut as barely to contain her swelling breasts, her eyes challenging every male and scorning every female of the company. James found it difficult, in the circumstances, to adopt the tone his responsible self felt to be fitting — especially as ever more it was his glance that those brilliantly magnetic eyes sought, caught, and held throughout her quite disgraceful sallies.

When toasts were being drunk, after the meal, to the King, to their host, to the memory of blessed Saint Ninian, the girl suddenly sprang up, goblet in hand, bold as any man.

"I give you a toast," she cried. "Drink with me to Archibald — who thinks he may bell the cat without cream! I give you the King's foremost subject, the Knight of . . . of the shrunken . . ." She paused wickedly. ". . . shall we say heart? Apt, for Douglas. The Knight of the Shrunken Heart!"

As the Douglas half rose in his chair, hawk-like features congested now, purple, quivering with rage, the veins of his bony clenched fists knotted, there was appalled silence in that thronged chamber save for the cracking of bones by the hounds amongst the floor rushes.

It was James who saved the situation, surprising himself by doing so. He raised his own goblet. "To the King's foremost subject," he repeated into the hush. "To my lord Chancellor." He smiled. "I swear it seems I must make him my Lord Treasurer, also!"

There was a prolonged shout of mirth, relief, acclaim, as the toast echoed and re-echoed to the rafters, and none feared to drink it, Angus slowly sank back, transferring his glare from the young man to the King. James, lifting one eyebrow at him, turned to Janet and their eyes locked. For moments on end they stared, oblivious of others, and then the girl's laughter pealed aloud.

"I congratulate you both!" she skirled. "Does Your Grace perchance think to make other claims on your Chancellor's . . .

goodwill?" She lowered her eyes in mock modesty. "For the King, of course, must be served!"

There was a further gasping from those who heard. James fingered his chin. "The Earl of Angus, I know well, would deny me nothing of his," he said, slowly. "Such is his leal fervour. Eh, my lord?"

After that the thing seemed to develop almost inevitably, James becoming quite frankly the young woman's accomplice in the teasing of the older man. It was barbed sport, spicy, rousing.

Where James was present there was usually dancing, and it was with the King of course that Janet Kennedy danced when the tables were pushed back and the rushes cleared away. He had partnered many tempting and enticing women in his day, but never with any so deliberately, blatantly seductive as this. Every movement of her splendid body was calculated, intended to rouse — and not only her partner. She saw to it, of course, that they danced ever in the vicinity of the scowling and unhappy Angus, where he sat with his uncomfortable and helpless host, two proud and haughty nobles reduced to impotence.

Abruptly, Angus had had enough. With a curse he got to his feet and without other words even to Kennedy, pushed unceremoniously through the throng of dancers, fiercely shouldering aside Janet and the King in the by-going. He stamped off upstairs to his chamber.

And at the very next measure, the young woman drew back from James's arms, curtly excused herself, and went off to dance with other partners.

As angry as he felt foolish, James fumed and fretted, only too well aware of the ill-concealed smirks of amused courtiers. He danced briefly with one or two other women, but his hot glance was never far from Janet's direction. When, during a pause, he saw her using her potent charms to coax Archbishop Blackadder to take the floor with her, driven by something other than his better judgement he strode over to her.

"Lady," he jerked. "A word with you, if you please."

She was stooping so low to the Archbishop in his chair that she had to hold her firm breasts in place lest they leapt wholly loose, one pink half-moon already visible. "Your Grace's pardon," she said coolly, "but I am already engaged to tread this one with my lord Archbishop."

"My lord will excuse you," James told her briefly.

The girl did not even straighten up. "The Archbishop would not disappoint me, I am sure," she declared, her hand out to stroke the cleric's sleeve.

Robert Blackadder had been a useful servant of the King, serving as envoy on a number of ticklish missions, a diplomatist rather than a pastor. But for the moment he was grievously disappointed with his liege lord. The old fox Shivas, Archbishop of St. Andrews, had died the year before, unlamented, and Blackadder had confidently expected to step into his shoes as Primate of Scotland. But James had appointed, or used his influence to cause the Pope to appoint, his young brother, the Duke of Ross, to this the premier archepiscopal see — this during his bad period after the Northumbrian debacle. He had done it partly for reasons of economy, with the Treasury so low, to save the cost of maintaining that young prince's establishment — for the St. Andrews revenues were very large; partly as a gesture to appease his brother's constant complaint that he was neglected, a resentful notion which Angus never failed to encourage — and which might have some slight basis of truth. The brothers James had never been friends — they had both been christened James, for at the younger's birth the elder had been sickly and not expected to survive; possibly the second son had lived with disappointment ever since. He had been handed over to Angus's keeping by the Privy Council, at his father's death, and the Douglas, failing to dominate the elder brother, had made sure of the younger. Ross was almost entirely under Angus's influence, and had been involved, in some measure, in many of the plots against the King. By giving him the foremost position in the Church, James hoped to take the edge off his envy.

So now the portly Blackadder rose to his feet, bowed first to the King and then to the smiling young woman. "With Your Highness's gracious permission," he said, and taking Janet's arm, moved out on to the floor with her.

Tight-lipped, James gazed after them. Then he too swung about and stalked to the door, uncaring that only some small proportion of the dancers noticed his sudden retiral, and hastily paused to bow and curtsy to his stiff back.

Watchful as always, Rob Bruce materialised at the King's elbow as he made for the winding stone stairs.

"We ride for Galloway at cock-crow," James snapped. "See to it."

"Yes, Sire," Rob said, heartily, in a sigh of relief.

A further two days were scheduled for the royal train to reach Saint Ninian's Candida Casa at Whithorn, on the southernmost tip of the Wigtown peninsula that thrust into the Irish Sea — but James in his present mood did the eighty miles in one, leaving behind him a scattered, broken cavalcade of outraged courtiers strung out over the intervening parts of three shires. At the saint's shrine itself he was equally precipitate, not being really in a state for profound devotions, and set off again northwards before noon the following day, before most of his company had arrived, to the astonishment of the Prior and his monks who had prepared for at least a week's banqueting — with suitable royal recompense to follow.

It had been intended that the return to Stirling should be in leisurely progress by Nithsdale and the Lowther Hills to Lanark, with the Lords Maxwell and Fleming and sundry abbots prepared to entertain the royal traveller and his entourage. But passing Drumlanrig and perceiving the Douglas Red Heart banner streaming from the castle keep, the King's enquiries revealed that the Earl of Angus had arrived at this house of his the day previously, and alone apparently save for his escort.

James rode on in silence after that for the best part of an hour, but when he reached the parting of the ways where the route to the north turned away right-handed out of the Nith valley, up the Mennock Water, he drew rein.

"I ride on. Up Nith," he told Rob Bruce. "Alone."

"But . . . Sire!" Rob protested. "We make for Crawford. Up Mennock Water, here."

"The others, yes. Go back and tell Sir Patrick Home to lead on to Crawford. I follow Nith."

"To . . . to Cassillis?"

"Aye. To Cassillis."

"I am sorry for it," Rob said heavily. And, when James did not reply, greatly bold he raised his gaze to meet the King's. "I am sorry . . . for the Lady Margaret."

James frowned. "The Lady Margaret is . . . secure. In my heart," he said shortly. "This is . . . other."

Rob sighed, but said no more.

"Inform Sir Patrick," James said tersely, and spurred his horse onwards. As Rob turned back to pass on the orders to the Master of the Horse, some way behind, without comment or question MacGregor of Glenarklet rode on after the King.

It took Rob Bruce two full hours to catch up with his master thereafter, joining him and the Highlander without remark or greeting as they forded the Afton Water preparatory to climbing over the great brown moors to Dalmellington and the valley of the upper Doon. It was early evening before the hard-riding trio came to Cassillis House — to the surprise of its lord.

James did not beat about the bush. "Where is the Lady Janet?" he asked, without delay or excuse.

"She is gone to my house in the town. In Maybole, Your Grace," her father said. "To spend my siller — or it may be Angus's siller — on gewgaws and siclike whim-whams. Was ever a man cursed with such a jade . . .!"

"Maybole? That is but a few miles. She will be back tonight, my lord?"

"Na, na — no' Janet. She'll pass as little time as she may under her father's roof, yon one! She'll bide in Maybole. Plenty swack lads in Maybole, see you . . .!"

"M'mmm. Angus, then, has not yielded? Given her what she wanted?"

"Oooh, aye. There's nae fool like an auld fool, Highness! Though mind, for the lave, Angus isna any man's fool. But a woman . . . yon besom! Aye, he's promised her Kilspindie. She has him where it hurts the maist! But she'll keep him dangling, as punishment for holding out. I ken her." He paused. "Your Grace . . . Your Grace isna sniffing round the same entry?"

"I have some unfinished business with that one," James told him briefly.

They rode on the five miles to the capital of Carrick of the Kennedies. There, even had the great town-house of the family not dominated the narrow High Street and all the lesser mansions of the Kennedy lairds, they would have known where to seek Janet Kennedy by the noise of music, singing and laughter that issued from the tall ornate building within its courtyard, and by the crowds of townsfolk who milled about in the street outside, flagons and mugs in their hands — for great barrels of ale were set up in the forecourt of the house, with scullions dispensing free drink to all comers.

Unrecognised, James and his two companions pushed their way through the noisy throng, into the house, and up the wide stairway where sundry couples were already in sprawling embrace, to the principal apartment. Here, to the music of gypsy fiddlers, a wild dance was in progress, half a dozen couples on the floor disporting themselves in abandoned fashion, led by the Lady Janet, all in vivid green — or such of her as was covered — and a heavily good-looking young man of muscular build and florid complexion.

James watched the spirited but indecorous scene for a few moments, grimly, and then strode forward through the stir to the leading couple. Janet Kennedy, much taken up with her gloatingly attentive partner, did not perceive the King until he was almost upon her. Then the laughter died on her flushed face as she stared.

James's hand descended upon the shoulder of the young man. "My friend," he said tautly, "permit me to interrupt. I would have word with this lady."

The other whirled round, hotly, eyes blazing. "The foul fiend seize you! Who in hell dares to . . . to . . .?"

"I do. Excuse us, sir."

At the authority in that, the man faltered, panting a little. But recovering himself, he let go of the young woman, and clenching his fists, moved up to the King, thrusting his face close.

James folded his arms but did not draw back, though his nose wrinkled. "You smell, fellow!" he observed. "I do not think I congratulate the Lady Janet. Stand back."

"Christ's death!" A hand was raised to strike.

Swifter than the eye could follow, the gleaming naked blade of a Highland dirk flashed up between them, within an inch of the other's red face. "Be off!" Glenarklet whispered, in his soft, sibilant voice. "You were hearing the King, sir? Be off!"

Janet Kennedy found her tongue, her laughter. "Poor Harry!" she trilled. "Bow, Harry! Kneel, Harry! Kiss the King's hand, Harry — lick his boots! Here's more potent power than lusty Harry Kennedy of Baltersan's! We all must bow to James of Scotland!" And she swept a mock curtsy.

The bewildered young laird stared from the wickedly flickering steel so near his eyes, to James's face, over to the girl, and back to James again. He was bereft of words, though his fists were still raised.

"Leave us, sir," the King jerked. "Here is no fault of yours. But . . . leave us." He turned to Rob Bruce. "Clear me this rabble."

"Ha!" Janet exclaimed. "You go too far, James Stewart! In this house, *I* command!"

"When the King is not present!" he snapped.

The skreak of Rob's drawn sword had the desired effect. Led by the gypsy musicians, the dancers and watchers began to scurry from the room. The young Kennedy laird backed away, at a loss. White with fury, Janet began to curse, and came at the King, clawing.

James suddenly laughed aloud, great shouted laughter. Beating down the girl's outstretched hands, he stooped, to throw one arm round her waist and the other behind her knees, and swept her up. Heavy as she was, and kicking, struggling, beating at him with her fists, he strode with her across the chamber to an open doorway where a narrow private turnpike stair wound upwards. Through this he pushed, not caring that he knocked her roughly against jambs and wall, to go stumbling and tripping up those twisting stairs.

At the first landing, he kicked at a shut door, but it remained firm. The second, his boot flung open, to reveal a bedchamber. Into this he staggered, and fell with the furiously wrestling girl bodily on to the bed. As she scratched at him, yelling, he slapped her twice, brutally, across the face, laying all his weight upon her heaving person. She sank her teeth into one of his hands, but with the other he began to tear at her clothing.

Suddenly, without warning, she stilled under him, her tense body went limp, her limbs drooped and flung wide, her lips parted and her eyes closed. He did not abate his furious tugging and ripping, but she lay like a dead thing beneath his urgent hands, even when he rolled aside to gaze down at her white loveliness, panting, groaning.

Then, as abruptly, she was alive again, her hand went up into his red hair, to clutch it, to force his head down to her own, while the other hand, busy, knowledgeable, was aiding him now. She swore again — but only at his chain.

Fiercely, violently, they came together, in raging, scorching passion — and the heat of their union dissolved all their world around them.

Rob Bruce closed the door on them, silently, and went down the stairs again, set-faced, heavy footed.

19

MARGARET DRUMMOND sat on the moss-grown stone seat at the edge of the high terrace garden of Stirling Castle rock, crooning to the child in her arms — another Margaret Drummond, now six months old — while near by the King played on hands and knees on the grass with his small son, Alexander Boyd, in as pleasant a domestic scene as any his realm could show that autumn afternoon. The sun was still warm, the Highland hills across the plain of Forth still glowed purple with heather, the tree-tops below them at the foot of the rock were glowing with gold and russet and scarlet, and all the land held a wistful loveliness. But it was to the woman, rather than to that fair prospect, that the man's eyes turned so frequently and lingered upon — to his son's impatience, who preferred his father as a spirited but single-minded charger. Margaret's loveliness had even increased with motherhood, her radiant warmth and calm serenity deepened.

Raising her own regard from the baby, she caught the man's adoring gaze, and smiled gently. "You are happy, Jamie?" she said.

"I am happy," he agreed. "I was never more happy, I think."

It was true. These last months had been rich, full, satisfying, for him. His evil humours and moodiness had evaporated, his domestic life here at Stirling was a joy and comfort, Scotland was at comparative peace internally and, thanks to the Spaniard, De Ayala, a born peacemaker and diplomatist who had a dual accreditation to both Courts, relations with England were better than could have been anticipated a year before. Henry, of course, was preoccupied with the savage business of reducing the power of his own nobles, and on the busy Ayala's advice even wrote to James begging him to act with mildness and mercy towards his Bishop of Durham who, from Norham Castle, had taken high-handed action against sundry Scots Borderers. All this had notably soothed James's feelings. Margaret was all that he could ever have wished for and more, he doted on the baby girl — and when the fierce restlessness welled up within him demanding release, there was Janet Kennedy to think of.

"I am glad, glad," Margaret murmured. "When you are happy, all your realm is happy also. And I am more than happy. Oh, that it may last!"

He nodded. "So long as you do not change, my heart, it will last," he asserted confidently.

"I shall not change, James. Nor will you, I think. But . . . others. Others may change much. Break our peace, our sweet accord — though never our love. I fear for it a little, my dear."

"Eh . . .?" Putting Alexander aside, he straightened up, though still on his knees. "What others? Who could come between you and me, Margaret?"

"None, I believe, I pray. Not even the Lady Janet Kennedy."

Slowly he rose to his feet. He opened his mouth to speak, and then closed it again. He took a pace or two away, to the terrace wall, and stood staring out.

"She came to Stirling, last night," Margaret went on quietly. "Did you know, James?"

He whirled round. "Here? She is here?"

"Yes. She lodges, I am told, with . . . my Lord of Gray!"

"Damnation! God afflict and confound them both!"

She smiled a little. "You see, my dear, how fragile a thing is our fine peace! I thought that you could not know."

Biting his lip he looked at her, "Margaret . . . this is . . . an ill thing. I did not know. I said that she should not come here — must not come here."

"Flaming Janet, James, is not notable for her obedience, I have heard!"

"I . . . I did not even know that you knew. Of her. Of this . . . this tangle."

"My heart — all Scotland knows what the King does. And half Scotland, what Janet Kennedy does! Think you that I would not be the first to be told? At this Court? Four ladies told me the tidings, in one day! Before you were yet returned from your pilgrimage."

"Then . . . dear God — you have known all these months! While we have been . . . while you have been so kind, so warm!"

"Why, yes. Should I not have been? I love James Stewart, and I know James Stewart. This is part of James Stewart. I have always known it. That you would need other women. It took me long to learn, you remember, that my love was stronger than my

337

woman's jealousy. For I am proud also, too proud. But that lesson I learned, in time. You would not expect that I forget it, now?"

He drew a long breath. "God bless you, Margaret!" he said, and came to her side. "Bless your dear, noble, generous heart! I am not worthy to touch the hem of your skirt! I know it. But . . . I love you, esteem you, need you, as I do none of these others. Something in them I need, yes—God forgive me! But you are my heart's heart, my life, my joy, my sanctuary. You and only you."

"That I know," she said simply, reaching up to take his hand. "And I never cease to thank God for it."

He kissed her fingers. "You know, the saints be praised. But do you understand? I' faith—do I understand, myself? There is at times a fire in me, hot, raging, brutish. You kindle your own fine fire in me truly—but not this fire. Never this fire, I thank Heaven!" He shook his head. "This Janet—she is a devil!"

"So I have heard. And you must tame her?"

"Yes. I must tame her. I *can* tame her. For a little. It is the same wild, raging fire, you see."

"It was so with Marsala MacIan?"

"Ah, no. No, that was other again. A better thing. A plague on it—how shall I explain it? What am I, in the name of sweet Ninian? What sort of man . . .?"

"You are James Stewart, King of Scots—and all of a man! The man to fill my heart, my mind, my body. What else? Mary-Mother—what else do I want? Do we want?"

They were silent for long moments, hand in hand. Then in a hoarse voice, James spoke.

"This Janet. She should not have come here, to Court. It is intolerable. She must go."

"Yes—she must go. From Stirling. Here she will harm you. Harm us. Harm the realm itself. It is not that I would be rid of her, if you need her. But . . . here she can only make trouble. You see that?"

"Aye, I see it. I forbade her here, I tell you. Janet Kennedy will make trouble wherever she is. But I will not have her troubling you . . ."

"It is not me, James. I believe myself to be safe and sure in your love. For me, she could stay. But she is hungry, that one. At this Court she will serve you ill. Either she reigns here supreme, or she will intrigue and fight and betray. She will use other men to work on your jealousy. And your enemies will use *her*! That she should now be with the Lord Gray . . .!"

"Aye – you need not tell me, lass. I see it all. I shall send her away, never fear. At once. And far away."

"And will she go? Stay?"

He frowned. "I am the King . . .!" he began, but there was doubt in his voice.

"James – tell me. Did you take this woman for . . . for herself? Or to spite my Lord of Angus? To take her away from Angus, who has injured you so deep and so often? Which?"

He almost groaned, knuckling his brow. "The fiend knows! Both, I think – aye, both. But now . . . now I need her, Margaret. Need something that she has. It is an evil need, perhaps . . ."

"What is she now, then? Is she your mistress? Oh, I know you have had her. But do you keep her? Or does Angus still do that? Who keeps her?"

"I do not. She has had but some trinkets from me. From Angus she has lands and houses. From others, God knows!"

"James – this will not serve," Margaret declared earnestly. "You have said you are the King. In this you must play the King, then. You say that you need her. So you must make her yours. The King cannot share a woman with all comers, like any trollop of the vennels! If you need her, make her *your* mistress – and yours only. Then you may command her – and keep her where you will."

He looked down at her, wonderingly. "This – from you, my love!"

"Why not? If you need her, you will see her, have her – that we both know. See then that you are master. It may be costly – but only this will serve. This, or put her from you. Give her her price, like a king. Do not chaffer. She loves lands, castles, they say. Give her a castle, a domain, large enough, fine enough, for her pride – but far from Stirling. Finer than Gray can give her, or than Angus will! Master more than her body, James – for your own sake! She will esteem you the better for it."

"Save us, Margaret! I had not thought . . . I would not have believed . . .! Is this sweet Margaret Drummond? But, by the saints – you are right! So it shall be. What shall I give her? Where shall I send her? Not . . . not *too* far away . . ."

"No – not too far!" She smiled faintly. "For I do not want to lose you for too long, each time your need comes upon you? But sufficiently far that she cannot come easily to Stirling . . ."

"Darnaway!" he interrupted. "The castle of Darnaway, in Moray! It stands empty. Huntly covets it — this will serve to keep him out of it. Aye, and it is great enough — a mighty pile in the midst of Darnaway Forest, the seat of the Earldom of Moray." He laughed. "Apt too, by the Rude! For it was a Douglas house, forfeit to the Crown by my grandsire, James Second, for the treasons of another Earl Archibald Douglas! Aye, Darnaway it shall be. She will come to little mischief there!"

Margaret rose, to pace to and fro, hushing the baby who had begun to whimper. "James — how will you tell her?" she asked.

"M'mmm. It will be difficult, perhaps."

"Yes. Do not let her make a triumph of it. Nor any display, before others. As I think that she might. I counsel you, do not let her appear at your Court, at all. Summon her privily. And swiftly. Before she can make an entry."

He nodded. "You have the rights of it. I will see her alone. Forthwith." He grimaced. "It may be a wild business, I fear!"

"Have her here, then. Before us both. In this garden, with none other present. That will irk her, hamper her, I think — to have me to face, with you! Were I in her shoes, I vow I should find it discommoded me not a little!"

James chuckled, he laughed aloud. "My dear, my pigeon — masterly! This is a Margaret Drummond I never knew! I felicitate you. So be it. I shall have Rob Bruce bring her here, forthwith. Alone. And as secretly as may be. And he shall arrange an escort to take her north to Darnaway thereafter . . ."

"The Lady Janet Kennedy," Sir Rob Bruce announced, and managed to get an astonishing amount of disapproval into the four words, even though he was not what could be called an eloquent young man. Straightway he turned and strode back up the zigzag path from the garden to the postern-gate in the frowning castle wall.

Janet Kennedy sank in a profound curtsy. "Your Grace's most humble subject!" she said, in her deep throaty voice. "This is a mòst signal honour, surely?" There was question there, and it was not at the King that she looked, but at Margaret Drummond.

James had prepared in his mind what he would say and how

340

he would behave towards her at what could only be a somewhat difficult interview; but the sight and sound of her played havoc with his strong intentions. "Janet . . .!" he cried, starting a pace forward, and then halting again. "Here's folly! Why did you come?"

"Why, Highness – because you sent for me!" She straightened up, smiling at her most dazzling. "Would any woman dare to do otherwise?"

"I meant, of course, come to Stirling. When I said that you should not."

She came slowly forward now, and she had a lithely graceful walk, after the fashion of a cat. "All Scotland seeks the sun of your royal presence," she observed. "Must I alone be denied the warmth of it? I, who know something of its goodly heat! Would not that be unkind?"

He frowned. "So you put yourself in the house of Andrew Gray! A man whom all know will do me dis-service, if he can!"

She raised arching eyebrows. "I put myself in the house of Your Grace's Lord Justiciar General – since I am less bold than to trespass in your own!"

Margaret coughed a little.

"M'mmm. Aye, Margaret. This is the Lady Janet, daughter to my Lord Kennedy. The Lady Margaret, who is . . . very dear to me."

"We have all heard of the Lady Margaret's good fortune," Janet declared. "So fair. So estimable. So immaculate." She was running a keen eye up and down the other's person. "And, on my soul, still so well-proportioned to be the mother of these two! This fine boy . . .!"

"H'mmm. That is . . . another," James said. "Alexander. He is, er, older."

"Ah, yes. Of course. I recollect. Another lady, was it not? The name escapes me . . ."

"I am rejoiced to meet the Lady Janet, Your Grace," Margaret put in, calmly. "Her fame has been known to me for some time – known to many. And with good reason, I see. She is very beautiful."

The two women considered each other. They made a most eye-catching pair, and a most extraordinary contrast, the one with a delicate and exquisite loveliness, the other with a magnificent, startling beauty. The man between them, so well aware

341

of the qualities and attractions of both, shuffled feet on the grass and cleared his throat.

"Yes. No doubt. That is so," he said. "As to this matter of Gray, now—I do not desire that you remain in his lodging, Janet. It is . . . unsuitable."

"On the contrary, for me, Sire, it is most suitable!" the other asserted coolly. "He is . . . very hospitable. He makes me most welcome. And the house, though small, is conveniently close to this Your Grace's castle."

"Nevertheless, I deem it unsuitable."

"Ah!" She smiled brilliantly. "You would have me come closer still? Here, to your castle itself? You are kind, Sire—but some might think that unsuitable also. For me! Some are apt to think ill of folk with red hair!" She glanced up at the King's auburn head. "Would that not be . . . indiscreet? What says the Lady Margaret?"

"That is not what I intended," James said shortly. "I would have you go to another house. And not in Stirling, Janet."

"You would, Sire?" Those fine greenish eyes flashed. "But I would not!"

"In who attends my Court, I decide, lady!"

"But not who walks in Stirling town, dwells in Stirling houses! I am no tame courtier, Sire. I am Janet Kennedy—and I dwell where I will!" She laughed briefly. "Ask my father! Ask my Lord of Angus! Ask any man who has sought to bid me do this or that . . ."

"I am not any man. I am the King. And I do not bid—I command!"

"You do not command me, by God! No man born commands Janet Kennedy."

"I commanded you once! Aye, and you were happy to obey . . .!"

"Lady Janet, I think, misunderstands," Margaret intervened, gently but firmly. "The house that the King would have you go to is no ordinary house. One worthy even of you!"

"I choose my own houses!" the other snapped.

"I think that you would choose this one—if you could."

Janet paused, searching Margaret's face. Then she turned to James. "What is in your mind?" she demanded.

He stroked his chin. "The Earldom of Moray," he told her.

"What . . .?" She wrinkled her brows. "Earldom . . .?"

342

"Even I cannot make you an earl," the King said, with his first smile. "But I can bestow on you the Earldom of Moray, its lands and revenues, and its great castle of Darnaway. How say you, Janet?"

For once, that young woman was short of words. She stared at him testing what he had said, weighing, questioning in her mind.

"How say you?" James repeated. "Do you choose an earldom . . . or Andrew Gray's lodging in the Broad Street of Stirling?"

"Darnaway Castle!" she said, at last. "You said bestow, did you not? Did I hear aright? *Bestow*, you said?"

"Bestow, yes. Not lend, or lease, or accommodate. I, James, King of Scots, bestow, give, convey and grant to Janet Kennedy, the Earldom of Moray with all the pertinents thereof, including the principal messuage-place, fortalice and castle of Darnaway, to have and to hold. For . . ." He swallowed, his eyes flickering towards Margaret. "For the love I bear her."

She looked from one to the other of them. "This is passing strange," she declared slowly. "To be so liberal, so prodigal, you must require much in return, I think?"

"Are not you, Janet, much? A costly jewel demands a costly setting! You, Janet, I require in return. Only you . . . but all of you!"

"I see. Yes, I see." She began to laugh, not her high whinny but a low chuckle of sheer amusement. "God's death — you are sore caught are you not! Sorely you want me — and sorely you would be quit of me! To buy so high." She eyed Margaret. "*She* contrived this, did she not? This is woman's work, I swear! Men ever wait to be asked. You fear me, Margaret Drummond. You fear that I might take from you something you value much — value more than an earldom and Darnaway Castle!"

"That is true," Margaret agreed, simply.

Levelly the two women regarded each other, unspeaking, probing, assessing, and undoubtedly each perceived in the other some quality that she might have wished for. James, in a moment of wisdom, held his peace.

"So!" Janet said, at length, "That is the way of it. I am to be the King's mistress at a distance, you to be the King's mistress at hand! The lady in waiting, and the lady in attendance! Which, in the end, I wonder, will cost the King dearest?"

When neither answered her, she shrugged, and threw up her

head in characteristic gesture. "Heigho!" she said. "When do I start out for Darnaway?"

"Eh . . .? Then . . . then you will go? You will do it?" James cried. "It is a compact?"

"It is a compact," she nodded. "Provided that I have a free hand at this Darnaway. I am still Janet Kennedy!"

"Aye — nor would I change you. As you will. You will ride forthwith. Tonight."

"Tonight? So soon. You must deem me potent indeed, Margaret Drummond!" She laughed her old high tinkling laughter. "On one condition then, I ride tonight. That the King rides with me! Escorts me to Darnaway, in person. Only so will I go this night!" Those eyes flashed their challenge at the other woman.

There were moments of silence, broken only by the baby's gurgling. James, biting his lip, looked at Margaret.

Slowly, that young woman nodded her fair head.

"Very well," he said tersely. "Tonight. We ride at sundown. And . . ." he paused. ". . . I warn you, I ride hard."

"So ride I!" Janet Kennedy declared.

20

THREE years of felicity, of peace and happiness, of progress at home and growing prestige abroad, thirty-six all too short months of satisfaction and harmony and emotional well-being, were granted to James Stewart. They were full and active years, of course, for they could have held little of satisfaction for that vigorous and zestful man had they been dull or uneventful. Perhaps three such years is as much as any man has a right to expect in a life such as James's. Living is not measurable in days and months and years, as is mere existence. The real living of many a lifetime may take place in a very small percentage of it. The King, at least lived to the full in the years of Our Lord 1499, 1500 and 1501.

Since to live and to love are surely basically linked, love played a large part for James in those satisfying years – his ever deeper and abiding love for Margaret Drummond, his strange, fiery and twisted love for Janet Kennedy, his very real father's love for his son and daughter – and on a different scale, the growing aware-ness of a people's love. This last, though vague, indeterminate and never actually put into words, nevertheless was a very important contributing factor to the satisfaction of these years. In a hundred ways, by small things in the main, James became gradually, almost subconsciously, aware of the esteem and affec-tion in which he was coming to be held by all kinds and classes of his subjects. This was something new, that a king should be loved. Kings were to be feared and obeyed, frequently hated, sometimes pitied; occasionally, though not often, they came to be respected by large sections of their people. But love and affection was something novel, something which no one visual-ised, no one planned for, no one really spoke about, the effects of which could not be foreseen. That this love, like so many another, should result in eventual great sorrow and tragedy for all concerned, certainly was not to be anticipated, despite all the lessons of mankind's long story.

In the affairs of the realm, the years were productive and constructive. In a fury and a huff at having his mistress stolen from him, and being made a laughing-stock, Angus resigned the Chancellorship and turned more or less recluse in his great castle of Tantallon in Lothian. Still he plotted and sought to engineer revenge, but the King's spies watched him constantly, he had lost the support of Gray, and moreover he was growing elderly if not old; his teeth were largely pulled. Even so, he sought to get Janet back, even going the length of offering matrimony, having a marriage contract drawn up and sent to Darnaway, nominating wide lands for her portion; their curt rejection hit him sorely.

Though it was by his sure hand that James mainly directed the ship of state, Bishop Elphinstone still refused the Chancellorship; so the King appointed Archibald, second Earl of Argyll, to the position, as a worthy if dull man who would not interfere with the activities of the Lord Privy Seal, and who moreover understood the problems of the Highlands. Through these two, much that was beneficial to the realm was enacted and accomplished, the burghs and townsfolk prospered, trade increased, crafts and land husbandry were encouraged and fisheries stimulated. Ship-building was a special project of the King's, who was determined that the new trade he was fostering with the Continent should not fail for lack of Scottish bottoms to carry it; he combined business with pleasure, and when he visited Janet in Darnaway always made a point of inspecting both the great timber-cutting operations in the forests of Speyside and the yards at Aberdeen where the wrights fashioned the ships. The new grammar-schools were proving successful, and the lords and barons sending their sons to them now without the threats and penalties of the early days. Elphinstone's university was not only proving its worth but was spurring on the older foundation of St. Andrews to fresh efforts, the more so as the new Duke-Archbishop saw opportunities here to shine in the world of learning and rival his brother's personal interest in Aberdeen. The Highlands, too, were as nearly at peace as the chronically feuding clans would ever allow, and no strong contender appeared for the Lordship of the Isles.

Abroad, James was seldom without special ambassadors in circuit of the courts of the Continent, for he was intensely conscious of Scotland as a part of Europe, and interested in the culture and habits of other lands as well as their trade. He had an especial pet project of reviving the Crusades, and leading a new army of Christendom to drive the heathen from the Holy Land, and though he could arouse little enthusiasm for this amongst his fellow princes, even the Pope, he kept trying. He concluded a defensive alliance with France and Denmark – for despite the treaty of peace he by no means trusted Henry of England; under this alliance, Denmark in fact soon called for aid to defeat a Norwegian revolt, and James was able and happy to send Scotland's first expeditionary force, in a Scottish fleet, to aid his mother's kinsfolk – and to serve as a warning to Henry Tudor that he need no longer think to dominate the seas around these islands.

Never had relations with England been so peaceable for so long. There had been treaties before, of course, some for peace perpetual and everlasting, but they had never been effective. There were still Border incidents, needless to say, for the Borderers on both sides obeyed no codes but their own, but these were private and sporadic affairs that need not involve the kingdoms. Henry and James loved one another no more than heretofore, but it suited the former not to have to worry about his northern frontiers in his present campaign to master his nobility, especially with his worsening relations with France. James had no illusions on this score. He used the breathing-space not only to build up his fleet, but to organise town guards and train bands amongst the burghs and citizenry, and to gather, equip and drill a nucleus of his own troops, as distinct from the small King's Guard, which he could use independently of his lords' retainers. The lesson learned painfully in Northumberland was not being forgotten.

It was not until the summer of 1501 that the first small clouds appeared in the clear sky. At the start, these clouds tended to blow in Henry's direction rather than James's. The English undoubtedly did not like that Scots expedition to help the Danes; it smacked of much too independent and confident an attitude for the comfort of southern neighbours. It was not lost on them that James was taking the opportunity to try out his new royal troops, and their reported success was not appreciated in London. Then, soon afterwards the new French king, Louis the Twelfth, took strong and vocal exception to the fact that in Henry's treaty of amity with James, the Tudor had styled himself, with his other titles, King of France – a thing that English monarchs had been doing for centuries – and which had inadvertently escaped the Scots' notice. It was James's haste to apologise to King Louis, and his fervent assurance that the Scots did not for a moment countenance such English impertinence, that worried Henry rather than France's complaint. In consequence of all this, the King of England sent a somewhat urgent representation to the King of Scots, indicating that these attitudes infringed the spirit if not the letter of the treaty of peace and amity, and requesting him as an assurance of good faith not to ratify the ancient Scoto-French alliance then due for renewal. James answered mildly but firmly that neither the Auld Alliance nor his affirmation on dynastic matters to Louis were to be considered as in the least skaithful or prejudicial to Henry's legitimate interests.

This situation, which smacked of comedy rather than serious international drama, much less tragedy, produced the unexpected result of Henry's suddenly increased urgency for his daughter's betrothal to James. He found it politic to adopt the attitude that it had all been settled in principle previously, and that all that was required now was a speedy settlement of terms and conditions, a drawing up of the marriage contract. James, taken by surprise, debated much, in his own mind and with Margaret, and, in a cleft stick as he was, played for time. After all, Margaret Tudor was still only twelve years old, and by the time that she was of marriageable age, his strength vis-à-vis England should be much improved, a son might have been born to Margaret Drummond whom he could openly name his heir, and the entire situation could be transformed. Accordingly, after as much delay as possible, he sent ambassadors to London with instructions to enter into preliminary negotiations only, to explore possible conditions — and to take as long about the process as they might.

The Scots envoys played their part notably — even though they were unaware of the true reason behind their required behaviour — spinning out the business for no less than five months. Henry however was no babe at this sort of thing, and took his own steps to pin James down. He made the issue both public and very official by requesting his Parliament to grant the vast sum of £90,000 to defray the costs of a suitable betrothal and wedding of a Princess of England to the King of Scots. Parliament, after some haggling, cut the amount to £40,000, but Henry no doubt had allowed for this in advance. To the legislators' doubts that even this was a high price to pay to the beggarly Scots, he pointed out that it was cheaper than maintaining a large army on the Border; and to observations made that the match might just conceivably

348

lead to a Scottish monarch eventually inheriting the English throne, Henry shrewdly replied that the greater always absorbed the lesser in the course of nature, and if this happened England would have wiped out the Scottish problem once and for all.

From far-away Stirling, James watched all this developing, with only faintly growing apprehension. The victory of the Danes over the Norwegian rebels, aided by the Scots force which made an excellent showing, however, together with renewed suggestions of a match between him and an Infanta of Spain, encouraged him to believe that time was still on his side. He was content to wait. Margaret was pregnant again.

James's royal potency was proved elsewhere, likewise. Janet Kennedy gave birth to a son, at Darnaway – and it seemed probable that it was James's. She declared that it was, at least. She queened it up in Moray, of course, and possibly had local lovers at Darnaway. But as well as rejecting Angus's advances, she kept all noble and important potential rivals at a distance, and gave James no cause for major complaint – however stormy were some of his visits to the north.

Janet's son was born in the midst of a hard winter, with the Highland passes to Moray closed with snow. James, in consequence, saw neither mother nor infant for two months after the birth. Then, in typical fashion, Janet made her presence felt. She managed to get a messenger through the snows to Stirling, with a letter. The letter contained a request, almost a demand, that her son to the King be forthwith created Earl of Moray, as was due and proper.

James showed the letter to Margaret, as they sat before a roaring log fire in their own private apartments of the castle.

"Janet remains . . . Janet!" he commented. "Read it."

Margaret scanned the large, bold writing. "She might well have asked it differently," she said. "But *what* she asks is fair, is it not?"

"You think it?"

"You gave her the earldom. Since she herself cannot be Earl of Moray, is it not right that her son should be?"

"It is less simple than that, my dear. I gave her the lands and revenues of the earldom, yes. But the title itself is otherwise. It carries responsibilities and special privileges. It is one of the most ancient and honourable in the land. Moreover, it was formerly held by the Douglases. How will that proud house view their forfeited honour bestowed on a king's bastard?"

"I do not know. But Angus, their chief, will not complain, I think – for Janet's sake. He must have a true fondness for her, in that he offered her marriage. And if Angus says naught, can any other Douglas speak?"

"It may be so. But there is still more to it. If I make Janet's son an earl thus early, what of Alexander? Mariot's son? My first-born. Is that just?"

She nodded. "There is that, yes. Little Alexander – you must likewise provide for him, James."

"I cannot make all my bastards earls!" He grimaced ruefully. "What would my Privy Council say?"

She smiled. "Never fear – if we have a son, I shall not ask that he be made an earl, my heart."

"No, he shall be no earl," James agreed. "He shall be Duke of Rothesay, Lord of the Isles, and Prince of Scotland!"

Mutely she shook her head.

"Yes, I say! But . . . leave it, for the nonce. I had thought of the Church for Alexander. He is a child of studious mind, though spirited. I am poor, as a prince – but the Church is rich. Too rich. This I can do for him."

"At nine years . . .?" she wondered.

"He would have an office without duties. Lord knows there are a-plenty such, mainly filled with the bastards of bishops and lords! Why not mine? My brother finds his archbishopric of St. Andrews well to his liking, with more siller to jingle in his purse than have I! He spends more on his back in a month than I do in a year. Aye, I was over generous there, I think. I shall appoint Alexander Archdeacon of St. Andrews, and cut him a slice from that fat haunch!" He sighed. "But this does not solve the problem of Janet's son."

"You will not create him earl?"

He examined his knuckles. "I needs must be sure that he is *my* son also, before I do that."

Slowly she smiled. "Poor James! What a pass for a king to be in!"

He looked up to meet her glance. "Aye," he said, sighing. "I know it. There are times when I think less than well of your James Stewart."

"Perhaps you are thinking less well of *Janet* than you ought? She is a strange woman, wild – but I think she is honest, after her fashion. I think she would not claim the child as yours if it was not."

"She must — or have herself proved a strumpet, a deceiver. How may I be sure?"

"Only by seeing her, and the child. Since they may not come here, you must go to them. To Darnaway. When the snow clears. I know you, James — we shall have no peace, else!"

He nodded. "You are right, as always. Save that I shall not wait until the snow clears — or I might wait for long. If this fellow who brought her letter can get through the passes, I can do as much. I will go forthwith — or William Elphinstone or some other will discover good reason why I should not!"

"As you will. All must ever be forthwith, with you, I well know! But . . . take me to Drummond Castle, as you go. I shall miss you less sorely there — and I long to see my mother and sisters."

"So? You will miss me? Even yet?"

"Now more than ever. I count each hour that I am not with you as an hour lost. So I have the more sympathy for Janet Kennedy in far Darnaway."

"I' faith, I doubt if Janet would be so thoughtful for you!"

"Poor Janet . . .!" Margaret said.

As always when James approached the great gloomy pile of Darnaway Castle in its forest by the Findhorn, he knew a little compunction for having exiled the spirited Janet to such a place. He never required to be with her for long, however, before such feelings wore off, and he was deeming Darnaway apt enough hermitage for her. Their three years' association had not mellowed her one whit.

She greeted him on this occasion with hot reproaches for not having come sooner, allied to accusations that it was only to see the child that he had come, even now. He was still protesting as she dragged him to her bed, travel-worn as he was. It was only afterwards that he was shown the infant.

One glance was enough to reassure him as to its fathering. The ruddy head was no proof, since her hair was even redder than his own, but the large lustrous eyes, the long nose, and the wide mouth above deep chin, were all Stewart. Indeed the little creature was uncannily like himself, so that James, bending over the cradle, chuckled warmly.

"Ha!" he exclaimed. "Little doubt who sired this morsel!"

"Doubt!" she took him up swiftly. "God's Blood — you

doubted? You came here doubting? Holy Mother of Christ — I believe that is what brought you! You came to see if . . . if . . .!"

"No, no! A pox, Janet — not so! You go too fast . . ."

"Do not fence or palter! I know you. Faithless yourself, like all men, you would paint me in your own colours! Name me whore, harlot!"

"I do not! You are unfair. I said the reverse, did I not? No doubts, I said . . ."

"Not when you saw the brat! But do you deny that you came here doubting . . .?"

"I came here, Janet Kennedy, to make your son Earl of Moray. And to see you. Not to be bearded and browbeaten."

"You will do it?" Like sun breaking from behind cloud, she changed. "You will make him Earl? Now? Earl of Moray — my son! Our son." Her hand was on his arm now.

"Aye. I had thought to do it forthwith. It means much to you?"

"Yes. For myself, I care nothing. But for my son. My father covets an earldom, but does not gain one. Had I a son by Angus, even had I married him, he would not be an earl."

He nodded. "I understand. It shall be as you wish. I have brought the papers with me. This warrior shall be Earl of Moray within the hour!"

She threw her arms around him, and her lips sought his. Swiftly, crazily, the passion rose between them once again.

James had intended to stay at Darnaway only for two or three days. But he lingered a day more, and another day, and another. Never had the young woman been like this before, so eager, so kind, so deliberately enticing. She was still Flaming Janet, of course, tempestuous, unpredictable, prickly, but her storms were brief, her reconciliations not long delayed, her peace-offerings heady. Undoubtedly she sought to detain him — which in itself was a new experience. Perhaps even that self-sufficient termagent could be lonely.

Letters and despatches would no doubt have followed the King daily had it not been for the difficulties of the journey through the snows. It was a week and a day, in fact, before the first courier from the south came seeking James. It was Sir Rob Bruce himself, drawn, weary, unkempt, who eventually found his restless master working off surplus energy by cutting down a dead pine tree for fire logs.

The King's welcome was spontaneous, hearty and affectionate

—but Rob did not respond. Drooping, silent, he stood beside his foundered steaming horse, eyeing James from under downbent heavy brows.

"Well, man!" the King cried, tossing aside his axe. "Have you come this long road but to glower at me like a bullock! What's to do? Out with it."

Strangled-voiced, the other spoke. "It is . . . the Lady Margaret."

James grinned. "Aye— I stay here over long," he admitted. "But did she not say that she was sorry for poor Flaming Janet! Of her charity, she can surely . . ."

Harshly, almost savagely, Bruce interrupted. "She is dead!" he cried. "Dead!"

Like the tree that he had so lately felled, James swayed on his feet as though he had been axed. Wordless, frowning, but blank-eyed he stood, a man stricken.

"Dead, I say!" Rob repeated, almost accusingly. "Foully done to death!"

With a great choking cry, James launched himself bodily forward in a single bound, to grasp the other by the sagging shoulders, to shake him with maniacal fury. "Liar! Knave! Dastard!" he yelled. "Oh, God! Oh, God!"

It was long before Rob Bruce could tell his story, or at least cause any of it to penetrate the King's crazed distraction. Indeed, it was Janet Kennedy who, coming out in search, discovered James sitting on his felled tree, head in hands, trembling violently and with his sweat cold upon him, and masterfully hurried him indoors out of the snow, while she plied Rob with questions.

His tidings were bald enough, in all conscience. Five mornings after James had left her at Drummond Castle, Margaret had taken breakfast with her two sisters, Euphemia, Lady Fleming, and Sybilla, in normal fashion—but they had barely risen from the table before all three were taken violently ill. Within the hour all were dead, in mortal agony.

"Poisoned!" Janet gasped.

"What else?" Rob answered dully. "None other in the castle suffered aught. Only these three."

"But who . . .? Why? Mary-Mother—who would do this thing?"

"Need *you* look far!" the other all but snarled. "Who but your friends?"

353

Hotly she jumped up. "Curse you—what do you mean? *My* friends . . .?"

"Aye—the English party. Angus. Or Gray."

"Christ-God—they would not do this! Slay Margaret Drummond."

He shrugged. "Only they have reason. To hurt the King. And to further the English match."

She stared from him to the crouching, silent James, and for once Janet Kennedy was shocked.

That night, for the first time in Darnaway Castle, James slept alone. He was up before daybreak, curtly shouting for food and, despite a cold thin rain, for horses. Nothing would do but that he rode south forthwith. Almost like a man sleep-walking, but utterly determined nevertheless, he set off, with scarcely a farewell to Janet, nor waited to see if Rob and the two grooms followed.

He rode like no sleep-walker at any rate, driving his mount, his companions and himself unmercifully, with as complete a disregard for safety as for time and distance, as though he sought thus to escape from the Devil himself. But James Stewart, that grim day, carried his own hell with him. Through melting snows and growing floods, in driving rain, he led the way, often so far ahead as to be barely in sight.

Sometimes Rob managed to keep alongside, and on occasion sought to pierce the King's terrible, wordless hurt by shouted talk. At first he avoided the dire subject of Margaret's death, speaking of anything else—without response; until, recognising that if this in fact was wholly filling the King's mind, some relief might well result from opening the flood-gates with words. At his second attempt, as they waited impatiently to be ferried over the flooded River Spey at Boat of Insh, James suddenly cut him short.

"That man. Of my Guard. The man-at-arms. Who, with you witnessed our marriage. Where is he?" he jerked. "I have not seem him for long."

"I do not know. He left the Royal Guard. With the money you gave him, he turned inn-keeper, I was told . . ."

"His name? You must find him."

"You think, Sire . . .?"

For a while the King did not answer. Then a torrent of words proved that however shattered he had been by the horror of it,

354

however seemingly distracted, his mind was now at least working clearly, effectively. He reasoned thus. This foul deed had been carefully planned, whilst they were parted and whilst Margaret was outwith the security of a royal palace. Why now? If it had been but to strike a blow at himself, however, it could have been done many times in the past years more readily than at Drummond Castle, in her own home. She had been killed now, because of changed circumstances. Because she was pregnant. But she had been pregnant before, and no attempt made on her, as far as he knew. But the English match was now much nearer, Henry's firm policy. This, then, was Angus's doing—Henry's tool. Angus. He had poisoned her before another child could be born. Why? Because he had learned that they were wed, and a son would be heir to the throne. Margaret Drummond had to die, that the King might marry Margaret Tudor—but only if it was known that he was already wed. A mistress would not have had to die. To think, when he declared themselves man and wife, that night, he was signing her death-warrant . . .

Rob groaned and cursed, but could not deny that the King's reasoning was sound.

Other than themselves and Rob, only one man knew of that secret marriage—the guard. That guard must be found.

Rob swore that he would find him.

James would talk no more.

Despite the grievous conditions, there was no halt or let up on that headlong journey. They came to Drummond Castle in Strathearn just before midnight. James stumbled, soaked and bedraggled as he was, straight to the chapel, where the bodies of the three sisters lay, and locked himself therein, without word to any other than the gatehouse watchman in that bedded household. Rob took up his own lonely vigil outside.

Sometime before daybreak James emerged, drawn, grey and wild-eyed. Nothing would serve but that the entire establishment should be roused there and then, family and servants alike, for questioning, interrogation, despite the anguished Lord Drummond's assurance that all had been done already, and drastically. The servants were all old and trusted, and the only stranger about the castle at the time of the tragedy had been a wandering friar, who had come the day previously and disappeared during the tumult that followed the calamity. Drummond had men scouring Strathearn and all his sheriffdom for this man.

The King's fierce and half-crazed investigations produced nothing new. Helpless with emotional exhaustion, frustration and physical fatigue, he declared that he was going back to the chapel, to Margaret, but stumbling over a bench in the Great Hall, sank down over the table and slid there into twitching uneasy sleep before their eyes. Drummond had him carried to bed, where Rob, as weary as his master, slept on a couch near by.

All day they slept, to waken in the evening, eat voraciously, ask if the friar had yet been caught, and slept again.

Next day dawned on a different James Stewart. Quiet, stiffly calm, armoured in reserve, he was the King of Scots again, all emotions controlled, master of himself and of others. He gave orders that Margaret's body should be placed in a litter, for him to take to the Cathedral of Dunblane, which she had loved, for burial — and when her mother pleaded tearfully that her daughters be not separated in death, agreed that the two sisters should be taken likewise. Rob was sent on ahead to Dunblane, ten miles away, to have all prepared. At mid-day the sad little cavalcade followed him.

Margaret Drummond, so very nearly the Queen, with her sisters, was laid simply to rest under the chancel of the little Perthshire town's modestly lovely cathedral, while a choir of priests and singing boys sang soft, slow chants so affectingly that the King gave orders there and then such should be sung, in her memory and for the repose of her soul, every day in all time coming, at his expense — and that when he himself should die, this service should continue with his name added to hers.

For long after all others had left the church, James remained, alone. It was thus that Bishop Elphinstone found him, and dared to intrude on his grief; Rob Bruce indeed, outside, would have allowed no other to enter.

Eventually, with these two, the King rode on the few miles to Stirling, the empty husk of a man, but set-jawed.

PART FIVE
Chain of Destiny

21

THE busy workmen directed William Elphinstone to the grassy slope at the foot of Arthur's Seat, where amongst grazing sheep two seated figures could be seen, a little way apart. Sighing, the Bishop turned away from the scene of activity in the new palace forecourt, and made his way towards the rising ground, waving his servants back.

James, idly plucking and chewing grasses, with Rob Bruce sitting stiff and unhappy a few yards off, scarcely greeted his elderly friend. His glance returned, almost at once, not to the stirring scene below where the barely completed towers and roofs of the new palace of Holyroodhouse rose beside the ancient Abbey buildings, but to the distant prospect, eastwards, where the fair Lothian landscape stretched over a score of fertile miles to the shapely green cone of North Berwick Law and beyond, to the abrupt bluff rock of the Bass rising out of the azure plain of the sea. The Bishop, noting the direction of that preoccupied glance, sighed again.

"Sire," he said, "much awaits your royal attention. In yonder new house itself, and up at the Council chamber. These papers I have brought for your signature, before I affix the Privy Seal — these are the most urgent. But there are others that require your eye . . ."

"No doubt," James interrupted. "And since they are so urgent, my Lord Bishop, most certainly they relate to that young female, Margaret Tudor! Is it another castle or lordship that she must have? Or new appointments to her household? Or more hangings for her bower and bedchamber? Or perchance, another humble address of welcome for the King of Scots to sign, on her deigning to set foot in his unworthy kingdom!"

"Not so, Sire. These do not concern the Queen. Or, h'm, but one does . . ."

"Spare me that, at least!" the younger man snapped. "If you will have her queening it before ever I have set eyes on the wench, I will not! Must I be burdened thus before my time, 'fore God?"

Elphinstone blinked. "You have been married to Her Highness, by proxy," he pointed out. "The Pope has confirmed the marriage and peace treaties, and given his dispensation. You have accepted King Henry's terms . . ."

"What if I have, God pity me! Must all my realm hang on the crook of her little finger? Enough that I must needs put up with her when she comes. Spare me her now!"

Troubled, the Bishop shook his grey head. "Your Grace – this surely is unworthy of you. To so await your bride. She deserves better than this in her husband, does she not? Be she king's daughter or the lowliest in the land?"

"Deserves better, you say? How much better do you wish for this English brat?" the King demanded. "What more must she have? I build a new palace for her. She is to have a Court and household larger than my own. A dozen castles are to be hers, and the gift of broad lands, whole shires and burghs. Gold and jewels and plate await her, such as never have been assembled in Scotland before – gowns and furs, tapestries, hangings, furniture, horses, servants. A pox on her – the land has been drained dry for her! And you say that she deserves better!"

"She deserves some little fondness. Friendship, if not love . . ."

"I swear that she has too many fond friends, for my taste, already!" James asserted. "Never a woman with so many, unseen and untried as she is." He glanced eastwards again, his eyes narrowed, only partly against the July forenoon sun. "Angus, yonder, was ever her friend – did he not prove his fondness in blood! Gray likewise. And my uncle Buchan. Ramsay. Lyle. Tod. These and others like them, were ever Henry's friends, and so his daughter's. But you, my Lord Bishop – you and Bothwell and Home. Blackadder and Forman and Brown. All these, all Scotland indeed, now seem to be her fond friends. She scarce needs me, I think, in this loving host!"

It was true, in a manner of speaking. In the eighteen months which had elapsed since Margaret Drummond's death, almost every man of influence in the land had weighed in in support of the English match. Never had the country seen such a campaign of pressure on a monarch to adopt a line of action. A sort of contagion had gripped the nation's leadership – though not the people themselves – demanding this clear and unequivocal token of alliance with the Auld Enemy. And James, broken-hearted, sunk in despair and lethargy, had been carried unwillingly along on the tide of it, caught in toils that were none the less sore for being partly of his own making.

Elphinstone considered his friend sorrowfully. "This is a great matter, Sire, to touch the minds and hearts of many — such a bond as this, between your realm and England. Never has there been the like. The two warring realms linked in marriage and peace. After centuries of fighting and hatred. Can you marvel that men see it as a wonder, a portent, the start perchance of a new age wherein love and not the sword may rule? That it is Your Grace's self, who has taught men to love you, who is the Scots link in this fair chain, is seen by all as right and proper. Indeed, no other king, I think, would have served for this. So men rejoice — not only here but in England. And since England is a rich land, her princess must needs be decked in the trappings of riches. Henry demands it, yes — but our Scots pride demands it likewise. We must not seem a poor realm. Hence the pomp and ceremony, the castles and manors and gear. It is fitting in this marriage . . ."

"This is not a marriage, man! This is a device, a merchand-ising, cold-bloodedly contrived by old men for their own ends. Do you deny it? Henry hopes to buy a secure northern border by selling his daughter. You, and the Council, think to buy peace and prosperity by selling *me*! Angus, to buy vengeance — and no doubt an increased pension from London! A marriage, to be fitting, requires nothing of all this."

The other bowed his head. "Your Grace is harsh, bitter. I understand your hurt. But, of your charity, at least do not hurt this child who comes to you. For she is little more than a child — fourteen years only. And nothing to blame, if blame there is. This may not be the marriage of your heart, my son — but can it be hers? I pray you to have pity on her."

James had not changed so greatly that this sort of appeal did not touch him. He frowned. "I shall not eat the wench, never fear!" he growled. "I shall play my part, since it is too late to do other. But . . . a truce to this fulsome talk of rejoicing and felicity. And no more queening her until she is Queen indeed."

"As you will, Sire."

"Where is she now?"

"Two nights gone she was at Durham. Two days hence she will be at Berwick-on-Tweed. The Council anticipates that Your

Grace will ride to meet her there, as she enters your realm. They suggest . . ."

"Then the Council anticipates amiss! I am not so hot for sight of Henry's daughter that I must go panting to the Border! Others more keen than am I may greet her there, if so they wish —yourself, Bothwell, Home, Blackadder. Let the Tudor come to me, not me to her."

"She has come far, already. From London . . ."

"Then another fifty miles will not injure her."

"Some may esteem it churlish, Sire."

"Then let them! I stay here, I say! Enough of this, my Lord Bishop. What have you brought me to sign? Have you ink and pen?"

"Aye, Your Highness—here." It was seldom indeed that Elphinstone called the King Highness. "The appointment of young Sinclair to the Sheriffdom of Caithness—he reached Edinburgh last night. Your royal pardon for the Northumbrian robbers Riddell and Appleby, that there be no outstanding causes between Your Warden and the English when the . . . when she comes. And the warrant for the payment of the stonemasons for this Holyroodhouse. It is much overdue, and should be paid before, before . . ."

James did not even scan the parchments unrolled for him as he signed them with the quill dipped in the ink-horn which the other produced from his pouch. Quickly his glance strayed away down that lovely coast again.

"There are many matters in the palace yonder awaiting your attention, your decision," the Bishop went on. "The Flemish painters ask your choice of designs for the Banqueting Hall. There are many hangings to select—merchants wait with them. A gift of plenishings from His Grace of Denmark, your uncle, has come, and the Master of the Household would know where they should be disposed. The Earl of Tyrconnel has arrived from Ireland for the wedding. Do you wish him to be lodged in the new palace, or in the castle?"

"Put him where you will," James said. "Choose you how all should be, in this house—since it is your palace rather than mine, I swear!" That was less than fair, even though Elphinstone had been foremost in urging the building of this handsome new royal residence. After Margaret's death, James had not been able to abide Stirling, with it speaking to him all the time of what he had lost. He had moved to Linlithgow, his father's favourite palace, but found it inconvenient for the transaction of the business of the state, its town too small to house all the Court, the public servants, the ambassadors and the like. More and more the King had come to dwell in the great castle of Edinburgh, rearing above the grey walled city, where his new royal troops were garrisoned and where much of the functions of government took place. But Edinburgh Castle was a powerful and gloomy fortress, skied on a high rock, and no place, declared Elphinstone and Argyll, to bring as a bride an English princess used to the spacious comforts of the palaces of St. James's, Greenwich, Hatfield and Woodstock. So the new house was built, at the foot of Arthur's Seat a mile away on the other side of the town from the castle, beside the Abbey of the Holy Rude, where there were gardens and orchards and green grassy slopes. It was not finished yet, nor would be for long, but at least the drum towers and main north block were near enough complete to be occupied, and the Abbey buildings near by had long been used for royal accommodation. No house in all Scotland had ever been planned, furnished and decorated as was this one – despite the lack of interest of he who was to occupy it.

Even now James's mind was elsewhere. "Is the Master of Angus yet come from Douglasdale?" he asked.

"No, Sire. Not yet."

"Bring him to me, so soon as he arrives. I have hopes of that young man."

Elphinstone groaned inwardly. He looked eastwards likewise, knowing well what ever drew the King's gaze thitherwards. Always James was staring down that Lothian coast, from the lofty windows and battlements of Edinburgh Castle, from any and all of the heights on which the windy city was built. Tantallon lay there, twenty miles away, between North Berwick Law and the Bass, Angus's stronghold, the most powerful private fortress in the kingdom, practically impregnable, unseen but seldom out of the King's thoughts. Not even Mons Meg, of James's cherished artillery, could get within range of it, on its sea-girt promontory; and the swirling tides around it were so sown with the dragons' teeth of reefs and rocks that no ship-borne cannon could some closer than half a mile to it. James had once besieged Tantallon, after the Highland campaign, before he had made Angus the Chancellor, and had had to withdraw, baffled and mocked. Angus could lie secure therein.

The prelate withdrew his gaze from Tantallon's direction, to look the other way, to where Rob Bruce crouched on the grass beside a whin bush, a score of yards uphill of his master. Their eyes met. But though Rob and Elphinstone were well agreed on most matters, in this of Angus they were not. The younger man was at one with the King here, at least. He had done everything in his power to find and expose the murderers of the Drummond sisters, without avail. He had traced the inn at which the former guard, Pate Lindsay, had settled — at Dunbar, significantly, no great distance from Tantallon — but one week before the crime the man had left suddenly and had never come back. The friar, too, who had so briefly visited Drummond Castle, had never been found, despite prolonged searching. Neither James nor Rob had any doubts that Angus and Henry Tudor were behind the killing, but they could prove nothing, strive as they would. Angus seldom left Tantallon, and nowadays never ventured forth without an enormous retinue of fierce Douglas soldiery to guard him. Nevertheless, the King still hoped and sought to establish his case against him, to bring him to justice somehow — and in this Rob entirely supported him. The Master of Angus, Bell-the-Cat's eldest legitimate son and heir, was the best of James's hopes in the matter, now. He was at odds with his father, who kept him short of money and treated him slightingly, a somewhat petulant young man who had married the Lady Elizabeth Drummond, Margaret's eldest sister — a match no doubt largely the cause of the Earl's displeasure. As the old man confined himself so closely to Tantallon Castle, more and more of the management of the vast Douglas estates inevitably fell to his heir, and in consequence more and more of the Douglas manpower was tending to look towards the Master for leadership. James was working on him, as was his wife, to bring him to the stage of being willing to discover and reveal some at least of his father's secrets.

Elphinstone, though fully sympathetic over James's loss and sorrow, did not support the quest for vengeance. If the murderers could have been uncovered and punished quickly after the event, he would not have objected — though he doubted even then the practicality of such a course. But, as a statesman as well as a priest, he deplored this prolonged preoccupation of the King's. No good now would come from the discovery, trial and sentence of those behind this political crime — even if it were possible to enforce. It would re-arouse intense national feeling and strife.

It was most unsuitable in the context of the forthcoming royal wedding, the success of which was so important for Scotland. And if it was indeed proved to be Angus's work, which seemed at least likely, the most powerful noble in the kingdom, linked to so many of the great houses of the land, could not be arraigned for murder without what would amount to full-scale civil war. Moreover, if Henry's hand should be disclosed behind it all — as James believed to be true, and would undoubtedly declare — there would be an end to good relations with England, and a fatal blow to the marriage. All this the Bishop had told the King many times. But in James's present mood of most unnaturally sullen brooding, his representations fell on deaf ears.

"Should the Master of Angus be arrived when I return to the castle, shall I tell him that he will find Your Grace dealing with matters in the new palace?" the older man asked, wearily persistent.

James actually smiled — and his smiles were scarce these days. "You do not give in readily, do you?" he charged. "I fear that I am a great trial to you, my old friend." With a touch of his old impulsiveness, he laid a hand on the cleric's threadbare sleeve. "I am sorry for that, for I know that you love me well. Aye — I will be in your palace." He rose. "Indeed, I will come down with you now, my Lord Bishop."

With a sigh of relief, Rob Bruce got to his feet, to follow them down.

The King rode slowly through the narrow cobbled streets of Edinburgh, nodding and bowing frequently when citizens recognised him and touched bonnets, gaped, or grinned according to disposition. He did not once smile, however, nor were his acknowledgements more than perfunctory. Nevertheless, he could not help eyeing with some interest the progress of the many triumphal arches, portals and ornamental erections with which the streets and wynds were being decorated, despite the waste of money and effort it all represented to him. Behind him, as was so usual now, rode only Sir Rob Bruce and MacGregor of Glenarklet.

James had a strange air of contrast about him. He was very fine in appearance, but sat his magnificent horse with nothing of an air of occasion. He wore scarlet and cloth-of-gold trimmed with fur, and a great sweeping ostrich-feather in his bejewelled bonnet, along with clumsy, heavy riding-boots, and with his hair merely tossed back and his beard untrimmed. His two attendants were dressed at their splendid best, Rob in gold inlaid half-armour and velvet, Glenarklet in vivid tartans and stone-encrusted silverwork; but there was no retinue, no heralds, guards or banners. Folk eyed them and wondered.

When the town walls were left behind them, and they faced the open country that rose in slow green waves to the castle-crowned ridge of Craigmillar, James did not spur into his accustomed headlong gallop. He did not even canter, merely trotting his spirited mount. His two followers exchanged glances.

Thus without urgency or enthusiasm they rode over the cattle-dotted hogsbacks of Craigmillar and Gilmerton into the wide valley of the Esk. Long before they reached the castle of Dalkeith, set above the river six miles from the city, they could see that the entire area was seething like a fair. Tents and pavilions, horses and gear, dotted the parkland like an armed camp, banners fluttered, men-at-arms lounged and servants hurried and scurried. Through all this press and activity the royal horseman and his companions made their way, almost entirely unrecognised now. Many of the devices on those flags and pennons were strange to them. Indeed, at the castle gateway itself they were curtly halted, not by its lord's, the Earl of Morton's, porters but by authoritative, heavily-armed, English-voiced guards in the Howard colours of red and white, and their business demanded.

"My business, friends, is with the master of this house," James told them, mildly enough.

"None enters here save with the permission of my lord Earl of Surrey!" he was told. "Your business, sir . . .?"

"Fools!" Rob Bruce cried, blazing-eyed. "Watch your ill tongues! You speak to the King of Scots!" Spurring forward he cleared a way through the astonished guards, hand on sword-hilt.

The same sort of exchange was repeated more than once thereafter before they reached the Great Hall, crowded with a gayly-dressed and chattering throng. Here James's identity was quickly perceived, and the word went round the crowd in a matter of moments that the King was here. Everywhere men hastily bowed – though not a few were uncertain in which direction to do so. Morton himself came hurrying forward, backed by Bothwell, Home, Archbishop Blackadder, Bishop Forman of Moray, and others, exclaiming at this extraordinary and unannounced entry,

James waved them silent, and asked the Princess Margaret's whereabouts.

The press parting for him hastily, he was conducted across the Hall and up a private stairway in the thickness of the castle wall. In the first room on the floor above two men sat at cards, both of middle age, both richly dressed, one a cleric. Both frowned at the intrusion of their privacy, and neither rose at the newcomers entered — until Morton barked out that here was His Grace of Scotland.

Even so, although the portly Archbishop of York was quickly on his feet, Thomas Howard, Earl of Surrey and Lord Treasurer of England, was comparatively slow in standing, and his bow less than profound. The shrewd, keen eyes that scanned the King's face were hard, unsmiling, and meeting them James knew that here indeed was a man to be reckoned with. He had heard much of this veteran warrior, England's greatest soldier, and renowned as a crooked awkward carle, as Henry's right hand was apt to be. Despite the circumstances of this their first meeting, their glances crossed like swords. James sensed no approval there. Presumably, then, Surrey did not esteem this match.

"My lords, I bid you welcome to my realm," he said stiffly. "I trust that you have had a fair journey. And that the Princess has not been overmuch wearied?" As stiffly he extended his hand for them to kiss.

The Archbishop murmured smooth greetings, homage and assurances, but Surrey merely cleared his throat, and rasped, "Y' Grace."

James eyed him thoughtfully. "You left your royal master well?"

"Well, Sire." Surrey was apparently a man of few words.

A little hurriedly Thomas Savage, the Archbishop, spoke. "This is scarce how we looked to have greeted Your Highness. Had you been suitably announced . . ."

"We were better prepared to receive you at the Border!" Surrey declared bluntly.

"Indeed? King Henry did not accompany his daughter far from London, I believe?"

"H'mmm." Still more hastily Archbishop Savage intervened. "I sent my coadjutor, the Lord Bishop of Durham, who has already had the honour of meeting Your Grace — I sent him towards Edinburgh. An hour ago, and more. To convey our reverences, Sire. With gifts and salutations from our liege lord. He is not here? You have not seen him . . .?"

"I fear that we have missed Master Fox—whom I well remember. When last I saw him, he was not bearing gifts!"

"No, er, that is so, Highness. But that, God be praised, is all blessedly past! Happy this day when felicity and love reign in the place of harsh memories. When all past hurts and pains are forgotten, and the two realms enter together into peace and concord for all time."

James looked at Surrey, and their glances held again, for a moment. "Aye," he said dryly. "No doubt. Now—I would pay my respects to the Princess."

"Ah, yes. Her Highness will be overjoyed, I swear. So long awaited this thrice happy hour! The longing of her heart at last to be . . ."

With something suspiciously like a snort the Earl of Surrey swung about, strode to an inner door, threw it open without ceremony, and called out, "His Grace of Scotland!"

There was a second or two of silence, succeeded by a babblement of female voices as though from a cageful of startled birds. James pushed past Surrey and strode into the inner room.

It was not a large chamber, and it appeared to be packed to bursting point with agitated women, all seeming to be anxious to move to somewhere other than they were, starting up from a table spread with more cards, tripping over lute, clavichord and tambour-frame, seeking to get one behind another, touching hair and costume, clapping hands over exclaiming lips.

James stared around at that scene of colourful confusion and panic, and his features broke into a smile, a grin, a hearty laugh. If that laughter was heard with mixed feelings, to some of the men behind the King at least it was a major relief—the first real laughter that they had heard from the monarch for months.

Gazing round so many flushed feminine faces and knowing not one from another, James swept off his feathered bonnet in a gallant gesture and made a comprehensive bow to include them all. "Sweet Ninian!" he cried. "Here's a bonny sight! Ladies—I greet you all!"

Amidst the gasps and giggles and the bobbing of curtsies, he scanned the company. There were more than a dozen females in that small chamber, one plump and elderly, one handsome and of middle years, and the rest all very young, and with one exception as James's quick eye noted, not markedly fair. Which was the Princess he had no means of guessing—although his glance lingered on the one lovely girl involuntarily, hopefully.

The handsome woman straightened up and perceiving the direction of the King's gaze, coughed and gestured towards the far side of the table, where a group of four girls stood bunched together. She sketched another curtsy.

James was grateful—though disappointed about the one bold-eyed beauty. But which of these four was Margaret Tudor? They were little more than children, all of them. Two were giggling foolishly, one plucking at her lips nervously and glancing at the fourth, who looked at him stolidly, unsmiling, from under heavy brows. His heart sinking a little, he inclined his head to the last.

When the older woman coughed again, this square-built, rather sullen-looking girl moistened her lips. "Greetings, Sire," she said levelly, tonelessly, as though repeating a lesson. "I have come to you over these long miles, that the Rose and the Thistle may be grafted into a flower both fair and strong."

"Ah . . . ummm." The King blinked, stroking his red beard. "Just so. No doubt. Very, h'm, apt. Indeed yes—both fair and strong! I . . . I congratulate Your Highness on your eloquence." And he jerked a brief laugh.

Some hint of bitterness in that laugh seemed to reach the girl. She was a round-featured, plain, dark-haired creature, somewhat pasty of face and prominent of chin, solidly made and well-formed for her age—but with no spark of grace to her. Though she appeared markedly insensitive, perhaps her looks belied her, for her lip quivered now at the King's laugh, and she looked down at her plump tightly-clasped hands.

James saw that quiver, and knew a swift spasm of compassion for this awkward, strained child before him. He came forward, squeezing past the others and round the table, to reach out for the Princess's fingers and raise them to his lips.

"You have come far indeed, and are welcome to this your new realm," he said, and stooped to kiss her pale cheek.

She flushed a little at that, but did not speak.

"You are weary, after your much travel?" he enquired.

She shook her head. "No, Sire, I thank you."

"M'mmm." At something of a loss, James glanced round at all the watching faces. "Your Highness has good company, at least. So much, h'm, youth and beauty!"

Much youth was there, at least, with fully half a score of young women, of her own age or a little older – and no doubt of the best families in all England. But beauty was another matter; a more uniformly homely assembly would have been hard to find, chosen undoubtedly so as not to outshine the Princess. James, a connoisseur of women, made a swift survey of them all until he came with relief to the only exception, the spirited, flaxen-haired comely piece with the roving eye and the provocative eyebrows; how she came to be included in this company it intrigued him to know.

All watched the King and Princess, and James who seldom lacked for words, especially where women were concerned, could think of nothing else to say to this silent girl. A rather evident pause developed.

The Archbishop of York came to his rescue, insinuating himself into the crowded room. "Your Graces – here is true joy and excellence," he gushed. "A sight to cause exultation in Heaven as on earth! Youth, devotion, and the very bond of peace!"

It is to be feared that the King was insufficiently appreciative. He frowned slightly. "Present to me these ladies, my Lord Archbishop," he requested.

The Princess recollected her duty, "*I* do that," she declared, with a strange mixture of diffidence and authority. She led him around the table, making for the handsome woman, whom she introduced as the Countess of Surrey. The attractive young creature with the fair hair moved closer at this, and she was thereupon named as the former's daughter, the Lady Mary Howard. So that mystery was resolved. The elderly woman was named as the Lady Scrope, presumably an outgrown governess, and all the plain-faced girls identified as the daughters of noble houses.

Another pause ensued – with James probably more aware of it than were the others, since for him such discomforts were practically unknown. He sought to enter into conversation with the Princess, but her answers to his remarks were monosyllabic, and since no one else in the room spoke in the royal presence, the non-success of the attempt was all too evident.

He turned to Lady Surrey and her daughter – and the difference was at once so apparent as to be almost equally embarrassing. He was smiling and chatting with the mother and daughter – especially the latter – with the easy interplay of glance, hint and suggestion, when he noticed Margaret Tudor watching them from under down-bent brows with a look that was not very far from a scowl. Sighing, he disengaged himself from the sour Surrey's attractive womenfolk and moved back to the Princess's side. And after another jerky exchange the silence returned.

James had seldom felt himself so foolish. Why he could think of nothing to say to this awkward, suspicious child, he did not know. It was clear that behind her somewhat bovine exterior she was far from stolid or acquiescent. The knowledge that this was to be his wife, was like a dull knell sounding at the back of his mind.

In a less than regal movement, as he turned to speak to the plump Lady Scrope behind him, in desperation, he all but stumbled over a lute which had been hastily set down on the floor at his appearance. As the lady, twittering in alarm, sought to bend her bulky person to remove the offending object, the King himself stooped swiftly and picked it up. Protesting anxiously, she tried to relieve him of the instrument, blaming herself that His Grace should be so incommoded, while he assured her otherwise. In the quite absurd struggle for the thing, his fingers drew a few jangling notes from the strings – and without the least intention of so doing, James, who was an excellent lutist, found himself countering the unfortunate noise by plucking true chords on the instrument. With a sudden shrug and half-laugh, he swung back to the Princess, bowed low, and on a pure liquid note thrice repeated, launched into a little rueful ballad about a lovelorn swain and his unresponsive mistress. He had a fine tenor voice – and though he felt a little ridiculous, it was less embarrassing than the heavy silence.

Clearly everyone else found the occasion improved also, the covey of girls cooing in delight at the handsome King's romantic and expert handling of theme and lute. Margaret Tudor showed no such delight, but at least she seemed relieved. Wide-eyed and lips parted, Mary Howard swayed her supple person to the melody and rhythm, her glance never leaving the King's face – although her father glowered disapprovingly from the open doorway.

The applause which greeted the end of the song encouraged James to offer another, and when he raised his eyebrows towards the Princess, she nodded – the first real communication between them. So, perching himself upon a corner of the table and signing to them all to sit down and be at ease, he gave them a selection of songs, some gay, some sad, some slightly scurrilous. By the time that Morton came back to announce that a repast awaited His Grace, Her Highness, and all the company, in the Hall downstairs, James had quite captivated his future Queen's ladies, whatever the effect on Margaret Tudor herself.

The meal went well enough, although the girl still had little to say; but she ate heartily, the King noted, though she drank but little. James had his host, at the other side, to talk to. In response to the toasts inevitable to the auspicious occasion, to the royal couple's felicity and the like, he spoke briefly, formally, with such grace as he could muster, the girl remaining expressionless.

After the repast, as was usual, the Hall floor was cleared for dancing — although this was an occasion when James would have been glad to have been spared his favoured pastime. When he rose, a little reluctantly, to the first measure, however, to seek the Princess's hand, she shook her head determinedly, and turned in some agitation to the Countess of Surrey, ever near by. She, after a whispered consultation, explained that Her Grace had not hitherto danced with men, and asked the King to excuse her until a more private occasion. Surprised, but by no means crestfallen, by this, James danced two measures with the Countess herself — and then felt free to seek out her daughter.

He found the Lady Mary fully as co-operative as he had anticipated, in his arms making a rousing partner indeed. It was during their second dance together that he received a further surprise, on discovering that the Princess was on the floor now, also, dancing with Lady Surrey — an unheard-of proceeding. Moreover, she was eyeing his own activities with undisguised disapproval; he was certainly holding the Lady Mary a deal more closely than Margaret did the Countess.

After the King had taken his partner for much needed refreshment in an ante-room, they came back to discover a distinct decrease in the number of women present in the Hall. It appeared that the Princess and her ladies had retired upstairs. James, Mary Howard in tow, followed them.

It was quite ridiculous that this fourteen-year-old Tudor should already be causing James Stewart, King of Scots, to feel at fault, almost penitent. He sought to please her now by complimenting her on her dancing — for despite her build she had seemed light on her feet — by declaring that he would teach her many new Scots dances, and seeking to describe these to her. She listened politely enough, answered his questions, but he could not feel that he was making any real impression on her. That he should be disappointed in this was in itself crazy, for he assured himself that he had no wish to impress her anyway.

At length, quite suddenly he had had enough. Getting to his feet, he announced that he was going. This seemed to startle the company; evidently it had been assumed that he would remain now with the Princess. He explained that urgent matters called him back to Edinburgh, that it was not suitable that Her Highness should come there quite yet, as the new palace was barely ready for her worthy reception — which was true enough — and that the city's preparations required a day or two more for completion. She and her train should stay at Dalkeith meantime, and he would return to see her on the morrow.

The girl at least did not seek to detain him, though she seemed a little bewildered. He kissed her, and declared himself well pleased at so fair a first meeting, striving to sound as though he meant it. Glancing up from her, with the feeling that all who heard must recognise the falsity of this, he saw Mary Howard watching him, with a particularly inviting expression, far from the critical one he somehow felt all must have. On an impulse he went round all the tribe of young women, kissing them, to a succession of muted squeals, gasps and gurgles. He kissed them all upon the cheek, however, until he came to Surrey's daughter. She turned and offered him her parted lips at the same instant that he sought them. It was only a brief contact, but those lips certainly stirred under his own. How much anyone saw of this he did not know, nor greatly cared. Clapping on his bonnet which, as an unusual compliment to his bride-to-be he had kept doffed throughout, he hurried out, down the stairs and across the Hall, taking courtiers and dancers by surprise. To Bothwell and Morton, hastening after him, he declared that this was as much as he could stand, for one day — let them tell Surrey and the Archbishop what they would.

In the castle courtyard he vaulted on to his waiting horse without touching stirrup, tossed a silver piece to the astonished English groom who held it, and digging in his spurs clattered out beneath the gatehouse arch. He was back to headlong riding again.

Rob Bruce and Glenarklet had to flog their beasts unmercifully to catch up with the King before the walls of Edinburgh came in sight. For a while thereafter they pounded along just a little behind, unspeaking. It was when they had to draw up to enter, at Peffermill, the long narrow causeway across the marshes at the head of Duddingston Loch, south of Arthur's Seat, that James acknowledged their presence, turning almost fiercely upon them.

"Was ever a man so accursed?" he demanded. "You saw her. Henry's daughter indeed! Proud, yet without looks or grace. Dumb as an ox—and not unlike one, 'fore God! Yet ready to carp and chide—at her age! At me, James! Sweet Ninian—it is too much!"

Neither of his companions answered him.

"I did what I might," the King went on, as though they were accusing him. "I sought to help her, to put her at ease, to draw her—and fiend knows I did not want to! But she would have none of it. To this I am to be married! This to be my wife! My *wife!*"

At the bitter hurt in that cry, Rob Bruce shook his head. "It may not be so ill, Sire. She is very young. Wearied, it may be, with her long journey. All strange to her. She is too young for marriage—a mere child. She fears it, and you, belike . . ."

"Have I not thought of that, man? I am not a fool! But it is more than that. There is a sullenness to her. A hardness. I abominate hard women! And this I must needs take to my bed —for all my days! Dear God! After . . . after . . .!" He swallowed. "For this, Margaret had to die!"

Abruptly, wildly, he was lashing and lashing at his horse again.

ONLY a little way to the west, four days later, James rode in very different style, at the head of the long and splendid cavalcade, approaching the city by the less direct route to avoid the causeways of the Duddingston marshes. Most of the nobility of Scotland rode in his mile-long train, with a dozen bishops and a score of abbots, not to mention the large English contingent. Margaret Tudor rode in a litter at his side, and all the way from Newbattle he had been having to rein in his mettlesome stallion to keep company with her sedate pacing palfreys. Directly behind rode Surrey and the three Scots ambassadors who had arranged the match, Bothwell, Archbishop Blackadder and Bishop Forman, followed by the Archbishop of York and the Princess's principal ladies. The great banners of Scotland and England flapped above them in the warm August forenoon air, and hundreds of lesser ensigns and pensions supported them as far as eye could see.

The Princess was dressed now gorgeously in cloth-of-gold and black velvet – and looked but the younger and no more regal for it. James jerked a word or two to her every so often, but had long since given up any attempt to maintain a conversation. This was their fifth meeting, for the King had ridden out to see her each day, forcing himself to his duty, first to Dalkeith Castle and then to the Abbey of Newbattle near by when an unfortunate fire had damaged the former establishment. He had made but little headway with the girl, however, force himself to try as he would. She remained stiff, awkward, unsmiling, seemingly wary, an unlikely bride indeed. Only the one link had James managed to establish – that she, like himself, was fond of hunting, improbable as this might seem. On this insubstantial foundation he had sought to build.

He had been gazing ahead of him for some time, and now he saw what he looked for – a group of mounted men led by his chief huntsman emerging from some woodland on the left near the mill of Nether Liberton. As they drew near the royal couple, the huntsman blew a high tantara on his horn, and the group of men opened out to reveal in their midst a handsome stag, hobbled with ropes.

The King gestured towards it. "Caught in my wilderness of Duddingston yonder but this morning," he told the girl. "Let loose, it will bolt back thither, for a wager. A mile. Come – will you course it with me, Margaret? It should give us a fair run."

Margaret Tudor stared at him. "Now? Me?" she gasped. "Course a deer . . .?"

"Why, yes. You say that you enjoy the hunt. My man here has a fine horse for you . . ."

"I could not course thus. Dressed so." She looked down at all her finery.

"Care nothing for that," he urged. "You can sit a horse as well in that as in aught else."

"No!" she cried. "No!"

"Ride with me, then. In front of me. This good bay of mine will carry us both. We may not catch the stag, but at least we shall see the chase."

She shook her dark head determinedly. "I thank you – no," she insisted.

James sighed. Almost he declared that he would run the course himself, thankful to get away from this weary pacing and her dull company for a little; but he reluctantly forebore, and shouted to the huntsman to course the brute himself, calling behind him to as many as could hear that all who cared to join the chase should do so.

The stag was then released and bounded off, and to a winding of horns and a great hallooing, not a few young bloods galloped off after the huntsman in hot pursuit. After watching for a little, as the riders and quarry grew small in the distance, the King gave the sign to ride on.

Half a mile from the city gates, another company awaited them. Here, on the greensward, an anonymous vizored knight in full armour, with a beauteous young woman beside him, rode forward towards James. When they were still fifty yards off, another knight, whom all recognised as Sir Patrick Hamilton, a famous jouster and friend of the King's, spurred furiously out from behind canvas screens, and bore down upon the pair, to seize the damsel's bridle and seek to ride off with her. The vizored knight emitted a hollow roar, drew his sword, and hurled himself upon the interloper. Thereafter followed a spirited tourney of expert sword-play and horsemanship, with the supposedly alarmed and bewildered young woman continually getting her horse between those of the two protagonists and only escaping the darting, jabbing swords by inches, to the excited amusement of all who could see. Presently, laughing, James pressed in himself, shouting for peace, shook hands with each of the panting contestants, kissed the lady, and waved on the cavalcade. Whether the Princess had enjoyed the spectacle there was no means of knowing.

At the gates themselves, they were met by a vast crowd of the citizenry and also two processions of ecclesiastics, Franciscan and Dominican friars, bearing the relics of sundry saints, which they presented to the royal pair to kiss. Having dismounted to do this, James asserted that since it was unsuitable that Her Highness should pass through the crowded streets in a litter in which few could see her, he had here a notable horse which she should ride. Once again the girl protested that she could not sit any tall horse dressed as she was, and seemed so obviously distressed when he insisted, that he shrugged and declared that he would take her up beside him on his own beast. He mounted to do this, but so upset was the Princess, by the high-spirited stallion's curvettings and prancings, that she set her strong jaw, stamped her foot, and announced with an unexpected oath that she would by no means mount this brute either.

So suddenly had this scene blown up that James was quite taken aback, astonished at her attitude, but more astonished by that dourly jutting jawline and the brief glimpse of haughty temper. He stared, and hundreds of pairs of eyes watched interestedly. James had a jaw of his own, however, and having said that she should not travel further in her litter, he made sure that she did not do so. Jumping down from his tall beast he strode over to one of the three milk-white palfreys he had sent to her as a present, vaulted on to its back, and pulling the startled animal round abruptly, spurred up to Margaret. He bent, threw an arm round her thick waist, and swept her up, gasping, into the air. Swinging round in the saddle, he deposited her, somewhat roughly, sideways on the beast's broad rump behind him, curtly ordering her to hold on to him. Without pause, he rode on through the gateway.

Behind him Surrey frowned, Archbishop Savage gobbled, and Bothwell slapped his thigh and hooted.

Just within the walls was a second barrier, artificial this time, of painted wood and canvas, depicting a turreted gatehouse. From a window of this, above the archway, leant a highly realistic angel, who all but fell out in his efforts to hold the city keys low enough for Margaret to take – which she did at the King's jerked command. From the turrets other angels sang joyous verses about the fairest of fair princesses come to Scotland to be Queen.

The Procession then wound slowly through the narrow streets, made narrower by the waiting crowds, the frequent triumphal arches and stands of flowers and greenery. Every window was filled with watching, waving folk, almost every house decorated, and all was smiles and laughter while the bells of every church in Edinburgh, jangled welcome. James put the best face on it that he could, recognising that this was such a welcome as had never before been seen in that ancient grey city, and since the sulky child behind him was a complete stranger to them all, its tribute must needs be for himself. He sought desperately to banish his dark resentment and presentiments, and laughed and waved and bowed, frequently even turning in the saddle to point out to the unsmiling girl this or that feature or landmark. As they moved on even Margaret Tudor appeared to become a little moved by the excitement of it all, her heavy features lighting up slightly.

Up the curve of the West Bow the cavalcade climbed, to the High Street, where at the new-painted Mercat Cross a wooden stage had been set up. Here, after a welcome by the civic dignitaries, grouped around a fountain which actually spouted red wine, three displays were mounted for the edification of the distinguished company – the Judgement of Paris, with the actors as nearly naked as might be; the Blessed Annunciation; and the Marriage of the Virgin – in rather peculiar juxtaposition, but all equally appreciated, according to the enthusiastic applause. James preferred not to enquire into the significance of the chosen episodes.

At the great church of St. Giles, close by, Gavin Douglas, the Provost thereof and one of the realm's foremost poets, presented another incongruity, in the shape of an ode to the Princess, florid and flattering, and in the other hand the arm of a saint for the lady to kiss. James spared her this last, at least, by doing it for her, and rode on down towards the Canongate.

Edinburgh was not yet finished improving the occasion. At the Netherbow Port, where the city proper ended and the ecclesiastical burgh of the Canongate of Holyrood began, four thrones had been erected, whereon sat the Four Virtues, Justice, Force, Temperance and Prudence, triumphing most realistically over Nero, Holofernes, Epicurus and Sardanapalus, which sinners writhed convincingly at their feet. English education being apparently rather less thorough than Scots, James attempted to explain something of this to his pillion-rider – but at the girl's unconcealed yawn he desisted, and thanking the protagonists, proceeded on down to the Abbey of Holyrood.

Here a most gorgeous company awaited them – James's brother the Archbishop of St. Andrews, and all the other bishops, abbots, priors and prelates of Scotland who were not already in the cavalcade, vested in their most magnificent, a vast and colourful array, sparkling with encrusted jewellery, gold and silver. Distinctly ruefully James eyed it all, as he listened to his brother's brief address. Here was three-quarters of the wealth of Scotland paraded – Holy Church most eloquently proving that it could far outdo any display put on by the King himself, the Council, the nobility, or the civic authorities.

A banquet followed, the sumptuousness and size of which had never been seen in Scotland before, with tables set, within and without, for no fewer than two thousand five hundred guests – the thousand of the nobility and gentry who had convoyed the Princess from Newbattle, her five hundred English escorts, a few representative citizens, and the solid phalanx of the prelacy. As the young Duke-Archbishop host showed the King and Princess to their seats at the head of the dais-table in the huge Abbey refectory hall, he perhaps might be absolved for smirking somewhat – for undoubtedly his puissant brother could not have afforded to mount a feast of anything like this splendour.

The vast company in the main hall had just sat down, James being on his brother's right, Margaret Tudor on his left, and Surrey seated next the King on the other side, when there was a fanfare of trumpets and a growing commotion outside. Then the doors were thrown open and in marched a great and brilliant company of fully a hundred richly clad gentlemen, led by a single tall and stooping figure that stalked grimly onwards looking neither right nor left. James caught his breath.

His brother was on his feet, smiling thinly, and all over the already crowded hall men and women rose in consequence. At the King's side, Surrey was preparing to stand, when he glanced at James, perceived his black frowning, and sat back.

"Ha — the old fox has left his hole!" he jerked — eloquence for Surrey.

"Welcome, my Lord of Angus!" the Duke-Archbishop cried. "Accept the hospitality of this house."

Crouching forward over the table, the King clenched his fists as the Douglas came stalking forward. All eyes switched between one and the other, the set-faced seated young man and the arrogantly striding older one. It was their first meeting for fully two years. With what seemed an almost physical effort James withdrew his glance, to look up at his host. That thin-faced, dark-eyed young man's always hectic colour was higher than ever. His smile now had broadened to almost a wolfish grin. Undoubtedly it was his moment of triumph, where he paid his brother back for hypothetical neglect and many an imagined slight.

James, of course, was as good as caged. To confront and accuse Angus here and now, on such an occasion, was unthinkable, before the Princess and all the other guests. Moreover, the Douglas had come well supported, as always — he had brought what was as good as his own court with him indeed, and no doubt outside would be the usual host of his men-at-arms; to be sure he had not come here to be taken into custody, and would show fight. A struggle now was out of the question — and it would mean civil war, should the Douglas be attacked and not held. This, on the day before the wedding, with guests there from all over Christendom! Scotland's fair name would never survive it.

All this, and more, flashed through the King's mind as he watched his arch-enemy approach, and gritted his teeth.

Angus came up on to the dais, leaving his train of laughing Douglas lairds behind. He bowed perfunctorily, as always, to the King, deeply to Princess Margaret, nodded familiarly to Surrey, and clapped the Duke on the shoulder like some grim uncle.

"Welcome under my roof, Cousin," the latter declared, loud-voiced, almost defiantly. "Here's a joyful circumstance, is it not? Long sought, i' faith!"

Well James recognised the significance of these remarks. By all the laws of hospitality Angus was safe now from physical or open verbal attack, since the Duke, as host, was claiming this as his own roof.

"My Lord of Angus," James said, striving to keep his voice steady. "I do not believe that you and Her Highness have for-

379

gathered — although, as all know, you love her father, King Henry, passing well!"

Men caught their breaths at the scarcely veiled accusation in that.

"That has not been my pleasure until this happy day, Sire," the other gave back, and looked the King straight in the eye. "A day I have striven for, in my humble way!" He moved over, to take the Princess's hand, but when he stooped it was to kiss her cheek not her fingers.

"Your reward, my lord, will no doubt well repay your long strivings. Now, and hereafter!"

"I seek no other reward than the felicity of this moment, Sire."

"Other reward, I vow, you shall have, sir!"

"You are too kind!" Angus croaked a short harsh laugh, and turned to the Princess again. "Child, accept an old man's benison. And this small gift." From the folds of his old black cloak with its moth-eaten fur trimming, he drew a parchment roll which he placed on the table beside her. "The castle and lands of Kilspindie," he mentioned.

The King sat very still, expressionless. Kilspindie! A princely gift — but the very place that Flaming Janet had so dramatically sought and which Angus had eventually so reluctantly promised her. Now, tossed to Margaret Tudor — but not so much as a wedding-present as a challenge and insult to the King, linking these two women thus scornfully. James would have liked to throw that parchment back in the other's face — but could by no means do so, in the circumstances.

The girl thanked Angus uncertainly, briefly, staring in something like alarm at his strangely threadbare and menacing appearance.

The Duke was making room for the Earl to sit at the other side of the Princess, between her and the Archbishop of York, when James started up from his seat — and perforce all the great company must rise with him.

"Here, my lord," he commanded, indicating a space on the other side, between Surrey and Archbishop Blackadder. "Sit here, next your old colleague and brother-in-arms, the Earl of Surrey! You have a deal in common, have you not? Many a close matter to discuss, in King Henry's cause! Here, I say."

Scowling, since he could not openly disobey such royal command, Angus had to come and sit by Surrey, Henry Tudor's open right hand, as he, in Scots affairs, had been his hidden left. The proud Howard, a despiser of plotters, spies and pensioners, greeted him but curtly and stared straight ahead of him. Black-adder, no friend of the Douglas, turned shoulder to him to chat with animation to the Lady Surrey. The King sat down, and all after him, room being somehow made at the lower tables for all the Douglas entourage. The banquet proceeded.

As far as the dais table was concerned, it was a less successful meal than the splendid and unstinted provision should have ensured. James sat almost completely silent, the Princess was never talkative, Surrey was a man of few words, and neither Angus nor the Duke had on this occasion much to say. A certain blight inevitably descended to affect the lower tables, despite the efforts of many diplomatic and hearty clerics and the effect of unlimited wine and cheer.

James grimly contemplated this travesty of a festive occasion. The representatives of a dozen countries were here in his honour, to celebrate his happiness and felicity. Yet, not only was there no happiness here for him, but every circumstance represented the defeat of his hopes and the triumph of his enemies. He had been forced into the English match, and Henry's friends were all around him, victorious. He sat in the capital of his own realm, helpless to punish or even openly accuse those who worked against him. He had to swallow insults and hold his tongue – he, James, King of Scots. How had it all come about? How, in God's name, had it happened? Most men would say that he had succeeded, as a king, in fair measure. Yet – this! He hitched at the chain around his middle. Was this his punishment, long delayed, for the death of his father? Had Ninian and the other saints achieved nothing in intervention for him with God Almighty for that evil day?

When the lengthy meal was over, James did not trust himself in another encounter with Angus. Nor did he feel in the mood for the traditional activities and cantrips of the bridegroom's last hours of bachelorhood. When he rose, after tersely thanking his brother for his hospitality, he made the excuse of showing his bride-to-be her quarters in the new palace, and, no doubt to the surprise of the vast hastily risen and bowing company, quickly led the girl out into the cool of the evening.

Avoiding the gardens crowded with tables for the lesser guests, where decorum was already a thing of the past and in truth the nuptial spirit was more truly in evidence than in the strained atmosphere of the great refectory, James was striding across the Abbey's orchard towards the palace when he realised that the Princess was almost having to run to keep up with him. Quite suddenly he relented, saw her then, flushed and a little breathless, not as Henry Tudor's daughter sent to be a millstone round his neck, but as a lonely and somewhat frightened young girl, out of her depth, fearing the morrow almost as much as he did, a pawn in the game of kings even more helpless than himself. He moderated his pace, and took her arm.

"Have you ever wished that you had not been born a princess?" he asked her, abruptly.

She wrinkled her brows. "No," she said.

"You are fortunate, then – in that." He paused. "Even so, you must have dreamed of marriage . . . other than this? Have you not?"

"No," she answered again, simply, factually. "Always I have known that I was to be Queen of Scotland."

"The devil you have!" he burst out – and then restrained himself. "Heigho – so you have thought of me always as the husband you were to have?"

"You, Sire – or your brother."

"Ha-a-a! Me . . . or my brother!" Sidelong he looked at her. "I see. Well – it is me that you have got . . . despite the efforts of some! I must commiserate with you!"

"I think that I would rather have you than he," she told him flatly, without emphasis.

He turned to her, smiling, his eyes lighting up. " 'Fore God – you do? Why, I wonder?"

She took a little time to answer that. "Because you are more of a man," she said, at length.

He took a deep breath. "I thank you," he told her, and there was no sarcasm now in his voice. Holding her a little closer, he guided her through the postern gate into the unfinished precincts of Holyroodhouse.

They were wed in the Abbey church next day, the eighth of August 1503, in the most splendid marriage ceremony ever seen in Scotland. At noon, the Princess was led by a procession of Scots bishops and nobility from her chamber in the palace, by way of the Abbey Strand and the cloisters, to the church, preceded by chanting choirs and incense-swinging acolytes. She was dressed in a robe of white damask, embroidered with gold and slashed to show the lining of crimson velvet, the long train, also lined with crimson, being carried by the Countess of Surrey. She wore a handsome crown especially fashioned for the occasion by John Currour the Court goldsmith out of eighty-three gold pieces which the King had found for him, and below this her somewhat limp and lanky hair hung loose almost to her knees. Her great Scots escort, pacing slowly, brought her to where Surrey and the Archbishop of York awaited her in the north aisle. She looked notably youthful today, but scarcely attractively so, the stiff lined damask of her gown by no means aiding her lumpish figure, and her heavy brows lowered in self-conscious unease. When she was in her place, Archbishop Blackadder of Glasgow, who was to perform the nuptual ceremony — since the Primate of St. Andrews was not in holy orders — led in, with Bishop Elphinstone, a glittering column of prelates, their colourful copes, vestments and mitres so ablaze with jewels in the sunlight, that streamed in from the clerestory windows, as to dazzle the eyes. These took their places in the choir. Then the chanting of the choristers was drowned in the high blare of trumpets, and the King's procession wound its way in.

James at least looked every inch a monarch. He wore a doublet of cloth of cold, with long crimson hose and trunks, under a loose jacket of crimson and black velvet; thrown over this was another robe of white damask, like his bride's, embroidered in gold with the arms of Scotland — and around his middle, worn outwardly on this occasion, to be seen by all, the incongruous links of an iron chain, polished with constant wear. On his head was a black velvet bonnet in which glowed and flashed a single enormous red ruby. He came forward, head high, his long red hair seeming to glow with life to match the ruby, where the girl's hung so dully. Before him went the Lord Hamilton bearing the Sword of State. Half a pace behind, at his left, stalked his brother the Duke-Archbishop. Then followed the great officers of state, Bothwell, Home, Erroll, Huntly and the rest, with the insigna, the crown, orb, sceptre, keys, spurs and other symbols of rule, and after them a lengthy retinue of nobles and knights — modest amongst the last being Sir Rob Bruce.

Reaching the Princess, James took her arm, pressing it a little

—but she did not turn her head to him. He led her onwards to pass under the rood-screen into the choir, where the ranked prelates waited.

The actual marriage, as performed by Blackadder, was simple and very brief, over almost before James had his mind fully schooled to take it in. It was the triumphant neighing of trumpets, echoing and re-echoing about the venerable lofty building that really brought the knowledge home to him, that the deed was done. With a void where his heart should have been he turned to look at his wife. She had changed neither expression nor posture, staring sullenly ahead of her. He sighed, and his shoulders dropped a little under his magnificence.

As the echoes of the trumpets died away, the Archbishop of York stepped forward to read the papal bulls that permitted and blessed the marriage. More trumpeting. Then the Litany was chanted, followed by Mass—this latter interrupted to allow for the anointing of her who was undoubtedly now the Queen, and the handing to her of her husband's sceptre.

Throughout that day, James could gain no sense of reality, no feeling that this was truly happening to *him*. It might all have been some lengthy, rather tedious pageant in which he was involved. His bride, moving through it without even a sign of interest, much less animation, contributed to this impression. In the festivities which succeeded the ceremony, the same air of illusion, pretence, make-believe, seemed to prevail—despite the substantiality of the provision. This feast was held in the barely-completed Banqueting Hall of the new palace, and to the accompaniment of music provided by a host of minstrels and singers, a succession of no fewer than fifty-two courses of meats, fish, fowl and sweets was presented to the great company, commencing with wild boar's head, gilded and adorned, roast cranes and swans, and ending with a vast quivering jelly decorated with the arms of Scotland and England. James merely toyed with his food and drink throughout the hours of this prolonged gastromomical marathon, marvelling at such unnecessarily lavish purveyance—though well aware that it was all part of the evidently urgent need on the part of his subjects to demonstrate to the English that Scotland was not the poor relation that she was esteemed to be. For once Margaret Tudor appeared to have lost her appetite.

Only the one detail impressed itself firmly, clearly, satisfactorily on James's mind; the Earl of Angus had most evidently absented himself from the entire proceedings.

In the display of masques, dancing, conjuring and ballad-singing which followed, the King and Queen took no active part. But as the interminable day progressed, and the evening advanced, James was well aware that this passivity, this drifting, could not continue much longer. The two principals had their traditional and highly personal part to play — and any resilement therefrom on his part would not only arouse enormous offence but possible diplomatic complications. It was a strange situation for James Stewart to dread a bedding.

At last, with drunkenness beginning to become evident amongst many of the guests, and the consequent risk of unfortunate incidents, James took a grip upon himself. He suggested that if it was Her Grace's wish, Lady Surrey and her other women should now conduct her upstairs. He would join her later. Stiffly he said it, and stiffly the girl, pale-faced and dark-eyed with strain and weariness, acceded. He strode outside to inspect the bonfires and festivities in the streets, and briefly show himself to his people where they milled around barrels of ale and roasting oxen at corners and open spaces. A train of his lords sober enough to follow him in this did so, but most awaited his return in the palace.

Loth as he was, the King presently turned back. Now a large company of the foremost nobles, prelates and guests received him, and with ill-suppressed high spirits and boisterous humour escorted their unsmiling monarch upstairs. On each floor of the northern wing of the palace, with its twin drum towers, there were four apartments. On the second floor there was an outer chamber, for the King's pages on duty, an inner ante-room for the ladies in waiting, with opening off this last a small corridor with a door at each end. Through the outer rooms, packed with a noisy crowd of men and women, a way was made for the King, and the left-hand, westernmost door thrown open for him. Here a cloud of steam met the excited company, from a great cauldron of water boiling on the well-doing fire in this the King's own bedroom, as yet unused by him. The heat, this August evening, was fierce, but it did not seem to damp the ardour of the escort at least. There was indeed an unseemly struggle to get in, on the part of more men than the only moderately sized chamber would accommodate, and Rob Bruce had forcibly to eject certain of the wine-roused gentry amidst shouting and clamour.

There had evidently been a drawing of lots for the privilege of what followed, since almost all the lords claimed the right to attend their monarch on this auspicious occasion – which presumably accounted for the fact that Andrew Lord Gray was prominent amongst them bearing a silver basin. Bothwell held a dish of soap, Home a ewer of cold water, and Huntly a towel.

Unprotesting but set-faced and stiff, James submitted to the time-hallowed ritual of the bridegroom – Rob standing close however, dourly concerned to see that there was no undue roughness or outrageous horseplay which he might prevent. The King was stripped of his fine clothes, every stitch, until he stood stark naked before them all. Amidst the sniggers and guffaws, not a few had the grace to remark on the fine figure of a man that he made, broad of shoulder, deep of chest, slender of hips and long of thigh, covered on breast and back by a mat of auburn hair. Despite the steam, none failed to note the strongly calloused band about the waist and loins where the famous chain had left its mark on his skin – even the parting it had worn in his body-hair.

With water from the cauldron, cooled from Home's jug into Gray's basin, many hands washed down the King's person. Not once did he open his mouth in protest or indignation. He met Gray's fleering eye on more than one occasion, but even so held his peace. Rob prowled around eagle-eyed, looking for prey.

Towelled enthusiastically rather than respectfully, and his handsome furred bed-robe being brought to him, James spoke for the first time in that room, two brief words.

"The chain," he said.

There were gasps, exclamations, even hoots – but the King's hand was held out authoritatively. Rob it was who handed him the thing, the same humble length of iron cable that had hung on the wall of Beatons' Mill at Bannockburn, with two or three links added as boy had grown into man. In silence James girded himself with it and hitched it into its accustomed lie. He nodded for the bed-robe.

Dressed only in this, and rejecting the goblet of spirits offered by his Cup-bearer, Home's son, the King gestured towards the door. Somebody threw it wide.

A great shout from the inner ante-room greeted the royal appearance as men and women jostled and struggled to see. In a noisy, pushing throng, he was borne forward to that other closed door at the opposite end of the corridor.

Bothwell, in front, banged on this with his great fist. "Open, in the King's name!" he shouted.

A skirl of high-pitched girlish voices from within rose momentarily above the din outside. There was a few seconds of pause, and Bothwell had his hand raised to knock again when the door was opened. Like an incoming tide, the crowd surged forward, carrying James into the room beyond.

There was steam here also ,and an almost throat-catching smell of hot women and strong perfume. This chamber was very different from its western neighbour. Instead of simplicity and panelling in oak, it was hung with rich draperies in red and blue and ablaze with candles. There were tapestries and mirrors on the walls, and chests and cupboards and tables on the floor that was strewn with rugs of skin. But dominating all, in the centre stood a vast four-poster bed, adorned and curtained with hangings, and having a canopy of cloth of gold bearing the royal arms. Sitting up, but crouching forward, so very much alone on the white sheeting of that huge furnishing, was the young Queen, huddled in a furred bed-robe not unlike the King's own. All around stood her flushed and giggling, gabbling ladies.

For a moment the girl stared wide-eyed at the eruption of loud-voiced men into the room. Then, putting her hands up to cover her face, she bent still lower, and so waited, motionless, wordless.

At the sight, as though at a given signal, another great shout arose. Men, Bothwell, Home, Gray and others, caught up the King bodily, grasping him anyhow, uncaring that his robe fell wide exposing long limbs and manly body. Forward they rushed with him, to throw him into the middle of the great bed, themselves sprawling over it, so as to knock over the crouching girl. Scrabbling hands pulled at them both, dragging aside their robes.

Abruptly James came out of his self-imposed quiescence, his patient but smouldering waiting. Exploding into violent action, he struck out right and left with his hands, clapping vigorously at red and grinning faces.

"Enough!" he cried, in a great voice. "Enough! Have done, I say."

It took several moments for the upheaval in that bedroom to subside, for the mass of the company to realise that the situation

387

had altered. Slowly men and women drew back, staring, panting. Sitting up straight on the bed, head high, caring nothing for the fact that he was half-naked, the King looked round them all, fine nostrils flaring, in distaste.

"It is enough, I say," he repeated, with entire authority, even dignity. "You have my royal permission to withdraw. Draw these curtains – and then be gone! All of you. Every one. By my command!"

At one side of the bed Lady Surrey stepped forward, and pulled the hangings into place, while Rob Bruce at the other side did a like service. The huge four-poster became a small shut-off room within a large room.

James turned to his Queen. "Have no fear," he said. "They are going. I am sorry. It is the custom. But . . . it is over now."

She said nothing.

As, at length, they heard the door close, and the noise of voices fade, and only the hiss and puff of the log fire sounded in that bridal chamber, James drew his disarranged robe around him and eased his way up the bed, to sit more comfortably with his back against the handsome armorial bed-head. He looked at the girl, who still sat crouched, unmoving, and he stroked his red beard doubtfully.

"It was unsuitable. Offensive," he said. "But to have forbidden it altogether would not have been well esteemed. A king, aye and a queen, is as much the servant of his people as their master, I have discovered. You . . . they did not hurt you? You are well enough?"

Almost imperceptibly she nodded.

"Do not be cast down," he went on, to her hunched back. "It is all past now." And when she gave no sign. "I am told that you have the same custom in England? This bedding? It has little to commend it, I think. But, 'fore God – it might have been worse!" He considered informing her as to what she had escaped – but forbore. In most beddings that he had heard of, the bride was not only stripped naked but her groom placed bodily in position atop of her, before all the company.

There was a pause. He considered her, brows wrinkled.

"Are you tired?" he asked, at length.

A brief shake of the head.

"You have long hair. Notably long."

388

"Yes."

"Will you not come up here? Higher? Lean thus. It is more comfortable."

She did not stir.

Sighing, he leaned over, jerked back the curtains at his side of the bed, and swung his legs over the high side. He stood up, and began to pace about the floor, littered with clothing, towels, basins and the like. He began to snuff out some of the host of candles.

"It is hot," he said. "Too hot. There is no air." He picked up clothing from the floor.

He found that she was watching him now. "Why do you that?" she asked.

James did not know how to answer her. "Do *you* not find it over-hot?" he demanded, instead.

"No."

He stood in front of her. "You are . . . very young."

"No, I am not. I am near fifteen years, Sire."

"Aye—and I am twice that, exactly!" He frowned. "It has been a long day for you. As was yesterday. Trying. Wearisome. Perhaps you should sleep, child? Now. Would you like to sleep?"

"No," she said.

"There is no haste, see you. No hurry."

"Are *you* tired?" she asked. "I have been told that when men are tired, they cannot do it."

Blinking, he cleared his throat. "No. No—I am not tired. It is but that . . ." His voice trailed away.

"You have had many women, they say," she went on, factually. "You will know well what to do, therefore."

"Aye." Heavily he admitted it. "You could say so."

Awkwardly, jerkily, she straightened up, and began to divest herself of her bed-robe, an entirely prosaic and matter-of-fact proceeding without the least hint of desire, the urge to arouse, or of coquetry. She lay back, completely naked, looking up at him without change of expression.

"This is how you would have me, is it not?" she asked.

He looked down at her, his face a study, scarcely knowing whether he should smile or weep. As he had realised, she was well developed for her years, but she was thick, fleshy, heavy, and somehow starkly white. Undoubtedly of all the women he had looked on thus, she was the least attractive. Nevertheless, she *was* woman, and young, and he was entirely masculine.

389

"This is . . . as you want it?" he asked of her, with what was intended to be gentleness.

"It is part of being Queen," she said, briefly.

"Aye," he agreed, on an exhalation of breath, and threw off his own robe.

She stared at him for a moment, and then turned her gaze up to the handsome royal coat-or-arms on the bed canopy above — no doubt a subject for inspiration and consolation. She made no comment on the chain, at least.

23

KING JAMES waved the flowery letter beneath his nose. It still smelled distinctly of a delicate scent, heavy, desire-rousing — vastly unlike the heavy perfumes his wife used so lavishly. "Write me Her Grace of France very kindly, my Lord Bishop," he instructed. "Separately from the letter to King Louis. Thank her warmly for this writing in her own hand. And tell her that it shall be as she asks. I shall indeed ride, for her sake, three feet on English ground, and break a lance for her! I could not do less for so gracious a lady!" James spoke with an illusion of lightness — but his eyes were sombre indeed.

Elphinstone sighed heavily. "It is war then, Sire?"

"Aye, my friend, it is war."

For a little the two men sat in silence in that lofty tower room of the palace of Linlithgow, looking out over the loch to the green cattle-strewn braes beyond. Both men had long known that it must come to this, sooner or later. For eighteen months at least. It had been only a question of time. Yet to the end the old prelate, experienced statesman as he was, had hoped against hope, acted always as though war might yet be avoided by not openly admitting its possibility. In this, at least, James had been consistently the more realistic.

In the unhappy years following upon the royal marriage these two had been drawn very close together. Although Argyll was still nominally Chancellor it had long been almost wholly through Elphinstone that James ruled Scotland. Though now in his seventy-sixth year, the Lord Privy Seal in his person hardly showed the passing of those ten years; always spare and frail-seeming, he appeared to be no more so than James had always remembered him. The Bishop indeed claimed that the rushing about Scotland in the train of his now chronically restless and seldom-still monarch, kept him so active that he had no time either to ail or decently to grow old.

"Must it be so?" Suddenly confronted with the long-delayed and dire decision, Elphinstone's voice quivered a little, and suddenly he was an old man indeed. "Is this truly the time, Your Grace? The occasion? Would something less than this not serve? Something less than invasion, outright war? Send aid, in men and ships, to France, yes – but not this, not to invade England!"

James did not answer him for a few moments. He was watching two of his sons, out there on the sunny loch, fishing from a boat – Alexander, now nineteen and for five years, since his uncle's death of a consumption, Archbishop of St. Andrews, no less; and James, Earl of Moray, Janet's eldest, a sturdy red-head of ten. It was good to see them together, fond of each other – although Alexander truly was fond of everyone, a sunny-natured happy youth, talented, brilliant indeed as he was friendly. Margaret too would be somewhere near, although this time she was not in the boat with them; she was never far to seek when Alexander was around – a sweetly affectionate child, with budding beauty and some hint of her mother's blessed serenity. James was fortunate in his children – those born out of wedlock, at any rate – and never failed to give God thanks for them, the light of his life. That he spent so much time with them here, at Linlithgow, at Stirling, at his new hunting place of Falkland, at Drummond or Darnaway Castles – this was sorely held against him undoubtedly by the Queen, at Holyroodhouse where she refused to set eyes on his bastard brood; but at least now she had a babe of her own that looked as though it might survive – the fifth in seven years, which her sullen, stubborn Tudor pride had demanded that she should produce to heir the thrones of possibly two, even three, kingdoms.

Sighing, James returned his undivided attention to the vital, the portentous matter on hand. "You beat the air, old friend," he said. "You know it, I swear. You know that the time for half-measures is past. I shall send men and ships to aid King Louis, yes. But that will not serve to halt this Henry. We both know it. Moreover, Louis and his Queen know it – hence this letter and De la Motte's embassage. We are in treaty bound to do all in our power to aid France if invaded – as is France to aid us. She is now invaded. My savage Tudor gude-brother now storms at the gates of Thérouenne, claiming to be King of France, to make a fact of his father's empty boast. Nothing will bring him back to England save an invasion of his own realm. And only I can effect that."

"But the price, Sire—the price!" the old man exclaimed. "You may save France—but what of the cost to Scotland?"

"Did we not count the cost when we signed the treaty? My word is pledged. You know the terms of it—for you helped to draw them. Would you have me repudiate what my seal and signature promises?"

"Your Grace has also a treaty of eternal peace and friendship with England!"

"Faugh!" the King snorted. "Name you that in the same breath? Did either of the Tudors pay the least heed to its provisions, once they had their daughter and sister married to me? They had me trapped, they thought, and the Scots muzzled. The English treaty was a device and nothing more. I knew it then, as I know it now. But none would heed me here. The Tudors, God's curse on them, intended that treaty as a trap not a compact. And neither of them ever honoured a signature in their lives!"

"Henry Seventh, your gude-father, kept the most of its terms after a fashion, Sire," the Bishop pointed out, but with only moderate conviction.

"Henry Seventh was a fox. He lived by stealth and cunning. He bribed my own subjects against me, worked ill while seeming to smile, supported my enemies, encouraged raids over my Border, withheld his daughter's dowry and jewels. His son, Henry Eighth, is liker a wild boar. What he does is done bullheaded. He attacks my ships and slays my seamen. He holds the galleon *Lion* and the pinnace *Jenny Pirwin* captive, and all within them. His ships assault French merchants in my very harbour of Ayr. He boasts openly that he is true suzerain over Scotland and that I hold the throne only in homage to himself—the old impertinence that Edward First propounded! Have I not warned him again and again not to invade France? Did I not send Drummond to him a year ago, offering to cancel and overlook all his injuries against me provided only he abandoned his ill project against France. You know his answer. He as good as spat in my face. He does not even respect the usages with which princes address each other. In the four years since his father died, we have been almost pushed into war many times. Now, at last, the die is cast!"

"But . . . need it be, yet? Not, Sire, because Her Grace of France sends her own ring and a woman's letter with fair cozening words and the lewd scent of her bed! Heed not such play-acting, my son. Send a fleet of ships, and an army of soldiers, to aid the French — this only, for the present. Perchance Henry will see the danger, at last. See that you intend to hold to the Auld Alliance indeed, to your treaty with France. Seeing this proof of it, he may return to England, lest you *do* invade. And so the day may well be saved. Short of war . . ."

"Man — can you not see it? Are your eyes growing dim indeed — you who were wont to see clearly!" James cried. "This is not Henry Seventh with whom we now deal. This is another, altogether. A prince who prefers deeds to words, the sword to the pen. Think you that if he returned thus, in rage, it would be to sit quiet in London, licking the wounds of his pride? He would march north, on the hour! We would have Henry on the Borders, with all his might. It would not be James invading England, but Henry invading Scotland. He intends to do so one day — that we well know. He has said as much. If I move to aid France — as move I must — better, is it not, that *I* cross the Tweed, not Henry? Better that we act while Henry and his main strength is in France, than await his return either in wrath or in victory? In either case, Scotland will be his next quarry. Would you rather have me face *all* Henry's might, or but a small part of it?"

The old man sat silent.

James stood up, to pace about the room. The ten years had but little changed him, in appearance. No grey hairs showed in the long auburn locks. He had shaved off his beard, at his Queen's request, but though there were lines now about nose and mouth that told their tale, they by no means caused him to look his forty years. Only the slightest thickening of his waist was evident — a link or two more on his chain — his restless energy no doubt contributing to keep him slim. It was not in his outward appearance that the years had taken their toll — but taken their toll they had.

When he spoke again, there was a different note in his voice — an almost eager note which the other had not heard for long. "How long will be required to have ready a force for France? To assemble, arm and provision it? Not over-large a force — for I shall need all the men I may be able to raise for my invasion over the Border. Ships will not delay the business; enough are all but ready now, and will but have to be brought together at one haven. It is the men . . ." James was really talking to himself, for he knew far better than the aged cleric the situation with regard to the enlistment and concentration of armed man-power.

The position was indeed vastly different now, in 1513, from that prevailing all those years ago when last James had sought to cross the Border in strength – he had made it his business to see that it was so. Now he could call upon a nucleus of four thousand highly trained royal troops, scattered in garrisons about the kingdom but capable of being brought together into a single experienced and hard-hitting fighting force at short notice, stiffened by veterans of the Norwegian and Swedish campaigns – and directly under the King's own command. Moreover, every city and large burgh now had a standing town-guard, which could be reinforced quickly from the ranks of the train-bands which he had caused to be set up amongst the citizenry. The Highlands, too, could now contribute large numbers of splendid fighting-men – although it would take a little longer to bring them to bear. All this he could assemble on his own authority, before he even called upon his former sole source of armed strength – the levies of his lords. With the navy which he had so assiduously built up, under the command of old Sir Andrew Wood and the vigorous Barton brothers, he was now able to assert his authority both within and without his own realm to an extent unknown to any of his predecessors.

"If we sent out the summons to muster forthwith, the fleet can sail within the week," he declared. "It is the twentieth day of July. The force will be with King Louis before August opens. And before another month is past, I shall have crossed Tweed."

"You sound . . . scarce displeased," Elphinstone said wearily. "As though all this was to your taste. Some sport or play to which Your Grace looked pleasurably. When, God knows, it is more like to be quite otherwise – a desperate venture wherein much blood will flow, wherein you hazard all . . ."

"Aye – hazard all!" James reached out, to grip the other's thin shoulder. "My good friend – are we so differently made that your heart cannot lift to such a hazard? To act, instead of talk only? To have done with dissembling? To have recourse to clean steel instead of lying letters and murky shifts and devices? Here is an end to uncertainty, to shameful fears, to the swallowing of insults. For too long I have had to play a part that has irked and vexed me. For years, ever since yon day I was tied to the Tudors, I have had to live a lie. You know it. Now, at last, I can be an honest man again!"

"Has it been so grievous, my son? Your marriage?"

"Aye."

"I am sorry. The more so that I myself urged you to it. Was I so wrong? I believed it for the best. Am I so apt to judge amiss, an old and stupid clerk who had been better to have stuck to his desk?"

"Say it not, man! I' faith — you have the wisest head in this realm, as well I know. Who can foresee all the turns of fate? But . . . enough of this. There is work for us to do now, in plenty. This matter brooks no more delay than it does question. My honour, and that of my entire realm, is at stake. The terms of my treaty with Louis declare most clearly that if England invades one, the other will at once make war with his whole power — each king swore on the Gospels that he would perform this. Henry knows it well — yet he has invaded France. So Scotland marches! Have the Council summoned, my Lord Bishop. Two days hence, at Stirling. Send to me forthwith my Lord of Arran. He shall command the French expedition. And bring me the French envoy, De la Motte. Aye — and Glenarklet, for the Highlands need to be apprised quickly. The fiery cross must be lit!"

"Aye, Sire." Heavily the Bishop said it. "And the Queen? What of the Queen, Your Grace? Her brother . . .?"

James frowned. "The Queen has known, as have we all, that it would come to this. She will be bitter, yes — but that can change nothing. I myself will inform her. When I have seen these others, I ride to Leith. To see to the ships. Wood is there. He is old, too old to send to France — but he will make all in readiness for the voyage. Then I shall go to the Queen, at Holyroodhouse . . ."

Deliberately the King did not turn in his saddle until his great white war-horse had reached the gentle crest of the ridge, when he drew rein. He had been waiting for this moment, waiting for long years. Standing up in his stirrups, he raised hand to brow to gaze southwards, into the early afternoon sunshine, out over Tweed. Then swinging round, he looked backwards, and eyes shining, he flung up his mailed arm in a wide sweeping gesture, and a great cry rose to his lips, a shout of mingled pride and challenge — a shout that was taken up by scores, hundreds, thousands of throats around and behind him, to go billowing like thunder back and back across the plain of the Merse, till the whole land seemed to quiver and tremble to the sound of it.

It would have been a poor spirit which denied James Stewart

cause for that surge of pride and satisfaction. Last time that he had stood on this spot, the long low ridge of Oxenrig, hurt, humiliated, retiring in failure, he had made a vow. He would be back, he had sworn, shaking fist not so much at England as at all the circumstances which had combined to tie and cramp and mock him. He would be back—and otherwise as to state and power. He was back indeed, and much otherwise.

Laughing, as none had seen him laugh for years, gaily, infectiously, he turned to the son who rode at his side, clad in magnificent armour emblazoned with the mitred arms of St. Andrews. "Look yonder, Alexander," he commanded. "There is a sight I swear never seen before in all our long history. There is no host, no army—there is a nation on the march, boy! A whole people, to follow me into England. Sweet Ninian—look at it!"

There was indeed a sense in which that was no exaggeration. If it was not all the nation which advanced in endless serried ranks behind them, it was at least the very cream of Scotland's manpower in almost every sphere and aspect, from the highest-born to the lowest, from Galloway to the Hebrides, from the towns and the country and the mountain glens, from the abbeys, the universities, the burghs, the merchant guilds, the craftsmen, the apprentices, the tillers of the soil. Never had the like been seen, not only in Scotland but probably in all Europe—the manhood of a nation following its liege lord to war for love of him.

For that was the truth of it, the basic reason for the King's pride and elation. This host, that marched thousand upon uncounted thousand out of the north, completely filling the plain, its rearguard lost to sight amongst the Lammermuir foothills, was there for love of James Stewart. He knew it, and they knew it—even though, being Scots, none would have said as much. No other man in Scotland's age-old story could have produced that astonishing assembly—for this was the first king who had thought to seek his people's love and esteem. Not one man in twenty was being paid for his presence there. The royal command could not have brought more than a very few of them, had they not desired to come. These were free men, in the vast majority, not hired men-at-arms this time, with their own armour and weapons, their own rations even, come marching under their own natural or appointed leaders because King Jamie asked them to come.

James himself had been astonished, overjoyed, at the answer to his call. He had long planned for some such result, yes – but never at his most sanguine had he looked for such unanimity of response, such enthusiasm, such touching faith in himself. The townsmen from scores of burghs marched behind their provosts and bailies; the merchants and craftsmen behind their deacons; the apprentices behind their elected captains; the countrymen behind their lairds; the clansmen behind their chieftains; the churchmen behind their deans, priors and abbots.

If it was unprecedented for a whole people to go to war thus, it was little less so for an entire government to do so; but that was here the case. Practically all the Privy Council, led by the Chancellor, was there, clerics as well as laymen – only the Lord Privy Seal remained behind, in Edinburgh, to manage the realm's affairs. The great officers of state all rode around the King – the Earl of Erroll, the High Constable; the Earl Marischal; Home, the Chamberlain; George Hepburn, now Bishop of the Isles, the Treasurer; Gray, the Justice-General; the Wardens of the Marches. Here were the Masters of the Household and the Horse and the Wardrobe, the Bearers of the Standard, the Sword, the Cup, and innumerable lesser officials. Thirteen belted earls rode there – including even Angus himself, unbidden, who had attached himself to the Douglas contingent as it passed through Lothian under his son, the Master; only four lords, in all Scotland, for reasons of extreme youth or age, were absent; and many of the most notable chiefs of the Highlands, under MacIan of Ardnamurchan, Lochiel, MacLean of Duart and Campbell of Lawers, had brought their tartan-clad legions. A round score of bishops and mitred abbots, armed like the rest, added their support.

Well might its King say that Scotland had followed him to the Border.

There was no need, on this occasion, to send forward Home's moss-troopers to ensure that the ford at Coldstream was open. All the fords of Tweed had been secured days in advance. Indeed, the lessons of that earlier ill-fated campaign had been well-learned. This time there was no looting and indiscipline; James was using his highly trained and tight-knit corps of royal troops – or three-quarters of it, for he had sent one thousand men away with the Earl of Arran to King Louis – as a sort of police force at this stage, to control the vast concourse of enthusiastic volunteers, to restrain the appetites of the lords' levies, to enforce the King's orders. Today, James was in sole command, in fact as well as in name.

In accordance with plans previously made, the great army, assured that no opposition awaited to contest its crossing of Tweed, fanned out hereafter to the major task of fording the river. To expedite the enormous exercise, this was done at three distinct points — at Coldstream itself, at Twizelhaugh three miles down beside the mouth of the Till, and still further down at Graden. James led his central array of the chivalry of Scotland to the middle crossing at Twizel. It would take two days, at least, to complete the prolonged operation.

"Why does King Henry not oppose us here, Sire?" the young Alexander asked, as together father and son watched the protracted process of getting the endless columns of men and horses and baggage across the broad swift-running river, swollen and brown after the rains of a notably wet summer.

"I do not know," the King admitted. "It is what I would have done, certainly. Perhaps Henry himself would have met us here. But Surrey, whom Henry has sent against me, thinks otherwise, it seems. All reports tell me that he has withdrawn Dacre and his Border forces to await him at Newcastle. A strange decision."

"Perhaps they have not had time to gather a sufficient battle to oppose us."

"They have had time in plenty. It is four weeks since I sent Lyon King of Arms to France with my declaration of war. I sent a herald to Dacre, the English Warden here, at the same time — although the Council declared that I should not do so, that there was no need. But I will not have it said that I played the game of war unfairly. I have sought to steal no march on the English. All has been done honourably. A week ago, I am told, Dacre had fifteen thousand men assembled in the valley of the Till. These, along this Tweed, could indeed have held up our crossing — for many days, no doubt. Giving time for Surrey with his main array to march north from York. But, no. Our pickets declare that all are now gone south to Newcastle, leaving only Berwick and sundry castles held against us."

"Can it be that they are but craven?" the young Archbishop said. "Knowing something of our great strength, they fear to meet us. Nor would I wonder at it, 'fore God! I would not care to meet all Scotland, Sire, with fifteen thousand men!"

James shook his head. "It is less simple than that, lad, I think. Dacre is no craven. Nor Surrey. I know these two of old . . ."

"There is no mystery here." A mocking voice spoke behind them, quavering a little but still harsh, vehement. Angus had come to join the knot of lords who listened and watched at the King's back. "Surrey, I have no doubt, *desires* that you cross Tweed. He would be a fool to halt you here!"

Frowning, James turned. It was his first real contact with the aged Douglas, other than the mere formal and cold exchange of courtesies when Bell-the-Cat had unexpectedly joined the host at Ellem in the Lammermuirs the previous evening. "Why, my lord of Angus, should Surrey so desire? Since *he* is no traitor to his liege lord, I think!"

The old man snorted. "He would, I swear, prefer to defeat you with your *backs* to this broad river! That you must needs cross it, in disarray, on your flight back to Scotland. Such as may! Thus shall his victory be complete indeed!"

A shocked silence greeted his savage words. Men stared at the ancient, stooping, venomous figure, then to the King and at each other. An angry, snarling growl arose from many throats.

James flushed, a boyish reaction which he had never managed to master. He opened his mouth to speak — then closed it again for seconds while he took grip upon himself. When he spoke his voice was controlled but vibrant.

"My lord, since I cannot think that you intend a jest, I must take it that this commotion, this great venture, has been too much for you after your long, h'm, retirement! You are not yourself. We encamp here, in this Twizelhaugh, until all are across the river. I urge that you have your pavilion pitched, and that you rest therein! Tomorrow, pray God, you will feel better."

The other was no whit abashed. "Your Grace need not concern yourself with my poor comfort," he grated. "I counsel, rather, that you look to the survival of this great multitude, this host of witlings and simpletons!" Angus flashed his scorn on the murmuring, frowning lords around him. "This mockery of an army!"

"Have a care, my lord!"

"Aye — *I* have a care indeed. Is it not for you, Sire, to have the care? Care for this foolish, careless, prideful legion that follow you. To their ruin, belike! To your realm's ruin! How think you Surrey will view this . . . this pantomime? Yon auld sly carle?

I swear that he rubs his hands and laughs aloud! Aye, laughs. I tell you . . ."

"Your Grace — must we stand and listen to this ill-mouthed dodderer?" Huntly interrupted hotly. "These are the ravings of a dotard . . ."

"Fool!" Angus swung on him. "Insolent puppy! Since when dares Gordon yap at Douglas! This is war, Gordon — war! What know you and your like — any of you — of war? You chase a wheen bare-shanked Hielantmen wi' whingers and dirks — and you call that war! Christ God — none o' you ken the meaning o' war. Not one o' you! You've seen nothing above a bicker or a bairns' squabble in this realm in twenty years! Thirty!" He turned back to stab a trembling talon-like finger at the King. "Tourneys! Joustings! Play-acting! That is your notion of war. You ken naught of true war, I say. Dare you speak to me, Douglas, who was old in war when you all were yet wet with your mothers' milk?"

He spoke truth, in some measure, of course. Thanks to James's efforts and policies, there had been no real warfare in Scotland throughout the quarter-century of his reign. Scarcely such another period could have been named in all the country's bloody history. That, and Henry Seventh's marked preference for cunning and manœuvre and plot, rather than the sword. No major English invasion of Scotland had taken place since that instigated by Albany and Douglas in 1483, five years before James came to the throne. Apart from the expeditions to Norway and Sweden on behalf of his uncle of Denmark — which affected only a few royal troops — there had been no more valid experience of full-scale warfare in James's Scotland than could be gained from clan fights and Border raiding.

"And because we have not fought in war, my lord, you hold that we must never dare?" the King charged him. "That we must abide Henry Tudor's insults? Must flee at Surrey's frown?"

"Frown, by the Mass!" Angus cried. "I tell you, Surrey does not frown. He does not need to frown. He laughs! He rubs his hands, did I no' tell you? He but waits to roll you up as I would roll a parchment! Surrey is England's most skilled captain. He has been fighting in wars, true wars, foreign wars, since he was a laddie. He doesna play with jousts and tournaments! Your Grace is but a lamb to Surrey's lion! He will devour you, I say — devour you!"

James mustered a smile. "Then, sir, he will have a notable meal to make!" He waved an arm to include all the vast host which was bearing down on Tweed from the north. "I vow all this Scottish lamb may yet give your Surrey his belly-ache!"

Bell-the-Cat's voice rose high through the laughter. "Think you that your multitudes will save you?" he shouted, passionately. "Numbers, I say, mean nothing. Nothing! Numbers, ill-led, untrained, but encumber the field. Who have you to outface Surrey's veterans? The scourings of streets and vennels! Packmen and weavers! Fat-bellied merchants and potmen! Capons from the abbeys! Red-kneed Hieland savages!" Angus hawked and spat, though less than efficiently. "That for your great array! How think you they will stand before Surrey's tight halberdiers and archers who have fought in a score of foreign wars?"

James drew a deep breath. He should have stopped this much earlier, he perceived, dismissed the man from his presence — although, even so, he would have gone on sowing his evil seeds of doubt and distrust and defeat. Now he had best be answered, unwelcome as was the task, for many more of the leadership had come up to listen, and despite the anger and offence, there was uneasiness writ large on not a few faces. This must be ended, and quickly.

"My lord," he said, schooling his tones to patience. "I think that you have too long played hermit in Tantallon! Our state is vastly other than you believe it. We are none so lamb-like! Untrained and ill-led, did you say? Think you *I* have been idle, shut up in a castle, these last years? Had you attended the wapinschaws which I ordained regularly in every corner of my realm, you would have learned better. The weavers and the merchants that you spit upon are trained to their weapons, fully as well as are the lairds. The town bands likewise. I have made it my business to see that it is so. The Highland clansmen are, I believe, the fiercest fighting-men in all this world, long schooled in battle. As for veterans, my own soldiers from the Danish wars are here, tight as any of Surrey's, I swear — three thousands of them. And cannon — I have all but a score of great cannon, the greatest that have ever gone to war. Four hundred oxen it takes to draw them! Besides unnumbered smaller guns — sakers, falcons, serpentines, and the rest. Never has so great an army, so well-trained and so well-accoutred, been seen in this realm. And led by all the chivalry of Scotland . . ."

"Chivalry!" the Douglas snorted. "These, you mean?" And he jerked his vulturine head at the glittering ranks of lords and knights in their brilliant armour and nodding plumes that surrounded him, in his plain black corselet and tattered threadbare cloak. "Daws!" he declared briefly, succinctly. "Of no worth . . ."

"Wait!" James commanded, hand raised. "Even if you think so ill of your fellow lords, *I* do not. Here are some of the noblest champions of Christendom — names to outmatch all Surrey's Howards and Percys and Dacres and Stanley's! But, if they mean naught to Douglas — even he will respect the French captains. Since he sets such great store by foreign wars! King Louis has sent me a great number of his famed long pikes, each as long as three men. With the like of which so many notable battles have been won. In the Low Countries. In Italy. And with them he has sent forty skilled French captains, masters of warfare indeed, to instruct us all in the use of them. Do you say that these likewise, my lord, are of no worth?"

Angus had eyed James sharply at the mention of the long pikes and French captains. Now, he shrugged his wide stooping shoulders again. "Still I say that Surrey desires this motley horde across Tweed!" he answered heavily. "That he may the more fully scatter and defeat it."

"I wonder indeed, then, that you thought fit to leave Tantallon to join so despised a company, my lord!" the King flashed at him.

"God's Eyes — I came, Sire, because two of my sons have brought out twelve hundred Douglas blades! Mine!" the old Earl cried fiercely. "That is why I am here. Is it no' my right to preserve these at least frae their doom, if I may?"

James inclined his head. This was a fact. The Master of Angus and his brother, Sir William Douglas of Glenbervie, headed a large contingent from the vast Douglas estates in Douglasdale, Angus and the Borders. "As you say, my lord," he returned stiffly. "Is it your intent to withdraw these from the array? If that is your wish, when all of Scotland marches — then I shall send for the Master and command him to turn back. To retire with you to the safety of Tantallon. With all his strength. It shall be done forthwith. Is that your wish?"

For long seconds they stared at each other. Then, with an explosive curse, the old man flung about and went pushing his way blindly, furiously, through the press, striking out right and left as he stalked, caring nothing that it was against hard steel that his knobbly knuckles grazed. Men gave him passage in silence.

Troubled, Alexander turned to his frowing father. "Sire — why is he so?" he asked. "Why does he hate you so?"

James sighed. "He has always done so. He swayed and mastered my father — but I, even as a boy, refused his mastery. He is . . . part of the price I paid for Sauchieburn!" And almost as abruptly as the Earl, the King turned away and strode off along the riverside, alone, his hand subconsciously reaching down to the chain about his middle.

With the booming of his cannon resounding in his ears, as they battered at the massive walls of Norham Castle, five miles away, James rode southwards up the valley of the Till early next evening. At his side rode only Sir Rob Bruce, and at his back a small escort of his own Royal Guard. They had passed Castle Heaton, which had surrendered that morning without a blow — its old belligerent lord Sir John Swinburne being dead and his son of a different kidney — and had glanced at the preparations for besieging Etal Castle, a little higher up the river, which still professed defiance. This English policy of leaving these individual castles unsupported to bear the brunt of the Scots might could not have been a popular one with Dacre and the other Borderers; Surrey's orders must have been definite and stern.

But the King's thoughts were by no means wholly on the strategy of war. He was frowning again, as he rode — and only partly in that he had rather brusquely had to tell Alexander to stay behind at Etal with the siege-makers; fond as he was of the son who seldom these days left his father's side, he preferred not to have him with him on this present mission.

"You say that she has changed?" he said suddenly, out of his musing. "It is scarce to be wondered at, I suppose — for it is seventeen years is it not? By the saints — seventeen years! Can you credit it, Rob? She was young then — not twenty. Though old for her years. And of a decided mind! Now she will be a ripe woman."

"Aye, Sire," Rob agreed briefly.

"Well, man — out with it? Be not so plaguey dumb! *How* has she changed? Is it her shape? Is she fat? Or skinny? Or is she more cold? Or more warm — since I doubt if she could be more cold, i' faith! Speak plain."

404

Rob Bruce shrugged. "I am no hand at describing women, Sire — as you well know. I but perceived that the Lady Heron had . . . changed. She was not as I recollected her. Something . . . something about the eyes, I think."

"Ha! The eyes? 'Fore God — the eyes are all-important in a woman! They tell all — or nearly all. What about her eyes?"

"I cannot rightly say, Your Grace. Save that they were different. In their look. They seemed to look at me differently."

"By the Rude, Rob — you can do better than that!" James declared in exasperation. "Looked at you differently! From what? How did she used to look at you? She used to look *through* me! Was she kinder with you? You thought well of her then, if I mind aright. You blamed me as unkind to her, did you not? Little you knew! How did she look you differently this morning? Were her eyes less fair?"

"No. She is very fair yet, I think. It is otherwise. I think that she may be . . . less noble."

"Noble! Guidsakes, Rob — *noble*! Here's a strange word. And from you! Was she noble once? Are fair women ever noble! Save . . . save . . ." James swallowed. "I do not take you, Rob."

"No, Sire," the other muttered, setting his chin dourly. "I did not think that you would."

If the Lady Heron seemingly had changed in appearance during the past years, Rob Bruce at least had not. A little heaviness as to shoulder, a little thickness as to neck and middle, was all the alteration that time appeared to have made to him. Otherwise he was still the same in aspect as in behaviour — stocky, craggy, four-square, a man uncompromising, unsmiling, but utterly faithful, reliable, and proud as Lucifer. He had been sent that forenoon on a special private errand to Ford Castle, which was held like Etal against the Scots. Under a flag of truce he had gained the presence of its lady — for lady it again was, her husband, Sir William, having languished for more than a year now in Fast Castle as a prisoner of Lord Home for being art and part in the murder of Sir Robert Ker, the Scots Warden of the Middle March, a deed actually committed by his illegitimate brother, the Bastard Heron. Rob had borne a message and request for the King, to which she had acceded at least sufficiently to permit of this private meeting — a meeting not announced to any at the royal camp at Twizelhaugh or before beleaguered Norham.

James found it strange indeed to be riding again along this

familiar road by the deep and winding Till. It seemed inconceivable that seventeen long years could have gone by since last he was here, with all that those years had meant. Now all that seemed as though rolled back, and the intense feelings, the emotions and frustrations of the trying but challenging Northumbrian interlude were strong within him again, as though it had been but yesterday. Only now he was in a state and position to master them.

The approach to Ford Castle's precincts only enhanced the impression of timelessness. All seemed as it had been. But as they drew close, they were twice held up for the curt inspection of suspicious guards, and it was apparent that every tower, embrasure and loophole of the castle was fully manned against attack. James, not even wearing half-armour today, submitted to the scrutiny patiently enough.

In the forecourt, they left the escort exchanging hostile stares with the castle garrison, and were conducted within. Lady Heron awaited her visitors in the Great Hall.

At sight of her, James swept off his bonnet gallantly — but his eyes were narrowed, keen, calculating. In this house he had received his greatest, indeed his only major defeat, as a man with a woman. He was not of a temperament to forget it.

The lady dipped low in curtsy — lower, notably, than she had been wont to do in the past. Nor was that all that was low about her; the neck of her gown, of black velvet, was eye-catchingly low as it had never been previously, and her forward-stooping posture most effectually presented her callers with the fullest benefit of a magnificent bosom. Long she held that position, eyes upturned. As slowly she rose, she was smiling — and at the same time closely searching the King's face.

James drew a deep breath. He saw what Rob had meant about the difference, especially in the eyes. Elizabeth Heron had always had fine eyes. They were no less so now, no less remarkable — but now, as it were they were unhooded, aware; they had always challenged, but coolly; now they challenged not so much warmly as knowingly, artfully. They had gained in depth and range of expression — but undoubtedly they had lost something also.

Otherwise, beyond question, the years had been kind to her appearance. She was now a most handsome and attractive woman, her auburn hair heaped glowingly on top of her head, complexion smooth and clear, her figure full and satisfying without being overblown, her whole carriage proudly, provokingly feminine.

"Your Majesty," she said, and her voice seemed lower also, throatier than he remembered it. "Welcome back to my poor house."

James had planned a shrewdly pointed speech of greeting that from the first would leave no doubts as to the changed circumstances, indicating mastery of the situation. Now, in his surprise, he recognised the need for a totally new assessment, and was the less eloquent in consequence.

"Madam — a pleasure! A joy. I . . . ah . . . am happy to see you . . . thus. It is many years, but . . ." He left the rest unsaid.

"The years have left but little mark upon Your Highness, I see," she took him up quickly but easily. "Alas for me, I fear, it is otherwise." And she spread her arms, looking down at herself in mock dismay.

"On the contrary, you are more beautiful by far, I swear!" he exclaimed. And then, recollecting himself and moderating his tone, "And you will remember, perhaps, that I ever esteemed you fair to look upon."

"You are kind. Perhaps, once, I was less so. I was very young. Now at least I am . . . wiser."

"And kinder?"

"Perhaps." She raised her brows enigmatically but by no means discouragingly. "Meantime, may I offer Your Grace the poor provision of my house? Above, I think, in my bower, would be more to our comfort than in this hall, would it not?"

"Indeed, yes."

"Come, then."

As he moved to follow her, James caught Rob Bruce's eye. Their expressions were remarkably different.

Up the winding stairs, which the King had last descended hot-foot in anger and alarm, he followed her rustling skirts. She did not chatter, and made no comment on the fact that Rob was not now at his master's heels. They crossed the ante-room of the floor above, into the same pleasant boudoir where they had held their last interview, and if she was thinking of its embarrassments, accusations and disclosures, she gave no least hint of it. The room was even more feminine in its atmosphere than it had been then, and redolent of a subtle perfume. Wines and sweetmeats were set out on a low table beside the smouldering log fire. James noted that there were goblets and platters only for two. This was indeed another Elizabeth Heron.

"My maid will see to Sir Robert's comfort. That he lacks nothing," the lady mentioned, following his glance. "Pray be seated."

He sat on the long low fender-stool, upholstered in tapestry-work, and his eyes were busy as she came over to him and stooped, very close, to fill his goblet with wine. She sat herself across the stool from him, near but not too near. They pledged each other wordlessly, looking over the rims of their goblets, and if their tongues were silent their glances were fairly eloquent.

In the silence of that warm room, the distant rumble and quiver of cannon-fire became the more evident. Elizabeth Heron raised her brows.

"There speaks a less flattering voice of Scotland!" she observed. "I have been listening to it all this day. What sad house is there meriting Your Grace's wrath?"

He stroked his chin at her change of tone. The old Elizabeth Heron was not entirely dead, after all. "That is Norham," he told her. "The Bishop of Durham's castle. A strong place. I offered them honourable surrender, but they defied me to do my worst. I could not leave such a stronghold held behind me, as you must perceive. That is one of the first rules of war."

"War!" She sighed. "And it is only in war that we meet!"

"It is unfortunate . . ." He shook his head. "But, Madam, it is in no warlike mind that I come to *this* house. I assure you."

"No? I rejoice to hear that, at least. What then, may I ask, is the object of this visit, Sire? This welcome visit."

He cleared his throat. "It was my desire to see you again. To renew our . . . association. I hope, to better it. I have often thought of you. Especially in the matter of . . . of Sir William. Your husband."

"Ah, yes." She leaned over, to offer him another sweetmeat. "Of course."

Surprised at the casual manner in which she acknowledged that, he eyed her quickly. "The matter is a difficult one," he went on. "As you will understand. But . . . something *might* be done."

"No doubt," she admitted. "To the King of Scots, I am sure, all things are possible."

He was taken aback. This was not the attitude that he had expected. He had visualised anxiety, pleadings for her husband's life, his release even, putting himself into a strong position to bargain. After the murder of Sir Robert Ker by the Bastard

Heron and his accomplices Starhead and Lilburn, the last-named had been captured by Home, and thrown into his castle of Fast on the Berwickshire cliffs. Heron, the leader however, a notably wild character, with Starhead, escaped back to Northumberland, and there defied both the Scots and his own Warden, Dacre, whose duty it was to apprehend him and hand him over to a Scots court for trial. Unable to lay hands on the culprit, who took to the wilderness of the Cheviots, on orders from King Henry who at that time was anxious to avoid an open breach with James, Dacre had arrested his brother, Sir William of Ford Castle, and delivered him to Home as surety. Since then, these many months, Lady Heron's husband had remained a prisoner at Fast, his half-brother uncaptured.

"You will greatly miss Sir William?" he suggested. "All these months . . ."

"Why, yes," she agreed. "Will you take more wine, Sire?"

"I thank you. It has, h'm, grieved me that he should have had to remain thus held, for so long. Grieved me for *your* sake. But he is fairly treated and in good health."

"Then that is well, Sire. I cannot expect more. I know that it is the Border custom. We must be patient. A younger man, no doubt, would find it more grievous." She looked up, from pouring out his wine, to meet his glance. "He is older than am I, by many years. Moreover, he was oft from home, always – full of affairs in Berwick or Newcastle, even York. These he will miss, I fear."

James swallowed. So that was the way of it! She did not want her husband back. This shed a new light on the situation. And destroyed the hold he had thought to have upon her. Unless . . . unless he used the contrary course. It might be more than not desiring her husband's return; she might even be eager for his continued absence.

"I must think more what I may do, here," he mentioned, sipping. "I had forgot that Sir William is older. It must be trying indeed for an older man to be thus confined, for so long. I must needs have a word with my Lord Home, the Warden. If still John Heron, his brother, cannot be found, perhaps we might think of some other way to serve the ends of justice, and have Sir William released."

"You are too kind, Highness," she said coolly. "I pray that you do not trouble yourself over our poor affairs. You have greater concerns, I swear. Have you not? This war. Your march south.

How far you go, and when. All this must come first." She paused. "Do you march for Newcastle, Sire? Forthwith? When . . . when Norham is vanquished?"

He smiled. "You wish to see the back of me, Madam?"

"Not so. Indeed, no. I but wondered."

"There are other castles holding out against me. Heaton has surrendered. But there is Wark. Etal. Barmoor. Doddington."

"And . . . and all must be conquered? Brought down? All?"

"All," he said. "And left so that they may not be used against us later. That is war."

"You mean . . . razed?"

"I fear so. Rendered unfit for defence, at the least."

"This house . . .?" she faltered.

"It would grieve me much to damage Ford Castle," he told her. "It is my hope that it may not be necessary."

Swiftly she searched his face, then looked away. "It is my hope, likewise," she said, low-voiced.

"Good! Then surely we may ensure it, between us. If there was no resistance to our arms. I might even take up my residence here, Madam—and so spare your house. By your leave?"

"Residence . . .?" she repeated. "But do you not march? Southwards?"

"Not so. That is not my purpose here."

She looked bewildered. "But . . . I thought . . . your great army . . .?"

"What would marching deep into England avail me? This is not such an occasion as all those years ago, when last I was here. Then I came seeking to set a claimant on your English throne. The Duke of York, as he styled himself. Then, I would have marched south, yes, had the English risen to aid the Duke as he vowed that they would. Now, it is quite otherwise. I do not seek Henry's throne—only that he returns from invading France, my ally. To that end I have invaded *his* realm. To that end I shall fight Surrey, since Henry himself does not give me that satisfaction. But I can fight him here, in Northumberland, as well as elsewhere in England. Better. The further I leave Scotland behind, the harder to feed and supply my great host. I am well content to await my lord of Surrey here. And Ford Castle, were it open to me, would well suit me as a waiting-place, I think."

"I see." Elizabeth Heron rose, to pace slowly over to the window that looked out over the great park. Dusk was falling and already the room was full of shadows. James could not discern her expression but there seemed to be calculation about her attitude. He returned to the attack.

"This matter of your husband, Madam — I think that it might be resolved while I am here. *If* I am here. Surrey is at Newcastle, and awaits his son, the Lord Admiral, with reinforcements by sea. He cannot be here for some days, at least. There is time . . ."

"No," she said from the window. "No. I thank you — but no. In this circumstance I think Sir William is better in Fast Castle. Meantime."

"Ha! You would not have me bring him back to your bed?"

"No. He might . . . but suffer for it. He might, amongst all your Scots here, be the worse for it. Speak them hard. He has a harsh tongue. Better as it is, I think. I pray you, Sire — leave him be." She half-turned to him.

Setting down his goblet, James rose and strolled over to the window also. He stood beside her, and looked out over the dove-grey evening. "Is it a compact, then!" he asked softly, almost a whisper in her ear.

She drew a long breath — but did not move away from him. "Majesty," she said, low in voice. "There is something else. I crave your . . . forbearance. You said, did you not, that you would reduce all castles and strong houses behind you? All?"

He nodded. "All save Ford. I can do no less."

"Even though they surrender?"

"If they surrender, they must still be disarmed. Rendered unable to be garrisoned against our rear. If they withstand me, they must be destroyed."

She pointed, out of the window, east by north. "Yonder, Sire, over the green hill, there is such a house. Duddo Tower. Four miles away. It is not a great castle — less strong than this. Or Etal. Or Heaton. A smaller place. It could not truly harm your great army."

"Duddo? I have heard of it, seen it on its hill. A place strong enough for its size. Well positioned and fortified."

"It would not injure you. If left standing. I swear it. Spare Duddo Tower, Highness."

"Why, Madam?"

"Because of he who holds it. Robert Clavering."

"Ah! Clavering. Robert Clavering of Duddo. You plead for this man? This man only?"

"Yes. He will not surrender, Sire. He is bold, headstrong . . . and young! He will not yield up his house, I know. He will fight, hopelessly . . . and belike die. Do not destroy Robert Clavering and his house, I pray you."

"Young and bold!" he said. "So that is it! And no doubt handsome?"

"Handsome," she nodded. "Spare Robert Clavering, Majesty." She looked up at him. "And earn my most grateful . . . submission."

He took a moment or two to answer here. "Submission," he repeated slowly, then. "Submission, Elizabeth Heron, may be a word for kings. But not for men. Not for James Stewart!"

"Then say, James Stewart — spare Robert Clavering . . . for love of me!" And her hand slipped into his.

"For love of you!" Suddenly he swept an arm around her shoulders and drew her to him. "A compact, is it? Duddo Tower not to be assailed. Ford Castle spared, and my resting-place. And Sir William to remain in Fast Castle! For love of Elizabeth Heron!"

She dropped her glance, but raised her parted lips to his.

After a little while, she pushed his urgency away, gently but firmly. "Sir Robert," she reminded. "Below. Waiting. Go send him away, Sire."

"Aye," he exclaimed. "To be sure. I shall send him back to the camp. To Twizelhaugh. To bring my gear. Here. Forthwith."

"Do that," she whispered. "Then hasten back. I shall await you . . . yonder." And she pointed to the open door of the same bedchamber that seventeen years before had so eluded him, to his humiliation.

24

LIKE an embattled city, like windy Edinburgh itself along its spine of rock, the two-miles-long ridge of Flodden Hill crouched beneath lowering, sagging clouds above the rolling plain of Till and Tweed, its broad crest packed, covered, seething with armed men, parading pipers, chanting friars, ranked horse-lines, artillery and their oxen, stands of arms, tents, shelters, portable shrines and fluttering banners. The smoke of a thousand cooking-fires billowed away on the south-westerly breeze to reinforce the leaden clouds, and, with the thin drifting rain which had for ten days been soaking the land, was equally reminiscent of the grey northern capital.

At the extreme south-eastern end of the long ridge, known as Flodden Edge, which was also its highest point, King James and all the might and chivalry of Scotland waited in the rain that forenoon of the ninth of September, drawn up in the panoply of war and in ordered ranks of battle, a stirring sight indeed. As once before, on the heights of Bannockburn, James had waited for his challenge to be answered, so again he stood to arms, ready, eager, impatient – but now with a confidence unknown before. For today his army was such as had never previously been at the command of a Scottish leader, and his position strong indeed – moreover reports set Surrey's force at anything from twenty to forty thousand men, a muster which James could all but double; again, this time there was no wondering whether the challenge might not be accepted, for Surrey was fully committed to fight.

Nevertheless, as the hour wore on towards noon that grey chill day, there was a growing concern, perplexity and even indignation in the Scottish camp. Where was Surrey? They ought to have seen his approach long ere this, from this lofty vantage-point. Admittedly visibility was poor under the ceiling of droop-ing cloud and driving curtains of rain, but even so the Scots position, hundreds of feet above the surrounding countryside gave a wide prospect; they could indeed see the smoke of Surrey's great camp at Woodend of Barmoor, four miles away to the north-east, at the other side of Ford, where the English army had passed the previous night. But though occasional small bodies of English troops had been observed all morning, moving here and there over the rolling intermediate terrain, there was no sign of Surrey's main force coming to the onset as arranged — and if it had indeed been on its way, surely it must have been seen, however much the low ground undulated in ridge and valley.

"We should have sent out prickers, spies, Your Grace," the Lord Home declared, by no means for the first time. "My moss-troopers would have kept us advised as to Surrey's movements. Or the lack of them . . ."

"So you have said, my lord!" James answered testily. "But what need should we have had of spies, in this? I have Surrey's word that he would meet me here by noon this day. The word of the Lord Treasurer and Earl Marshal of England."

"That for Surrey's word!" the Earl of Huntly cried, snapping his fingers. "I'd as soon trust a scorpion!"

A growl of agreement rose from a score of noble throats.

"My Lords," James said loudly. "Surrey represents his master, King Henry of England. He sent one of the King's heralds. Rougecroix Pursuivant, in answer to my own challenge, two days ago. To say that he would do battle with me, by noon this day at the latest. Moreover his son, the Lord Admiral of England, wrote discourteously to the same effect. I have his letter here — and intend to make him eat his unmannerly words, by St. Ninian! Whether or no we trust Surrey as a man, here he speaks as the mouthpiece of his liege Lord Henry. Kings do not lie in such a case, my friends."

Helplessly the others exchanged glances. To declare that they would trust Henry himself as little as they did his representative was scarcely possible, James's own brother-in-law as he was.

"Sire," Home persisted boldly. "Surrey sent Rougecroix again but yesterday, offering to fight you down yonder in the plain. By the river at Milfield. It was but a device to coax you out of this strong position. We know that he did not move his army to that encounter. If that was but a ruse, a deceit — why not this?"

"Because this is an agreement, a compact. That insolence I did *not* agree to. This, to which we both agreed the day before therefore still stands. I sent Islay Herald to say that I would await Surrey here. This he accepted. My honour is engaged."

Tactfully Argyll, the Chancellor, intervened. "It may be that Your Grace's notion of honour is greater than that of my Lord of Surrey," he suggested. "It lacks now only thirty minutes until noon. If Surrey was to keep his word, he must needs have appeared below us here in force long ere this. So, Sire — he keeps *not* his word. Or his master's. *His* honour therefore is lost . . ."

"He may have been delayed. A great army may not be moved to and fro like a troop of horse. I shall await him for another hour . . ."

"Honour, Christ God!" Angus had kept to his tent almost entirely during the two days in which the Scots army had been encamped up here on Flodden Hill, after spending over a week at Ford Castle a bare two miles away. Now he came thrusting through the throng around the King. Unlike the others, he wore only a breastplate as armour. "Who prates of honour in this pass?" he cried. "This is war, have I not told you? This is no fools' tourney! Surrey is a soldier, and a cunning one — not a mummer or a court popinjay! His purpose — aye, and his plain duty — is to smash this Scots array, however he may. No bairn's-talk about honour will weigh with the Howard more than a belch of belly-wind! He wasna bred in that school, by the Mass!"

For once, Angus might have had most of his hearers with him, had he said his say otherwise — for the majority would have admitted that he talked sound sense on this occasion. But his scurrilous, angry speech, and his disrespect to the King, told against him as ever, and no voice actually supported his protest.

"Your opinion of your former companion-in-arms may be low indeed, my lord," James told him coldly. "But *my* honour is my business! I do not toss it aside because my opponent's is in question."

"Your business, Sire!" the old man took him up fiercely. "Is your business no' rather the safety and weal o' this host? You are no' in your lists now. I'd mind you! Leave you your talk o' honour there. Here sterner work is toward."

"What would you have me do, then, my lord? Thus sternly?"

"Retire back over Tweed, Sire — while you yet have time," the other cried. "The way is open. It is but five miles to Coldstream. Beyond Tweed, Surrey cannot come at you . . ."

"'Fore God — are you mad, man?" James blazed. "Retire beyond Tweed! I — James Stewart? I' faith — I did not bring this great host into England to turn tail and flee at Surrey's approach!

415

I have more men than Surrey. And better men – the pride of a nation! We are rested and he is not. We hold a notably strong position . . ."

"What use is your strong position here if Surrey will not assail it?" the old man broke in. "He is not such a fool! You may wait all this day. Whatever Surrey does, he will not throw his men away on such a folly. He will leave you here like a treed fox . . .!"

Angus's harsh croaking voice died away as a commotion at the rear turned all heads. A group of heavily-armed moss-troopers in the Hepburn colours were pushing their way forward, despite the frowns of knights and lords. Adam, the young Earl of Bothwell who had succeeded his father Patrick a few years before, went to them. He came back bringing their hard-bitten leader with him.

"Sire," he exclaimed. "News of Surrey! He moves. The Admiral also. Down Till. Towards Tweed!"

"Tweed! Save us – what mean you? *Down* Till . . .?"

James's words were lost in the hubbub as men exclaimed and demanded. The King had to beat his mailed fist on his gold-inlaid breastplate to gain quiet.

"Speak, man!" he ordered the Hepburn captain. "What folly is this? What prating report?"

"No prating, Lord. Truth it is," the newcomer panted. "The English have been on the march since daylight. North. Towards Tweed. We've seen them."

"But . . . how, man? Where? Since *daylight*? How know you this? Out with it. Quickly."

"We saw it, Lord. We were at Ford. Guarding the castle, as you commanded. A laddie told us. Told us that men were crossing Till at Etal. Many men. We rode to see it. Truth, it was. All the valley was full of them. They were coming down a bit burn, hidden. From Barmoor. Into the Till valley. Crossing at Etal. The Admiral's men . . ."

"How do you know that? The Admiral?"

"We caught a pair, Lord. Captured them. In a bit wood. We made them talk – dirk at throat. Och, they talked – Englishry frae the south. They told us. This was but a small part o' the Admiral's array, they said. To hold the far side o' the ford at Heaton Mill, further down. Where Surrey and the main battle crosses. The ford below yon castle. Three miles down . . ."

"Surrey crosses Till? At Heaton?"

"Aye. He's moved fast, the auld yin! He's been marching since cockcrow. By the low ground. Wi' the rearguard, they said. The Admiral crosses lower still, wi' the van. Down at Twizel Bridge, they said. Near Tweed. Three crossings . . ."

"God in His Heaven!" James cried. "The knaves! That crooked dastard Surrey! While we awaited him here . . .!" He took a grip of himself. "What means this, then? Does he make for Tweed? Twizel is only a mile from Tweed. Then why does Surrey himself cross higher, at Heaton? And this at Etal? What means it?"

Talk swelled in an excited babblement, as the lords debated, argued, questioned, cursed. Anger rather than alarm was the general reaction — anger that they had been made to look and feel foolish, waiting inactive up here on Flodden Hill while the English secretly used the valley system of the Till's flood plain to steal away unseen to the north, by devious routes. Although this Flodden Edge was a notable vantage-point, owing to the rolling wave-and-trough formation below, such a manœuvre was perfectly practical. But that was how raiders, cattle-rievers, freebooters and broken men, might act — not the armies of great kings, surely!

More time and breath was expended in condemning Surrey's behaviour than in questioning his purpose. But some did that. Various assertions were put forward. The most widely held was that the English meant to steal secretly across Tweed, then turn and hold the fords against the Scots, preventing them from getting back to their own country and their source of provision; the Admiral at Twizelhaugh and Graden, Surrey making for Coldstream. The Etal crossing would be merely to cover Surrey's flank.

What to do now? Whatever Surrey's intentions, the Scots army was now miles behind him, and facing in the wrong direction, set in array of battle, its cannon's muzzles trained southwards. Its strong position was valueless.

If King James was for the moment bewildered, nonplussed, he might be excused, forgiven. This was not how any battle of which he had ever heard was fought. After preliminary manœuvre and positioning, the great onset, the head-on clash, the true trial of strength, was axiomatic. He was faced here with not only a totally unexpected situation, one for which nothing had remotely prepared him, but with one of the most difficult tasks known to man — the turning around of a vast army of infantry, cavalry, artillery and hangers-on, with all its equipment and impedimenta, in a very limited space. For a little his mind boggled at the thought.

He had no lack of advice, at least. Some counselled not a reversing of front but a march on and down into the low ground, there to swing round and follow down the Till valley in the rear of the English. Others advised that they swing off due north-wards, in an attempt to drive a wedge between Surrey and the Admiral; this would have to be done swiftly, however, and could only be attempted by a mounted force — so that the footmen would be left behind unused. A third proposal was to wheel round north by west, and make for the Tweed fords higher up, in the Wark and Birgham areas, so as to cross and meet Surrey on Scottish soil, descending upon him from the west; but this would first entail crossing much hilly and broken country, pitted with bog — impossible for the heavy cannon. Some lords even suggested that the army stayed where it was, being in a strong position; let it be Surrey's worry to bring the business to battle.

Presently James held up a hand for silence, and eventually made himself heard. "My lords," he said, "I have listened to you all, and weighed your counsel. I will not divide my host — as I must if I seek to drive between Surrey and his son. To do so I needs must leave behind the foot and the cannon. Nor will I cross these hills westwards, to the Tweed at Wark, for that would break up any army and lose us our cannon likewise. This host is a great and mighty one, and I will keep it so, in one. I will not go down into the low ground and follow down Till; in that narrow valley we should be constrained and strung out for miles. At our weakest. Such might well be Surrey's ruse, to tempt us off this hill. But neither shall I stay here, as though palsied. This great upland is two miles long, my lords. We turn and go back along it, above the plain. At its northern end, at Branxton Edge, we shall halt, facing Scotland. From there to Tweed at Cold-stream is but three miles. All fair level ground. We shall see from there what the English do — how they are disposed. It will take time — but we shall be still one, and secure, on this hill. How say you, my lords?"

Out of the surge of discussion, it was clear that the great majority accepted this decision as probably the best that could be devised in the circumstances — although the more experienced pointed out the confusion, if not chaos, that must arise out of turning so great a concourse as it were on its own axis, back to front, in the different arrays of battle, left, right and centre, van and rear, foot, horse and artillery, all to take up new positions in a very restricted area, indeed through a standing camp. Impatiently James waved them quiet, declaring that well he knew the difficulty — but at least here on this hill they could carry out the process in their own time and without fear of being attacked whilst so disorganised.

"Let it be done, then," he commanded. "Every leader to his due place in his own array. Messengers to me, here, when each is ready to make his turn. The right will move first, becoming the left. The right rear, under my lords of Erroll and Crawford. Then the right van, with my lords Huntly and Home. Not until they are in position will the left move, to become the right, The rear first under my lord of Bothwell and MacLean of Duart. Then the van, the main Highland host, under the Chancellor, my lord of Lennox and MacIan of Arnamurchan. Finally my own central division. Is it understood, my lords?"

Into the chorus of acknowledgement, Angus raised his voice once more. "Before it is too late," he called out, "I bid you heed me. You, Sire — and all your foolish lords. Hear a man who kens the meaning of war. What you purpose will but serve Surrey. This great manœuvre. The holding of this hill. It gives the English what they need most — more time. Time to fulfil *their* purpose. I tell Your Grace — two ventures now you can make, and only two. Send a strong force of your chivalry down yonder, at all speed, to ride between Surrey and his son. To keep them apart, while they are on the march. And you, with your main force, make for Wark and Tweed, westwards across these hills. Abandon your cannon. They will only hold you back. This you can do, and Surrey cannot stop you. Beyond Tweed you can face him, secure. Your chivalry can cut their way down to the ford at Lennel. It will serve horsemen, but not foot. Do this, and the day may yet be yours."

Even James was reluctantly impressed by the authority with which the old man spoke. He had forsaken his ranting, sneering abuse and spleen for a more reasoned and dignified representation, with almost a note of pleading behind it somewhere. But his moderation came too late, years too late. The King shook his head.

"No, my lord," he said. "I flee for no man. The day will be

ours more surely by keeping this great host as one than by dividing it. I did not labour to forge all these cannon that I might abandon them unused on an English hill-top!"

"They will hold you back. Give Surrey more time . . ."

"Why should time be so precious to Surrey, man? You, Bell-the-Cat—tell me, does not time favour the cat rather than the mouse? We are the cat, this day, and Surrey the mouse. We are stronger, of greater numbers, better provisioned and equipped, rested. Time, my lord, is with us and against the English."

"No! No, I say!" Suddenly Angus lost his brief precarious patience and became his violent, peremptory self again. "Time is never with the bungler and the simpleton!" he shouted. "You have squandered your time ever since you started on this fool's progress—precious time! It is two weeks since you crossed Tweed. Two weeks! We have idled here waiting for Surrey, while you whored with yon Heron woman at Ford! The folly of it—waiting for one o' the masters of warfare!"

"Silence!" James commanded hotly. "This is too much! I will hear no more of you, sir! If you are so afraid of Surrey—then you have my permission to go home! Go, my lord!"

It was as though the other had been struck. His lined features grew purple, as if he sought for air as for words. Then he seemed to sag and shrink, to collapse upon himself. "Afraid . . .!" he muttered. Shaking his head, he turned to peer around him, almost dazed. "Afraid? Douglas?" As with an enormous effort, he drew himself up. "My age," he said thickly, "renders . : . renders my body of no service. No service. And my counsel is despised. I . . . I . . ." He could say no more. Swaying unsteadily round, he stumbled away from the royal presence. Near by his two sons, the Master of Angus and Sir William Douglas, stood, set-faced, watching, unmoving.

James threw up his head in characteristic gesture. "My lords," he cried. "I likewise give my full permission to all and every other who feels as does my Lord of Angus. Go now—the way to Tweed at Wark is open! Go if you will."

Silent, motionless, the great company stood, the only movement that of the old man stumbling towards his tent.

"So be it," the King nodded, presently. "To your duties, my friends."

Whether or not time was an ally or a foe, it was in short supply upon Flodden Hill that wet September afternoon. The operation of turning the army around upon itself took even longer than James had anticipated, and for hours disorder reigned on that ridge, broad as it was, however theoretically disciplined and regulated the exercise. For almost four hours indeed the King supervised and directed, rode hither and thither, cursed and fumed. Never had men and oxen and horses, by their own scores of thousands, seemed so maddeningly awkward, unmanageable, stupid. Never were material things, tents, clothing, armour, stands of arm, particularly those eighteen-feet-long French pikes and the massive lumbering cannon, so hostilely inert and cumbersome, always in the way. Never was terrain itself so unhelpful, the rain-sodden land churned up into deep and cloying mud ribbed by outcropping reefs of rock.

By nearly four of the afternoon, however, all was practically in order again, even if tempers were frayed. Flodden Hill was a lengthy saddle-shaped eminence, two miles long by perhaps three-quarters of a mile in width, with a large, wide sag in the middle, almost a valley, in which the land sank for fully one hundred feet. On the gently-sloping sides of this great declivity the army was now reformed in six main lines of battle, van and rear in a centre and two flanks. Satisfied, James at last rode forward towards the northern escarpment of the hill, Branxton Edge. He overtook the long line of heavy cannon being painfully dragged and man-handled thither.

The hill ended quite abruptly, in a long grassy slope which fell fairly steeply for some three hundred feet to a wide hollow through which a burn meandered. There was a slight rise beyond and then the land levelled off to the plain of the Tweed, across the right-hand corner of which the Till wound its serpentine way. Unfortunately all thus had to be seen by the eye of faith alone, from up here, partly because of the driving curtains of rain, but mainly on account of the billowing smoke clouds which drifted over all on the south-westerly breeze. These were caused by the rearguard of the Scots army burning all the unwanted encumbrance of gear, tentage and rubbish accumulated by the host, a Highland campaigning habit which James had now cause to rue.

Lord Home, who had been sent forward in his usual advance role, with a detachment of his Borderers, was awaiting the King at the brow of the hill. "God's curse on this smoke!" he cried.

"What fool ordered this burning? I can see nothing. I have sent men out, down the hill, Sire—probing, searching. I could do no other."

James peered into the hazy mirk, northwards. The weather had been growing worse all day, and now the heavy rain clouds had blotted out all the Cheviot foothills to the west, even fairly close at hand. The vista northwards over the plain would have been much restricted anyway, but the rolling smoke hid everything, even the foot of their own hill. The hoped for information as to the enemy's movements was not to be had.

"There will be no fighting this day, I fear," James said heavily. "It will be dark early. In three hours. At least, we are in good position to pass the night, secure on this hill. But where is Surrey? Will he have yet crossed Tweed? From his crossing of Till at Heaton it is but four miles to Coldstream. But fording Tweed will take much time—as we know."

"Listen, Sire!" Home interrupted. "Horses, hard-ridden. And up this hill . . ."

Out of the eddying smoke below a couple of riders materialised, spurring their beasts savagely. One of them called out while still many yards from Home.

"My lord—they are there! Below. Directly below. Coming into the valley. They near had us. English."

"What? Here? Below us? Here at Branxton, man?"

"Aye—no' half a mile frae us! Marching into the valley—frae yonder." The moss-trooper pointed north-eastwards. "Many. A host, my lord."

"A host!" James took him up, spurring closer. "You are sure of this? A host, you say? Not some troop, lost? Some wandering band of English . . .?"

"No, Majesty—a host. Horse and foot. Banners . . ."

"Sweet Ninian—here below us! What means this? A plague on this smoke! Why should any part of Surrey's army come thus close? To this hill? To have come here from Heaton, or even Etal, they must needs have turned *back*! Can it be . . .?"

"Your Grace." Rob Bruce, at the King's back, leaned forward in the saddle first to touch James's arm and then to point.

Some trick of the wind was rolling the smoke clouds away at that side, further round to the east, leaving a corridor, ever broadening, not entirely free from haze but clearer by far. Half-right, the corridor extended, north by east.

All the staring men caught their breaths at what they saw down there. Like an enormous snake winding its way across the plain from the immediate valley of the Till, marched a great column of men, mounted and on foot, in companies a score abreast at least, flags flying, an army of many thousands, silent, disciplined, inexorable. Into the valley immediately below, this human flood was pouring—and although smoke still hid the western outlet of the hollow, it was apparent from the way that the foremost ranks were breaking up and fanning out that it was no through passage that this multitude intended. The valley was indeed their goal and destination.

"By the Rude!" James exlcaimed, almost below his breath as though he might be heard by the enemy below. "They come to battle, after all! It is not the Tweed. They have turned round. This is no straying company, but a great array . . ."

"Aye, Sire—and see yonder!" Home was pointing now, further over, almost due north, where the thinning smoke was temporarily permitting an ever-expanding vista. Indistinct but not to be mistaken, was another and even greater host advancing from the north, over a mile away yet, coming over more level ground from the direction of Cornhill-on-Tweed. "More of them!"

The King nodded, frowning. This still larger army must be the main body of the English—therefore Surrey himself. That below must be his son the Admiral's array. Thomas Howard, more impetuous no doubt, had travelled faster than his veteran father. But . . . both were making for the same point, this valley. They must be aware of the Scots' new position therefore. And since they could not see the Scots army, and the move here was only decided upon at noon, the English must have been informed of it.

"Who told them?" James rasped. "How know they to come here? What turned them both back in this direction?"

"Treachery?" Home jerked.

"Who left our camp, Rob? After I had given permission for any who would to follow Angus? Who went?"

"I do not know, sire. In the confusion many may have slipped away. But no lords with their full companies went, I think—save only one. My Lord of Gray."

"Ah! Gray! Gray followed Angus in the end, then? It could be . . ."

"Your Grace," Home said urgently. "What matters Gray now? Here is our opportunity. If you bring up your chivalry and attack now. Swiftly. We can scatter and defeat these, the Admiral below, before Surrey can come up. There is just time, I swear. They are still in line of march. Cannot be formed up to battle yet awhile. We could sweep them away like chaff, with a charge of horse. Round the side of the hill yonder – for this bank is too steep . . ."

"My lord," James stopped him. "What folly is this? We are not now on one of your Border forays, I'd remind you! The fair name of Scotland is here engaged. I came not here to outwit the English but to meet and defeat them. Even though Surrey does not keep his word, the King of Scots does, I say! We meet the enemy face to face, as true knights should – not seek to cut them down, unready, like cut-throat robbers!"

"But, Sire – we need not wait until they are at their strongest! Throw away our opportunity . . ."

"Enough!" the King said coldly. "I meet Surrey in fair fight, or not at all. I have not brought the pride and glory of my realm into England to throw it away in dishonour. So I told Angus, and so I tell you, sir! Wait here, my lord, and keep watch. I go to bring up our host."

As James swung his horse around, a bulky elderly man came running up from further along the brow of the hill, on foot, red-faced and panting. "My Lord King!" he cried. "Yonder bridge! Down at the mouth o' this valley. That they cross. I have three great cannon in position now. The bridge is within shot. The banks o' the burn are steep – fine I can see it. I pray leave to open fire, Your Grace. Now. I can bring doun yon bridge under them – break their column in two. Your permission to fire, Sire."

"No, sir. Not yet," he was told, shortly.

"But, Your Grace – yon bridge broken will greatly hold up the enemy. The banks are ower steep for horses. It will much delay them. They'll no' get their guns across . . ."

"I say no!" the King cried. "Would you also have me play the cut-purse? The robber-baron? Think you I fear to wait until I may meet Surrey on equal terms on a plain field? Does a knight stab his opponent while still he dons his armour? Hold you your fire, Master Borthwick, until I give you leave. You understand?"

"Aye, Sire."

Rob behind him, James rode back over the summit of the hill and down to the huge waiting concourse that filled all the great hollow in the centre, drawn up now in formation of battle. The smoke was thinning and dying away as the fires beyond burned low, and the King's heart rose in pride and emotion at the gallant and tremendous sight.

"My standard here, Rob," he directed, drawing rein on a slight eminence, as young Alexander cantered up to meet him. "Trumpeters to sound the rally. All leaders and captains to me here." To his son he smiled. "All is well, lad," he said. "The English do not disappoint us, after all."

Trumpets blaring out their stirring summons, men came hurrying. The Standard-Bearer took up his position behind the King, under the great Lion Rampant of Scotland, young Alexander of St. Andrews at his left, Rob Bruce as Sword-Bearer, at his right, backed by the great officers of state, members of the Privy Council, De la Motte the French Ambassador, and such lords and prelates as were not actually leading their own companies of the army. In front assembled the commanders of the host — earls, bishops, abbots, barons, knights, provosts, deacons, stewards.

Raising his hand, James spoke, his voice quivering with excitement and fervour. "My lords, my friends, my people!" he cried. "The hour strikes, at last! They approach! The English come to the onset, after all. Late in the day — but they come, praise God, they come! Below yonder hill." He turned in the saddle, pointing. "There they assemble, Our waiting, my friends, is over."

A great shout, led by those who could hear him, and then taken up by all the massed ranks of that mighty army, far and near, rose and swelled, echoing and re-echoing about the hill and its neighbours like the waves of an angry sea, a stirring, indeed a terrifying sound. It was some time before the King could resume.

"This day I have awaited for long, for many a year," he went on, hoarsely. "All Scotland has awaited it. We have a long score to settle!" He had to pause again, as the savage acclaim rose. "Henry Tudor, like his father before him, has well earned a lesson! We shall teach him it this day? Would that King Henry was here himself, and not only his sour servant, my lord of Surrey! Wait! Wait, you! Hear me. Although today we shall settle our own debts right gladly, let us not forget that we are here for other reason — in the sacred cause of friendship. Performing our pledge. Faithful to our trust. Henry has invaded France, our ancient ally. With his armies he devastates that fair land, claiming insolently to be its rightful lord. I warned him, and warned again. King Louis and his bonnie Queen have sought our aid – under the terms of our treaty. We are here, then, in honour bound. And since for honour we come, let our every act this day be honourable. Let honour strengthen our hearts, sustain our wills, guide our hands. A captured Englishman this morning declared that King Henry's sternest orders to Surrey are that in his fighting with the Scots there is to be no quarter, no mercy shown. No prisoners are to be taken, all wounded slain. Such is Henry Tudor! The Scots are to be ground down . . ."

The harsh growl that issued now from thousands of throats was like the rumble of distant thunder, ominous, filled with menace.

Again James waved his hand for silence – indeed he was turning to a trumpeter to gain quiet for him when the savage sound at length ebbed and died away.

"Such commands but little honour their giver, or those who would carry them out," he went on. "They are worthy of a monster, rather than a Christian monarch! Mine to you, my friends, are otherwise. We shall fight hard, to be sure, as Scots have always fought. But we shall fight fair, taking no advantage and asking none. If we win – and win we shall, I say, for we are the better men – we shall be merciful. But it shall be a fight to the finish – for this is the day of decision! There shall be no leaving the field short of victory. You hear me? Victory, my friends – we win . . . or we die! It is Scotland that stands on this Northumbrian soil this day, and Scotland does not deal in half-measures! Enough, then. I have said enough." He turned. "The sword, Rob."

Taking the great brand that had been the Bruce's, James raised it in both hands above his head, standing in his stirrups. "The time is past for words!" he cried. "It is time for action. May God and Saint Ninian be with you and with me, this day. My friends, I give you . . . Scotland!"

The deafening roar of voices mounted and mounted and maintained.

CHAPTER

25

BRANXTON EDGE inclines slowly down from its long green summit for almost a quarter of a mile before its brow is reached and the land then falls more sharply into the valley below. Over the crest and down this grassy slope the Scots army marched in perfect order, a mile wide, centre slightly forward, flanks curving back with the formation of the hill, rank upon rank, endless, covering the entire upland, ever new lines appearing over the ridge. The centre and left marched to the high bugling of scores of trumpets, although away to the right the Highland host strode, almost ran, held back like hounds on leash, to the fiercer music of their own bagpipes. Like a forest on the move all advanced, the thousands of long eighteen-feet pikes, King Louis's gift, held upright, and streaming amongst them in the rain-laden breeze the banners, ensigns and pennons of every arms-bearing family, clan, abbey, burgh and craft in Scotland, hundred upon hundred.

In the very centre of the long front line James himself marched on foot, carrying a pike like the rest, only the crimson and gold of the Lion banner above him marking him out. No single horseman rode in all that vast array. This was by the King's express and unpopular command. Scores of thousands of horses were left behind, despite the fury of protest, in that great hollow beyond the hill. This was no terrain or battle for horses, James had decided. The hillside was too steep, the ground too sodden with rain. The horse would only out-run the foot and the line of battle would be broken. So had vehemently advised De la Motte and Louis's French captains. Charging horsemen would negate the value of the long pikes, which had to be used in strict formation. Moreover, James had added darkly to Alexander, if there were no horses, there would be no temptation to flee the field, to ride off with loot and booty, the bugbear of every Scots commander. So all were dismounted, and thousands of heavily armoured nobles and knights and lairds marched clankingly, cursing but obedient, on foot beneath their banners.

James, like the others, was having to use the butt of his unwieldy pike frequently to steady and support him as he strode heavily forward over the slippery and water-logged slope. Already he was sweating, for the great weight of full armour was no help to difficult walking. Beside him, Alexander laughed and exclaimed excitedly, never less like an archbishop. At the other side stumped the portly Bishop of the Isles, a purple cope over his armour, with the Earl of Cassillis, Flaming Janet's brother, at his elbow. Immediately behind, Rob Bruce stalked, grim-faced. All around, in that central division, marched the very flower of Scotland.

When the King came close to the actual brow of the hill, where the land quite suddenly dropped more steeply, he threw up his hand to check the advance, signing to his trumpeter. The shrill summons to halt rang out, and all along the mile-long front the command was repeated and the serried ranks came to a standstill, gazing downwards.

The smoke had thinned to a mere haze, now, and all the English army was spread out below for them to see, almost as though on a map. The major part of Surrey's force had now come up, to join that of the Admiral, and everywhere men were wheeling into position, mixed horse and foot. Their formation was very similar to that taken up by the Scots, a long front divided into four distinct groups. The first-comers, the Admiral's array, had split into two and now formed the right wing, facing the Scots left. Keen eyes scanned the leading banners there, to identify the heraldic devices. The extreme right was marshalled under a flag well known to the Scots – that of Lord Dacre, the English Warden of the Middle March. Most of his troops were mounted men, his own Northumbrian and Cumbrian Borderers; with them, however, was a large contingent of foot under a Howard banner, no doubt that of Sir Edmund, Surrey's other son. Not all these were in sight from the Scots centre, owing to the curve of the hill and the valley at its foot. The Admiral's own formation came next, filling most of the valley and the gentle slopes behind it. A little left of centre, Surrey's own main force was taking position at the wide grassy eastern mouth of the hollow, where the land levelled off, although there was one rounded eminence at the back, on the summit of which the royal banner of England flew proudly. Away to the east, facing the Scots right, and again largely out of sight following the turn of the hill, was the enemy left, which must be Stanley's force of Lancastrians and Midlanders.

For tense minutes the two great hosts stared at each other, weighing, assessing, separated by less than half a mile of steep slope. The situation was a strange one, indeed, militarily as in other respects. Although so near, neither army was in a position to come to grips with the other without a major weakening of its position. The Scots obviously were in the better case, in a commanding situation on the high ground; for the English to attempt to scale these heights to attack them would have been suicidal. On the other hand, the Scots advantage was purely defensive, and the very steepness of the slope before them meant that if they advanced to the attack they must do so over a most difficult descent. With two cautious commanders, it could have been stalemate.

All this was not taking into account the presence of artillery, however – and artillery had long been one of James's especial interests. Now, he took the initiative, and signed to Robert Borthwick to open fire at last.

The long-awaited signal had barely been given before the cannon thundered out their mighty challenge, and all the land shook to the deafening crash of a bombardment such as never before had been heard on English soil. A great shout arose from the Scottish ranks. Large cannon and small belched shot, flame and smoke, from batteries dug in along the brow of Branxton Edge. The mass of men below seemed to shrink and cower visibly under the terror it.

On and on the cannonade went, Borthwick's gunners serving their beloved pieces like men possessed, while other men's heads reeled to the stouning clamour of it, new smoke clouds eddied and drifted, and Flodden Hill seemed to tremble to its very foundations.

Nevertheless, to James, as to others who could see beyond the smoke and sound and fury, it became quickly evident that something was far wrong. The cannon-balls were doing but little damage, falling too far back, amongst the skirts and baggage of the English host, not amongst the fighting-men. After the first numbed cowering beneath the blast of it, the enemy, realising that the shot was hurtling above their heads, pressed forward further into the valley. The Scots guns spouted and roared – and tossed up fountains and cascades of turf and mud and divots.

Desperately Borthwick and his gunners sought to depress the barrels of their weapons. But they were too highly sited on the brow of the hill. They could have kept all that English army from entering the valley had they been allowed to do so, but now that they were therein the guns could not be brought to bear upon them without a radical change of position, a re-siting down the forward slope itself. Tears of fury and vexation streaming down his red, smoke-begrimed face, Borthwick turned towards his monarch, helplessly.

All too well James perceived the folly of a continuing waste of precious shot and powder. His hand cut down in a curt slicing motion. Raggedly the guns fell silent. He swung on Rob Bruce.

"Men to aid Borthwick," he jerked, pointing. "To move the cannon. Further over. Down. Quickly, man!"

Now it was the English turn to shout, as the Scots fell silent. Wild relief, cheers, taunts and jeers surged from thousands of throats as their owners watched the desperate efforts above to manhandle the massive unwieldy guns out of their pits into new positions on the slippery rain-sodden slope. But there were more than cheers and jeers. Sharp clear orders were being given, by men who well knew their business. The clamour was drowned once more in the bellowing roar of gunpowder as the English artillery open up in turn.

Surrey was not so well equipped with cannon as was James, either in quality or numbers, Henry having taken the best of it to France. Moreover some of his heavier pieces had not yet come up. But such as he had were excellently placed just over the lip of the green eminence on which Surrey's own litter stood under the English standard. Here, on a slight uphill slope, the guns were able to point directly at the brow of Branxton Edge. There was no problem of raising or depressing muzzles. The gunners needed only to aim and sight and fire.

The first English balls smashed into the hillside slightly below the position where the Scots cannon were being manhandled. Quickly the fall of shot was perceived and adjusted, and one of the next salvo made a direct hit on a Scots gun itself, scattering its busy crew like chaff. Thereafter all the English fire was concentrated on the Scots artillery position, with deadly effect. Borthwick himself was one of the first to be slain, and all around him his men, and those aiding them, fell like ninepins.

Set-faced James watched the carnage, and saw the end of his cherished artillery. But he did not gaze for long, as the angry murmur of his host swelled behind him. A diversion there had to be, and quickly. He turned left-handed, gesturing in that direction. His trumpeter sounded a pre-arranged signal.

Far to the left, Huntly's pursuivant bugled acknowledgement. The famed battle-cry of "A Gordon! A Gordon!" came drifting down on the breeze, to be heard between the erratic burst of English cannon-fire. Slowly, firmly, in good order, Huntly's array moved forward.

The slope was much less steep at both sides than in the centre, although it was still a major descent. Slipping and stumbling a little but on the whole keeping fair formation, the massed ranks marched steadily downwards towards Edmund Howard's Cheshiremen and Dacre's Borderers, five thousand men of the North-East. There had not been sufficient of the French pikes for all, and few of this array were so equipped. All eyes turned from watching the slaughter at the guns to this stirring and disciplined advance to battle.

Half-way down the hill, the Scots were met by a sustained hail of arrows, the dreaded cloth-yard shafts that had been England's pride and stand-by in so many bloody encounters. But most of Huntly's front ranks were Aberdeenshire and Buchan lairds and their retainers, clad in full or half-armour, morions and breast-plates, and the archery appeared to do comparatively little damage. On the marchers strode, but faster now, and the distance between them and Howard's waiting legion dwindled and dwindled.

Surrey, from his litter on the little hill-top, acted. He switched a number of his cannon round, and directed their fire at Huntly's advance. Only some six guns were involved and the angle of fire was an awkward one. The result was far from devastating, although casualties there were, lanes cleared in the solid phalanx of men. The cannonade had its effect, however, a mainly psychological one. The steady disciplined marching was no more. With a great shout Huntly's ranks broke formation and, swords out, hurled themselves upon the enemy at a lumbering run.

Howard's Cheshiremen reeled back before the onslaught. In a brief minute or two the entire far left of the conflict became a chaotic mêlée of hand-to-hand fighting, fierce and furious. Dacre's mounted Borderers could do little but circle the perimeter of it, smiting where they could, so inextricably mixed were friend and foe. It soon became apparent, however, that the drift of battle was northwards. The English were being forced back, there archers and artillery ineffective in this pass.

The unengaged majority of the Scots host were not left to appreciate this struggle undisturbed however. Surrey, too shrewd either to waste his cannon or to leave them unused, abandoned his battering of the silent Scots artillery at last, and turned the whole weight of his guns upon the centre of the Scots line. The tight-clustered banners, surmounted by the magnificent Lion Rampant sewn by the ladies of the Court, made it sufficiently clear where James himself was stationed. Thitherwards all muzzles were directed.

As the balls began to crash amongst the close-packed ranks, James bit his lip but stood firm — and all around him men did likewise. One of the Scots cannon had been pushed into a good position at last, and had opened fire again. On an impulse, the King sent his son over there, to the right, to take Borthwick's place, to seek to bring other guns to bear now that the English fire had switched. Even a few shots landing amongst the enemy cannoneers would help. And it was better that he himself should not cringe at every report, lest the next English ball would strike the lad at his side.

When it was apparent that his brother's force was collapsing, the Admiral detached some portion of his own division to their aid. This manœuvre was what James had foreseen and awaited. Whenever he perceived it, he signed to his trumpeter to blow the second signal. The inner Scots left cohort, under Erroll the High Constable, Crawford and Montrose, directly above the Admiral, moved down to the attack.

From the first this was less successful than had been Huntly's advance. For one thing, the ground was much more steep and made footwork difficult, especially for men accustomed to fighting on horseback. Moreover, this division was equipped with the eighteen-feet-long pikes, and very swiftly it became evident that however valuable these enormous spears might be in static defence or in slow controlled advance over level ground, they were nothing short of a tragedy for men slithering down a slippery hillside. Despite the frenzied shouts of the French captains to keep them up, to keep them high, stumbling, blaspheming men could not control the unwieldy, top-heavy weapons, three times their own height. More and more of them swayed, slewed and fell in all directions, tripping up their bearers and those around them, packed tight as they were. Before the front ranks of the array were half-way down the hill, all semblance of formation was lost, men were casting away the encumbering poles and drawing their swords instead — such as could keep their feet. The lengthy littered pikes then became an added hazard for those who followed on. Into this confusion, Surrey, ever the opportunist, turned most of his artillery fire. It was not a proud array but a maddened, chaotic, stumbling mass of angry men that bore down on the hastily re-formed Admiral's division, more or less driven on by the momentum of the ranks behind and above.

There could be little doubt as to the outcome of such an encounter. The Admiral's men, who had come by sea to join Surrey at Newcastle, were mainly veterans of the Continental wars. Grimly they awaited the confused and indiscriminate assault, their halberds and bills like an iron-bound coast on which the tempestuous waves of disorganised Scots hurled themselves to their death. Erroll, Montrose and Crawford themselves, in the van, were amongst the first to die. Their thousands fought bravely, savagely, when they could fight at all, waiting their turn to face the unbroken line of thrusting eight-foot halberds with their three-foot swords. The rear ranks, hemmed in by their own fellows, could only wait. It took a long time for so many to die — but die they did, in as complete an annihilation as any large body of men in history. There was no retreating; not only the King's command, but the steep bank behind saw to that.

Groaning, James watched the early stages of it all from his vantage-point on the hill. If only Huntly could be diverted to their aid, to attack the Admiral in flank, his own victory over the Cheshiremen almost complete, much might be saved. The King was about to send a runner to him when Huntly himself perceived the need, and started to draw out his triumphant fighters from the chaos, to turn them eastwards against the Admiral. This however was Dacre's opportunity. He massed his frustrated Border cavalry, to bear down upon the disengaging Scots.

The King was watching this development in an agony of apprehension uncaring that the cannon-balls were once again crashing into the ranks around him, when swift movement still further to the left drew all eyes. It was horsemen that they saw, a fiercely yelling cascade of cavalry, hundreds, thousands strong though not all of it was in sight, pouring over the lip and down the hillside yonder. A ringing shout of relief rose from the Scots centre.

"Home — thank God!" Bishop Hepburn, at James's side, exclaimed.

Cassillis actually grabbed the King's arm. "Look, Sire! Home rides! Home rides!"

"Aye." The King swallowed. He himself knew sudden elation. But it was only momentary. "He rides. He rides – against my royal command!"

"But, Sire – if he saves the day! If he holds Dacre . . .!"

"If he fails in one command, he may fail in another. Well I know how these moss-troopers fight! Pray God this day Home remembers that he fights for Scotland, not for Home!"

Rob Bruce was back. "My lord of Home was not present, Sire, when you gave your command," he reminded. "You left him here to watch the enemy."

"Aye. And think you none of his people, none of these he now leads, told him of it?"

"The Borderer without a horse is only half a man!" Rob declared stubbornly.

"But on a horse, man – when will he stop riding? We saw how it went, years ago . . ."

James's words faded away. The action they watched left words irrelevant. With irresistible élan and at headlong speed the Scots Borderers swept down upon their English counterparts, and the clash of their meeting for the moment drowned every other sound on that battlefield. Nothing could withstand the force of that impact, and Dacre's horsemen were hurled back, knocked down, over-run and scattered in a shocking pandemonium of flailing steel, lashing hooves and screaming horses. On up the long slow slope beyond their impetus carried the yelling Homes, Scotts, Turnbulls, Kerrs and the rest, clean through the entire English lines, foot as well as horse.

"Sweet Ninian!" the King exclaimed. "Send Home now the wit to see it! To swing round. Round behind Surrey. God be good – he could change all! Round, man – round!" he cried. "Before the cannon can be turned or the archers brought back!"

Half a mile away Home was waving his men round indeed – even though by no means all of them were paying him heed. Many saw, in full view before them beyond the slope, much of Surrey's baggage-train, guarded only by servants and camp-followers, most of them already bolting. The temptation was too great, and on to the booty they rode in the age-old tradition of their kind. The majority, however, obeyed their chief and his lairds, and swung their careering mounts around. But it was not eastwards, half-round behind the main English rear that they turned, but fully round, back whence they had come, against the scattered and reeling remnants of Dacre's horsemen, their hereditary foes. Dacre, seeking to rally his dazed and dispersed forces into some sort of order, himself saw what was bearing down upon them, complete and utter extinction – and did not await the outcome. Wrenching his own horse around, he spurred for respite, for safety, the only way that he could turn, westwards along the valley, away from the battle – and all around and about him his people did likewise. By the time that Home's moss-troopers had completed their tight circuit and were pounding back into the hollow beneath the hill, the entire cavalry of the English right wing – or what was left of it – was streaming away at the gallop westwards towards the mist-shrouded Cheviot foothills in headlong flight. And without pause or hesitation the Scots swung after them in equally headlong thundering pursuit. Only the dead and dying, the staggering wounded and crazed riderless horses, were left in the western mouth of the valley.

"Precious soul of God!" James's left fist was upraised, to shake as did his voice, in helpless, heart-sinking rage and disappointment. "Come back!" he yelled. "Fools! Fools – come back! Saints in Heaven – I knew it! I knew it!" He swung on his trumpeters. "The recall!" he ordered. "Quickly! Sound the recall, I say! They may yet hear. By the Rude – get them back . . .!"

It was of no avail, of course. Those pounding shouting moss-troopers, even if they heard the high neighing of distant trumpets, paid no heed. In complete triumphant victory they pursued their vanquished enemy out of the battle.

That trumpeting, however, was not without its effect – its dire effect. The Scots right wing, in all this while, had fretted inactive, unable to see because of the lie of the land what went on else-where – and this was the fiercest and most impatient division of all the Scottish array, the Highland host. For long they had been straining, creeping forward, held in by their leaders with the greatest of difficulty. Now, they heard this peremptory trumpeting at last, mistook it for their own signal, and with a mighty roar surged to the onset.

The situation on this front was entirely different from else-where. Instead of a recognisable valley before them, the land here sank in waves and ridges to a lower area of hummocks and knolls and hollows — difficult country for a unified defensive battle, excellent country for wild, individualist Highland fighting. Surrey knew it well. Knew also that Stanley's troops, who constituted his left wing, were the least experienced and reliable of his whole army. Moreover he could not bring his artillery to bear on the Highland position without altering its central siting because of the basic sweep of the hillside. So, out of his long experience of war, he had sent thither secretly, almost his entire force of archers. Up amongst the hollows and hummocks they had moved quietly, mainly unobserved, to a position on the flank of Stanley's waiting Lancastrians. Now was their moment.

A Highland charge is the most fearsome attack to await known to man — and some fifteen thousand clansmen here came roaring down in barbaric might and pent-up fury. While the front ranks were still three hundred yards off, the waiting Midlanders began to waver and sag. Then, in almost a moment, all was transformed, as the ranked archers crowning the crests of the hillocks received their delayed orders to shoot. Thousands of bowstrings twanged almost in unison.

The effect was scarcely believable. The entire Highland front crumpled and disintegrated in shattered and bewildered confusion. Well had Surrey calculated where his bowmen could do most damage. Only here in all the Scots array was there no armour, no steel helmets and breastplates, only tartans and bonnets, cowhide jerkins and round leather targes or shields. Into these the English yard-long shafts drove by the thousand to maximum effect. Never, in centuries, had English bowmen had such unprotected targets.

The slaughter was stupendous, utterly without precedent, as the archers, with practised speed and skill, kept up a continuous dense shower of arrows, and the pride of the glens and the isles were transfixed and died in heaps and swathes and ranks, in blazing wrath and dire astonishment, their broadswords falling unblooded to the blood-soaked grass. Never had the clans had to face this sort of warfare.

On and on went the deadly hail. On and on surged the Highlanders from behind, to clamber over the mounds and ridges of their fallen comrades, to die in their turn without ever coming to blows with the foe. Few indeed of these, the fiercest swordfighters in Europe, ever came to grips with Stanley's almost equally astonished pikemen and halberdiers.

Appalled, his heart seared with pain and anguish, scarcely believing what he saw, James watched this disaster, his mind almost too numbed by the scale of the carnage to be capable of thought, of coherent decision. It was a cannon-ball smashing into bloody pulp the Abbot of Inchaffray quite close to him—for Surrey was again concentrating all his artillery-fire on the great central division of the Scots battle-front—that brought the King back to his senses. He stared around him and behind him at the serried waiting ranks, torn and gapped as they were by the bombardment, but standing fast, his eye wild, his face pale.

"We have stood here sufficiently long!" he cried, to no one in particular. "I stand no longer. while my friends die!" He swung on his Armour-Bearer. "My helm!" he demanded.

All this time James had been bareheaded though otherwise in full armour. Now he donned the massive war-helmet, banded by the gold circle of the crown and crested with the representation of the red Rampant Lion. A great sigh rose from all around him who could see this gesture. He pointed to the trumpeters.

"Sound the advance!" he commanded.

"Sire!" That was the Bishop Hepburn, at his side, thickly. "You mean . . . to go down . . . yonder?"

"Aye."

"But . . . is it wise, Your Grace? The day goes but ill. Here we are safe—save only for these thrice-damned cannon-balls! They dare not scale these heights . . ."

"If safety was what I sought, my Lord Bishop, I would not have left Scotland!" James snapped. "We came to do battle, not to skulk in safety."

"But the cost, Sire! Already this day has cost Scotland dear. Would you lose more? All, may be . . .?" He was shouting, above the blaring of the trumpets.

"Are all to fight, man—save the King? This is my main battle, the main weight of my realm. I send others to the fight. Shall we now hold back? We can yet save all . . . or . . . or at least, save the day . . ."

"Aye, 'fore God! No more standing! No more talking!" the Earl of Cassillis exclaimed. "Sir Priest—if you have no stomach for the fight, turn back. But let others be doing!"

"On! On! Let us have honest steel! Instead of these accursed cannon-stones!" somebody yelled.

There was a general shout of agreement—though some around

the King expressed doubts, suggested delay, claimed that they were throwing away a strong position. James cut all short with his upraised hand.

When the trumpets died away, he spoke hoarsely. "Honour forbids that we retire, unblooded. We cannot stand here idle, longer. We have a cause to fight, a name to uphold, and comrades to avenge, my friends. Who follows James Stewart?"

The centre of Scotland's main array surged forward to a great shouting, in which even Bishop Hepburn's voice was upraised, over the lip of Branxton Edge.

There was a fall of some six hundred steep yards to the valley floor, where Surrey's main strength waited – the steepest part of the entire escarpment indeed. The Scots had been warned, by seeing what had happened to Errol's and Crawford's division. Nevertheless few were really prepared for the crippling difficulty of that descent down an apron of rain-sodden turf and bare red earth, for thousands of men clad in heavy armour and bearing enormous pikes. It was next to impossible to keep a footing for more than three or four successive paces, and so tight-packed necessarily were the ranks that every man who toppled cannoned into those around him, overbalancing others. The pike-shafts just could not be kept vertical – and once otherwise became immediately an even greater menace than the slippery ground, tripping, stabbing and confounding all around; once the shafts were broken and splintered, as happened in many cases, the sharp points thus produced speared and gouged many whose lower parts were unprotected by full armour – the more so in that ever greater numbers of those behind were casting off heavy boots in order to keep a footing on the greasy slope made worse by the feet of those in front. The cursing of King Louis and his vaunted French pikes rose like a breathless antiphon from the entire floundering host.

In the circumstances it was impossible to keep any recognisable formation – although the entire strategy of pike-fighting demanded the closest and most disciplined disposition and order. If the front ranks made the bad ground even worse for those behind, these in turn by their very weight pressing down made a controlled advance almost impossible for their leaders. Added to all this, the cannon-fire at ever closing range, and the rain of arrows which, though less effective against these armoured ranks was galling nevertheless, made a further hellish chaos of the descent.

James himself fell many times — and regaining the upright in full armour was no easy matter — but he still held his pike tight-grasped when, perhaps two-thirds of the way down that devilish slope he found himself being aided to his feet by his son Alexander.

"Boy!" he gasped. "What do you here? I sent you to the cannon."

"The cannon may no longer fire, now that you close with the foe. Moreover, my place is at your side, Sire."

"No! No — not here, lad. Back. Not here in the forefront . . ."

"Aye, here, Sire," the youth insisted. "Is it not my place? By my father's side?"

"Y' Grace — you it is who should be back, i' faith!" Somehow old Lord Lindsay of the Byres was now at the King's side. "Here's no place to direct a battle! In the foremost front," he panted. "Go back, Sire — back where you may see all, govern all. More surely."

"Never!" James cried. "Would you have me craven? In the rear, urging others to the onset, myself secure?"

"Is Surrey craven? Where he sits in his litter? On yonder hillock, directing all? He kens the general's part, I say . . ."

"And I ken mine, my lord! Where the fight is thickest you will find the King of Scots, I promise you! Whom should I direct, in safety, from the rear? All is now committed. It is win or die. For me, as for us all."

"And for me, Sire," Alexander declared, stoutly.

His father shook his head but said no more.

Somehow that grievous descent was made, although at terrible cost. Quarter of a mile wide, the Scots front reached the Branx Burn which wound its way through the valley-floor, already running red with blood shed higher where the Constable's and the Admiral's forces were locked in deadly slaughter. All cannon now had fallen silent, for fear of hitting their own men. Surrey's archers too could only fire at the Scots rear. The main enemy front was a bare hundred yards away, and slightly uphill. Even so the massed footmen stood still, firm-planted, behind the bristling layers of pointing halberds, tier upon tier of tense, glaring men. Behind them the mounted knights waited in all the panoply of coat-armour and heraldic blazon, hundred on hundred. And further still, half-left, on the summit of the green knoll, amongst the massed banners, Surrey stood beside his litter, a crooked, stooping but menacing figure, motionless.

Panting for breath, James dashed the running perspiration from his eyes as best he could through his visor. Having waded the burn and clambered up the little bank beyond, he steadied himself against the tall pike-shaft, for the moment not pressed onward by the weight of men behind. Personnel close to him had kept changing in that disordered downward progress, but Rob Bruce ever remained immediately at his master's back, and one of the trumpeters at least was still near by. In the face of the grimly waiting foe, so near, to this man the King turned.

"Sound me a summons!" he ordered. It would give them precious moments, at least, to prepare, to reform.

Somehow the trumpeter managed to collect sufficient breath to blow. Ragged but high, challenging, a flourish ran out over all that blood-stained valley. In the comparative hush that followed its choking finish, James raised his gasping voice.

"My Lord of Surrey!" he called out, at the pitch of his heaving lungs. "You did not keep your word. To meet me. By noon this day. At Flodden Edge. Redeem your honour, now! And that of your King Henry. Come you down! Come here. Meet me. In fair fight. As true knights should. Your fame . . . may yet survive. Come—and bring your sword, my lord!"

There was an uncanny quiet now from all near by against the background of more distant battle. It maintained for seconds on end. Then Surrey's creaking nasal voice sounded, thin, cold, contemptuous.

"Come *you*, Sir King! A little further—since you have come so far! I am well content here. Come! I await Your Majesty! Come—if you can!" That ended in a brief high whinny of laughter.

The cackle was taken up and magnified into a great shout of laughter, first by the English nobles and knights sitting their chargers around the hillock, and then by the mass of the waiting soldiery.

Hotly, furiously, James flushed within his helmet. Raising his unwieldy pike which he had borne so far, he hurled it from him, in the direction of the distant Surrey, as though it was a gage thrown down between them. "The sword!" he cried, turning half-round, to take the great two-handed weapon which Rob Bruce held out to him. "I come, Surrey—I come!" he yelled. "Saint Ninian! Saint Andrew! Bring me to him!"

A pace or two ahead of his charging line, the King of Scots flung himself forward on the waiting ranks of halberdiers, smiting.

It was a full hour later, the most terrible hour in Scots history, that James Stewart perceived that his son was dead. For long now the King had stood in that one place, savagely, crazedly as he had forced his way onward until then. He had been straddling the body of the fallen youth who, after fighting well, had been first dazed by a halberd blow which knocked off his mitred helmet, and then pierced through the throat by a spear which had penetrated beneath his gorget. Long Alexander had taken to die, it seemed, for so mortal a wound, gazing up at his father with eyes which only slowly lost their lustre, gradually glazed. Frequently, between thrusting and lunging and flailing, James had glanced down at him, spoken brief gasping words to the lad who could by no means speak back, whose lips only bubbled blood. It had been a difficult stance for the King to hold, to balance himself upon — for they were high above the reeking grass here, mounted on a pile of bodies, of friend and foe, seven or eight thick, and not all of these bodies lay still.

"He is dead, Rob," James croaked, tonelessly, dry-throated, even as he drove his red sword-point expertly in at the arm-hole of a breastplate — and as expertly wrenched it free again before the screaming victim could bear it down with the weight of his falling body.

"Aye," Rob Bruce panted flatly, wearily. Rob was very tired, and his strokes were beginning to flag. He was wounded, of course, in two places — but then, so was the King, whose fierce and feverish energy seemed to have abated nothing in all that nightmare of killing. James's left arm hung useless, and the sword which he now brandished was no longer The Bruce's famous brand, which took two hands to wield, but the lighter weapon which had hung at his side. How many men these two had slain between them in that ghastly hour, there was no knowing — but many indeed, for there had been much competition amongst Surrey's knights, as well as the common soldiers, for the honour of bringing down the King of Scots; James had indeed, early on, himself killed five men with a truncated pike snatched from the dying grasp of the Bishop of the Isles — before its spearhead was chopped clean off by a halberd blow, and the

441

King, in casting it away and drawing his personal sword, had lost the use of his left arm.

Now he darted a swift glance at his friend. "Up, Rob! Do not . . . . fail me now!" he cried. "God has Alexander! Aid me . . . to Surrey!"

That had throughout been James's goal, driving him on with almost superhuman fire and fury—to get to Surrey. Here, on this pile of dead and dying, they were indeed on the same level as the English commander—for they were near the top of the round hillock, green no longer, and their stance raised them higher. Thirty yards, no more, separated the two leaders, and had done for the past quarter of an hour, whilst father stood above son. Behind them, the wide causeway of dead piled thus high as it climbed the hill, plainly marked the path that the King had taken to reach his chosen quarry—a causeway in which lay the very flower of Scotland. All around, beneath the trampling, struggling, battling men, the fallen were thick, in swathes and heaps—but not so thick as in this broad corridor, nor so illustrious, where the nobility of a whole realm had taken it in turn to bear the monarch forward on the bloody road of his honour.

James was now pressing on once more, himself the apex and spearhead of a tightly knit phalanx of fighters, wedge-shaped, which in turn formed the steel point of the completely surrounded remnant of the Scots central division. In this, shoulder to shoulder, each man supported his neighbour, sword in one hand, stabbing dirk in the other, all pikes having long since been abandoned. Within the wedge itself were others, regaining their breath, ready to step into the places of their comrades who fell. These men close to the King were, by a process of elimination, the toughest and most skilful sworders of the whole host. The composition of this group, this embattled bodyguard, had in the early stages changed frequently and almost completely—but not latterly; now it merely grew gradually smaller. To it had belonged such renowned warriors as the Earls of Atholl, Bothwell, Cassillis, Rothes, Caithness and Glencairn, the fighting Dean of Glasgow, the Lords Lindsay, Sempill, Hay, Livingstone and Elphinstone, the Masters of Angus, Fleming and Cathcart, and innumerable others. All these had fallen. James himself had long lost all awareness of the identify of his immediate colleagues—indeed most of them now were not nobles at all, or even knights, but unknown stalwarts with a gift for survival. Even the royal banner, which still flew bloodstained and tattered above the King, had had fully a dozen upholders after the Standard-Bearer had been slain in that first mad charge, and who it was who bore it now, snatched from the dying grasp of the giant Hector MacLean of Duart, James had no idea.

The King's sword-work, though still strong, astonishingly so, was no longer consistently accurate; frequently his slashes and stabs missed their target altogether. He was not alone in this, however, for there were no fresh fighters left in all that valley, Scots or English. He had long cast away his great helmet, as an encumbrance, a handicap to vital sight, and his auburn hair was now clotted with dark blood from a glancing scalp wound. All his hopes, fears and efforts were now reduced and limited to two immediate concerns – could he reach Surrey, and would Rob Bruce, who had saved him times without number, last out even until then? At what stage James had finally recognised that the day could not be won, that the Scots cause was doomed, it would be hard to say – but there was no question as to when he had accepted in his own mind that he himself would not survive this field; that was when, at a dire moment when his great sword had been wrenched from his grasp and for seconds he had reeled defenceless, facing swift death, his hand had subconsciously slipped down to his middle, his loins, where, beneath the chain-mail that other heavier chain should have been – and he had realised that indeed it was not there. The chain which he had worn throughout all his life, the sign and symbol of his purpose, the token of his vows, lay in Elizabeth Heron's bedroom at Ford Castle. She alone of all the women that he had bedded with had prevailed upon him to lay it aside; in the haste of that morning's rising, on the false alarm of an enemy feint, he had forgotten it. The Englishwoman had, in the end, not failed her people, it seemed. Even though Rob Bruce had saved him once more on that occasion, the assurance of personal doom had struck the King then with entire certainty. Alexander's fall soon afterwards had been but the confirmation of it.

Twenty yards to go now, no more, to Surrey. Above the helmets and plumes in front, James could frequently glimpse him, still standing beside his litter, holding on to one of its uprights, and always looking towards himself, peering through the thin rain and the early dusk, a spare, stooping figure in rich armour under a long cloak.

Only from immediately in front could English assailants effectively strike at the King, protected as he was by his close supporters. It was all swords here, near Surrey—knights and nobles; the halberdiers and pikemen had been left behind. So tight was the press that never more than three of the enemy could at one time cross blades with Rob and himself who fought side by side. Their partnership had been a match for any combination against them so far, their flanks and rear being so well defended; but now Rob was beginning to fail, and sword-points were ever more frequently reaching within their guard, to strike against steel armour. James knew that his time was desperately short.

With consequent suitable desperation he sought to redouble his own slackening efforts, although with dizziness, pain and utter weariness it was ever more difficult to drive his point where it could be effective, at the seams of armour and junctions of pieces. By sheer fury of attack he knocked aside a knight's helmet before him, and as the other's sword went wide as a result, scraping over his shoulder, he drove in with his foreshortened blade to the suddenly grinning face. As his victim, a heavy man heavily clad, toppled backwards, he knocked off his feet a slighter man behind, and both crashed to the ground.

For moments there was a gap, a clear corridor of view above the fallen, before others could surge in to fill it—a brief slender corridor that led straight from James Stewart to Thomas Howard. Their glances met at a bare dozen yards, blazing blue and steely grey. James opened his mouth to shout the final challenge which he had battled his way through unparalleled slaughter to deliver —and even as he did so, knew that it was too late. He had waited for, visualised this face-to-face moment; but so had Surrey. Even as he stared, the King perceived the man close to the other's side, an archer, bow raised, arrow levelled, string drawn. James looked his death in the face, perceived it well—and actually threw up his head to receive it, his flaming scorn flashing, burning, upon Surrey.

The arrow, therefore, took him not through the eye and the brain as it ought to have done, at that short range, but through the right cheek, transfixing the throat, and out at the base of the skull beyond. Backwards James staggered, against Rob Bruce and the man who bore the Rampant Lion.

Without a moment's hesitation, Rob dropped his sword and threw his arms around his monarch and friend, gently to lower him to the ground. Above them the steel clashed with renewed fury and the standard dipped and swayed.

Staring up, James sought to speak. Though his lips worked, words would not come. At last painfully he got it out. "The chain . . ." he whispered. "The chain!"

"Sire! Sire!" Rob sobbed, tears beginning to run down his face.

"Weep not, Rob," the King mouthed, his face contorted with pain. "Not for me. Weep . . . for Scotland! Whom I love . . . I have slain! My realm . . . my son . . . Margaret!" Twitching convulsively, he struggled to sit up, actually half-raising himself within the other's arms. "Margaret!" he gasped. "Sweet Margaret!" and smiling even as his head jerked back, he choked to final silence on a red flood.

Amongst the trampling feet Rob Bruce remained on his knees, cradling his lord. He did not seek to rise or to defend himself – and when the inevitable thrusting blow came, he did not even look up to meet it. Down upon his bent neck, between helmet and gorget, the blade drove, and he pitched forward arms still round his friend.

The man with the royal banner lasted only seconds longer, his eyes distracted by what was done at his feet. He sank down, sprawling, and the Red Lion of Scotland covered King, knight and commoner alike.

A few yards away, Thomas, Earl of Surrey, Earl Marshal of England, turned away, and like a very old man climbed up into his litter. Huddling there, he drew his cloak around him tightly.

"It is cold," he said. "Cold."

NIGEL TRANTER

The Wallace

William Wallace — a man of violent passions and unquenchable spirit, the natural leader of a proud race

Scotland at the end of the thirteenth century was a blood-torn country under the harsh domination of a tyrant usurper, the hated Plantagenet, Edward Longshanks. During the appalling violence of those unsettled days one man rose as leader of the Scots. That man was William Wallace. Motivated first by revenge for his father's slaughter, Wallace then vowed to cleanse his country of the English and set the rightful king, Robert the Bruce, upon the Scottish throne. Though Wallace was a heroic figure, he was but a man — and his chosen path led him through grievous danger and personal tragedy before the final outcome . . .

CORONET BOOKS

NIGEL TRANTER

The Wisest Fool

'A vastly entertaining addition to the historical
novels of Scots author Nigel Tranter'
Glasgow Sunday Mail

In this colourful portrait of James the Sixth
and First we meet one of the oddest kings ever
to ascend a throne. Neither noble nor heroic,
he was shrewd enough to reign for fifty-eight
years, survive countless plots and never go to
war.

'The book swings along in great style'
The Times

CORONET BOOKS